THE CITY BELOW

Books by
James Carroll

Madonna Red
Mortal Friends
Fault Lines
Family Trade
Prince of Peace
Supply of Heroes
Firebird
Memorial Bridge
The City Below

JAMES CARROLL

THE CITY BELOW

Houghton Mifflin Company

BOSTON NEW YORK

Library of Congress Cataloging-in-Publication Data
Carroll, James, date.
The city below / James Carroll.
p. cm.
ISBN 0-395-59070-1
I. Title.
PS3553.A764C58 1994 93-40837
813'.54—dc20 CIP

Printed in the United States of America

QUM 10 9 8 7 6 5 4 3

Book design by Melodie Wertelet

for

Paul Lannan

and for

Larry Kessler

—✧—

Brother of my heart,
don't you know there's only one
walking into the light, only one,
before this light
flashes out, before this bravest knight
crashes his black bones into the earth?

— GALWAY KINNELL

✧ 1960 ✧

I

ON A BRISK SPRING MORNING in the year that John F. Kennedy began his run for president, a pair of burly micks in overalls and tweed caps sat on the bench in front of the monument on Bunker Hill in Charlestown. One was in his fifties, and looked it. He seemed relieved to be idling. The other was younger and seemed agitated, his eyes scanning the scene like a radar dish. The older man gazed serenely, straight ahead, blank-eyed. The grass sloped away from them toward the street, which was lined with stout brick houses, stately Federal bowfronts, the kind Bostonians associated with Beacon Hill, not Bunker. There was a puritan-pleasing simplicity to the unadorned pillars and lintels of the entrances, but it had been years since the people using them had understood what a shine those brass door knockers would take.

In the distance sat the egg-sucking, indifferent city, with the spire of the Custom House, the white steeple of Paul Revere's church, the peaked roof of the Boston Sand and Gravel tower. Otherwise the skyline was flat. Nothing had been built in the city below since before the Depression. In Boston the Depression wasn't over yet.

Deebo McCarthy — Brian — was the Charlestown waterfront boss. His young sidekick was Dick Burke, his hack. Along the piers and in the warehouse districts, not only of the Town, as it was called, but of the Irish territory out the long peninsula of South Boston, McCarthy's rule was absolute. The Irish neighborhoods were his complete domain. He had begun as a roustabout, and he was still at ease in work clothes. He always had a wet cigar in his mouth. Burke tried to carry himself like Deebo, that air of fuck you. But he couldn't pull it off. He was worried.

For his part, McCarthy had always been unable to look out at the rest of the city without a sharp sense of what was not his. He had succeeded in walling himself off from that feeling now. This morning he would settle for the turf divisions as they were. The pristine steeple there, so close he could almost hit it with spit, marked the Italian North End. Italians dominated East Boston, on another side of him, and the Everett and Chelsea banks of the Mystic River on yet another. Downtown, Italians ran the great commercial storage wharves, the former icehouses, along Atlantic Avenue up to Fort Point Channel, which marked the boundary with Southie. The Teamsters were controlled by Italians out of New York, and only a month ago McCarthy's own Longshoremen's Union had voted with the hod carriers and the luggers from Logan Airport in Eastie, electing its first wop slate. The balance of their version of the earth had shifted then. The dago takeover of the forever Irish union was the signal, Deebo knew, that things were changing. This morning was his turn at bat, and if he took his eye off it, the greased-up ball would hit him. The era of sharing the waterfront loot in Boston would be over. He had to crowd the plate, stare back at the fuckers, make them think he didn't give a shit.

When he'd gotten the call from Tucci, he'd been suspicious. Guido Tucci was more than McCarthy's counterpart. He controlled the Italian waterfront organization as Deebo did the Irish, but his sway had extended to the citywide rackets — gambling, loansharking, black markets — since the thirties. For most of those years, he and McCarthy had respected each other's turf, mostly because the Irish had settled for the lucrative but limited acreage around their own neighborhoods. But now? When Tucci had proposed this meeting, McCarthy had suggested this site in his own territory, cut off from the Italian districts by the harbor and by the Charles and Mystic rivers. He'd thought Tucci would never agree.

Yet here the fucker was, pulling up in a car he was driving himself, no bodyguard even. The car was dark and large. It rolled to a stop at the foot of the broad granite steps that led up from the street. Neither Burke nor McCarthy moved as Tucci got out of the car and came up the stairs toward them. A small man, he was dressed like a mortician. McCarthy had known him since '38, and he recognized the slow, deliberate walk, the slightly bent posture, the right hand forward with each step, as if he were using a cane. Tucci had cultivated the personal style of a gentleman from the old country. He was born in Worcester at the beginning of the century, but he'd been raised in a strict Sicilian household, and he still spoke English with a heavy accent. He conducted himself as if slick American ways were foreign to him.

"Hello, Brian," Tucci said quietly, approaching.

McCarthy nodded but said nothing.

"I had hoped we could talk alone." Tucci turned his gaze on Burke, who felt the chill of it.

Burke said, "Nothing doing. I'm Mr. McCarthy's assistant."

Tucci wearily raised his arms, making them like wings. At that invitation, Burke stood and patted him down.

Tucci let an amused sparkle show in his eye as he looked at the much brawnier McCarthy. "I am honored that you regard me still as capable . . ." He let his voice trail off. Tucci's skin was dark and smooth, but at his eyes and mouth it was wrinkled. His body had begun folding onto itself.

McCarthy stood up and nudged Burke. "Let it go, Dick. Jesus."

Burke was satisfied by then anyway, so he stepped back.

"Could we walk?" Tucci asked quietly. "Could you show me . . . your estate?" He grinned.

"Sure I could."

"Boss, we —"

"Never mind, Dick. What would you like to see, Mr. Tucci?"

Tucci shrugged, but he let his eye drift up the line of the towering obelisk.

"Two hundred and ninety-four fucking stairs, Guido. I don't think either of us is young enough for that."

"It is beautiful, nevertheless, from here."

McCarthy shrugged. "Yankee idea of a monument, if you ask me. Like a cross without the corpse. Like their wooden churches. Now that" — he pointed to the gun-toting statue of Colonel William Prescott, a literal rendition — "tells you something."

"What?"

"Fucking battle. Whites of the eyes. That shit."

"The British won this battle, I believe," Tucci said.

"No, we did."

"We?"

"Americans."

"If you choose to think so."

McCarthy looked across at Burke, the surprise of a new idea sharp on his face. "We won that, right?"

But Burke had not heard what they were saying. He shrugged.

"No, I'm sure we won," McCarthy said with forced expansiveness. "Yankees put this thing here. They don't raise monuments to defeats. Only the Irish do that." McCarthy laughed. "I'll show you something.

Come on." With abrupt enthusiasm, he led the way around the monument. Tucci followed.

Burke called after him, "Boss, should I — ?"

"Forget it, Dick. Meet me at the clubhouse."

On the west side of the monument McCarthy stepped onto the grass at a point where it sloped sharply down. He gestured toward a huge granite building across the street, four stories high, a façade ornamented with seven false columns, an American flag wafting gently above the entrance, below the words CHARLESTOWN HIGH SCHOOL.

"See that?" McCarthy pointed.

Tucci smiled. "I see it, yes."

"That's where Jack Kennedy announced for Congress in 'forty-six. Right there, in the auditorium. I was there. This is Kennedy's first district." McCarthy turned toward Tucci, his face transformed by a rowdy expression that said, Match that, you fuck.

But Tucci's face remained impassive.

"What's with you, Guido? At least he's a Catholic, right? Don't you want a Catholic president?"

Still Tucci did not react.

"I don't get it. Don't you people give a shit?"

"You people?"

"You know what I mean."

Tucci turned and sent his eyes up once more, tracing the lines of the massive granite shaft.

"So what did you want to talk about?"

"Can we walk?" Tucci asked. "I prefer to walk."

McCarthy's impatience flared. He made a show of looking around. There were no watchers. No one could hear them. What was this?

But he thrust his hands deep into the pockets of his overalls. "All right. I'll show you where the fucking British landed. One if by land, two if by sea. They came by sea."

"Not that day." Tucci pointed to a plaque mounted on a stub in the grass. Both read in silence: *NW corner of redoubt thrown up on the night of the seventh of June, 1775.*

"Paul Revere," Tucci said, "was in April."

"How do you know that?"

With the slightest turn of his head, Tucci glanced in the direction of Revere's church, the white steeple a mile — but a world — away.

McCarthy laughed, a sudden recognition of their absurdity, a mick and a wop scoring on each other about the mythic exploits of the old

Americans whose descendants disdained them both. "Come on," he said, setting off at a clip.

He led the way north, toward the Mystic River, which formed one side of the tight peninsula. If McCarthy walked with a sprightly energy, perhaps it was because he liked leading Tucci even deeper into the heart of his own turf. They took the two steep downhill blocks to Bunker Hill Street, where, to the right, the Town housing projects began. Curley's projects, just one of the great things the late mayor had done for the Town. A baby's cry wafted into the air above the tidy brick enclave. Young mothers could be seen sitting on benches surrounded by carriages. McCarthy's nose supplied the smell of ammonia and soiled diapers.

To the left, across the flattened land, a broad, ill-tended ball field ran toward the narrow inlet beyond which, along the riverfront proper, stood the wharves and warehouses of the Charlestown docks. Two huge cargo ships were at their piers, cranes towering over the holds of the ships, pallets dangling. McCarthy eyed it all proudly.

When it had become evident that the stooped, slow Tucci was not going to keep up, the Irish waterfront boss eased his pace with a show of resentment, but also with a sly smugness at his old enemy's physical decline.

That was why it came as a surprise when, on the far edge of the ball field, Tucci, while still walking, said simply, "We will have a new arrangement, beginning now."

McCarthy stopped, staring after him as Tucci kept walking toward the channel. The inlet was a narrow gut lined with walls made of granite monoliths. Its bank was an apron of pavement six feet across. When Tucci reached it, he turned to face McCarthy.

"What do you mean, 'new arrangement'?"

Tucci did not answer.

Something told McCarthy to stay where he was, but the image of the frail, vulnerable old man drew him. The fuck. "What do you mean?" he repeated, approaching.

"Your people will be working with mine now."

"What, in Charlestown?"

"And in South Boston. Things have changed, Brian."

"The fuck they have."

"The union is mine. The airport is mine. The big ships don't come in like before. The old division doesn't work. I want you to help me make a new one. The waterfront must be one operation, controlled by one organization."

"Yours."

"Yes."

"No fucking way, Tucci. Things have worked in Boston because we've kept apart. My people will never lug for you."

Tucci shrugged. "It will be you lugging for me."

"It don't play that way with us."

"Why do you say your people would not accept this when it is *you?* Are you afraid to say it is you who refuses me?"

"No. I ain't afraid to say that. I've spent thirty years building what I have. You think I just hand it over, you got shit for brains." McCarthy turned as he spoke, covering the act of reaching inside his coat. "What sparks this, Guido? The fucking union vote? The union vote don't mean a damn."

"Except as a sign of the times, Brian. You know what's happened in Providence and New York."

"Boston's different, always has been. Separate turf, that's the rule here. As it was in the beginning, is now, and ever shall be."

"Until now. On the water, on the harbor — action goes through one organization. One juice collection from the ships, one loader's fence, one distribution."

"Yours."

"I said that."

"You said it, yeah."

"Then you understand."

"The question is, do I agree?"

"Yes."

"You've got some fucking nerve. Do you know that?"

"Brian, Brian. I've come here myself, against advice, to give you a chance. Between the two of us we could make the adjustment smooth. We are old men. The young ones have not seen what we have seen, how bad it goes when —"

"Forget it, Guido."

"You would be my *capo*."

"Your flunky. Your hack."

Tucci shook his head mournfully. "Do not do this."

"This?" McCarthy began pulling his gun. "This?" A primitive urge carried McCarthy forward, as if to push the bastard backwards into the oily water. "This?" He showed the gun.

McCarthy had made his move so swiftly that he was on Tucci before seeing the flash of the knife — it came from Tucci's sleeve, one of those arms he had so willingly held up for Burke. The blade was visible only for an instant, until it disappeared in its ample new sheath, McCarthy's own stomach. Jesus.

McCarthy's last sensations were the unforgiving crunch of the cement against his face and the roar of a motor in his ears. He had life enough to realize that Tucci would make his escape now in some dago's souped-up speedboat, swirling into and out of the channel, out to the harbor, across to Eastie or the North End. Two if by sea, the fucks.

✧

In quick order, in the days following, even before Easter, McCarthy's chieftains in Southie, Savin Hill, and Fields Corner, in Union Square and Winter Hill in Somerville, were eliminated, all but one in public executions calculated to make a point. The takeover, to succeed, had to be swift and brutal. If the Italians, for their part, misjudged the Irish, it was in assuming they would need a hope of victory before putting up a fight. The old-country Irish impulse was to make their defiance at least as brutal as it was futile, and that spring and summer they did.

Guido Tucci's nephew was run down on North Washington Street, coming out of Polcari's. Afterward the mick driver stopped, got out of his car, went back, and, in front of the young man's mother, Tucci's sister, cut off his ear and threw it at the woman's feet.

With no overt warning, killings became rampant in the areas where Irish and Italian neighborhoods overlapped: Dorchester, Somerville, Chelsea, and Everett. The two Irish peninsulas, Southie and Charlestown, because of their geographical isolation, were the most concerned but the least affected. The murders spilled over into downtown, into Scollay Square, and even, three times, the Common. At first every lurid slaying — a corpse thrown from a sedan at Farragut's statue, a restaurant owner shot through the eye amid the bright morning crowds of Haymarket, a fish handler drowned in a holding tank on Rowes Wharf — hit the front pages, often with photographs. But eventually the press, the police, and the citizenry itself became inured. The violence continued into the fall.

Old Boston was confirmed in its most cherished views of both peoples, the Irish and the Italians. The closed systems of Boston's caste society and the city's economic stratification were at last justified by the primitive blood lust of those who'd been kept out. Their viciousness shocked even those whose disdain had been absolute. Corpses showed up in the cold-storage vaults of the waterfront, a naked flogged body was found hanging from a light fixture in the workers' bathroom at the

Park Street station. See how the Catholics kill one another. To the denizens of Back Bay and Beacon Hill, the gang war was proof that the long-held attitudes for which they'd been so ridiculed were perfectly true. The City on the Hill had fallen to men of no virtue, and was ruined.

✧

One day in May of 1960, a year after Guido Tucci had murdered Deebo McCarthy, a pair of dark-eyed, slick-haired punks came into the Kerry Bouquet, a flower store across the street from the Charlestown Common, on the lower slope of Bunker Hill.

Ned Cronin, in the corner by the ivy trellis, sized them up without lifting his head. He was a large, white-headed Irishman with a reddish nose, the same age as the century. He had the build of a scrapper, but, as the flower king of the Town, he spent most of his time with women, the parish biddies and nuns who kept him in business. So the arrival of the toughs drew his absolute attention.

He had been making one of his trademark shamrock boutonnieres, and when the two came in, he redoubled his focus, knotting a wire, yet watching them. One wore a shiny black suit, a lilac shirt, and a tie a deeper shade of purple; the other wore an argyle sweater with red and blue diamonds against a field of cream. The sweater had suede lapels, one of which the man cockily fingered.

"What'll it be, fellows?" Cronin looked up, letting his glasses slide toward the end of his nose. He held his concoction delicately between thumb and forefinger, four shamrocks and a spray of baby's breath, held together with wire. The shamrock lapel flowers were silly things Ned had put together one St. Patrick's Day, but Townies liked them, and he could always sell whatever he made.

The pair ignored him to make a show of inspecting the shop. The one in the suit was an unwashed, pimply version of a rock 'n' roll crooner, that ducktail, the lithe jittery body of a car thief. With exaggerated nods at each separate bunch of irises, tulips, and carnations, he took a series of audible whiffs — in contrast to the other, who grimaced as he pushed the foliage aside, giving off the authentic, pungent air of anarchy, a stink of it.

Cronin tilted back in his chair. He picked up a can of artist's fixative and sprayed the shamrocks. Even when shellacked, they would last only an evening. He put the can and boutonniere aside, to rest his shoulders against the ornate brass cash register. In all these years he had never been robbed. He could feel the baroque relief pattern of the brass cash drawer through his shirt. Jesus, Mary, and Joseph, now what?

"How can I help you, pal?" Cronin addressed himself to the one in the sharkskin suit. But anxiety had pushed its way into his voice. He heard it himself, knew they would, and he wanted to curse.

But Squire must have heard it too.

Cronin's grandson, and his chum Jackie Mullen, came out of the back room. They'd been putting together wreaths for a funeral. Each one wore dungarees and a T-shirt with the sleeves rolled up. Squire, one of Cronin's two grandsons, was his after-school helper, a lanky kid with slick red hair combed in a modest but unmistakable pompadour. A bridge of dirt crossed his nose where he'd rubbed it with his hand. Despite the ominous presence of the Italians, he stood easily on the threshold, lighting the room with his habitual grin, a boy born to bring flowers.

Mullen was harder to read. A shy, cautious boy, he'd hit his stride the previous autumn as a fullback. He was strong and unafraid, but those qualities alarmed Cronin as he saw the sour expression on Jackie's face.

Cronin saw his grandson move his left hand behind his leg. The lad was still holding the curved blade he'd been using to trim stems.

Cronin thought back to the K of C gala the year before, when he himself had been raised to the Fourth Degree. As a joke, in the cathedral hall where the beer was flowing after the ceremony, he had brought the flat of his new Eminent Commander's sword down on Nick's shoulder and dubbed him Squire, his second in battle, his armor polisher and weapons carrier. They love a nickname in Charlestown, and "Squire" had stuck. Now the kid was standing there so bravely with that blade, as if about to leap to his old grandpa's defense. Knight's squire indeed.

"We've come for the dues," the pimply face said.

Cronin found it possible to smile, as if this were repartee down at the Flower Exchange, but he could not summon the response that would make the situation funny. With a weary grunt he stood, grateful to find that he was taller than the intruders. "Dues? What club?"

"New merchants' association. You know about it."

"No, I don't believe I do."

Squire was smiling in a friendly way, but as concealment. His hand had tightened around the cork handle of his hidden knife. His eye moved from his grandfather to the strangers and back.

It was Squire to whom Mullen kept looking for a signal. His hands were flexing and unflexing, wanting the ball. When Squire sensed Jackie's eagerness, he hid the knife from him too. The knife took over Squire's mind. What would it be like to slash at the pimples on that one's face?

"Twenty a week," the Italian said. "Beginning today. And for your money, you get a smooth operation, guaranteed."

"Thanks. I already have a smooth operation." Cronin turned to Squire and Jackie. With an impatient flip of the fingers of both hands, like the monsignor shooing altar boys, he gestured them toward the back room. But neither Squire nor Jackie moved.

Without warning, the acne-faced one leapt at Cronin, grabbed his shirt, and smashed his face with a chopping punch. The old man's nose immediately gushed blood, and he crumpled. The Italian's fist was bound in a set of brass knuckles.

Mullen charged forward, but the second thug hit him from the side. The blow landed on his cheekbone with a dull *thunk*, another brass sucker punch. Mullen went down, coldcocked.

Squire used the hatred he felt as fuel for an act of deep memorization. One face, then the other — the bastard who'd decked his grandfather. He dropped the trimmer's knife into the potted plant behind him. Without a glance at Jackie or Cronin, he walked to the cash register. He rang up No Sale; the drawer popped open. "Twenty, you said?" And he held out two tens.

The one with the acne released Cronin, who fumbled for his handkerchief. The punk crossed to Squire and snatched the bills. "We'll be back once a week, get it?"

"Yes, sir. You bet."

The punk stuffed the bills in his trousers pocket and turned to a bucket of carnations. He snapped off a flower and put it in his lapel buttonhole, a trophy. "How much for the rose?"

"No charge," Squire said.

Jackie looked up at his friend with shame and disappointment. The guy who'd hit him still stood over Mullen, fist cocked. The other was turning to lead the way out when Squire, still at the register, said, "Does this mean we don't have to pay the other guys?"

The two looked at Squire.

"I mean, you take care of them for us now, right?"

The Italians exchanged a glance. The suit said, "What other guys?"

"Mr. Triozzi," Squire answered. "He said not to tell his name, but it's okay for you to know, right? What's your name?"

"Triozzi?"

"He said he was somebody's cousin. Weirdo, or something."

"Guido?"

"Yeah, that's it. Guido. Guido Tucci. That's what he said. He's Guido Tucci's cousin."

Again the two looked at each other, but now the one in the sweater flashed with anger, and his partner muttered defensively in Italian. In three broad strides, he crossed back to the cash register and slapped the twenty dollars down, then turned and left the store. His comrade followed, whining, "Goddamnit, Mano, I told you —" Then they were gone.

Mano. Squire repeated the name to himself.

Ned Cronin took one last swipe with his handkerchief. He brushed the remains of the shamrock boutonniere from his shirt, then joined his grandson in helping Mullen to his feet.

"Triozzi?" Cronin asked. "Who the hell is Triozzi?"

When Squire did not answer, Cronin realized what his grandson had done. He looked nervously toward the door, then back at his daughter's kid. "You made that up? Jesus, Mary, and Joseph, you made that up?" A grin slowly overspread Cronin's face. With amazement and disbelief, he repeated, "You made that up?"

Still Squire did not answer.

Cronin grasped his grandson's forearm. "You had me fooled too. I thought there must of been some guy come in here while I —"

Squire was looking at his grandfather with rare solemnity.

"How did you know what name to mention?"

"Triozzi." Squire shrugged. "It's the wop name that popped into my head."

"They wouldn't of believed you if you'd just said Tucci, if you hadn't played so dumb. 'Weirdo'! You said 'Weirdo'!" Cronin laughed.

"I'm sorry the guy hit you, Gramps. I'm sorry I just stood there."

Cronin pressed Squire's arm. Of course, the kid *hadn't* just stood there, which was the point now. "Hell, I'm okay." He turned to Mullen. "You're the one who took the crack, Jackie."

"The wop bastard." Mullen's cheekbone was aflame, the hollow under his eye already mousing up. His fingers jittered at his face.

Cronin wanted to shake the stunned Mullen: Didn't you see what Squire just did here?

Squire picked up the bills from the register. "Here's your twenty back, Gramps."

"That's yours, kid." Cronin laughed again and pushed his grandson's hand away. "That's protection money, and you're my protection now. Wait'll the boys at the Exchange hear what you did."

"No, Gramps." Squire spoke with grave authority. "You shouldn't talk it up. Not at the Exchange and not here in the Town. We should let it sit for a while. We should find out who else these guys have hit. *Them* we talk to. We tell *them* about Triozzi. We treat Triozzi like he's real. One by one, we sign up the other stores on Main and on the square."

"And the fellas at the Exchange —"

"No, Gramps. Just Charlestown. We keep this thing in the Town. Marin, O'Brien, Jocko — the ones we trust. But we all treat Triozzi like he's real. Get it?"

Cronin nodded slowly, his gaze fixed upon his grandson, seeing something new in him.

"Lou Triozzi," Squire continued, "who operates out of Revere, where Tucci lives."

"How do you know where Tucci lives? Or are you making that up too?"

Squire shrugged, knowing not to say. Ambiguity could be a hiding place. Even he was surprised by the sureness with which these moves were coming to him, like in the heat of a basketball game.

Yes, Tucci lived in Revere. And yes, Squire had seen him. But there was no question of explaining that to his grandfather. His many trolley rides to the northern terminus had begun innocently enough. Wonderland, Revere Beach, Oceanside Park with its roller coaster and midway, had for decades been popular destinations for Boston's streetcar vacationers. But the gang wars had ended that. Revere was a step up from the North End and Eastie, but it was solidly Italian and its new Keep Out was implicit in the headlines. Lately, the MTA trolleys often arrived at the turnaround empty. And hadn't exactly that comprised much of the allure for the gang of Charlestown boys, Squire and half a dozen chums, all sixteen or so, who'd trekked to Revere the summer before? Each had draped a towel around his neck, a vestment signifying the innocent purpose of swimming. But once they'd set out, they'd become a raucous, towel-snapping platoon. They were charged up more by the prospect of trespass than by the pseudo-danger of any roller coaster. When they'd dismounted the trolley, though, they found themselves alone, a set of isolated intruders on the edge of an off-limits enclave. And they'd become instantly subdued.

Their instinctive wariness had been justified at once as a group of lean figures approached from the Wonderland dog track. Five of them, no older than the Townies, they were greasers. But they sauntered forward in their dark clothes like a motorcycle gang, juvenile delinquents, street fighters. Their T-shirts were rolled to show biceps and cigarette packs. They wore slick hair, pointy shoes, pegged pants. Purple thread marked the seams of one kid's black trousers, like an officer's stripe.

"Get the fuck back on that train," one of them yelled from across the circle.

Behind the Italian boys, still in the shade of the dog track's marquee, stood a knot of girls in calf-hugging pants and tight summer shirts. They pointed like spectators and cupped their mouths at each other's ears. Squire understood that they made the boys dangerous.

The streetcar was about to embark on its return trip. The bell clanged urgently. The Charlestown boys knew better than to look at one another as, one by one, with no swagger, they climbed back aboard, as if summoned by nuns.

The last to do so was Squire. At the time he was still known as Nick, and that was the name Jackie Mullen hissed at him, to get him to come.

When the trolley, with its screech of iron wheels, began to roll away, the Irish kids, in an explosion of nerve, began to jeer back at the Italians, hanging out the windows, flipping the bird, crying, "Wop cocksuckers!" The Italians gave chase, but the Irish knew there was no danger they'd catch up to the accelerating streetcar. The driver was a mick too, and he laughed as he said, over his shoulder, "You showed them, I guess, huh?"

Squire had been at the window, jeering like the others, but it had been more an act in his case than in anyone's. His skin burned with that shock of humiliation, and inwardly, on the instant, he resolved to return to Revere and violate its every precinct. And he would do it without the others, who were already slapping each other's backs, snapping towels again, an absurd display, an implicitly phony claim of victory. He would go back alone.

And he had. He'd discovered that as a solitary idler, he could go anywhere in Revere unchallenged. He'd returned numerous times in the summer and fall, and even a few times in winter, indulging a fascination with the decrepit seaside realm. That it was enemy territory had made him a spy. He had browsed unnoticed at comic book racks in candy stores and had sat unobtrusively on rocks while olive-skinned children skipped stones into the lapping surf. He had collected seashells in good weather and tonic bottles from trash bins on the boardwalk when the weather turned. He had cashed the bottles in at the corner grocer's, as if the pennies were what he wanted. Before long he'd begun to nod at people he recognized. In those candy shops and grocery stores, on benches along the boardwalk and on boulders by the water, Squire had listened to the agitated talk, sometimes in Italian but mostly in English, of beatings, gun-downs, and disappearances. He heard the story of a particular fishing boat at a nearby pier that at least once had set out at night to dump a stiff into the sea. He heard of a gas station owner in Everett who kept pickled human ears in a jar by his cash register. Italian kids younger than Squire regaled each other with tales of the war their brothers were winning against the micks down in Beantown.

Squire had heard the name Guido mentioned repeatedly, and it took him a while to realize that Tucci was being referred to. It was in April, a week after the body of Paulie Mack, a City Square newsstand owner and numbers operator, was tossed out of a car near the donut shop, that Squire had first seen Tucci. A carpenter replacing planks in the Revere Beach boardwalk had pointed him out, a lone figure walking in a hat and long overcoat with his collar up against the springtime wind. Squire had watched the black form grow steadily smaller as he receded to the far end of the boardwalk. When Tucci turned to come back, Squire saw two men who'd been trailing behind step aside for him, and he realized they were bodyguards. That told Squire to keep his distance, and he did. But even so, he watched Tucci for a long time that day, following him finally to the end of a particular street three blocks back from the beach. Another day, picking him up on the boardwalk again, he followed Tucci far enough into the street to see him enter a prim bungalow between two vacant lots. Squire saw the bodyguards get into a black Buick which, then, they did not start.

Yes, he knew where the infamous Tucci lived. He *was* a spy. If he'd uncovered a secret, it was that the great enemy had a small but rounded stomach, walked with a slouch, and seemed lonely. Was merely a man.

Squire held his grandfather's eyes. "Lou Triozzi," he repeated. "Guido Tucci's cousin. We'll talk him up bit by bit. We'll accept his protection . . ." The young man spoke so coldly that Ned Cronin glanced at Jackie Mullen, but the boy was still too dazed to be marking this phenomenon. "Until we can get protection from one of our own."

2

GROWING UP IN CHARLESTOWN, they were just the Doyle boys, old Cronin's grandsons, the double pulse of Flo Doyle's heart. Terry and Nick — the sight of one so evoked the other that people in the Town never imagined they would turn out to be so different from each other.

Their father had gone late to the war, and had not come back — Battle of the Bulge, Flo always said. That was why she and her babies had moved back in with her father above the store. Cronin's own wife had died in Ireland giving birth to Flo. No one referred to it, but in the Town, Cronin and his daughter were regarded as if they had replaced each other's spouses. Slightly strange.

But the boys were alike in their bright normality, as American as Irish. Toddlers around the store, they were favorites of the Altar Guild ladies, who praised them for their freckles. As altar boys they always served together, gliding across the polished sanctuary of St. Mary's in cassocks that hid the movement of their legs. But they were headlong players in the neighborhood too, on their bikes and clamp-on skates, shooting hoops at the playground and stealing Pepsi bottles like other kids, pelting cars with snowballs and lying for each other when they were caught. Only a year apart in age, they had the air of twins, which served each well when he needed to deny something.

At Charlestown High — by now they were tall, well built, and lithe — they'd become famous outside the parish as a pair of hot-handed forwards who could hit each other with passes without looking. To the Townies in the stands, there was no mystery in the magic the Doyles worked on the court: their being brothers was what gave them their mystical connection. In the heat of a game, even old Cronin had trouble telling them apart.

Not that he didn't have a secret preference. Nick, the younger, was the one who'd been declaring, ever since he could talk, his intention to be a flower man. He hung around the store, drawn by the current of Cronin's particular affection. But that seemed only fair, a compensation for Flo's all too obvious preference for Terry. He was the long-dead father's namesake, and on him, years before, Flo had fixed the stare of her own ambition. Her first-born son was going to be a priest, which was the only large distinction available in the dreams of her kind, and was always the first thing she'd ever said about him. Terry cooperated in her expectation, which set him apart from an early age in everyone's eyes, except in Nick's.

"You, Nick! You!" Ned Cronin had called out that night after the K of C ceremony. The crowd had filed down into the large crypt hall below Holy Cross Cathedral in the South End. Cronin was wearing a satin cape and a plumed hat. Cardinal Cushing had greeted him with the once-over and the crack, "Your haberdasher, Ned, or mine?" Now Ned was near one of the beer kegs, waving at his grandson. "You get over here!"

Nick pressed forward, leaving his brother behind. The other men could tell them apart tonight because Nick was in chinos and a corduroy jacket. Terry wore the black suit his mother had bought him, as if he were already in the seminary.

When Nick presented himself to his grandfather, the circle closed around them. Cronin raised his new sword high over Nick's head. "Kneel ye!"

The men pushed closer to watch. They had their beer and their cigars, after choking through the interminable convocation upstairs, in the cathedral proper. Their ties were loosened now, and their shirts were open at their throats.

"Bow ye!"

Nick bowed his head.

And though this was a game, the encircling men felt a common shudder of delight as they recognized Nick's posture, with his robed grandfather towering over him. "I dub ye Squire! Squire to the Knight!"

Nick raised his head to look his looming grandfather in the eye. When he said in a firm, loud voice, "I, Squire, pledge ye, Knight, my fealty and devotion," the men let up an approving cheer.

Squire got to his feet. The men were slapping his back, but the boy ignored them and leaned toward his grandfather and whispered, "What about Terry, Gramps?"

Cronin blinked. What about him?

"Do one for Terry, Gramps."

Only then did Cronin realize what a hole he would blast in their brotherhood if he did not call Terry forward too. These boys made their moves together, and it was like Nick to have said so. Nick and Terry were a pair.

Cronin stretched to his full height to look for the kid. With his plumed hat, Cronin was taller than anybody there. He spotted Terry back by the sandwich table. "And behold," he bellowed, "the Knight spies his Chaplain!"

The men stopped and listened again. Terry stepped aside.

"The Royal Chaplain!" Cronin added.

Terry stood where he was, a stricken look on his face. His grandfather sensed how he'd have preferred to be ignored, but Cronin had no way to know why being singled out like this — *as* this — was Terry's nightmare.

"Chaplin!" one of the men cried raucously. "*Charlie* Chaplin!"

The Charlestown gang laughed. Another nickname, a beaut. Some people would call Terry Doyle Charlie long after the originating joke had been forgotten by everyone but him.

✧

Terry was sitting on a bench at the foot of the obelisk on Bunker Hill. He often came here, just to look out at the spine of the city — the Custom House and the harbor at one end, the Hancock Building with its hypodermic-needle spire at the other. In between, he pictured the men and women who lived and worked in those buildings, who stood at the wheels of sailboats in the harbor, who spread cloth napkins on their laps to eat breakfast in the restaurants, who drank cocktails in the hotel bars. He pictured students at their desks at all the great colleges, the blue books in which they wrote their exams.

It was a magnificent spring afternoon, with an army of clouds in retreat across the sky. The light was so clear that the lines of the mortar in distant brick buildings flashed, the air sparked off the angles of new leaves. A pale green haze draped each tree. As he sat staring out of Charlestown, an unusual peripheral sense had made Terry feel aware both of the view and of what was behind him a few dozen yards away, over the lip of the hill, down the grassy slope — the high school, where he'd learned that the feelings he had, sitting here, were disloyal.

The school had let out hours ago. He was supposed to be home for dinner already, but he'd become transfixed by the view of downtown, the clouds streaming overhead from west to east, which had maybe hypnotized him. He was suspended in a mood of uncertainty and longing. The sight of the distant buildings soothed him, but the images they evoked — men in topcoats hailing cabs, women getting out of those cabs, leading with one spiked heel, one perfect leg — filled him with anxiety. The few tall buildings were modest compared to the skyscrapers in other cities, he knew, but to him they were the pickets of a world of sophistication and accomplishment, a world of which he was meant to know nothing.

He took out a cigarette and lit it. He knew that the impression most outsiders had of Charlestown came from the fearsome, low-rent end that abutted the Mystic River Bridge from which commuters looked down. They saw the rough industrial district dominated by the Boston Sand and Gravel tower on one side and by dilapidated wharves lining the crotch of the harbor on the other. Outsiders could see the Bunker Hill monument, but they knew nothing of Monument Square or the streets leading into it where fine Victorian houses stood, proudly kept not by the wealthy who had built them, but by the large, intact families of Irish firefighters and cops. They knew nothing of Main Street where storekeepers greeted every shopper by name, or of the tranquil Common where he lived, or the elm trees, the wide sidewalks, the tidy squares of grass, the hedges and flower beds, the neighbors minding each other's children, burying each other's dead. They knew nothing of the churches — his own St. Mary's, but also St. Catherine's and St. Francis de Sales — where the people, all the people, met each other regularly in one common acknowledgment not only of needing grace but of having it.

The views into Charlestown from the elevated bridge ramps featured, in addition to the blank walls and smoked windows of the warehouses, the housing project that North Shore suburbanites would see as one of the grim neighborhoods they associated with the decaying inner city they left behind each night. They would imagine vacant-eyed, unattended teenagers with freckles bridging their noses, and pregnant mothers tugging at their children's ears. They would picture Irish gypsies, young hooligans and drunks, knowing nothing of the lengths to which those mothers went to keep the threadbare clothing of their children clean, or of the natural genius corner boys had for cracking jokes, or of the rare camaraderie of tavern haunters who thought nothing of putting half their gin rummy winnings in the St.

Vincent's poorbox, which sat by the pickle jar on every tap counter in the neighborhood.

Passersby would see none of that from their autos, and in fact, from his vantage on Bunker Hill, neither did Terry. He had no need to. He saw nothing of the Town but the slanted asphalt-and-shingle planes of the rooftops he took for granted, as he took for granted the essential virtue of the people who lived in the rooms below them. The city proper was what he saw and what he wanted, without knowing why.

"Hi, Charlie," a girl's voice said from behind the bench. The sound was close enough to startle him, but because of the name, he did not assume she was speaking to him.

She was, and when he realized that it was the damn moniker they'd laid on him at the K of C, he bristled, even before he knew who she was.

He stood up and faced her.

The girl took a few steps toward him in the shoulder-bouncing, hand-flapping style of Charlie Chaplin. A decent imitation, in fact. When he only stared at her, she stopped.

"Your mother called to see if you were out here."

He recognized Didi Mullen, Jackie's sister. She was a tall, thin girl who'd graduated the year before. That crucial year had, in the social system of Charlestown, kept her and Terry from being friends, and now that she took the train out each morning for her job in an office downtown, the gulf between them was wider than ever. The Mullens lived on Monument Square.

"She said you're late for dinner."

"Hi, Didi. I was just going to finish this smoke." He held up his cigarette. "Want one?"

At first he thought she hadn't heard him, but then her face broke into the goofy, wide-mouth grin for which she'd been teased in high school, the flat-chested Martha Raye. She held her hands out and he tossed her the pack. She laughed when she caught it, and he thought, You shouldn't use so much lipstick, or not such a bright red, or something.

"You're no gentleman, Charlie," she said. She lit her own cigarette, then approached his bench.

"I'm no 'Charlie,' is what you mean. You may call me Terence." He sat as she kept coming. His casualness was not quite the act with her that it was with girls in his own circle. If he blushed, it was because he felt she'd just caught him at something.

She smiled and threw her head back to clear her hair away from her face so she could put the cigarette to her lips. Her hair was a rich, shimmering red, the best thing about her. Terry remembered seeing her from behind in the school corridors, that very hair pouring down over her shoulders, a promise that when she turned around, this would be one beautiful girl. When she did turn it was always a surprise. Her mouth was made for a bigger face, her chin was pointed, the rims of the glasses she wore curled above her brows, making her look bug-eyed, more Eddie Cantor than Charlie Chaplin. Didi's offbeat appearance, Terry thought, was what made her try to win you over by being a little silly. And her offbeat appearance, more than her silliness, was probably what had put him at ease with her in ways he rarely was with the pretty girls. The offbeat he knew about, if of a different kind. He was good looking enough for a guy, and played basketball. But he had interior features that clashed. He was always turning around, as it were, and seeing shadows of disappointment fall across the faces of those he'd hope to impress. He reacted not by being silly, but by being, as they said, quiet. And no one had ever been surprised — this had been assumed of him in Charlestown since grade school — that God had blessed him with a vocation to the priesthood. Lucky bastard: many are cold, few are frozen. Kids left Terry Doyle alone.

Didi wore a tan blouse and a dark skirt and snappy high heels, but it was like her that she also wore, as if it were a jacket, an oversize man's shirt that was navy blue. The sleeves were rolled back at the cuffs, and the bottom button was fastened so the shirt flowed around her like an artist's smock, gave her the air of a beatnik. Terry noticed stitch marks on the sleeves and realized patches had been removed. Didi's father was a cop. This was a shirt of his. Beatnik, hell.

When she had drawn close enough to hand him his cigarette pack, he gestured at the bench beside him. "Have a seat, Miss? Is that what a gentleman says?"

Didi grinned at him, and when she took a deep drag on the butt, he was more conscious than ever of her big lips. She exhaled dramatically, letting him see the pleasure a hit of nicotine could be. Only then did she sit. "What are you doing?"

"Just looking. I come here sometimes."

"I know you do. I see you from my window. You sit here by the hour."

"Not by the hour. By myself."

"Doing what?"

"Sometimes my homework."

"What else?"

"Looking." He shifted his gaze toward the downtown buildings.

She let her eyes follow. "Oh, you just have a case of senioritis. I used to do that last year. I can see downtown from my bedroom."

"You see a lot from your bedroom."

"I used to sit there by the hour too, trying to picture it, hoping I could get a job downtown."

"And you did."

"But it's not so great as a high school senior thinks it is, take it from me. I bang a typewriter all day. See that building there?"

"The Hancock."

"That's me. Hancock Insurance. Seventeenth floor, typing pool. I sit in a room . . ." She put the cigarette in her mouth and began to mime the act of typing. Each time she hit the carriage, she made a *ding* sound. It was true, she had a Chaplinesque flair. Finally she stopped, and when she looked at Terry, it was with a sudden solemnity. Then she looked away again. They spoke, each with eyes on the distant skyline.

"You don't like it?"

"I like it okay," she said. "I'm a lot faster than I was."

"But you —"

"— see the rest of my life flashing before me. I'm nineteen. There are girls in the typing pool who are forty, still living with their mothers. I'm afraid if I blink, I'll be old. Maybe I'll spend my whole life filling out the forms of other people's accidents. They're not even my own accidents, Charlie."

"I really wish you wouldn't call me that."

She looked at him with surprise. "You don't like your new nickname? How would you like 'Horseface'?"

"No one calls you that."

"Me?" She was shocked. "I was talking about my brother."

Terry stared at her, trying to fend off the feeling of horror, that he'd so insulted her. He'd never heard Jackie referred to as Horseface, but —

But then she laughed. Her strange face broke into an expression that said, Gotcha! At that moment Terry, feeling a release of his own, was sure he saw a flash of real beauty in her. What he saw was the charm of a girl laughing at herself, and the self-acceptance such a thing implied was as far removed from his experience as the downtown buildings were.

He snapped his cigarette away, but instead of getting up to go, he reached into his pocket and pulled out another one. Didi held out her cigarette to him, and he leaned toward it to take a light. He cupped his hands around the tips. His hands shook slightly as the cigarettes touched, then flared.

"Like dragonflies," she said.

Terry wasn't sure what she meant. He inhaled with an excessive show of pleasure, as she had, and he leaned back. He became aware of her legs, one crossed over the other, her knee peeking out from her skirt. She was wearing nylons. As he watched, she shifted her legs, turning toward him, nearly touching him. He had never noticed before the line a woman's calf muscle makes as it falls to the hollow of her ankle.

She looked at his face and waited until he looked back. "Speaking of brothers, that was something, what yours did today."

"What?"

"You didn't hear?"

"No."

"Some Italians came into your grandfather's store. They wanted money —"

"A robbery?" Terry's alarm brought him forward.

"Not exactly. They said they wanted payments."

"Protection?"

"I guess so. Squire fooled them. Jackie said he made them think your grandfather was already paying it. Jackie said they couldn't get out of there fast enough. Lucky for him. You should see his eye."

Terry felt that he was supposed to be in two places at once: at the Bouquet, seeing this thing happen — what, Jackie getting slugged? Nick scoring somehow? Terry felt he should have been there stopping anything bad from happening — but also here. He was supposed to be here, with this girl whom he felt he was meeting for the first time. The scent of her perfume hit him only then; he'd never noticed her perfume before. He was aware of her chest, inside her father's shirt. He took in a glimpse of her tan blouse as if it were underwear.

There was life in her legs as she uncrossed and crossed them again; the sound made him think of satin.

Moments passed.

Terry wanted to put his hand on Didi's knee, but she spoke before he could do so, not that he ever would have tried.

"Your brother is special," she said. "Everybody says so."

Terry leaned back and let his eyes follow the clouds. They were running across the sky like horses, and all he knew was that he wanted to be one of them. He said nothing. How could he?

After a long time, Didi pinched the small butt to her lips like a truck driver. Then she flipped it away, somebody in a movie. She put both her arms behind her back, pressed them against the bench, swelling her breasts. On purpose? She said, "So are you."

"What?"

"Special."

"Why do you say that?"

"Because it's true. You're going to be a priest. That's special."

"But I'm not," he whispered, not daring to look at her. Usually when he had this feeling he was in bed, crushing his pillow, raging. But now he was taut, his back straight, his hands on the cold wood by his thighs. Though a space of only inches separated them, it might as well have been the whole city.

"You're not what?"

"Not going to be a priest."

He had never said it aloud before. Until now he had not understood that this was his problem. Where there was supposed to be faith — that cavity in his chest, his heart, his soul — was instead this feeling; this feeling of loss and longing was what he worshiped.

"Why not?"

He said simply and quickly, "Because I'm not worthy."

It was the truth, but also it was miles from being the whole truth.

"Have you told anyone?" she asked quietly.

He shook his head.

Having told you that, he thought, may I touch you now? An obvious deflection from what he'd just declared, his new longing for her. An instance of his unworthiness? If that's what it was, he did not care. The elements of her face were concentrated into the dark pupils of her eyes, which had locked on him. How could he ever have thought her unbeautiful?

How many times had he peered at the backs of the heads of girls who did not know of his existence, thinking, Look at me! Turn in your seat right now and look at me! They never had.

But Didi *was* looking at him, openly marveling. The world is round, he'd said. The earth moves around the sun!

"What is it like?" she asked.

"It's like being a hypocrite. Everybody treats you like you're a little god, when inside you know you're just . . ." He shrugged.

"Like everybody else."

He took this in. All he'd wanted was that she wouldn't laugh. She wasn't laughing. "That isn't quite the feeling," he said. "I have some kind of calling, I mean for something special, but just not necessarily the Church."

"If it's something special, it has to be the Church." She said this so simply. It was an absolute truth of their kind. An absolute cul-de-sac. "I thought about being a nun."

"You did?"

"But only as a way to get out of Charlestown. How's that for a noble motive? Talk about unworthy! The religious life is the only way a girl like me gets out of here. The Medical Mission Sisters was what I thought about."

"But you —"

She leaned into him. "I decided the Town, with my dippy brother and his friends — no offense — was better than a leper colony in Borneo."

Terry laughed.

"Of course what I got, since it *is* my dippy brother and his friends, is a leper colony in the Town."

And then *she* began to laugh. They both did, at the joke of their impossible situation. Born to be special, but born here. They laughed and laughed. In a few minutes they would not know what had been so funny.

Finally Terry stood up, and then Didi followed. He said, "Anyway . . . now you know my problem."

"You've got two problems — God and your mother."

"Guess which one is worse."

"So just go home and tell her."

Didi seemed so practical all of a sudden, as if she thought nothing of telling the truth to her mother.

"And then what? I graduate next month. If I don't go in the seminary . . ." His voice trailed off, and once more he lifted his eyes to the city in the distance.

"You do what the rest of us do. You get a job. Maybe you get a girlfriend."

"But what about that other feeling, of being called to something else? I think . . ." He faced her, feeling rushed now. What had he said? What had he done? When she brought her eyes right back into his, he felt the bolt of his strength again, what he'd needed before. He said, "I think I'd want to go to college. I mean, maybe I would just postpone the seminary, you know what I mean?"

"That's what you'd say to her?"

"No. It could be true."

"Postpone, Terry? What? Giving your life to a God you don't feel worthy of? You don't want to be a priest any more than I want to be a nun. You just want out."

"I'm not saying that, not yet."

"Wait a minute, bud. Are you nervous because I said 'girlfriend'?"

"No. No, that's —"

"I wasn't talking about me, you stupid shit."

"Neither was I, Didi."

She stepped back, feigning incredulity. "You're in high school, Charlie! Do I look like a cradle robber?" She kept backing up, now pointing at him while cupping her mouth with her other hand.

Terry felt dizzy with confusion. Offending her was the last thing he'd meant to do.

"Do I look like a church robber?" Didi threw her head back and laughed. Her hair caught the feverish light of sunset and seemed afire for an instant. She made a cackling sound, then turned and minced away, twirling an imaginary cane, her head cocking from side to side. The perfection of her Charlie Chaplin showed him, somehow, the depth of her wound.

✧

That night Squire and Terry were lying in their beds against opposite walls of the small room with the slanted ceiling. It had been their room forever.

"Nick, you awake?"

Terry was rigid, his hands under his head. He'd been trying to make out the seam in the ceiling where the inclined plane met the horizontal one.

"Nick?"

What is this called? he wondered, thinking of the shape of the room. Trapezoid cube? It reminded him of questions on the College Boards. He wondered if he could use the results of the test he'd taken to get into the seminary. Not cube, rectangle. Box. Bedroom.

He looked to the side, just able to make out the form of his brother under a dark mound of blanket. Mushroom.

"Come on, you dipstick."

The mound stirred, but settled again.

Nick had said so little at dinner. It had been a momentous day for him too, but Terry's announcement had usurped all the energy in the room. Their mother had stiffened with surprise, her fork suspended above her plate, a piece of potato stuck in the air. Her free hand had danced at her throat as the color came into it, the blood puls-ing through her arteries, her hypertension, what always threatened to make her swoon.

Ned Cronin had said, "What, what's that?"

"I've been thinking about maybe a couple of years of college before going to the seminary. For the experience, you know? I'd still go, but not now, I mean."

He had repeated the exact words twice. But before that, he had said them in his mind a hundred times, all the way down Winthrop Street from the monument, around the tidy Common across from the store and house.

"But you're accepted already," Flo said. "You sent in your forms. I've started sewing name tags on your shirts. Monsignor already wrote the announcement for the bulletin." Her cheeks were aflame now. Her fingers had moved to her temple, which she was pressing.

"But he didn't print it yet."

"He bought you a present."

Terry stared at his mother. She was forty years old, but looked fifty. Her hair was white. Everyone said she had the nicest smile, and it was true. She could go on about her blood clots — she discussed her medi-cal condition as if it were a job — but she always ended by "offering it up," as she would say, "for my dear Terry," by which she meant the boys' father. With her purse full of pills and the white elastic stockings she wore for her varicose veins, she was regarded as one of the parish hypochondriacs, but the truth was that a clot had nearly killed her once. She expected it back, like a planet in a slow but certain orbit. No wonder she was preoccupied. No wonder she wasn't practical. Her father had long since stopped using her help in the store. Instead, she was in charge of bringing flowers to St. Mary's. Every day she fussed over the altar as if the Blessed Mother were coming. If she wasn't feeling lightheaded, she could be counted on to help serve the meals that the parish offered after funerals to families too poor to provide their own. She needed nothing for herself, that was her theme. Except for one thing, one thing only had she allowed herself all these years to need. A son a priest. Him.

"What do you mean, college?" she asked now. "Who's going to pay for that?"

Terry looked away, stunned. But Nick said, "That's not the point, Ma."

Her voice was shrill. "We can't send you two to college. We can barely —"

"Nobody's talking about me," Nick said. "Terry's the brain. He should go to college if he wants to. Money's not the point, is it, Gramps?"

Old Cronin looked helplessly at his grandson. "You know how we operate in this family. What's good for one is good for the other."

"Nobody ever said that when it was Terry going to the sem."

Terry leaned toward his brother. "Nick, never mind. I'll —"

"You have a right, okay?" Nick said "That's all I'm saying."

Terry stared at his brother, too grateful to speak. The ocean in his chest had become an ocean of love for Nick.

A killing silence descended on the table. Finally Flo stood, pressing her temples now with both hands. "I'll get seconds," she said. She put the corner of her apron in her mouth, sucking as she left the dining room. Terry knew she'd be taking a pill out there, along with a hefty swallow of her sherry.

In her absence Cronin leaned toward Terry. "You shouldn't be agitating your mother. You know what the doctor says."

"I didn't mean to, Gramps."

"Well . . ." Cronin looked from one boy to the other. "It's not your fault. It's nobody's fault."

"But he can go to college, right?" Nick asked.

Cronin covered his mouth with his napkin. His wet eyes glistened, turning on Terry. "Don't you worry. You can do that if you want. It's what the cardinal did, a couple of years with the Jesuits at BC. You tell your mother Dick Cushing did that very thing." Cronin spoke intimately of the cardinal because they'd become friends years before, when a younger Cushing had helped out at St. Mary's.

"Would *you* tell her?"

"I will indeed. She can wait. So can Monsignor's present."

Terry felt that he could breathe again.

But then his grandfather had added, "Experience, that's right. And some Jesuit training. You'll be a better priest for it." He'd fixed Terry with a cold stare. "Your mother is counting on you. And so am I. But the main thing, boyo, it's a sin to reject a divine calling, and we all know you've got one. Right? Right?"

Now, in the bedroom, Terry said into the darkness above him, "I know you're awake."

"No I'm not."

"Come on, Nick."

"Squire."

"You like that name? You don't think it's phony?"

Squire sat halfway up. Terry could just imagine the expression on his face: Who's phony?

"All right, *Squire*. All right."

Squire flipped onto his back and punched his pillow up.

Terry said, "I heard what happened. Jackie's sister told me."

"Told you what?"

"At the store. Those guys."

"Wop cocksuckers."

"How'd you do it?"

"Just said we were already paying some asshole. Said everybody on Main Street was. Lou Triozzi." Squire laughed quietly. With Terry, now that he'd asked, Squire could enjoy it.

"Won't they find out?"

"We *are* paying. That's what I've decided. Us and everybody."

"Paying who?"

"Me."

"For protection? That's nuts. They never —"

"Gramps agreed. He's calling the meeting. The Lou Triozzi Benevolent Association. It's about to become famous. Punks like the two that we saw won't know it from the Black Hand."

"Does Mom know?"

"Come on, Terry. What does Mom have to do with anything? You shouldn't worry so much about her."

"I really let her down tonight."

"That's catshit, Terry. Hey, do you want to be a priest or don't you?"

"I don't know."

"It's your life, kid."

"But she's sick. I really get worried."

"That isn't your fault. Anyway, who the hell knows how sick she is?"

"I just wish we could keep her from getting so —"

"Maybe she gets that way to keep the leash on. Don't get railroaded."

"But *you're* getting railroaded. You're the 'Knight's Squire.' That's a leash. A year from now it'll be you who's graduating, and you'll be headed for the flower shop full time."

"Hey, as long as I don't have to take your place in the sem." They laughed. Then Squire said, "The shop is okeydokey with me."

"Really?"

"Yes. I fucking love the place. Especially now."

"Because you're Lou Triozzi, you mean?"

"I'm going to organize the pansies around here. Moran's, the Shamrock, Flanagan's, the drugstore, all of them."

"You're in high school!"

"The two wops that came into the store were no older. What do you know?" There was a defensive meanness in Squire's question, and Terry felt the shove in it.

They stopped speaking.

The silence from Squire's side was blunt, and Terry was disoriented by it. Once, Nick had deferred to Terry in everything. Nick, hatching a plan, would have wanted to know what Terry thought. But this was "Squire."

"Charlestown is changing, Squire."

"No it's not."

"These Italian guys coming into the shop like that proves it. The whole city's different. We just may as well face it. Wops come into our turf. Some of us go out. It shouldn't bother you so much."

"What fucking bothers me" — Squire sat up angrily — "is watching Gramps get slugged to the ground."

"That happened?"

"You didn't notice the mark on his head?"

"I thought that was —"

"What, he got drunk and passed out? Jesus Christ, Terry, you can really be an asshole, you know that? I mean a fucking asshole! This is the real world I'm talking about, not BC."

"What does BC have to do with it?"

Squire fell back in his bed, silent again.

"No, seriously. Why does BC bother you? You were the one who said I should go."

Squire did not answer.

Terry felt the weight of a new recognition. Despite the way his brother had supported him, Terry was letting him down too. Squire had read Terry's feelings, the way he always could. Terry wanted to say, It's not you I want to get away from. But instead he said, "You have to be careful, Nick."

"I am careful, Terry. And I'll tell you something. Those wop cocksuckers won't be coming in again."

"Yeah, thanks to another wop."

"Named Triozzi."

"Named Tucci. Isn't that his name?"

"I'm surprised you know it."

"You didn't scare those guys off, Squire. Their Al Capone did, and he won't like it if he finds out what you and your Benevolent Association are pulling off."

"He won't find out unless I tell him."

"Oh, Jesus, Squire, listen to yourself. You should leave this stuff alone."

"They didn't leave *us* alone, Terry. The two wops came to us. That was *my* calling. And I agree with what Gramps said: it's a sin to reject it. You do what you have to do. No problem. But the same applies to me, okay? That's the point, the one you seem unable to get. So go to BC. Have your malted milks at the sock hop, go to the big game, rah, rah. Get your A average. Get yourself a car coat."

"Why are you pissed off at me?"

"I'm not."

"You sound pissed off."

"You need a girlfriend, Terry. Get yourself a girlfriend."

"Jesus, Nick, why do you say that? I mean, that really —" Terry rolled with a grunt toward his wall.

"Gets you?"

"It all gets me, okay? Let's drop it."

"You brought it up. You fucking woke me."

"You were awake and you know it. This is all bullshit, Nick. All of it. Including the 'Knight's Squire' and including your junior G-man protection racket. It's crap like this that makes me want to get the hell out of here."

Squire said nothing. He lay there under the weight of knowledge he didn't want: how different they were after all, how fucking different. He thought of Jackie Mullen, his friend. He didn't need Terry.

He pictured the two punks, the acne on the one's face, the other's ridiculous sweater. He wanted them to come back. If he had to, he would go after them. He wanted to see the glint of fear in their eyes again. He wanted to cause it. "Crap like this," he said quietly to the blackness above, to himself, "makes me want to stay."

3

IN SEPTEMBER John Kennedy was the nominee, and at Boston College the air was charged. Students at Catholic schools all across the country felt the jolt of politics that fall, but at BC the unprecedented energy shot through everyone, students and teachers alike, even the wizened old Jesuits long committed to a holy ignorance of events outside the classroom and the cloister. Kennedy made nuns giddy, and he made monsignors regret having become Republicans, but his candidacy was no mere replay of the Al Smith effort three decades earlier. John Kennedy's appeal went far deeper than religion, and the success he'd achieved already, simply by the character of his arrival on the national scene, gave his first constituents a visceral sense of vindication. His importance for Catholics, for the Irish, and especially for the Irish Catholics in the neighborhoods of Boston who had elected him to Congress lay in the way his new prominence made them feel connected to the larger world he was storming — the world beyond the parish, beyond the neighborhood, beyond the parochial school, the Holy Name, the K of C, the Catholic societies and clubs that had kept separate not only sacristy ladies but lawyers, doctors, and even foresters — connected to the world beyond the streetcar schools for the Catholic kids who were, almost all of them, the first in their families to go to college.

BC was as far from Charlestown as it was possible to go and still be inside the city limits. It was a gracious, sprawling enclave straddling the border between Boston and Newton. Terry Doyle arrived there with no notion of the cultural assertion made by its sham Gothic architecture, or of the social meaning of the college's location, near Chestnut Hill where the Brahmins lived. The cardinal's residence across Commonwealth Avenue was a more telling point of reference. He noted the mansion as the streetcar passed it, but he was focused on the college as the car slowed for the turnabout at the weather shed that marked the end of the line.

Much as he'd wished otherwise, his thoughts on the interminable ride from Charlestown that first morning had kept returning to the world he did know. As he'd left the house, Nick had wished him luck. Gramps had pinned one of the famous lapel shamrocks on his new corduroy sport jacket. And his mother had put a special sack lunch in his hands and kissed him. But he was sure they'd exchanged glances behind his back as he'd adjusted the clover flower on his coat and tugged his necktie into place.

In the reflection of the streetcar window Terry had played over and over vivid scenes of his life in Charlestown. All summer the thought of this first day of college had filled him with eagerness, but what he kept seeing now in the mirror of the streetcar window had undercut his every pulse of happiness. The flower store with his red-nosed, nip-sucking grandfather, the attic room with his brother, the rooms above the store with their shelves full of pill bottles and Madonna vases, their pictures of Curley, Cushing, and Pius XII — these were the places he belonged. What was he doing going off to college? Who did he think — in the masterpiece kneecapping question of his kind — yes, who did he think he was? One night Nick had laughed and said Terry's feelings were only fitting, since surely he'd been kidnapped in infancy by tinkers and sold to the peasants at the Kerry Bouquet. That not even Nick understood his feelings had been the real surprise.

By the time he hopped off the streetcar opposite the entrance to BC, he felt hung over. He hadn't noticed them until now, but six or seven other guys got off too and headed toward the campus. They were as gangly and awkward as he was, with fresh haircuts that made their ears stand out dangerously. At Charlestown High, ears like that would get snapped from behind. All the boys wore new shoes and an air of timid isolation, but to Terry Doyle they seemed supremely at ease, upperclassmen probably.

None was carrying a brown paper lunch sack, and that stopped him just as he was about to trail across the street. Without consciously making a decision, but also fully aware of the meaning of the deed, he turned back abruptly to the streetcar platform and went directly to the green trash barrel into which commuters stuffed stale newspapers. He pushed the bag his mother had given him deep into the newspapers, appalled at himself yet knowing he had no choice. Just as automatically, he pulled the shamrock off his coat and stuffed it in after the bag.

The demands stern Jesuits made on him that morning purged him not only of his morose self-doubt but of all feeling. "No salvation," he imagined them thundering, "outside of class!" In a welcome state of numb compliance, he went from intimidating orientation sessions in a succession of classrooms to the slow, snaking lines of course registration in the big gym. Even his ability to be impressed by the turreted campus was dulled when a warm, late summer drizzle began to fall. The rain made the figures passing each other in the quads slouch into themselves, yet Terry had concluded that not even his fellow freshmen were as lost in this new world as he was.

When he had finally accumulated all seven of his class-admit cards, he went to Lyons Hall where a temporary bookstore had been set up at one end of the large cafeteria. He bought his textbooks and terraced them under his left arm the way other guys were doing. His heart sank as he prepared to go back out in the rain. His books would be ruined before he got home. None of these other fellows had even looked at him. Nobody had said so much as hi. He felt lonelier and more displaced than he ever had — was this possible? — in the Town. This whole thing was a mistake.

But then Terry saw the tables against one wall of a congested corridor outside the cafeteria, each with a knot of guys clustered at it, each table, he saw then, with signs and barkers. Campus organizations were working to draw recruits. ROTC, he read, GOLD KEY SOCIETY, THE HEIGHTS. Terry walked slowly into the bustle, afraid that the disappointment that had so dogged him was evident. What would these eager, laughing upperclassmen make of him? He dreaded being branded.

Then he saw it, a card table with a felt banner skirting its front edge reading YOUNG DEMOCRATS. Above the table a professionally lettered cardboard sign running vertically on a pole, like a delegation banner at a political convention, displayed the one shimmering word, blue caps against white. Not IOWA but KENNEDY.

Doyle pushed through the ebullient throng to that table, but when he got there his point of reference changed entirely. The student standing by the table, clipboard in hand, waiting to sign him up, was a Negro. He was taller even than Terry, and much thinner. He wore the uniform chinos and blue oxford cloth button-down, but the deep brown skin of his hands and face set him absolutely apart from the others. He was the first Negro Terry had seen at BC that day. His eyes were big and round, and the whites of his eyes looked like glass, and set against that skin his teeth seemed made of china. Doyle had never seen such a smile on a man.

"Why don't you take a picture? It'll last longer."

Terry had not realized he was staring.

"I'm Bright McKay." The young black put his hand out.

Terry took it.

"What's your name?"

"Terry Doyle."

"Hi, Terry. I'm a sophomore here, history major. Can I talk to you about Jack Kennedy? I think he's your kind of guy."

"Yeah," Doyle said. "Yeah, you can."

McKay's bony wrists and hands protruded from his sleeves like sticks, and it was easy to picture him on *The Ed Sullivan Show* with Harry Belafonte, singing the "Banana Boat" song. His cheeks were hollow, and his nubby hair was cut close to his scalp. A barber's clipper had furrowed a part on the left side of his head.

As McKay rattled off his spiel — "a chance for our future . . . our time has come" — Doyle backed away, feeling as if he'd answered the door to a magazine salesman. *Jet*, he thought. *Ebony*. "A turning point in history," McKay was saying, "when our country turns to us and we provide the leaders —" Suddenly he stopped. "What's wrong?"

"Nothing's wrong," Terry answered, but he knew he was blushing.

"You look confused."

"You said, 'We're the leaders now.'"

"Yeah, that's the point."

Doyle sensed McKay's mystification, but hadn't a clue how to explain himself, that "we're the leaders now" meant, in his world, the Irish, the Catholics.

"Wait a sec." McKay leaned in on him with eyes digging. "Wait a sweet goddamn sec. You think I'm talking N double-A C P. You think I mean 'we' as in 'We Shall Overcome.'"

"No I don't."

McKay laughed. He sat back against the edge of his table, hugging his clipboard. "Terry, my man. Terry . . . Terry . . . Terry. 'We' as in 'You and me, brother.' As in 'Young men shall dream dreams.' As in 'Our time has come!' People like us, people our age . . ."

A door burst open in Doyle's mind. For the first time in his life he was being invited to think of himself as belonging to a group that was not his nationality or his race or his religion. He and this colored guy were "youth."

McKay had read his mind, and Doyle wanted to ask, How do you do that?

But McKay had resumed his spiel. "America under Ike has gone soft because there is no vision, and where there is no vision, the people perish . . ."

As Terry listened, he was struck by the fact that the kid's accent was nothing like what it should have been. Belafonte: there *was* a lyrical curl in Bright McKay's voice that made him sound almost as if he were singing, and all the time he spoke, his smile never quite left his face. McKay repeatedly referred to the candidate as "Jack Kennedy," with such an air of familiarity that, at one point, Terry almost interrupted to ask, Do you know him?

Where did you learn to talk like that?

Even before McKay had finished, Terry Doyle had admitted to himself how drawn he was to him.

"Any questions?" McKay said finally.

"Yes, one," Doyle answered with a jauntiness unusual for him. "Where do I sign up?"

McKay's grin grew, if anything, wider. He held his clipboard steadily in front of Doyle. "Right here, my good man. Right here."

Aware of the relief he felt — landfall! Kennedy! And was this a friend? — Terry Doyle wrote his name as if that were what he'd come all this way to do.

✧

Kennedy headquarters were on Tremont Street just down from the Parker House. Three afternoons a week that fall Terry Doyle interrupted his streetcar commute back to Charlestown to stop there and work. A cigarette between his fingers, his cord sportcoat flung over his shoulder, his tie loosened, Doyle put a picture in his mind, as he arrived, of young Jimmy Stewart. His personality had never seemed so vibrant. His status as a college student, entirely involved by day with people who had not known him before, gave him license to reinvent himself, and that's what he was trying to do. Often he arrived at the campaign in the company of other guys from BC, and they all instinctively adopted the manner of candidates, slapping shoulders, cracking jokes, aggressively inviting other workers to like them. That one of the BC guys, a leader of the group, was a Negro made Terry's experience of his new situation all the more exotic.

The other campaign volunteers were mostly older people, retirees and housewives, middle-aged hooky-playing city workers, men in sleeveless sweaters and women wearing little hats like Jackie Kennedy's, or eyeglasses shaped like cat's eyes with rhinestones at the corners. They waved at the friendly college kids, youthful examples of the jaunty American masculinity of which Kennedy himself was the beau ideal. What a relief for Terry, a secret relief, to be out from under the low, dark ceiling — pallium — of his mother's wish for him. Down here he was no longer an apprentice priest. He could live without the good opinion of the nuns. He could be virtuous — the cause of freedom! — without being pious. And he could look at girls, want them, have one.

The Young Democrats were pulled together from several area colleges, and had their own section of phone banks and Ditto machines in the far rear of the huge open space on the first floor of headquarters. Warrens of campaign offices filled the floors above, but those were staffed with the pros who ran the whole country. Kennedy's brothers and sisters, Larry O'Brien, Ted Sorensen, Richard Goodwin, Kenny O'Donnell — word was they all had offices upstairs, though no one ever saw them; they were always on the road. The volunteers' domain was this room the size of a roller rink. As Terry Doyle, Bright McKay, and three other eagles crossed it one day in October, they rattled off their greetings.

Terry stopped once to snuff his cigarette out in an ashtray. Except for McKay, the others kept going. The blue-haired woman at one of the desks grinned up at Terry. "That's a nice crop of daisies," she said. She had a pleasing Irish accent like his mother's, and was about her age.

"Daisies?"

"Freckles."

"Thanks, dear," Doyle answered. He liked the woman, but he felt his skin heating up.

"You know what freckles are, don't you?"

"No." He squinted at her through the smoke of his last drag. He had not come this far in life to have attention drawn to his freckles. One summer he had applied Man Tan to his face every day for most of a month to blot the damn things out. His mother had said he looked like a coal miner. He hadn't stopped until his brother began calling him Smoke.

"Angel kisses," she said. "Every freckle is a place where an angel kissed you."

Bright McKay had been hanging back, but now he pushed himself between them, opening his hands, ta-da! "Well, look what them angels done to me!"

The woman's face froze, and Terry did not need to wonder why. He took McKay by the arm and waved at her while pulling him away. "You're the angel, sweetheart. See you later." Then, when they were several desks away, he said to McKay, "And they call you Bright?"

McKay took his arm back and stopped, halting Doyle too. He channeled his reaction into an arch pompousness. "My name is not a comment on my mental acuity, Terence. As an alternative to Neville, I accept it." He smiled impishly. "Neville McKay. How 'bout that flag? I'll take Bright any day. In our part of town it means light-skinned, as in mulatto."

"But that's ridiculous. You're so . . ."

"Black? You can say it." He was speaking a little loudly, as if he wanted the biddies to hear him. "It's a joke, Terence, a joke of opposites, like calling Fats Waller Sprat. My skin was always this black. One huge freckle from Ghana. A less ironic people would have called me Shine."

"Shit, Bright, I'm sorry if she —"

"Some brogue, that lady. A voice like that is a colored man's warning bell."

"Relax. My mother has a voice like that. Take it from me, she'd hate the British a lot sooner than she'd hate you."

"Then I'm in double trouble. She probably sensed it that my father still sings 'God Save the Queen.'"

"What?"

"My guv is British," McKay said with a sharp new accent.

Doyle stared at him.

McKay burst out laughing, slapped Doyle's shoulder. "Yowsah, Mistah Da'll. Camptown races, do-da-day!" McKay did one quick hoedown dance step, then shifted completely to draw himself up like a butler, snapping his words off. "And, my good sir, you are of the conventional conviction that all British subjects are of the Caucasian persuasion."

"No, no. I'm not."

"I can read your mind," McKay said simply.

And once again it seemed to Doyle that he had. Could he read feelings too? This confusion? This distress at having said something wrong? But what? Some insult? Why was McKay angry?

"My father comes from Barbados." McKay smiled with sudden warmth. "My mom is from cotton country, but they met here. I'm Boston through and through, Terence. Same as you."

"You think you've got yourself a thick mick here, don't you? Puncturing his neat assumptions." Doyle was aware that he could have said this bitterly, but bitterness was not remotely what he felt.

McKay shrugged. The bustling room around them had fallen away. "I hadn't expected that this would necessarily happen. But it had to if we were going to be friends."

"What do you mean 'going to be,' asshole?" Terry deflected the uncool impulse to express affection. "You've got some neat assumptions of your own."

"Like what?"

Doyle tossed his head toward the blue-haired lady and the other busy middle-aged Irish volunteers. "That they were all Joe McCarthy's people. Since Nixon was too, that they should be with him. That they're only here because Kennedy is Irish Catholic."

McKay showed those teeth of his again. "But that's true, isn't it?"

They laughed. Hell, maybe it was true. But Terry wanted to repeat himself. These are good people, he wanted to say. They don't know you, that's all. I love these people.

McKay put his arm around Doyle's shoulder. Terry was aware of Bright's hand falling across his sweater as they started across the floor again. He was aware of the volunteers watching them now.

"And I've got other surprises for you," McKay said.

"No you don't. Your father's a Brit? Nothing could surprise me more than that."

McKay said, "He's a priest."

Doyle stopped, sliding out from under his friend's arm. McKay continued for another step and a half, then froze with his leg in midair, a bit of slapstick.

"What?"

McKay swiveled around. "An Anglican priest, man. Ever hear of St. Cyprian's?"

Terry shook his head. There was a lot he'd never heard of.

"On this same street, Tremont Street, out across Mass. Ave., in the Berry. You've heard of the Berry?"

Doyle did not react.

"Roxbury, Terence. St. Cyp's is the Turkish parish."

"Turkish?"

"West Indian. My dad is the rector."

"He's a minister?"

"A priest. Just like the priests at BC. Mass every morning. Chasuble, alb, transubstantiation."

"But he's got a kid, so we're talking Protestant, right?"

"Christ, if my father ever heard you say that. As if he were Baptist, as if he were fucking Methodist! St. Cyprian's Episcopal Church. Not AME! C of E!"

"Okay, all right." Terry put his hands up, surrendering the point. But only because it had been made: Episcopal was Protestant. "Now I see why you're excused from theology class at school. Because you're Episcopal."

"Episcopalian, actually. And yes, that's why I draw a bye. But" — McKay raised his hands now too, calling this game off, this one on one, this keep away — "the truth is, unlike my father, I am not a Christian, period." He leaned in, and Doyle could smell his cologne, spicy and sweet. "Don't tell my old man when you come home with me for Sunday dinner — you *will* come home with me, won't you?"

"Yes."

"Don't tell him or Mom either, but I'm an atheist."

The stark expression on McKay's face hit Terry, the dead earnestness at last. He understood that there was more integrity in that statement, more virtue, than in all the easy, countless credos he himself had made. He answered quietly, "I'm not an atheist, Bright. But I have my version of the same thing. I am supposed to be a priest. And I mean *priest!* I am the elder son. It's the landless Irish version of primogeniture. They still expect it of me."

"Shit, man, and you want no part of it."

"Right."

"Don't blame you. Who in hell could blame you? Tell you what." He slugged Terry's shoulder. "Stick with me. I'll teach you a thing or two."

McKay turned and strode back toward the Young Dems' corner. He glanced back and said, "Come on."

But Doyle did not move. For a moment he just stood there watching McKay and thinking, You already have, you bastard. You already have.

✧

On another afternoon he stood inside the front door for a moment, just in from Tremont Street, having come down from BC alone. The room had been enlarged by the removal of walls and false ceilings, and it sprawled from the front of the building to the back. Light bulbs hanging in factorylike tin cones made a checkerboard of light and shadow. There were dozens of card tables, metal desks, folding chairs, and wooden benches, most piled high with cartons to be opened, sheets of paper to be folded into flyers, envelopes to be stuffed and addressed.

Doyle watched the workers checking off names, moistening wads of envelope flaps on sponges, dialing telephones — all brimming with the edgy happiness of former athletes. In Boston politics, volunteers could be pros too.

Not only the lift of the campaign lightened Doyle's step as he crossed the spirited room. One of the things that had heightened his interest in the far back corner where the college kids worked was the fact that, as the weeks had passed and the momentum picked up, more and more of the Young Dems were girls. "Young Debs" was what McKay called them. They came from local women's colleges, Regis, Emmanuel, Radcliffe, Wellesley, and Wheaton. They were suburban extroverts, flirtatious and surprisingly sexy in their blazers and pleated skirts. They seemed completely free of the feeling of displacement that he took for granted in himself and had sensed in the girls he'd known in Charlestown. In their double-your-pleasure levity, in their twin-sweater sets and penny loafers and pageboy hairdos, it was easy to picture the neatly trimmed lawns in front of their family houses — barbecues and patios out back — in white-collar Forest Hills, Roslindale, and even Wellesley and Winchester. What an anti-Xanadu the pinched, tavern-ridden milieu to which he returned at night would be to them. Much was made in the Town of Kennedy's having started out there, but the truth was he'd never had anything to do with the place. Some of these girls, on the other hand, were daughters of men who knew Kennedy. They were English majors, or history or poli sci or even economics majors. They were smart. They talked of going to Washington when Kennedy won. They talked of working for him after graduation. The Kennedy girls gave no indication they thought the world was made for anyone but them.

But there was one thing the debs couldn't do so well, which was use a typewriter. That afternoon's crisis in the Young Dems' corner was about typing.

While Doyle draped his sportcoat over the back of his chair, he listened as the team captain cruelly berated a girl, waving a page of typescript in her face. He was Ed Lake, a Harvard senior whose blond hair fell across his forehead. "Where'd you learn to type, Ginger? At Disneyland?" he shrieked. "Or was it a home for retards? You have a dozen erasure scars on here, and they're a mess." Lake swung around to his audience of eight or ten Young Dems. "This letter is going to fifty college deans! It asks to get our people excused from school for the last push. It has to go out tonight, and it has to be perfect! Can't anybody here use a goddamn typewriter?"

"If perfection is what you want, why don't you do it yourself then, Ed?" one of the other girls said.

Terry liked her guts, and he looked for her eye. When he got it, he winked, Good for you. But the girl looked at him as if one of them were dead.

The typist was crying softly in front of Lake. It's fun, making girls cry. Lake made a show of collecting himself, taking a deep breath, boosting his shoulders, bunching up the letter, and tossing it in the wastebasket.

Terry felt he was watching a performance in a war movie, an officer confronted with a case of shell shock. A British officer.

Lake turned away from the girl and said calmly, all leadership now, "Seriously, folks. We need this typed. We can't send out a generalized mimeo. These are deans. We need the letter typed fifty times, each one separately, before Ken O'Donnell leaves tonight, so he can sign them."

"If Kenny has to sign them, why doesn't his secretary do it?"

"Because it's our job, that's why. Shit!" Lake banged the table, bouncing the telephones, jolting their bells. This is my shot, Terry imagined him saying, at a job upstairs!

As the bell sounds faded into the awful silence, Terry, from his place behind Lake, said, "I know a typist."

Lake faced him.

Terry looked at his watch. "If I catch her as she's leaving work, I could have her over here inside an hour."

Lake's eyes bulged. "Go! Go!"

Doyle did not move. He said quietly, "I wouldn't think of bringing her over here if it was possible you'd talk to her like you just talked to Ginger." Somehow Terry found it possible to keep from blinking as he held Lake's eyes.

Lake shrugged. "Okay, buddy. I'll be good. Promise."

Terry glanced across at the girl who'd looked through him before. She wasn't looking through him now. To Lake he said, "Apologize to Ginger, Ed."

"You're shitting me."

"If you want a typist, you apologize."

"You're the kid from BU."

"BC, Ed. Big difference. Eagles, not Terriers. What about that apology?"

Lake let everyone see the trouble he had believing this. But finally he looked back at the girl slumped in a nearby chair. "I guess he's right, Ginger. I'm sorry. I was out of line."

Terry hooked his jacket and walked away.

The Hancock Building was across Boston Common, a few blocks up Boylston Street at Clarendon. He arrived at the main entrance in time to light up. He leaned against a parked car and enjoyed his smoke and the cool air on his face. Beyond Copley Square the sky was red with the coming sunset. A feeling of calm acceptance came over Terry, and it reminded him of the feeling he'd once associated with church.

Girls began pouring out of the building at a minute past five. They were heading home to neighborhoods like his own, but they were dressed like women in magazines or, even, movies; not like students. They wore a lot of makeup, dresses with petticoats and cinched waists, hats, and, some of them, gloves. They must spend most of what they earn, he thought, at Jordan's or Filene's.

He didn't see her. He dropped his cigarette and pushed clear of the car, pulling himself to his full height. Had she quit? he wondered suddenly. He hadn't seen Didi Mullen, except from a distance, since the May afternoon on Bunker Hill, and if her life had changed as much as his had —

But then he saw that hair in the grand doorway. She had it pulled back in a ponytail, but still it framed her face and set her apart, as it always had. Her hair was the color of the sky at the end of Boylston Street.

"Didi!" He called her name twice more as he cut through the crowd, waving. The girls made way for him. "Hey, Didi!"

She stopped on the stairs. Other office girls flowed around her. Terry crossed to stand on the pavement just below. "Hi," he said.

"Charlie!" she said, with an air of Anything can happen downtown.

He raised his fist in mock anger.

"Okay, okay." She laughed. "Terence." Her eyes sparkled behind the big round lenses of her glasses. Her arms went out. He thought for a moment she was going to leap, hugging him, which made him pull back. He couldn't help it, but his first feeling was disappointment. He had remembered her as pretty, but she just wasn't. Now that he saw her face again — her pointed chin, her big lips with the wrong lipstick, her gangly neck, even her smile, which seemed goofy — it all made a sharp contrast to the pert good looks of the girls at the campaign.

"Hey, Didi."

"Hay is for horses."

He felt himself blushing. "How you doing?"

"Good, Terry. *Really* good." She hunched her shoulders girlishly, an unconscious emphasis of what could only have been happiness.

"You *look* good," he said, and as if his statement had changed her, he saw the way in which she did look good, her face transparent with affection, shining with feeling, unprotected. Her eyeglasses moved and he thought, Dragonfly! Their cigarettes touching, how foolishly sexual he'd felt for a minute that late afternoon, and how the sweetness of their accidental, unrepeated intimacy had lingered. Now she didn't seem at all older than him, and the connection between them seemed far closer than the fact of her being the sister of his brother's friend.

"What are you doing here?"

"I came to find you."

"Me?"

"Didi, I need a favor. I'm in really big trouble."

"You are?"

"Did you know I work for Jack Kennedy?"

"I thought you went to college."

"I do. I go to BC. But I'm a volunteer in the campaign, and we're in the homestretch now, and —"

"He's going to win, isn't he? Everybody says he's going to win."

"The polls don't say that. Ike is working hard for Nixon now, and with Lodge, even Massachusetts —"

"But *you!* You said *you're* in trouble."

The office workers were still streaming around them.

"Which way do you go?" Doyle asked.

"The MTA at the library."

"Shall I walk you?"

Didi fell into step beside him, but she kept her eyes fixed on his face, and walking was awkward. As they headed across Copley Square in the wrong direction, away from the campaign, Terry felt stupid. How had he ever imagined that she would agree to drop everything and rush to Tremont Street? Or, if she would, that she could handle what went on there?

"What trouble?" She asked this with such earnest alarm that he realized he had conveyed the wrong thing. She thought he was talking about himself. Hon, he wanted to say, in politics we always talk personal, urgent, end of the world. Relax.

She continued looking at him while they were walking, and he had to nudge her once to keep her from bumping someone. He fell back on a briefer's neutral tone. "My office in the campaign coordinates getting college students onto the bandwagon."

"I'm not a college student."

"I know. That's not why, I mean . . . we hit a major snag today." He saw it coming, the insult she would feel. If he could have touched a button and disappeared — Captain Video! "I mean, like twenty minutes ago. They sent me over, like desperate, to see if you would help?"

"Help Kennedy?"

"Yes. At the campaign headquarters near the Parker House."

"Is he there?"

"Kennedy?" Doyle burst out laughing. "No, Didi, no. The candidate is anywhere but in his headquarters. I've been working there a month, and I've never seen him."

"Well, but what — ?"

"A typist, Didi." Terry stopped, then she did. They faced each other. Behind her the brilliant sky glowed, making her hair seem spun of the purest light. "We need a typist, right now. We need one bad."

Terry had himself braced for her reaction, but he knew so little.

"Really?"

"Yes."

Her face filled with delighted surprise. "You need me?"

"You can type, can't you?"

"A hundred words a minute. I won a prize last month."

Doyle's eyes took a light from hers. "If you come with me, you can win one next month — but for Kennedy. Will you?"

She seemed very young to him, despite her more formal clothes. She was so unlike the charging people he spent time with now, and sure enough, without a hint of the mortification he'd have felt saying such a thing, she answered, "Yes, I'd love to. But I have to call my mother."

She was great. She sat at a typing table in the corner, her fingers flying. Other girls took the letters as she finished them, fed her fresh sheets of bond, carbons arranged, and crossed out the names as she moved down the lists. She rarely hit the wrong key, but when she did, she erased as if by magic, leaving no perceptible mark.

Bright McKay had arrived after she set to work, and he, crossing back and forth for phone calls and for coffee, sent signals of approval toward Terry — winks, three-ring signs — as if Didi's accomplishment were his. Or was that his meaning?

Her work sparked that of others, and soon the Young Dems were bustling among the tables, pushing voter lists at one another, barking into telephones.

All the bustle made Didi pull into herself, the way she could in the middle of the vast typing-pool floor at Hancock. She'd been shy when Terry had first made the introductions, but she'd tried to compensate by being funny. When they'd shown her to the typing table, she'd cracked, as girls did at work, "Now to knock off some hen tracks on my roll-top piano." But no one had laughed. A couple of girls eyeballed each other without even trying to keep her from seeing.

Terry encouraged her to take a break at one point, but she refused. She let the coffee he brought grow cold. He sensed her need to avoid having to make small talk with the other girls, to whom her presence had to be a rebuke. She resembled them hardly at all. With her garish costume jewelry, bangles on her jumping arms, and oversize earrings she looked more like the middle-aged housewives licking envelopes across the room than the girls in bobby sox and loafers. Terry wanted to see her getup as offbeat, but the truth was Didi seemed like an adolescent in her mother's clothes. In that company, he wanted to protect her.

It was almost ten when she finished. Except for the Young Dems' corner, the vast room was nearly deserted, and all but the hanging cone lights had been turned off. Their corner glowed, however, and the eight kids who remained gave a rousing cheer when Didi snapped the last letter out of the machine.

Ed Lake put the stack of pages in an accordion folder and hurried across the room, through the door that would take him upstairs.

Doyle saw Didi rubbing her neck. He stood behind her and put his hands on her shoulders and began to massage gently while the others congratulated her. Didi twisted in her chair to look up at Terry. The ripeness in her face made it clear that a sense of his pleasure was all Didi Mullen really wanted. The other kids saw it, and they fell silent to hear what Doyle would say — which of course made his saying anything impossible.

Didi excused herself to go to the ladies' room. Terry watched her go, unsure why he felt sad all of a sudden.

Ed Lake returned and reported that the gods above were well pleased. "And so am I," he said. "Thanks, gang. You're the best."

"Praise from Caesar," one of the girls snapped. Lake struck a self-mocking pose that made everyone laugh, and made them like him again too.

"Cow time!" Bright McKay cried, and a Tufts guy named Thatch countered "Chugalug!" Which meant the Grill Room of the Parker House. There were noises of agreement while they grabbed their coats and bags.

Lake said to Doyle, "Is Didi gone already?"

"She's in the head. I'll wait for her. I'll see if she'll come."

"Tell her dinner's on the candidate. I hope she'll . . ." Lake hesitated.

"Sign on?"

"That's what I was going to say, but I guess she probably . . ."

"Probably what, Ed?"

"Probably wouldn't." Lake stared at Doyle, hard. Doyle sensed his dislike, and realized Lake had just decided something, but it had more to do with him than with Didi.

"You could ask her," Doyle said.

"I don't think so, no. Young Dems is a little different. If she wants on, she could hook up with the church-supper ladies." Lake tossed his head toward the main part of the room. "They need a typist for those voter lists."

"That way, if *you* need one again, you can just raise your hand and snap your fingers."

"Give it a rest, Doyle. Anyway, tell her the offer stands. About dinner, I mean. Dinner's on us."

"Tell her yourself." Terry indicated Didi, who was coming toward them from the far side of the room. Her rich red hair was loose now, brushing her shoulders.

"No, you do it." Lake glanced at her as he put his coat on and moved away. "See you at the Grill."

By the time Didi reached Terry, Lake was gone. "Where'd everybody go?"

"The Parker House. It's sort of a tradition, if we're here this late. Everybody's hoping you'll come." *He* was, anyway. With her hair down she looked less prim, more like one of the debs, ready to go out. He caught a whiff of her perfume. It stirred him to think she'd just applied it. "In fact, the campaign wants to buy you dinner."

"Oh gosh, Terry, I don't think so."

"No, really, Didi. You saved the game tonight. That was really important, what you did."

"Terry . . ." Unconsciously, she leaned toward him, a gawky posture. Her neck was so long. Her hair fell forward on her face. "I'm glad you asked me. I mean, I liked doing it."

"So come have a sandwich or something. Then I'll take you home."

"No, I'm sorry, but no."

But hadn't she just prettied herself up? Had she done it only for going home?

Terry realized she had just this moment changed her mind. Watching Ed Lake, that bastard, she must have grasped it that they were finished with her now, ready to send her back across —

Doyle did not have the language to describe the gulf that separated

Didi from his new friends, the gulf on both sides of which his feet had been planted for weeks now. He'd been a big shot, a comer. But Didi knew him. He was a fumbling adolescent pretending to be a man.

"Well, let me take you home then."

"You don't have to, Terry."

"No, really. I'd like to."

"I have cab money. Ma makes me take a cab at night."

"Are you downtown that much at night?"

"Not really, but at work sometimes . . ." She let her voice trail off. Downtown? What would he think when he saw what downtown was to her — the world in which she worked, and the world from which she fled?

He put his coat on, feeling slightly sick. "Well, anyway, I can walk you to a cab stand."

"Sure you can, big guy." Didi tried to defuse the glumness by bumping her hip into Terry, a stab at Mae West, but it didn't come off.

They crossed the room, Terry leading the way between the tables and desks. He imagined reaching back to take her hand, but knew how out of the question that was. Instead, he reached up and slapped a light fixture, which began to sway behind them, playing its beam back and forth across the shadows.

On Tremont Street the air was cold and wet, blowing in from the harbor. The pavement glistened with the mist of a coming rain. The streetlamps wore halos.

There were no cabs at the stand in front of the Parker House. At the curb, a limousine sat with its engine running, a driver at the wheel. Two men in business suits were standing at the open rear door, talking. As Terry and Didi approached, he recognized Ken O'Donnell. He had the accordion folder pressed under his arm.

On an impulse, Terry did then take Didi's hand and go right up to the men.

"Mr. O'Donnell," he said brightly.

O'Donnell interrupted himself to look blankly at Doyle.

"I'm one of the Young Dems, sir. Terry Doyle, from BC." Terry Doyle, ace bell ringer, back slapper, junior candidate. "I wanted you to meet the girl who dropped everything to type those letters for you." Terry indicated O'Donnell's folder. "Not one of our regular crew, an emergency volunteer." Terry brought her forward. "This is Deirdre Mullen."

O'Donnell could be imperious with his own people, but he understood that this was an outsider. "Hello, darling," he said warmly. "You did a great job tonight, and we appreciate it." He put his hand out. When Didi took it, he turned her to his companion. "And say hello to Ted Kennedy."

The sound hung in the air.

Didi and Terry both turned slowly. Kennedy. He was looking at her, nodding. What occurred to Doyle to say was, You should see how she erases.

Kennedy was a big man with dramatic features, a head of wavy dark hair, a powerfully dimpled chin, eyebrows that nearly touched above his nose. Doyle had rung a few doorbells himself by now, and he knew about smiling, but it was impossible that the warmth on Kennedy's face was not genuine.

"How are you?" he asked, but with a rote inflection that contradicted the light in his face. He shook Didi's hand, then Terry's. "BC? You both go to BC?"

Terry's heart sank, but before he could protect her, Didi let out a loud laugh. "Oh, no, Mr. Kennedy. Not me. I'm too smart to go to college!"

Kennedy stared at her for a moment, then he laughed too. "So was I," he said. "*Much* too smart." He winked. "But not as smart as you, because I went anyway and hated it." He roared, a great, loud, infectious bark of a laugh that echoed off the walls of the buildings above them.

Terry loved Didi for having put it that way, and for having so surely touched something in Kennedy.

O'Donnell said to her, "But you're on the team now, right? We need you, Deirdre."

Didi glanced at Terry, who nodded.

"Yes, sir. I guess I am."

"That's great." He squeezed her forearm.

And Kennedy said, "My brother appreciates what you're doing for him." He looked right into Doyle's eyes.

This Kennedy was less than a decade older than Doyle, the baby of the clan, the playboy who'd recently married a blond dish and who drove a convertible. Yet Terry felt as if the man had just blessed him. He veered from the thought, its association with priests. "We're working for your brother, but for the country too."

"That's true. What's your name again?"

"Terry Doyle."

"And Deirdre Mullen," O'Donnell put in, demonstrating his skill — his first service to the family — at catching and keeping names.

"Well, thanks, Terry," Ted said. "And thanks, Deirdre."

"'Didi,' actually, Mr. Kennedy."

Kennedy laughed again. "Then 'Teddy,' actually." And he leaned over quickly and kissed Didi's cheek.

A moment later, Kennedy and O'Donnell were gone.

Terry faced Didi. A soft rain had begun to fall, but neither had noticed.

Terry said, "Gosh, now you can't wash your face again."

Didi, too moved to joke, stared at the darkness into which Kennedy's car had disappeared.

"You're on the team, Didi. Handpicked by the head coach."

She looked at him. "So I guess I better eat with you, huh?"

"Yep." He took her elbow, and they walked to the Parker House entrance.

"Wait a minute, Terry. Who's going to be there?"

"The kids you met already, or if you didn't meet them, the ones you saw."

"Are they friends of yours?"

"Not really . . . Well, one is. Bright McKay."

"Which one is he?"

"He's another BC guy."

"Does he know . . . ?" She glanced toward the street, then let her eyes settle on Terry's. "You told me something last spring that I didn't forget."

"What?"

"That you weren't so sure about the priesthood anymore, and then, the next thing I hear, you're going to BC instead of the seminary. I mean, I was amazed, Terry, that somebody I knew would actually do something about his life."

"Talking to you that day helped me make up my mind."

"Not that I would have known that."

"I would have told you, but —"

"But your mother told my mother that you're still going in the sem, only later, after a couple of years at BC. That's what you said you might do. So you're still going to be a priest."

"I wouldn't, I mean . . ." He felt humiliated that she should have glimpsed his confusion, and cowardice. There was no question of his having told his mother the truth, but had he told it to himself? He'd thought his new fever for politics would have released him from the curse of the priesthood, but in some ways it was worse. Doyle's deepest wish was to be like John Kennedy, but how was that remotely possible for a boy like him? A new image of the priesthood was half formed in his mind, one that had less to do with the parish biddies of Charlestown — it appalled him to think of the mothers discussing his vocation — or even with the brilliant Jesuits, than with the as yet ill-defined joining of the moral and political purposes he associated with Senator Kennedy. Something special: he was called to something special, he just did not know what. Christ, couldn't they leave him alone? Couldn't she? Didi was giving him the feeling he always had at home, and he hated it.

"I'm just trying to get things straight about you, Terry. That's all."

"What things?"

"Why you came to get me today."

"Because we needed you."

"That's it?"

"Yes," he said coldly, "that's it."

"Okay, Charlie." She pushed through the revolving doors into the lobby of the hotel. When he followed, she kept going, but said over her shoulder, "Where is this joint?"

"Straight ahead."

She began to walk like Charlie Chaplin, twirling a make-believe cane, her head jerking, her feet pointed to the side with each step. The bitch.

The Young Dems had pushed into the usual crescent-shaped booth at the far side of the bar. The Grill Room was crowded, but there were a pair of empty chairs nearby, and Ed Lake pulled them up.

"I'm glad you came," he said.

Didi shook his hand. Terry realized she had no idea what a prick he was.

All of the kids greeted her with special warmth. McKay wasn't there, but Terry saw his lighter on a Luckies pack at a vacant place.

Once they'd sat, Doyle announced, "We just met Ted."

"No shit," a Northeastern kid named Mark Sanger said, his tone dismissive and envious at once.

"He was very nice," Didi said, and even she sensed that she had just passed some of them, moving closer to the center.

Terry found Ed Lake's eye. "Ken O'Donnell put Didi on the team."

"Well, good for you." Lake picked up the beer pitcher and poured for Didi. "Good for us." He seemed to mean it.

"Chugalug!" Sanger cried. "We were just about to go." He hoisted his glass, as did two other boys, none of the girls. "Ready?"

Lake finished pouring, but Terry didn't touch his beer.

"Set?"

Suddenly Didi lifted her glass to hold it in front of her nose.

Terry almost leaned over to whisper, You don't have to . . .

Sanger yelled, "Go!"

Three boys and Didi upended their glasses at their mouths. The beer flowed into gullets. When Didi banged her empty glass down, she was a perceptible instant ahead of the others.

Lake's arm shot toward her. "Winner!"

The others pounded the table, hooting.

"What else are you fastest at?" one of the debs asked coyly.

Didi was ashen-faced as she tried to get air into her throat. She pressed her hand against her chest, in such distress that the table fell silent, watching her.

At last she recovered. She looked at Lake. "I do that with my brother. He wins contests against his friends. He makes me practice with him." She grinned. "But we use milk."

"Milk!" Lake cried. "No fair!"

"Rematch!" Sanger demanded.

They all laughed.

Didi felt them liking her. "No rematch. The champ retires."

Pitchers were passed around again. Didi leaned to Terry and said quietly, "Jackie makes me do it every morning. I like the beer better."

He touched her arm: Good for you. Then he gestured toward her other side. She looked up. A colored man was standing beside her with his hand out. "Hi. We didn't meet, you were so busy, but I admired your work. I'm Bright McKay."

"You're — ?" She flinched.

"Bright McKay."

Didi swung back to Terry.

"My friend."

She felt woozy. The beer was hitting her. She took McKay's hand, couldn't keep from staring at the black fingers encircling hers. "Bright," she said. "I like your name."

He sat next to her. "Light-skinned," he said solemnly, "which is a joke."

"Oh, well, I love a joke." She pushed her glass toward Lake, who filled it eagerly.

When the group broke up after midnight, Terry was aware of her unsteadiness as she got to her feet. He took her elbow as she stumbled, but she fell the other way, into McKay. Bright put his arm around her. She looked into his face and said easily, "Thanks. I'm okay."

Bright gave her a squeeze. "You *are* okay." And the warmth of the smile they exchanged relieved Terry.

He still had her by the elbow. "I'll take you home, kid."

"You're damn right you will."

A few minutes later they were in the back seat of a taxi. Didi was leaning against Terry. "I'm drunk," she said.

"I'm feeling pretty good myself."

"Good enough for this?" She brought her mouth up to his and kissed him.

He put an arm around her and kissed her back. Then he pulled away, glancing at the indifferent driver. "But I don't want to mislead you."

"Don't worry about that, Charlie."

He stiffened. "I hate it when you call me that."

"Charlie, Charlie, Charlie," she said, a broguish Cary Grant.

He faced away, looking out the window. His arm remained awkwardly around her shoulders. His pants bulged with his erection, but also he wanted to throw the cab door open and jump out. They were cruising past the bakery on the corner of Causeway Street. The lights were blazing and the aroma of bread filled the night air. They crossed the Charlestown Bridge, the navy yard on their right. He pointed at it. "My father shipped out from there. I don't remember it, but my mother says I stood on the pier waving at him as the ship pulled away. I never saw him again."

Didi snuggled closer. "Geniuses all lose their fathers when they are young."

"Where'd you hear that?"

"It's true. Einstein, Darwin, Elvis . . ."

"Jesus Christ, Didi."

"Him too?"

"I never know how to take you."

"Just take me."

"Are you making that shit up?"

"What, that you're a genius? Relax, I read it in *Reader's Digest.*"

Despite himself, he laughed.

And she kissed him again, but now she slid her fingers under his tie, between the buttons of his shirt. "God, Terry," she whispered, "you don't wear an undershirt. That really makes me —"

He swung around on her, kissed her harder. Her mouth opened, and his tongue found its way between her teeth. She began to suck on it, with noises that made him think of the driver again. But fuck the driver. Doyle took her tongue into his mouth, then *he* made the noises.

He felt dizzy with desire and hope. Finally he was doing it. He began rubbing her body through her clothes, as she was rubbing him. When he felt the firm pressure of her breasts, and when she made no move to stop, he pushed his fingers inside her dress, inside the wires of her bra.

"Here we are, kids," the driver said.

They came up like a pair of divers, blinking and gasping, the bends. The cab was at the curb in front of the Mullen house. Above and across the street was the hill park of the square, the fierce steeple of the monument outlined against the moon.

Didi pulled her clothes together while Terry paid. The cabbie said, "Thanks for the show, lover boy." But Terry ignored him and helped Didi climb out of the cab. She had to hold on to him to keep from falling.

He looked up at the windows of her house. A light was on in the living room. To his horror, he saw a curtain move.

"Your mom is there."

Didi straightened up and got her distance at once. "Oh, that bitch."

"Didi, don't."

"I'll never get past . . . I feel sick." She began to giggle. "She'll never believe me, I met Ted Kennedy."

"You were great tonight, Didi, really great."

"And I got drunk. Oh, God."

"Didi, your mother —"

"It's *your* mother you're worried about."

"No it isn't." But it was, and now that he saw it, Doyle made a decision. He took her inside his arm again. "The hell with mothers, right?"

"Right."

Terry kissed her. It was a chaste kiss compared to the others, but in its way it was the most adventurously erotic of all.

She leaned against him. "Thank you."

"Didi, what I said before wasn't true."

"Which of the many lies you told me?"

"The one about why I came to get you. It wasn't only for the campaign, for the typing. I'd been wanting to see you again."

"Well, now you did. And without misleading me."

"I didn't mean that either."

"Well, what *did* you mean, Charlie?"

He kissed her, his tongue brushing the space between her lips. "That."

Her eyes were closed when he pulled back to look at her, but she opened them, and they were brimming. "I want to tell you something, Terry Doyle. I see right through you. And I like what I see."

"Didi, I —"

"No, listen to me. I *know* what's going on inside that eggnoggin of yours, and I don't mind. I'm your friend. No strings. You sort things out. I'll be here. Okay, Terry?"

"In that case, you can call me Charlie."

"I only call you Charlie when I'm mad at you. And I'm only mad at you when you get scared."

"I'm scared all the time, Didi." To his horror, his own eyes began to fill now. He had never made such an admission before. It was true and it was incomplete: he could not have said what he was afraid of.

"You got to believe in yourself, Terry. If I can, why can't you? You've got a lot more going for you than I do."

"That's not true. You're a very special person. You're gutsy and honest."

"I'm 'Horseface.'"

"A thoroughbred is what you are. Everyone saw that tonight."

"Watch out for those people, Terry. Especially the girls. They're ponies. I mean phonies."

"McKay's no phony. I talk to him like I've been talking to you."

Didi shrugged. She didn't mean the colored guy. A colored guy was Terry's business. "I mean that Harvard hot shot."

"I thought you liked him."

"I mean those girls with the sunny names, Ginger and Pebble, give me a break. Switzerland and the islands in Greece, enough already. And that guy with the pilot's license, offering to take us up."

"You, Didi. Offering to take *you* up."

"Tweed. What the hell kind of name is Tweed?"

"They've been around —"

"They don't know half of what you know. I'll tell you something. People like that, with their fancy schools and their vacations and their oil paintings of their grandfathers and ladies like my grandmother cleaning their houses — they love the Kennedys. And do you know why? Because deep down where it counts, the Kennedys are not like them. But *us*, Terry. *We're* what the Kennedys come from. Us! Right here! A neighborhood like this! Scrubwomen on their knees. Children who grow up hungry for something not food! Like we did! Like us! *We* are who the Kennedys are, and the Kennedys are not ashamed of it. So don't *you* be ashamed either. Certainly not of where you come from. Ted Kennedy recognized *us* tonight, didn't you see that?"

"I'm not ashamed, Didi."

"Enough of that 'I'm not worthy' crap, then."

"That was about God."

"You don't have to be ashamed with him either. He made you, didn't he? He died for you, right? What the hell, Terry. How bad could you be if God did that?"

"I'm not sure I believe it," he said.

"If you were sure, it wouldn't be believing."

Terry smiled. "How do you know so much?"

"I know everything." She kissed his cheek. "Good night, sweet T." She turned and went to the door of her house. Just as she was about to take the knob, the door opened.

Jackie Mullen was standing there in pajamas. "Hi, guys," he said.

"Oh!" Didi jumped back.

He grinned, eager to let her know she owed him a big one. "Mom was out of her mind about where you were. I got her to go to bed by saying I'd stay up. You're lucky Pa is on the shift." Didi pushed past her brother, not deigning to acknowledge him. He turned his shit-eating grin on Terry. "My mother called your mother. Then she called back twice. Your ass is grass, Charlie. And your mother is the lawnmower."

Terry's face began to burn. Listen to this. Think of it. How could Didi seriously expect that of him, not to be ashamed?

4

AWAY FROM CHARLESTOWN, with his Marlboro cigarettes and raunchy black coffee and his beers at the Parker House; with his pressed chinos and his new crew-neck sweater; with his razzmatazz teammates who themselves could get the country moving again; with the stagy Tracy-Hepburn routine that marked him and Didi off as a stylish duo, but never in the neighborhood — Terry Doyle had simply become someone else altogether.

So it jolted his eyeteeth, one evening in late October, to look up from a list of New England NSA chapters and see Nick standing there. Squire.

Didi was running the mimeo machine a few feet away. Bright McKay poked at the typewriter keys on the desk beside Terry. Four or five others, boys and girls both, worked the phones at adjacent tables. The third debate was two nights away, and the push was on for TV parties in college dorms from Rhode Island to Vermont. As usual, the Catholic schools — Providence, the Cross, St. Mike's, St. A's, and a dozen smaller ones like Assumption, Merrimack, and Salve — were turning out the real numbers, which had the Young Dems from Harvard, BU, Wellesley, and Tufts fetching coffee for the BC, Emmanuel, and Regis kids who made the phone calls. The debate parties were important because they would kick over to supply bodies for the New England grand finale at Boston Garden. The arena proper would be full of pols and party hacks from across the state, gathered by the campaign officers upstairs. The Young Dems' job was to pack the rafters and streets outside with "jumpers," the wildly cheering kids who would start the pandemonium when Kennedy arrived.

Terry brought his swivel chair forward with a thunk. "Nick! What are you doing here?"

Terry's brother grinned amiably back. *Born to bring flowers, that boy:* Terry could hear their grandfather's boast. Who didn't like Nick? And having lost him, who wouldn't feel regret? They still slept in the same room, but Terry was rarely home for meals anymore. Sometimes, very late at night, Terry would look up from studying to find Nick staring at him with a sad expression. "What's wrong?" Terry asked once. Nick shook his head and rolled over, his only statement in the way he pulled the covers up.

Jackie Mullen was standing behind Nick, bigger than ever. Unlike the forever cool Squire, Jackie seemed uneasy here, shifting feet, glancing first at Terry, then at his sister, whom he did not quite acknowledge, then back at Terry and over to Bright McKay. Mullen took out a pack of Pall Malls, lighting up with patently false nonchalance. The pair looked awfully young in their high school dugout jackets, the red wool body, the white leather sleeves, a varsity *C* on each right breast, the number *61* on each left shoulder, their names curling in a nun's perfect script — *Squire, Jackie* — on their left breasts. Terry knew that arching across their backs would be one proud word, *Charlestown*. He wanted to tell them, Don't wear your coats downtown, fellas.

"Hey, Charlie, how goes?" Mullen blew a quick set of smoke rings.

"Easy as it comes, Jackie." Terry winked. "Hi, Nick."

"Hey, brother." Squire offered his hand and they shook. "Nice to see you when you're awake, Charlie."

Bright McKay said, "Charlie? What's that, for Charlestown?" No one answered, so he got half up from his chair and offered his hand to Squire. "I'm Bright McKay. Terry's told me about you."

Squire smiled easily. "I wish I could say the same. Terry tells us nothing."

Jackie put the cigarette into his mouth, pointedly taking it deep between his lips. Then he took it out and offered it to Squire. "Want a drag?"

The end of the cigarette was wet with saliva, a full inch of it. Squire took the butt and held it up, a display. Nigger-lipped.

Terry nearly reached across to slap the thing out of his brother's hand.

Squire eyed the cigarette, then looked at Terry with an apologetic wince: Do you believe this crude asshole Mullen? "I think I won't," he said. He mashed the cigarette out in an ashtray in front of McKay. But he had made Mullen's gesture a success.

McKay's fabulous smile had not faded. He sat there in his starched shirt and perfectly knotted narrow tie, hands clasped serenely behind his head, and Terry realized with relief that a jerkoff like Mullen couldn't touch the classy Bright McKay.

Terry stood and made as if to move Squire away, as though they had nothing to discuss that wasn't highly confidential.

But Squire did not budge. Instead, he scanned the room, sizing up the Dems, disarming them with his smile, the girls especially.

Didi had gone back to cranking the mimeograph, saying everything she felt about this intrusion by ignoring it.

Terry turned to Jackie. "What gives, fellows? What's the rub?"

Jackie shrugged. "We thought, you know, we could help."

"Help?"

Squire answered, "The thing at the Garden."

But now Terry did take his brother's arm. "I can't hear you with that mimeo machine. Come on. I'll buy you a drink." Terry led the way toward the center of the big room, far from his colleagues, near a U-shaped arrangement of tables at which, in daytime, the ladies sat addressing envelopes. No one was there now. A water cooler stood nearby.

"What," Squire said, "you don't want me to meet your new friends?"

Mullen tugged at Squire's sleeve. "Did you catch that bitch sister of mine? She wouldn't even look at me."

Terry said, "She looked at you, Jackie, long enough to see that stunt you pulled with your fucking cigarette."

"What stunt, Charlie?"

Terry went to the cooler and filled first one paper cone with water, then another. "Here, have a drink."

Jackie sipped his, and his face went sour. "Jeez, Charlie, somebody's been putting water in your booze."

Terry leaned back against a table, but his rigid white mouth betrayed his feelings. "What are you doing here?"

"Terry, you seem different." Nick was grinning broadly. "Even the way you talk is different."

"Yeah," Mullen piped in, a sudden recognition. "What happened to your voice?"

Squire raised a hand to silence Mullen. "Lay off, Jackie. Can't you see how embarrassed he is?"

"I'm not embarrassed."

"Yes you are. But why, I wonder. Because we give your new friends an eyeful of where you come from? Or is it earful? Do we talk funny, Charlie? Do me and Jackie have dem Townie accents? Or are you embarrassed because of what *we* hear?"

"Neither. But I still don't know what you're —"

"'What's the rub'? Did you ask us that? What kind of phrase is that? And how *do* you do that with your voice? It's lower, ain't it? You're talking through your teeth."

"You're full of shit, Nick."

Squire opened his hands to show how harmless he was. "Hey, Terry, it's nothing to get pissed off about."

"I'm not pissed off," Terry said, but so vehemently that even he laughed.

Squire was relieved. "You can't fool me."

The brothers looked at each other, nodding, the way they had in basketball games after a score. "I know it," Terry said. "I'm not trying to fool you, Nick."

Nick held his eyes for a long moment. "I miss you, brother."

Terry was surprised, a direct affirmation, no hint of sarcasm. It would have been natural, because it was true, to reply, I miss you too. But he did not.

"So," Squire said, "what about the Garden?"

"How do you know about that?"

"Didi told us."

"No, I didn't." Didi had come over from the Young Dems' corner, and beside her stood Bright McKay. "I told Ma. She must of told Jackie."

"What's the dif?" Squire said. "When Kennedy comes back to Boston, there'll be a big hoopla. Is that some kind of secret?"

"No. We sure hope not."

"When is it?"

"The night before election day."

"Which makes it . . ."

"November seventh."

Jackie and Squire exchanged a look. Jackie said, "Plenty of time."

Terry cocked his head. "For what?"

Before Squire answered, an apparently oblivious McKay stepped between the brothers to help himself to water. He swallowed some, then crushed the cup, glancing at Jackie as he did. McKay was taller than Mullen but far thinner, no physical match. But for that moment he seemed a threat. And then, in the next instant, the cloud had passed. McKay offered his hand to Mullen. "Bright McKay," he said. Mullen put his hand in McKay's, who squeezed it hard. "I don't think we've met."

"I'm Jackie Mullen."

"Sullen?" Bright's smile was like a harbor. An ocean liner could sail into it.

"Mullen," Jackie corrected, having missed the blade.

"Didi's brother?" Bright swooped his arm back toward her. "Didi is the queen bee here, aren't you, Didi?"

"Who's the king," Squire asked, "the guy in charge?"

"Of our team tonight? I guess that'd be me."

"You?"

McKay took the cigarette pack from his pocket and snapped a couple free. "Smoke?"

Squire had to admire the bastard. He took one. So did Terry. Mullen refused.

McKay flicked his lighter, lit his cigarette, then Terry's, then Squire's. While Squire was drawing on the flame, Bright said, "Third man unlucky." He snapped his Zippo shut. "You know why they say that, don't you?"

"No."

"The war. GIs lighting up in a foxhole. By the time the third guy has the flame in his face, the enemy sniper has his aim. Bang."

Squire exhaled a cloud. "Maybe that's what happened to my old man." He smiled weirdly, then leaned to the water cooler for another cupful. "I hate these fucking Dixie cups, don't you?"

Bright laughed. Fucking Dixie, fucking A. He liked the guy.

"So, do you want to hear my proposal or not?" Squire asked.

Terry couldn't tell whether Squire's nonchalance was an act. He had never felt quite so much the observer of his brother.

"Sure," McKay said. "Why not?"

"So the night before the election, you got all these kids out in the street cheering for Kennedy, right?"

"If we do our job," McKay said. "On Causeway Street, down Canal, all the way to North Washington Street."

"For the cameras, right?"

"It'll be on television."

"And you'll have all these beautiful young college kids going crazy for the guy."

"We hope so."

"Any colored people?" Jackie put in.

Squire's hand shot up in front of Jackie, a command, but a late one.

McKay didn't miss a beat. "Sure. Plenty." He smiled. "A lot of colored kids go to college these days."

This blade caught Mullen. He leaned toward his sister and hissed, "*You* don't go to college. What are you doing with these creeps?"

Now Squire took Jackie's arm and moved him back. "Will you please?" A mask of impassivity fell across Mullen's face.

Squire turned back to McKay. "So all these beautiful young people are waving something, right?" Squire swiveled to Terry. "Right?"

"I don't know what you're talking about," Terry said.

"It's television," Squire said like a pitchman. "I mean, they got to have something that makes an impression on the moms and dads in the living rooms of America."

"What," Terry said wryly, "like hankies?"

"Like flags," Bright said.

"Wrong." Squire dropped his cup into the trash. "You are so wrong. Flags aren't Kennedy. Flags are Nixon. Flags are what schoolchildren wave, like hankies" — he bit at Terry here — "are for war brides. Besides, what happens to flags after? Thousands of flags. Dropped? Tossed aside? They get walked on, how would that go over? That's . . . whatta ya call it?"

"Desecration."

"Right. No, you want something else. Something sexy. You want something the people can *throw* if they feel like it. All the better if they do." Squire looked for support to Jackie.

"Like a bullfight," Jackie said, on cue.

"Yeah," Squire said. "Ever seen a bullfight? What do people wave at the matador? What do the fans throw at him? Isn't Kennedy our matador? The Irish matador?"

Terry touched McKay's shoulder and he said wearily, "Flowers, Bright. He's talking about flowers."

"That's right." Squire took McKay's other sleeve. "It could be roses, but we think carnations, with long stems."

"Christ, Nick!" Terry came off the table and turned to go back to the corner.

But Bright stopped him. "Wait. It's not necessarily a bad idea. We had been talking about confetti or ticker tape, but the buildings aren't high enough around the Garden, and it'll be dark."

"But Bright, pay attention," Terry said. "My grandfather is —"

"In the flower business, I know."

"And this is my brother. He works in the store. He's just selling. He's down here *selling!*" Terry whipped around to Squire. "You could have talked to me first, goddamnit!"

"You're never around, Charlie."

"Quit calling me that!"

Squire and Jackie, and Bright too, pulled back. Terry said, "Have you ever heard of conflict of interest?"

Bright touched Terry's arm. "I don't necessarily —"

"But he thinks because I'm here, because Didi's here, he can sell —"

"I'm not selling," Squire said firmly. "I'm talking about donated flowers. Not just Gramps's shop, but the whole fucking Flower Exchange. They all love Kennedy down there. Dineen and Reynolds are the biggest wholesalers in Boston, both micks. They'd give Kennedy flowers by the truckload if you asked them to. It won't cost Kennedy a dime. I can arrange it. I know these guys."

McKay raised an eyebrow at Squire's jacket. "You're still in high school."

"I'm at the Exchange every morning before school — if I get to school. The Exchange is what I do."

Bright glanced at Terry, who nodded and said, "He does know them."

"Then what's your problem?"

Terry shrugged. What could he say: I love my brother but he's an operator, always has been?

McKay made a show of studying Squire. A young Negro, yet his authority was complete finally. "It's worth running by Mike, upstairs. Can you hang around?"

"Sure." Squire let his weight fall back against a table edge. "There are a couple of things, though."

"What?"

"The flowers won't cost you . . ."

As Squire talked, Mullen slid toward his sister, who had remained at some remove.

". . . but you have to, you know, place official orders with the various wholesalers. They'd want credit for the donations."

"That's reasonable," McKay said.

"And also, of course, you wouldn't have to do it this way, but . . ."

Didi ignored Jackie even as he drew close to her. He put his mouth by her ear and whispered, "How's your love life, sis?"

Her face bloomed. She turned — how she hated him! — and walked back to the Young Dems' corner. What a defeat, to have him enter this special world of hers, so easily claim a place in it.

"I'd appreciate it," Squire was saying, "if you or Mike or whoever could make the deals through me, so my grandfather can get *his* credit with the suppliers."

"No problem," McKay said. "I'll make the point. Anything else?"

"Yeah, actually there is." Squire flashed one at his brother. "I guess you could say there *is* a little selling here. Was the campaign going to buy flower arrangements for the big platform? You know, where Kennedy will stand? What they speak from, inside the Garden?"

"I have no idea."

"I think usually platforms have floral displays."

"Like I say —"

"I mean, if they were going to buy flowers anyway, maybe you could put in a word for —"

"Buying them from your grandfather."

"Exactly."

McKay shrugged. "You'd have to raise that with Mr. Gorman, if he wants to see you, which is what I'll find out."

Squire was pointedly not looking at his brother. "It's just that a thing like this would be the peak of his life. He loves Kennedy." Now Squire did face Terry. "We all do. Gramps would donate the money right back, but the commercial transaction would get him a foot in the door at the Garden."

"That's bullshit, Nick. Gramps doesn't care about the Garden."

"How would you know? When were you last in the store?"

"I know a crock when I —"

"Hold it, guys." McKay pulled Terry away, to a partition beyond the U-shaped tables. "This isn't a bad idea, Terry. Gorman might go for it."

"I'm out of the flower business, Bright."

"Let it go, man. Whatever it is with you and your brother, let it go."

Terry looked back toward Squire with a vague sadness. McKay caught it and said, "Squire'll be one of those guys who has his name on his shirt. First his letter jacket, then his green uniform."

"Mullen maybe, but not Nick. He's a very ambitious guy."

"That's what you are. So you're more alike than you think."

"We used to be alike. Not anymore."

"Maybe that's what's bugging him. He holds it against you that you left."

"That's the problem, Bright. I *haven't* left. That's what his being here means. It's a feeling I don't like."

"It's a feeling you should shake. This flower thing is a chance for *you*, Terry. It's a whacky idea, carnations in the streets, but Gorman might buy it. And if he does, the connection with the campaign is *your* grandfather. *You* handle it. *You're* where the action is. If Kennedy loves the sight of ten thousand people waving flowers at him, you're made. That's how we get ahead in this business, get an idea and go with it. Either that" — McKay grinned and held up his hand — "or get yourself some black skin. We're talking How to Succeed in Politics in the Sixties."

Terry laughed. "You never quit, do you?"

"Hey, you mick meatball, take a look." Bright held his hands out. "This train is leaving the station. I don't want to leave my buddy behind." He pumped his hands, choo-choo. "Come on, Terry. It's an idea. They fucking *love* ideas upstairs. Anything that turns up the volume, and this would. Come upstairs with me."

Terry glanced back toward Didi. She had returned to the mimeograph, but she was staring across the vacant room at him. Without effort he read what was written in her expression. Why did they do this to us, coming down here? And Terry wondered for both of them, Why had it seemed so important, keeping this world separate, keeping it only theirs? He faced McKay again. "Okay, let's go."

They started toward the stairwell, but Squire called out, "One more thing." When McKay and Terry turned back, he said loudly, "We could probably get the carnations dyed. They could be green, like for St. Paddy's Day."

McKay said, "Jesus, you're not kidding, are you? We'll go with the matador theme, Squire, not the leprechaun."

One of the Young Dems working at a postage meter machine by the wall snorted. McKay continued to make his way across the wide room toward the heavy fire door.

Terry remained where he was for a moment, staring back at his brother. He knew damn well that while Squire had not been kidding about dyeing carnations, he had not meant it either. Leprechaun, shit. Squire had fired a parting shot was all, and now he stood there grinning, the friendliest brother a guy could ever want. He had puffed his chest out to flaunt his puerile jacket, asinine name on his chest, and Terry saw him suddenly as a pot-bellied, strutting, middle-aged fart, turning the circuit from City Square out to Old Ironsides, *still* wearing that thing after all, a true Townie male forever.

Only Terry Doyle could read the question hidden in his brother's phony smile, his wearin' o' the green: Who the *fook* do you think you are?

✧

The "bull gang" at Boston Garden was famous for the speed with which it could transform the parquet basketball court into an ice arena or a boxing ring or a dirt corral. Rigidly unionized crews of carpenters and mechanics did the massive nightly work of preparing for circuses, rodeos, revivals, concerts, sports events, and political rallies. Services and equipment that the Garden crew itself could not provide were contracted out, but there too, strict controls were in place, and the levers belonged not to the Garden owner or the sports team owners but to certain union leaders and, as it happened, to a few of the Garden's North End neighbors. Particular caterers, liquor and soft-drink distributors, printers, sign painters, even veterinarians had locks on the right to service Garden events. They were known euphemistically as "preferred suppliers," but the relationship went beyond preference.

The Garden was only a quarter of a mile from City Square in Charlestown, but the river boundary had been absolute, and the rule extended to flowers. Since 1947, the preferred florist was Joe Lombardi, whose modest shop on Endicott Street had been a North End fixture for decades. In his time, Lombardi had decked out pulpits for Bishop Sheen and Billy Graham, stages for Liberace and Tommy Dorsey, floats for the Ice Capades, and podiums for Eamon de Valera, James Michael Curley, and Winston Churchill. His arrangements, featuring long birds of paradise and gladioli spiking out of fanning palm branches, along with sprays of mums, delphiniums, and hollyhock, always looked the same, but Lombardi knew what selections showed up from one side of an arena to another, and he also knew that nobody ever looked twice at flowers in such a place. When Sonja Henie performed, or when Mrs. Roosevelt spoke, or when some big shot's wife went with him to the platform, the same dozen roses always turned up in her arms. When Tony deMarco, a welterweight who grew up on Salem Street six blocks away, took the world title from Johnny Saxton in 1955, Lombardi himself climbed into the ring with a huge bouquet and presented it not to Tony but to the beaten Saxton. The flowers were lilies, and the fans loved the joke.

When Walter Brown, the Garden owner, called to tell Lombardi that the Kennedy people were supplying their own flowers for the election eve rally, the old Italian reacted with silence. Brown thought they'd been disconnected. He took the phone's handset away from his face to stare at it, then put it back to his ear. Finally Lombardi asked simply, "Why?" Brown said with a shrug in his voice that Kennedys write their own rules; they weren't even paying Garden costs. Even Cardinal Cushing, when he used the place, paid costs. Lombardi thought of Dineen and Reynolds, the Irishmen who ran the Flower

Exchange. They wrote their own rules too, and Lombardi understood implicitly that some mick friend had gotten to Kennedy and was using him to redraw boundary lines. "Relax, Joe," Brown said, "it's a one-time thing." Instead of answering, Lombardi hung up. The next morning he got his son to drive him up to Revere, to see what Guido would say.

A fortnight later an exhausted John Fitzgerald Kennedy returned to Boston — 77,000 miles, 45 states, and 237 cities in ten weeks. It was already dark. One hundred thousand wildly cheering supporters lined the streets on both sides of the harbor tunnels, territory over which P. J. Kennedy had ruled as an East Boston ward boss, and over which the North End's "Honey Fitz" Fitzgerald had presided as mayor, and which had launched Jack Kennedy himself as the 11th District congressman.

The plan was that he would speed through the old neighborhood, then stop and change shirts at his downtown hotel, but because the cars moved so slowly, and because cameras were waiting — television would be the real meaning of this event — the decision was made to go right to the Garden.

The overhead lights on North Washington Street illuminated the crowd, and sure enough the jumpers were there, cueing the crowd's hysteria. Sharp-eyed political operators saw right away what the Young Dems had accomplished: the spontaneous, overwhelming emotional outburst had been carefully prepared for. Screaming boys and especially girls — was this Sinatra? — roared without stopping, "We love yuh, Jack!" Just because their leaders had rehearsed them didn't mean it wasn't true.

"Where you want love," Bright McKay had said, quoting his father quoting John of the Cross, "put love and you will find love."

"We love yuh, Jack!"

The motorcade turned onto Causeway Street, but it was completely jammed, and the police were unable to clear the last several hundred yards even by bringing their clubs down on heads. For a few awful moments, it seemed Kennedy would not make it to the arena, not alive anyway. Was this South America?

But the drivers kept their cars inching forward. In that last stretch, the look of the crowd changed, for in front of the Garden itself, it was entirely college kids swarming around the vehicles. The Young Dems had turned them out from campuses all over New England, afraid they would be the only ones in the street.

And none of the spirited students was waving flowers, no long-stemmed carnations, no palm branches either.

Inside the Garden, twenty thousand people let up a roar when Kennedy appeared. Party hacks from all across the state; ward heelers from Springfield, Worcester, New Bedford, Fall River, Cambridge, and Boston; machine pols and state committeemen and volunteers from the suburbs — all had been transformed, by the mere sight of Kennedy, into holy-roller worshipers, worshiping him. Cameras filmed the scene as the crowd continued clapping, stomping its feet, blustering approval for nearly ten minutes.

Kennedy waved back at first, but then he let his arms hang as he stood immobile on that platform, taking all that they were giving him. He displayed a preternatural calm which, amid that pandemonium, made him seem even more dignified, even more unlike them. He received the outpouring as if it were appropriate, but he had not expected it.

Then he was speaking. "And in a free society the chief responsibility of the president . . ." Now he was hitting the crest of his speech. He stabbed his finger at them as the waves of his voice rose into the high reaches of the Garden, above all those rapt Irish faces, above the red-white-and-blue bunting, the huge photographs of himself, the banners emblazoning his name, the flags. The throng sat absolutely silent now, each person leaning forward, ready to leap and move, listening as intently as before they had cheered. ". . . is to set before the American people the unfinished public business of our country . . ."

His words soared above the black superstructure from which the clocks, scoreboards, and nests of loudspeakers hung. His words carried all the way to the narrow catwalks, the network of girder bridges and klieg lights up near the roof. ". . . that this is a great country. But I think it can be greater . . ."

Terry Doyle was perched on one of the catwalks in the shadows above the lights, his legs dangling. Didi Mullen was beside him. Other Young Dems sat like crows along the rafters. Doyle wasn't sure about Didi, but he had a bad case of the whim-whams up here. Given what had happened that morning, Terry might well have been dizzy and afraid in any case, but the height sure wasn't helping. His left arm was in a cast and sling. His ribs were wrapped with a broad elastic bandage that bulked under his shirt. He wore a white bandage on the side of his head.

Didi wasn't hurt, thank God. She'd stayed with the truck. Her brother and Squire were beat up about like Terry, but Bright — oh, Bright! He was in the hospital, and would be for a while. Terry wouldn't have come here without him, even to see Kennedy, but Bright had insisted. Now Terry was trying to concentrate on the speech, to hear every word, to know each nuance, so that he could tell his friend all about this climax of their effort.

". . . can do better . . . I think we can make this move again . . ."

But Terry kept losing him. He couldn't focus. His mind kept drifting back to what had happened. Didi looked at him, then turned away. He knew she could not stand the sight of his kicked-in face.

". . . for in the final analysis, our greatest common challenge . . ."

Kennedy, in the beam of the champion-of-the-world spotlight, was a finger-size but sparkling mote bracketed on that platform by the crescent of politicians behind, some in boater hats, and in front, below, by a bank of flowers that separated the podium from the audience. Terry Doyle's puffed and aching eyes kept snagging on the flowers. Even from that distance he could identify the birds of paradise and gladioli shafts spiking out of the palm branches, blue delphiniums, and the showy hollyhock.

They had rented a twenty-four-foot panel truck that morning. Bright McKay had been authorized by Gorman to sign for it, but he was afraid to drive the rig, so Terry was at the wheel. Squire was with them in the cab, sitting by the passenger door. In the back, with the cartons of cut flowers, rode Jackie and Didi. Gramps wasn't along, which had been an issue between the brothers. Squire had counted on pulling away from the Exchange before Gramps got free to join them. Given how close Gramps and Squire were, that should have been Terry's first warning. Squire hadn't wanted Didi to come either, but she'd been on board already, and she'd insisted.

It was shortly after ten when Terry pulled into the alley that ran between North Station and the huge Garden service building. The alley became a tunnel under the third-story bridge between the arena and 150 Causeway, then it opened into a cinder courtyard that abutted the Boston & Maine storage yard where rolling stock sat idle. The enclosure reeked permanently of elephant urine and horse manure — all those circuses and rodeos.

The courtyard was clogged with deliverymen, concession stockers, bull gang workers, and the easily identified campaign staffers: effete young men in button-down shirts and prim women in wrap-around khaki skirts. A dozen trucks of various sizes were backed against the dock that ran the width of the building. Supplies were being offloaded by forklifts, dragged onto wheeled pallets, and tractored up broad ramps into the arena above the railroad station.

Terry tried to seem relaxed as he struggled to find reverse.

"Grind me a pound, Charlie," Squire said as he and McKay elbowed each other.

Terry grunted as, with the gears screeching, he rolled the truck backwards toward a narrow space between a Coca-Cola truck and a laundry van. He pulled forward, then backed up, and forward again. The secret was to move slow.

When the guys in back finally yelled out "Whoa!" as the rear bumper kissed the loading dock, Terry shut the ignition off and slumped over the wheel with relief. He rubbed his hands together, noticing for the first time how wet they were.

Bright nudged him. "Where'd you learn to drive like that?"

"Right here, just now."

"Shit, you told me you had experience." But then McKay slapped his thigh. "My God, we're *all* becoming like Kennedys. We can do anything!" With sudden exuberance, he threw an arm around each of the brothers and pulled them close across his own body, so that their heads almost touched.

Terry pulled himself free to look at McKay — dark-eyed, black-skinned, and determined. Bright had been cautious in Nick's presence all these weeks, but Terry sensed now that this display of affection was more than the infectious enthusiasm of the campaign. That McKay could include Squire in their friendship moved him and opened the door on his own oldest feeling for his brother. The bond between them was unbreakable, no matter what. Bright still had Nick's head in the vise grip. Terry reached over and rubbed his knuckles on Nick's scalp, the old Indian burn.

"Don't fuck with the hair!" Squire slipped free and swiftly knotted the college boys' ties together. "And *don't* you" — he broke into song, hopping out of the cab — "*step* on my blue suede shoes!"

By the time Terry and Bright had untied their neckties, Squire and Jackie had the two hand trucks out and were unloading the boxes of flowers. As he piled one carton onto another, Squire kept jitterbugging, "Blue, blue, blue suede shoes . . ."

Didi was in the truck pushing the cartons out, and she danced too.

When the dollies were loaded, Jackie and Squire each took one. Before rolling his off the loading dock, Squire said to Didi, "You stay here, okay?" He tossed his head toward the fifteen cartons of long-stem carnations still in the truck. "Somebody's got to watch those. We'll be back in a few."

Disappointed, she glanced at Terry. This was his second warning, but he missed it.

When the Doyle brothers, McKay, and Mullen emerged from the low-ceilinged entrance tunnel, the sight of the arena stopped them. After the ill-lit, smelly passageways and ramps leading up from the street, the cavernous space wrenched open their eyes and, for that matter, mouths. Workers stood on ladders and craned over railings to drape the red-white-and-blue and to hang the huge posters. Technicians in the rafters were adjusting lights, and television men were setting up cameras on perches jutting out from the balconies. At the far end of the arena floor, where one of the Celtics' baskets should have been, carpenters hammered away at the speaker's platform. Even though it wasn't finished yet, soundmen were already wiring the microphones. In front, on floor level, a lone man was bent over cartons that struck Squire Doyle, for one, as familiar.

Despite the activity, all four boys noted the vast emptiness of the Garden. They'd been to dozens of games there, but they'd never seen the thousands of seats vacant before, the glistening wood, orange in the lower levels and green in the upper. In the absence of screaming fans, the buzzers and horns, the place seemed, despite the hammers and drills, almost silent.

"Jesus," Squire said. And he knew that the impulse that had prompted his thrust into the tiny opening between Kennedy's new power and the old turf boundaries had been right. *This* was worth it, and after today Kerry Bouquet would have a toehold here, which he would make into a niche. Squire thought Terry wanted a like toehold, but with Kennedy. Both boys wanted to cross the river into Boston itself, the route the Pilgrims had taken out of Charlestown three hundred years before. "Beautiful," Squire said. The Garden was Boston, pure and simple. That's why Kennedy was coming here. Squire too.

Terry touched his brother's sleeve. "Jeez, Nick, wouldn't you love to play here? Don't your fingers itch for the ball?"

"The fast-break twins."

Their eyes met. "Yeah," Terry said. "The good old days."

Nick shook his head once. "We're going to miss you this year, kid." He hit Terry's shoulder. "We're all coming down here to see you play for BC. Enough of this politics, Charlie. Get back on the old parquet."

"I'm going to."

"Oh, really?" McKay said, taking Terry's other arm. He pointed up to the press box, which floated, a fluorescent rectangle, under the ledge of the second balcony. Inside the box were three men who stood looking down like gods.

"That's Mike," McKay said.

Mike Gorman was head of the campaign in New England. He had been one of Kennedy's buddies in the navy, and his present status as one of the candidate's true inner circle made him seem to shimmer. In Terry's weeks as a volunteer, he had dealt with Gorman only in relation to these flowers. Gorman's presence here, now, attending to pre-rally minutiae, reinforced Terry in the feeling of his own importance. And to think he'd fought Squire at first on their bringing flowers into this.

"And that's Larry O'Brien," McKay added.

"Christ," Terry said, "it is!"

"Let's go, fellows," Squire said, "before you wet yourselves."

The four young men moved onto the raw plywood flooring over which the fabled parquet would be laid for basketball.

"Hey, Cous!" Jackie called over to Squire, two-stepping his hand truck between racks of folded chairs.

"Pick!" Squire cut by a stack of risers. The Cous, Ramsey, and Russell — Terry would have joined their skylarking, but just then he was distracted by the figure of the stooped man below the speaker's platform. The man straightened up, unfurling a large bunch of palm branches.

Squire saw him too, and instantly understood what he'd refused to take in before. He looked left and saw figures — eight or ten men in suits — moving down the aisles of the stands from the deep shadows of the rearmost seats. "Shit," he said.

Terry saw the cloud in his brother's face before he saw what caused it. He had heard the sick alarm in that word "shit," but he didn't understand it, any more than he understood that his brother had been trying to pull a tablecloth out from under crystal and china here. And now the crystal and china were going to break.

The thugs had cut them off and were on them so quickly that the three Irish kids, and the one black, had no real choices to make. Squire shoved his hand truck at the one who came at him, a would-be body check. But the man sidestepped it and reached for him. Squire ducked and had his belt pulled halfway out of its loops, his only weapon, but another man hit him from behind. Jackie Mullen leapt over chairs and seemed about to get away when he was caught. He landed one solid punch, and he felt the cartilage of the man's nose jolt, which was one small satisfaction as he was then savagely pummeled.

Bright McKay and Terry fought back briefly, but a knot of four or five men beat them down. Terry's teeth sliced much of the way through his own tongue. He gagged on blood. Bright lost consciousness when the toe of a stout black shoe connected with his head. "Nigger! Nigger!" The man repeated each time he drew his foot back and then swung it forward. He kicked McKay's head again and again in a fury. "Nigger! Nigger!"

Long after Bright stopped hearing the word, Terry, crumpled beside him, would hear nothing else.

Squire had covered his head with his arms, an apparently defensive posture, but he uncoiled twice, a pair of well-aimed, vicious kicks, one of which visibly snapped his assailant's jawbone. That man would have killed Squire, but his comrades dragged him off.

The television technicians, carpenters, bull gang, and bunting hangers all stopped what they were doing to watch. Only the man unpacking flowers at the platform continued his work.

The dark-suited, silent men — silent except for that "Nigger! Nigger!" — continued hitting the boys in clear view on the spot, approximately, where the boxing ring would stand on Friday night. No spectator moved to help at first, although one woman on a ladder with streamers draping her shoulders let out a scream when the blade of a machete appeared above their heads. From the distance, it looked like a pirate's cutlass. The machete came slicing down not on the boys' heads but on the cartons of flowers. A dozen swings was all it took. The brilliant red of chopped petals sprayed into the air like blood.

A few dozen more swings of the blade — with a terrified but unharmed Didi pushed up against one panel of the truck outside — was all it would take, moments later, to shred the entire lot of long-stem carnations. So much for hailing the matador.

But in the Garden now, a man's voice pierced the silence. "Hey, stop that, you! Stop! Leave them boys alone!"

One thug released his grip on Squire, straightened up, and peered into the vacant stands. Perhaps twenty rows back stood a lone Negro in a green shirt and green pants. "You stop that, you hear? I'll call the police." The Negro held a push broom, the handle pointing like the barrel of a gun.

The thug crashed through chairs and jumped a railing to go after him. Light sparked off the man's fist as he raised it, the polished bar of brass knuckles. The janitor tried to run, but the man caught him. Two punches broke his teeth. He fell in a heap.

"Jesus," Jackie said later, "the only one who tried to help was this old spade." And still later that would come to seem a kind of proof, as if the janitor had responded only to McKay, that spades stick together.

Terry was still conscious when the men in suits left, but in his memory of the event long afterward, it would seem he wasn't, because he could never quite get the time right — not the year it happened, not the city, and not even who was attacked and with what. He was sure now that his ribs had been cracked right into his heart. He was sure he was dying, but dying was less to him already than a deep feeling of shame. Bloody and smashed, he was finally naked — here was the feeling — before God. And God was averting his eyes.

He found it possible to look over at Bright. Bright was dead. His face was a mass of blood. One eyeball was hanging outside its socket on his cheek, hanging by a pulsing blood vessel.

"This is a great country . . ." It didn't sound like Squire, because the words were pushing through a thick-lipped, broken mouth. And then Terry realized that his brother was speaking even at that moment in a broad, stock imitation of John Kennedy. "But I think it can be better. I think we can get this country moving —"

"Shut up!" Terry screamed. The pain in his tongue! Spittle fell back onto his face, and he told himself to get up, but he couldn't move. "Shut the fuck up!"

"Fuck yourself," Squire said.

"Fuck *you!*" Terry knew nothing of what had happened, except that Nick had caused it. Nick had betrayed him. Bright was dead, and Nick had killed him.

Terry lay there for a long time. His head was positioned so that whenever he opened his eyes, they went right to the figure inside the press box. Terry wanted to yell up, "Tell Senator Kennedy that I'm sorry!"

Mike Gorman was staring down at them, like a householder waiting for the garbage men to come and sweep the dogshit away.

Here was where Terry's memory became confused. Sometimes, over the years, instead of the indifferent Gorman high above that carnage, he saw an image of Lee Harvey Oswald looking down on Dealey Plaza. Italians hired Oswald to kill the president — that was the absurd notion he would never be able, quite, to disbelieve. The melee at the Garden seemed an a priori proof. Italians killed Kennedy. Giancana, Marcello, Patriarca, or Tucci — it didn't matter which one or why. Push across boundaries, was the lesson, and the boundaries push back.

"Fuck you, Nick." As if Nick were the one staring down from the heights. As if *he* had kicked Bright's eyeball out. As if *he* had shot the president and ruined everything more or less forever.

5

THANKSGIVING CAME and the Irish praised God for Kennedy. A few days later, Squire made his way by streetcar up to Revere. It was a cold, wet day. Outside the streetcar window, the muddy flats of backwater wetlands stretched toward the Saugus hills. Shy of Revere, the rain started to fall. The half frozen raindrops hit the window like pieces of rice.

Squire was still wearing a small bandage on his ear, and his left eye was still shadowed by a small dark crescent. But mostly he'd recovered, like the others, except for McKay, who was blind in his left eye now, and always would be. Squire saw things more clearly than before, and that was why, unknown to anyone, he was going to Revere.

He wore an orange canvas rain slicker — what longshoremen wore — and a tweed cap pulled down on his face. He looked like nobody. Even in the Town he would no longer wear clothes, like his dugout jacket, that said so blatantly who he was. He kept his hands inside his coat pockets, his right closed tightly around a roll of quarters, his left clutching a brown envelope. The clacking of the steel wheels, the side-to-side jostling of the streetcar, and the monotonous sight of the dull tidal landscape combined to soothe him, putting him almost to sleep at one point, asleep everywhere except in that hollow place in his chest where part of him was always awake now.

At the end of the line he got off, walking into the rain as if unaware of it. On the boardwalk, going north, he had to lean into the wind. At the pavilion, his marker, he stopped and faced the rolling sea to watch the storm.

A few minutes later he was on Tucci's street. He left the sidewalk for the middle of the asphalt so the men in the dark Buick would see him coming. As he approached, the car doors opened. The two men got out, exactly as he knew they would. He took his hands from his pockets and held them away from his sides as he walked. They waited.

A dozen feet from the Buick, he stopped. "My name is Nicholas Doyle," he announced. "Mr. Tucci has business with me in Charlestown."

The two men exchanged a glance now that they had seen what a kid he was. Squire had no memory of the thugs' faces from the Garden. For some reason, he did not feel afraid. He indicated his pocket. "I brought something."

One of the guards nodded.

Squire took out the envelope. As he handed it to the first, the second grabbed his free arm, twisting it back, wrenching his wrist well up against his shoulder blades. Despite himself, Squire let out a yelp of pain. The other roughly frisked him, finding the roll of quarters.

The envelope and the quarters. The guard weighed one in each hand. The envelope was sealed, and he knew better than to open it. The heft was familiar, and was what made it impossible to dispose of this kid without first checking inside. He nodded to his partner, turned, and went up the tidy flagstone walk. Tucci's house was a three-story bungalow with faded yellow stucco walls, brown trim and shutters. A veranda protruded off the first floor, and behind its screens forlorn summer furniture lay stored against the wall. The guard mounted the stairs, pushed a doorbell button, and waited. When the door opened, he went inside.

Squire and the second guard stood outside for a few minutes, staring at the house. But nothing happened. The sleet fell harder than ever. The guard opened the Buick's passenger door for Squire, then circled the car to get in on the driver's side. Suddenly Squire felt cold. Only now, in shelter, did he find himself shuddering.

Half an hour passed in silent detachment. It was not true, of course, that Squire had no stake in what was about to happen, but acting that way made it feel true. Where had he learned this, that the value of seeming not to care was in the structure it imposed on the secret anarchy of his caring too fucking much.

The first guard came out at last and got him. He brought Squire into the house and then left.

Guido Tucci was sitting behind a long table in a dark-paneled room just inside and to the right of the door. The table held stacks of ledger books. File cabinets lined one wall, but instead of seeing the room as an office, Squire saw it as the dining room it had been before.

Beside Tucci, to the rear, stood a middle-aged man, overweight and bald, nobody's guard. He had his lips prissily together, but there was a malevolence in his eyes that made Squire not meet them.

A shawl covered Tucci's dark suit and black bow tie. Seen this close, his smallness was a surprise, especially in contrast to the bigger man behind him, but it made Squire more aware of his power. Also, Tucci was old, as old as Squire's grandfather. His hands were placed carefully on the table, flat in front of him, one on each side of the still unopened brown envelope and the roll of coins. Tucci looked at Squire as from behind a wall. And another wall, it seemed, stood between Tucci and the other man. If Tucci can ignore him, Squire thought, so can I.

"I'm Nicholas Doyle. I'm eighteen years old. I live in Charlestown, on Common Street. I go to school there. But also, beginning last spring, I serve as the manager of a merchants' association. I collect the dues, which is the money in that envelope."

"You bring it to me?" Tucci's accent sounded nothing like Squire had imagined, an actor on *The Untouchables*. There was no crispness in his voice, and he spoke very softly.

"Yes. The money is yours."

"Why?"

"In the envelope, you will find bills and a list of merchants and tavern keepers up and down Main Street, from City Square to Sullivan Square, thirty-seven of them. One is my grandfather. They have nothing to do with the trouble between your people and McCarthy's, but you know what happens. Last year, men came into their stores wanting money. I told the store owners they need insurance, but they didn't know where to get it. I told them to pay me, I would arrange it. Out of respect for my grandfather, they do. They trust my judgment. My judgment was that insurance from you was what we needed, but why would you give it to us? I have told everyone that a relative of yours is our sponsor. It is a lie. But it worked. No one bothers the businessmen in Charlestown now, but it is because of you, even if you don't know. I have come today to pay you what is yours, to ask you to make my lie the truth." If the explanations seemed a speech, it was. Squire had practiced it.

Tucci picked up the envelope and, with the nail of his forefinger, slit it open. He emptied it on the table, several banded stacks of bills, hundreds, fifties, and tens.

"Ten dollars per week," Squire said, "for six months, from thirty-seven members. A total of eight thousand eight hundred and eighty dollars. It's all there."

A lot of money to the Irish kid. The fact that it was not to Tucci made no difference. The shops in Charlestown, unlike those on the waterfront, made no difference to him either. He sat staring at Doyle. The deep pools of his eyes were like that ocean out there gone completely calm.

To Squire it was as if someone had lit a fire in the fireplace on the wall behind, the fresh warmth in the room was that palpable. He had come here hoping to gain a foothold in the wall of Tucci's confidence, to become his formal representative among the Irish in the Town. It had never occurred to him to hope for, or want, a personal affirmation, yet that was what he began to feel.

He looked at the man behind Tucci, saw the resemblance, and realized that he was Tucci's son. His role, Squire sensed, was to do only this, and do it always: watch.

"Your grandfather," Tucci said at last.

"Yes?"

"What business?"

How the fuck did Tucci know to ask that? Squire nearly laughed. He would have to make an admission now that would associate him with the Garden, which would ruin everything. In the confessional, Catholic boys learned to say nothing that could prompt the priest's direct question, because it was unthinkable to lie in response to it. Yes. Here it was, confession. "Flowers." He touched the bandage at his ear. "You offer insurance to the flower man at the Garden. I was the one who crossed the line there. You stopped me. I learned my lesson." He gestured at the money. "I want to work for you on my side of the line, my side of the river. In Charlestown."

"But you already do."

"A presumption until now." Squire grinned. "Is that what you call it? I only claimed a connection to you, hoping to make it true eventually."

"Or hoping that, with Kennedy, you could replace Lombardi."

"Who?"

"The North End, the Garden."

"That was the flower business, something separate, something for my grandfather. A mistake."

"You're bold, aren't you?"

Squire did not answer.

"I like boldness. Although, in the young, more often it is foolishness. Are you foolish?"

"What do you think?"

Tucci had not had this experience before, studying a young Irisher.

Instead of seeing the hairline crack along which Doyle could be broken, Tucci saw an image of the fierce, unbreakable man he'd been himself.

"What do they call you? Nick?"

"Squire."

Tucci smiled for the first time. "An old-country idea. A liegeman. A man with an oath. Whose squire are you?"

"Yours." Squire answered without any sense of treason because he did not mean it.

Which Tucci knew. He also knew it was the exact answer he'd have given. He picked up the money and put it back in the envelope, all but one band of ten hundreds, which he pushed toward Doyle, who took it — the symbol of their deal. "You collect ten per week from each one?"

"Yes."

"Make it five. You tell them Tucci personally makes it five."

"They'll like that."

"I expect you back every other month, the first Monday. Only you."

"You honor me." Such solemnity was strange in Squire, but it had come spontaneously, as if Tucci's presence required it. Squire glanced toward the son, who still showed nothing. What had he made of this? Could he tell it was true, what Squire had just said about being honored?

Squire pointed to the roll of coins on the table. "Your men took those from me outside, a measly handful, but it belongs to someone else."

Tucci pushed the roll across to him. "Take it, then. Now leave."

As Squire's streetcar headed south, back toward the city, he remembered another time on this route, when he and his Townie chums had been chased by a gang of dagos. What would they think now? Squire allowed himself a brief rush of satisfaction, then deliberately blanked his mind. He kept his hands in his coat, his fingers clutching, in one pocket, the thousand dollars, and in the other, the roll of quarters.

The streetcar passed through Winthrop and Chelsea and rode for a time under the shadow of the Mystic River Bridge. The houses were ramshackle, the businesses depressed. Oil storage tanks and warehouses dominated some streets; blind-windowed taverns and weedy vacant lots dominated others. The streetcar stopped periodically, but few passengers boarded. Then it entered Maverick Square in East Boston, a lively intersection lined with colorful stores and dotted, that day, with umbrellas. The MTA stop was crowded. Many of those waiting wore uniforms, and Squire realized they were airline employees just off from the early shift at Logan.

Squire stood, and with a sweep of his hand and a pleasant smile offered his place to a woman in a cleaner's uniform. He positioned himself in the aisle, apparently set, but then at the last moment, just before the driver threw the handle over, slapping the door shut, Squire pushed past a burly Pan Am worker and dropped through the door like a parachutist through the hatch of a transport plane. One of Mark Clark's boys dropping behind the lines into Italy.

Squire waited under the shelter until the streetcar was gone, though it made no rational difference if its riders saw which way he headed. Fuck Mark Clark, he was no commando. An image like that could put a fellow in the wrong mood.

He set out, concerned now because rain this hard could screw up his plan. He pulled his hat lower on his face. From Maverick he went down the street that led away from Logan to the waterfront. Two blocks along he turned right, into the more private realm of a residential street. Now he realized that the rain was a friend, and he could hustle along without being noticed. The windows of the houses were blank. Not a curtain stirred. This was the city neighborhood into which North End Italians had been spilling, across a narrow finger of the harbor, since the war. At the next corner was a butcher shop, which had hanging in its window the skinned carcasses of whole rabbits and what Squire, when he'd first come here, took to be dogs, but then had recognized as lambs. Even in the rain, the stink of foreign food registered. He turned left and came to a small bakery, and he smelled its strange licorice bread. He kept going.

The Dello Sport Café. It was across the street at an angle from the bakery, the first floor of an unpainted three-story clapboard building. A large plate-glass window dominated the sagging façade, and through the window Squire made out the figures of men holding sticks, playing pool. He watched for a moment, until satisfied that the one he wanted was there. He continued along the sidewalk to a point beyond the house opposite the café, an alley into which he stepped to hide from view. Across the street, the same alley ran beside the café into a warren of fenced yards, collapsing garages, and precarious rear porches. Squire leaned against a building, set his collar again, and prepared to wait.

Wait. How un-Irish it had been of him. Instead of impulsively and suicidally charging his enemy, he had waited. He had followed. He had watched. He was at the end of one period of waiting, however, because he was at the start of another, a much longer one. It was time to finish with the first.

More than an hour passed. During that period the rain eased off, and he took it as a good sign when the pool players opened the door of the café to let in air. From previous visits, Squire knew that the toilet was in the rear of the building, off the alley, and that customers had to go out the front and around to reach it.

Finally one man came out and went into the alley and disappeared into the closetlike jakes. He reappeared moments later, zipping his fly, and returned to the café. A short time later another man came out carrying his pool cue, and then went back. Still not the one Squire wanted.

The fourth to appear was the kid with the stooped shoulders, the shiny suit, and the cocky, dipshit gait that formed the larger part of the profile Squire had memorized. He remembered the guy's name, Mano, which had enabled Squire to track him. Squire came alert when the punk stepped outside, paused on the wet sidewalk to take one last drag on his cigarette before snapping it into the street.

Mano must have just taken a game of eightball, because he stretched with satisfaction, up on his toes like a smug cat. He headed toward the rear of the building. Squire waited as Mano went into the head and closed the door, then he pushed away from his wall and quickly crossed the street. In seconds he was at the door. He kicked it open.

What a picture the bastard made, hunched on the seatless crapper, his precious pants carefully hooked at his knees to keep them free of the wet, filthy floor. He looked up at Squire with utter stupefaction. His acne-pocked face, with a wispy new mustache but the same stringy sideburns, was the smaller part of what Squire had memorized. He had seen it in the haze of his first sleep every night since May.

Doyle was at his most efficient. He had imagined this. He said, "A flower store in Charlestown — remember, asshole? Off the Common? An old mick at the cash register? You did this." Before Mano could react, Squire slugged him on the side of the head. His fist, wrapped around the roll of quarters, came down like a rock. Irish brass knuckles.

Mano collapsed into the gap between the toilet and the wall, his upended ass smeared with shit. He looked groggily back up at Doyle, who reined an impulse to hit him again. He had not only imagined this moment, but he'd anticipated its decisions. Blow for blow, a strictly equal act of retribution, a disciplined response, and a message, the beginning of a method of operation.

Squire had no urge to avenge the savage Garden beatings, not his own and not even the sickening blinding of Terry's friend. Whether the high-flown but stupid colored guy, or Terry, or even Jackie had known it or not, the four of them had spun the wheel that day and lost. They'd tried to push across the, what was it, Rubicon? Tiber? The fucking Charles. In other words, they'd asked for it.

But not Gramps. Gramps had just been sitting in his own place, making his damn shamrock whatzits. He was old, his fighting days over. Gramps had treated the wop assholes with respect. This was the one who'd pounded him. The bastard started to get up. Squire leaned over him to hiss, "You cross into Charlestown and I'll know it, and I'll kill you."

He had never said those words before, and he had not intended to now. It was no part of his dream of this. What shocked him more than having said such a thing was realizing he meant it.

Nick Doyle broke the roll of quarters and spilled the coins on the slumping, half-naked figure, an impulsive final gesture, not planned either.

Gramps. Watching his grandfather get hit and doing nothing; watching his grandfather fall and bleed; watching his grandfather look around for help, for him. His grandfather by whom he measured the meaning of love. His grandfather who had tapped him, dubbed him, consecrated him Squire.

✧

The campaign had chartered dozens of buses to bring the Boston contingent of the New Frontier down to Washington for the inauguration. But two days before, on January 18, Terry's mother developed symptoms. Real ones.

"She can't catch her breath," Terry told the doctor. It was midnight. He clutched the phone, pressing it against the bones in his face. "I've already called the ambulance."

"What about her pulse?"

"Wild," Terry said. "Her pulse is wild."

"Has she been taking her Coumadin?"

"Yes, I think so. I mean, unless she got confused. She takes a lot of stuff."

"But you don't know for sure?"

Terry looked across at his blinking, shaken grandfather. Nick was in the bedroom, bundling up their mother. "No," Terry said. "I don't know for sure."

"I'll see you at the hospital. Make sure they take her to MGH, because it's closest. I'll call ahead."

Terry hung up the phone as the wailing siren drifted up from the street. The sound released the knot in his chest, and panic surged through him.

An hour later the doctor appeared in the threshold of the visitors' room. His white coat was open over a misbuttoned flannel shirt. The brothers and their grandfather stood. "She survived," the doctor said. "She's had a pulmonary embolus, but she survived."

"That's what she had before," Nick said.

"Yes. But she's developed a new clot, almost certainly in her leg. A piece of it broke off and went to her lung. We find that if they don't kill a patient right off, then the patient usually does fine."

"So she'll be okay?"

"We have her on heparin, an instantaneous blood thinner. It will take a while for the clot to organize."

"What?"

"For the body to reabsorb the clot. Until that happens, the danger remains that it will break off again."

Ned Cronin stepped between his grandsons. "But she always wore those elastics. Always."

"That's good, Mr. Cronin." The doctor's solicitude was laced with condescension. "But she was also supposed to be taking her Coumadin."

"She did," Nick said angrily. "She took it every damn day. I made sure of it."

The doctor glanced at Terry.

Nick leaned in on the doctor. "So why did this happen? You said those pills would —"

The doctor backed away. "We don't know, son. The Coumadin should have kept the blood from clotting, but if there was trauma in the wall of the vein —"

"She knelt too much," Cronin said.

Terry took his grandfather's arm, but the old man shook him off. "I told her. Novenas. Holy Hours. The daily rosary. Her knees were always swollen."

The doctor kept backing away, as if the three men frightened him. He said, "Bed rest. That's the thing now. She won't be critical after tomorrow. We'll keep her on blood thinners and in bed for a few days. I'm sure she'll do fine."

"You're sure?" Terry asked.

"Yes."

"When can we see her?"

"You can look in for a minute, but she's asleep. Wait for the nurse to come out. Tell her I said you could look in." The doctor turned and went off down the corridor, the tails of his white coat flapping.

It was the next afternoon when Flo told Terry to go to D.C. anyway. Nothing doing, he said, not a chance. But she insisted. The color had returned to her face, her blood pressure was near normal, and she seemed herself again. The nurse had said she was doing great.

In the hallway outside her room, Terry took Nick's elbow. "Christ," he said, "what am I going to do?"

"Do? What do you mean, do?"

"I mean, should I go?"

"You just told her nothing doing."

"But she insisted."

"Yeah, right. 'Don't worry about me, boys.' Well, I'm worried, Terry. Aren't you?"

"But if she's just going to be in bed . . . I'd be back before she got out of the hospital. Meantime, I don't think she really needs me, Nick."

Nick stared at his brother. In a million years, he would not have put his reaction into words: But me — what if *I* need you?

"I'd call in," Terry said. "I'd call in regularly."

Nick winked and struck his brother's shoulder softly. "Like the good son you are."

The next day, inaugural eve, a blizzard hit Washington. The buses from Boston arrived in the early afternoon, just as the snow began to really dump. While the president-elect, his inner circle, the party regulars, and the major contributors attended a concert in Constitution Hall that night, the Young Democrats would be having their own belly rub at the gymnasium at Georgetown University. Kids from colleges all over the country were coming in, and they were being put up on couches, makeshift cots, and spare mattresses in the lounges and hallways of the dormitories of the local colleges. The Boston contingent was slated for the dorms at Georgetown itself, just down the street from John Kennedy's own house. This coup was arranged through the BC-Jesuit connection, through Bright McKay, in fact, who'd played it like a trump card when the best Ed Lake could do was a setup at Johns Hopkins fifty miles away. Didi and the two dozen other girls from Boston would be at Visitation, the convent school that shared one high wall with Georgetown. The debs from Radcliffe,

Wellesley, and Simmons had arched their eyebrows at that news, but it had enabled Didi's mother to overcome her reluctance to let her daughter go.

Terry and Bright claimed a choice corner in the lounge of Healy Hall, the spired old building that stood like a black-robed Jesuit in the center of the campus. They unloaded their sleeping rolls and duffel bags onto a pair of adjacent leather couches, confident that the gear was claim enough.

"I got to make that phone call," Terry said.

"Good luck. I hope she's okay."

"She will be. She is."

Terry found a telephone in a dark hallway and called the hospital. The nurse said his mother was asleep. His brother was there, but he'd gone down to the cafeteria. Everything was fine, not to worry. The nurse took Terry's message: It's really snowing here. I'll call later.

McKay had gone on ahead, and Terry found him in the formal sitting room off the main entrance of the musty old building. On one wall was a portrait of George Washington. Bright was standing in front of the portrait on another wall, and Terry, as always now, was aware at once of the off angle at which Bright held his head whenever he looked at something carefully. He took a place beside his friend.

The painting was of a bishop, the red robes, the three-sided stiff hat, the ring flashing from the folded hands. But this bishop was a colored man, with unmistakable brown skin, flared nose, and wide lips. *James Augustine Healy, SJ*, the plaque read. *The Bishop of Maine, 1830–1900.*

"Who's that?" Terry asked.

Bright had to turn his face entirely around to look at him. The wound was mostly healed now. He had been wearing a black leather eye patch since before Christmas, but it was a shock every time Terry saw it. Bright had missed the last half of the first semester, returning to school only when classes resumed last week. Their friends at BC still did not know what to say, not that Terry did.

"Never heard of him," McKay said, "but I'm not that surprised. It was easier for a Negro in this country seventy-five years ago than it is now. There are no colored RC bishops today, are there?"

As far as Terry knew, there were no colored priests; Floyd Patterson was the only colored Catholic he'd ever heard of. Bright looked at him with the grave sadness that rode on his shoulder like a bird now, piercing Doyle every time he saw it.

On the bus early that morning, as the Young Dems happily piled on board, a pair of BC guys had taken the seat in front of Bright and Terry. One, meaning no harm, had cracked, "Hey Bright, can you get me a discount on a Hathaway shirt?"

Terry wanted to slug the guy, but Bright didn't miss a beat. "Sure. Shall I have them stuff it for you? Or do you do that yourself?"

Everybody in the nearby seats laughed.

But McKay fell silent once the bus was moving. He faced the window, making it impossible to talk. A little while later Terry began to doze, but he came alert when he realized Bright had said something. The bus was just leaving the far western fringe of Boston behind.

"What?" Terry asked.

"I hate that fucking city. I'm going to enjoy being gone."

Hate Boston? Such a thing had never occurred to Terry. But then he realized that Bright was talking about his eye, a first.

"You blame Boston?"

"Sure I blame Boston. Wouldn't you?"

"I'd blame the bastards who —"

"Tribal warfare, Terry. Boston's tribal warfare." Bright's one eye, when it concentrated on you, could start a fire. "What I can't get over is, it wasn't even my tribe. Negroes had nothing to do with it that day. I mean, we weren't the fucking issue. Nobody was out to skin a coon. I got caught between you guys, wops and micks. Not my fight. Do you know what kind of dickhead that makes me?"

"Hey, come on. Don't put it on yourself."

"Everybody has an enemy in Boston. That's what tribes do for a place. You know your friends and you know your enemies. All those different groups, Terry — WASPs, wops, micks, Jews, Chinks even — the one thing you all have in common, one tribe you all hate." He didn't have to name it. "Which you all basically ignore until some nigger is stupid enough to make you notice. And then, boy: Nigger! Nigger! Nigger!"

So he *had* heard it too. Terry could think of nothing to say. Bright faced the window again.

After a few minutes Bright said, "Washington is better. A good old down-south city where, when they kick the shit out of you, at least it's you they'd set out to get." The first rays of dawn were backlighting the snow-covered Blue Hills. "After I graduate," he said, as if to himself, "I'm signing on with the New Frontier and heading south."

McKay's eye socket and that entire side of his head were acutely sensitive to the cold. Now, when he and Terry left Healy, setting out into the snow-blown city, McKay pulled his navy watch cap down to his left brow. The freezing air hit his head like a hammer, and he knew it would take a while to get used to the pain, but he would, and no one would know about it.

They picked up Didi and a girl named Sally Fitzgerald, with whom Didi had hit it off on the bus. Sally was a sophomore at Regis, a nuns' college in Weston. She had not joined in with the debs' nervous jokes about Visitation. ("If we get pregnant, we can say it was a miracle.") Sally was friendly in the breezy way of overweight girls.

For all Didi knew, the Young Dems had disbanded after the November election. She hadn't seen that much of Terry either, and in hindsight she'd realized that what had happened between them that drunken night had scared him as much as her. And there was the mystery of what had happened at the Boston Garden that day, the most terrifying experience of her life. No one had bothered to explain to her who those men were. Because of how mean Jackie was about it, she knew better than to press her questions. She had visited Bright in the hospital several times, but had not seen him since he'd been released.

That she had met Edward Kennedy had come to seem as much a dream as kissing Terry in that cab, or watching a maniac chopping up cartons of flowers with a sword right in front of her. But then Terry had called about this trip to the inauguration. He had bulled right over her initial reluctance, insisting the trip was the Young Dems' reward, *her* reward therefore. She had felt thrilled that he had called her, then he'd admitted he was calling everyone, going down a list like they did on the campaign. She had fortunately channeled her anger into the act of doing something nice for herself for a change: she'd said yes. On the way down to Washington, the bus had been sleepy at first, but when they'd stopped on the Connecticut Turnpike, she and Sally had begun to talk. Sally had a way of making her feel a part of things, and it didn't phase Sally when Didi said she was a working girl with no intention of going to college.

Now they had five hours before the dance began, and they were in Washington, D.C., even if it felt like Antarctica.

"How's your mother?" Didi asked.

"She's good," Terry said. "She's over the hump. I just called. She'll be fine."

"At least she's warm," Didi said, hugging herself. Terry put his arm around her as they walked, amazed at how relaxed he felt, how normal this adventure seemed.

The four set off in the snow, their collars closed against the wind. They wanted to see it all, the Lincoln Memorial, the Capitol where

JFK would speak the next day, the White House where he would live, and the monument built in imitation of their own Bunker Hill obelisk.

But the gusts were too raw. The city was blanketed and more snow kept coming. There were no taxis. Terry linked arms with Didi, and likewise Bright with Sally. They pushed into the wind, determined, four members of a new generation of Americans come to claim their places.

They stopped for hot chocolate at a hamburger joint on M Street, a tiny lunch counter called the Little Tavern. The counter man was yellow-toothed and scrawny. Wearing a soiled white paper hat, he stood with a spatula over a spread of sizzling meat patties. Grease stains freckled his shirt, and a cigarette perched on his lower lip. When he saw Bright McKay and Sally Fitzgerald holding on to each other, the man's eyes flashed. Sugar and spice! "Nuh-uh, not in here," he said. "Your kind don't eat in my place, nuh-uh!"

"What?"

"You heard me. You can say we're closed, on account of the sudden bad weather."

"Oh, brother," Bright said, though without surprise. But Terry remembered what he'd said on the bus, that Washington was better.

"What do you mean closed?" Didi demanded. She leaned across the counter aggressively.

Terry said, "You're not closed. You're still cooking."

"That's for my dog. You all get out."

"We will not —" Didi began.

Bright took her arm. "Let's go. It's not worth it."

Didi and Terry faced him, but it was Sally who drew their attention. Aghast, clearly stunned by the implicit accusation that she was with McKay as a girlfriend, she was backing out.

Bright tugged Didi along, but he turned his eye on the counter man. "Do you know what tomorrow means, mister?" He spoke in the steady, firm voice that had first drawn Terry to him months before. "It means your days aren't even numbered. They're over." With that, he led Didi and Terry back out into the storm. On the sidewalk, Bright knew not to take Sally's arm again. "Forget it, okay?" he said. She found it possible to nod.

Terry grabbed Bright's arm. "Forget it, hell! That son of a bitch can't do that to you."

"To me? Was it to me he did that?"

"Us, I mean. He did it to us."

"That's more like it, brother."

"But we're just walking away?"

"What do you propose, Terry? That we go back in and kick his eye out?"

"Jesus Christ, Bright."

"Then forget it, okay? If you're not ready to jump the guy, forget it. Those are the fucking choices. Wise up."

"Why are you mad at me, Bright?"

The two stared at each other across a gulf that neither had, until now, admitted was there. The wind swirled a cone of snow around them. Terry dropped Bright's arm, quite aware that his question had gone unanswered because the answer was obvious: You fucking kicked *my* eye out.

Terry said, "I'm sorry."

Bright shook his head. "That ain't it, Terry. That ain't it at all." He grinned. "We didn't come all this way to sing the blues, did we?" He turned to Sally. "Do you sing the blues?"

"No." She looked helpless.

"Then what say, folks, aren't we going to see the monument? Wasn't that the plan?"

"What about Lincoln?" Terry said. "With malice toward none." He tossed his head back toward the Little Tavern. "Except that asshole."

Half an hour later, Terry and Didi were on the Mall heading, they thought, for the Lincoln Memorial. The wind and snow were worse than ever, and they could no longer see where they were going. They'd become separated from Bright and Sally, which had worried them at first, but now all they wanted was shelter. Away from the street, they'd become disoriented. Even the towering Washington Monument was blanked out. This was tundra. At one point, Didi stopped and fell against Terry. "I can't catch my breath. I can't breathe in this wind."

"Take it easy, take it easy," Terry said, but he was thinking, Symptoms! Shortness of breath. Pulse rate. He opened his coat around her, a cave. She leaned into the hollow of his body, burying her head.

"I'm scared, I'm scared."

"Don't talk, Didi. Deep breaths, in and out. Come on now, in and out."

They kept going. They found the edge of the Reflecting Pool, a step down into a field of snow, and they used it as a line to follow. Soon the huge white temple, pillars and pediment, loomed above them. Terry kept his eyes on it as if the thing would disappear again. A mansion in the clouds, a Parthenon.

They moved into the vacant circular road. Beyond the memorial, the cloud was punctured eerily by headlights moving along the Potomac Parkway, but no cars came here. As quickly as they could, they crossed the apron and began to mount the long, broad stairs. But that side of the temple was more exposed to the river wind than anyplace yet, and Terry practically had to carry Didi up. At the top they fell into the cavern in which Daniel Chester French's marble Lincoln sat, big as God.

Terry led Didi around behind the statue to get away from the dangerous weather. "Are you all right?"

Instead of answering, Didi leaned against the wall, struggling for breath. Above her head, a line etched in the marble caught his eye: . . . IS ENSHRINED FOREVER.

Neither knew the word "hyperventilate," but that was what she had been doing. Nothing to do with varicose veins, an organizing clot.

Didi had expected to suffocate at any minute, which had made her panic, which in turn had made breathing nearly impossible. She was more afraid than she'd been since pressing herself against the wall of Terry's truck while the madman had swung his sword in her face. She held on to Terry now as she'd longed to do then. Once she could breathe again, she began to cry.

How fragile you are, he thought. He closed his arms on her.

He had always liked her for being strong, full of verve and wit. Yet here she was so needy, needy for him. He stroked her sides, rubbing his hands lightly up and down. Aware of the thickness of her tweed coat, that she could not feel his touch, he pulled his right glove off with his teeth and let it fall. He crooked his forefinger at her cheek and began to gently stroke her there. How fragile you are, how sweet.

"Why haven't I seen you?" she asked.

"After what happened in the Garden, I shut down inside."

"It was scary."

"It still scares me, Didi. Sometimes I dream about it. And what happened to Bright, I feel —" He stopped because what he felt had yet to present itself in words.

Didi said, "This wind's scary too. Will they still have the inauguration?"

"I think they have to. He has to take the oath, right?"

"I guess." Didi pulled back and found his eyes. "What do you think of me, Terry?"

"I think you're my friend."

"That isn't how you make me feel."

"I'm sorry, Didi." He closed his eyes and leaned against the marble. Christ, all he could do was say he was sorry. Where was Bright? Where was Sally? If something happened to them now, would that be his fault too?

Leaning together — it could have been all that occurred between them, two young people, lonely and afraid, consoling each other. But Terry's physical sensations, which moments before had been concentrated in his nearly frostbitten face, slowly began to settle in his groin. He opened his eyes and looked at her. He noticed her lips, too red, too big. He remembered having her tongue in his mouth.

He kissed her. She kissed him back. He slipped his ungloved hand inside her coat, into the crevice between her belt and her blouse. She pressed against him.

Moments later he stopped, pulled back, made her look at him. "Is this okay?" he asked. She nodded. He removed his second glove and dropped it. He unfastened the buttons of her coat, carefully, as if something might spill out, then the buttons of her blouse. It was cold; each understood that the parted shirt was as far as this undressing would go. His hand inside her bra, he found her breast. The palm of his hand had never seemed so sensitive as when it pressed the small, hard nub of her erect nipple. He kissed her again. When she opened her mouth now, he sucked as if her tongue would give him milk.

✧

The only Young Democrats to show for the party at Georgetown were the ones staying on campus, plus a few who dragged themselves through the storm from GWU. Sixty or seventy kids in the huge McDonough Gymnasium, with beer and chips enough for ten times that many. The band did not make it either, but some local genius hooked up a record player to the PA system, and the randy voices of the Everly Brothers began to bounce off the towering empty bleachers. The panicked refrain of "Wake Up Little Suzie" echoed across the vaulted space, vibrating the red-white-and-blue streamers and the poster photographs of John Kennedy and Lyndon Johnson. For a long time that song alternated with "All I Have to Do Is Dream," because apparently they were the only records that could be found.

The Young Dems weren't complaining. They jitterbugged to the one song, slow-danced to the other. Eventually someone arrived with other records, but by then the night belonged to Don and Phil.

Terry and Didi were not the only couple to drift up into the dark privacy of the vacant stands, but the gym was so big, and its nooks so numerous, that they might as well have been. They were both half blitzed, but they moved purposefully, holding hands. They found an isolated corner in deep shadows behind the highest row of seats. There were barbells arranged neatly by a bench. Exercise equipment was attached to the wall. The cement floor was covered with vinyl mats, which both took as absolute permission, an act of fate that obliterated what few of their inhibitions remained. They faced each other, kissed tenderly, then went slowly down.

Given all that they had to overcome, their lovemaking was a first-time success rare for their kind. It was passionate, but without the usual pretense that they were being swept away. Perhaps because he was drunk, Terry felt freed from the obsessive self-awareness that had always undercut him. He was focused instead on Didi, on her wondrous body, her breasts, her mouth, her tongue, her thighs, the deep cavity between her legs; his fingers swam in it. As for his own body, in its nakedness and freedom, it felt like someone else's.

Didi helped by seeming so unlike the virgin he knew she was. When he stopped at the crucial moment to say, "Jesus, should I get a — ?" she covered his mouth with her hand. "Never mind," she said. "Where would you get one now?" And she smiled with such abundant acceptance that he put the thought of birth control aside. With her other hand she guided him in, and then they began to move together so naturally, it seemed they'd been joined like this before. She bridged up under him and suddenly began saying, "Good, good, good!" How did he know to do this? "Good," she said, "Oh, sweet T, good!"

A loudspeaker blared above them, "All I have to do is dream . . ." If Didi Mullen had any sense of doing something wrong, it was in thinking, even while Terry caught the rhythm of the music inside her, what a perfect memory this would make someday. To leave the present for the future, that's what is sinful.

Terry allowed the idea of wrong nowhere near his mind until the next morning, when he awoke under a suffocating blanket of it. Despite the frigid air around him, he was wet with perspiration. He found himself on the couch in the lounge of Healy, with no memory of how he got there. On furniture and mattresses around the room, boys slept. He realized he had slept. He had dreamed.

When he sat up, a mass shifted in his chest, like a bubble in a bottle. Not air, panic. The bends. The hangover clangbird clawed at his head. He looked at the mound on the couch across from him, softly falling, rising, falling again. He saw the black arm protruding from the blanket. McKay.

Without thinking, Terry tossed his own blanket aside. He saw that he had slept in his shirt and trousers, like a drunk. He went over and shook his friend. "Bright. Bright."

McKay came to slowly, bewilderment in his one eye. His patch was in place. "Huh? What? What?"

"I need to talk to you. Something happened."

McKay sat up. "What's wrong?"

"Jesus Christ, man, I think I made a huge mistake last night. I'm not sure what I —"

A sly smile came across McKay's face. "You mean you and Didi?"

"Yes."

McKay freed his hand from the blanket to slug Terry's shoulder. "Don't be a jerk, Doyle. It's about time you got laid. You said it was great. You said you never felt better." A cheesy grin had transformed his friend's face into something awful, and Terry saw, as if reflected in McKay's one good eye, an image of his own ridiculousness. Didi was one issue, Bright was another.

"I wanted to tell you I was sorry."

"Sorry for what?"

Terry just stared at his friend, unable to say it: For your eye. Finally he managed, "Just sorry for everything."

"Can the self-flagellation bullshit, Terry, will you?"

Is that what this was? Self-flagellation about his first girl? About a black man with one eye? "Sorry I woke you, I meant." But Bright had rolled over and seemed asleep again. Jesus Christ, Terry thought, he's blind. Blind in that eye — it only fully hit him now — for life.

Terry stumbled back to his couch and fell on it, but he faced the window now instead of the room. The sky was blue above the snow-crested college buildings, the storm had passed, but not the one inside Doyle. John Kennedy's inauguration would go on as scheduled, to be followed by a splendid parade, more parties, and a new day in America. But not for him. Where was this misery coming from? Getting laid? Altar-boy guilt? Making Didi think he loved her? Not even the first clear recognition of Bright's fate accounted for the feeling. Terry asked, and asked again, What? What have I done?

Across the quad, Georgetown students were trudging through the snow toward the chapel. Puffs of vapor came out of their mouths, only to disappear instantly in the cold. Some walked with hands covering their ears, a sight that made Terry want to block his senses too. His mind. He got up again, found his shoes and coat, and stumbled to the bathroom, where for a long stretch of moments he stooped over a toilet bowl expecting to vomit.

In the corridor outside the lavatory was the phone booth. Terry went into it. He dialed the long distance operator and asked for Mass. General.

The ward nurse told him his brother wasn't there, and neither was his grandfather. When he asked how his mother was, the nurse did not answer. The silence seemed unending. Finally she said his mother wasn't on the ward any longer. She asked him to hang on while she paged the doctor, who would talk to him.

He hung up and dialed the operator again, to call home. Nick answered on the first ring.

"It's me," Terry said. "What's going on?"

And again, that silence.

"Did Ma come home? They let her out already?"

"No, Charlie. They didn't let her out."

"What then?"

"She died. She died last night. We called down there. They said they couldn't find you. You were supposed to be at some dance, but they couldn't find you."

"She what?"

"She died. She died, Charlie."

"How? She was over the hump. What —?"

"She fell out of bed, okay? She hated the fucking bedpan, and she wanted to go to the bathroom, and she fell."

"She fell? Wasn't anybody watching her?"

"Yes. I was. I was watching her. She fell, and the blood clot broke and killed her. Because I went to sleep, okay? In the chair beside her bed I fell asleep. Okay? Because I couldn't watch her alone."

"What?"

"I fell asleep, didn't you hear me? And she fell out of bed, get it? And you didn't even fucking call. You said you'd call."

"She's dead?"

"She's dead, Terry." Suddenly Nick's anger dissolved in stifled sounds of weeping. After a moment he managed to ask, "Are you coming home?"

"Of course, I'm —"

"I can't handle this alone, Terry. Gramps is useless. We need you."

"I'll catch a plane. I'll get there as fast as I can. Jesus, Nick." It struck Terry how far from weeping he himself was. "I'm sorry, Nick."

"Me too. Oh, me too." And then Nick hung up.

✧

Terry pushed through the drifted snow, crossing the campus toward Visitation. There, a nun answered the door. He asked for Didi and the nun showed him to a bench in the cold vestibule. When Didi appeared, he saw in her face that she knew. "What's wrong?" she asked.

"Ma's dead."

They stared at each other, not moving.

Terry said, "I got to leave right away, and I didn't want you to think —"

"What? Wait a minute. What?"

"Ma died last night. They looked for me at the dance, but they couldn't find me."

"Your ma?" Didi closed the distance between them, instinctively ready to embrace him.

But Terry put his hands up, stopping her. "It's because I wasn't there."

His statement jolted her. "What do you mean?" she said.

"She fell because Nick and Gramps couldn't take care of her alone."

"That's ridiculous. She was in the hospital. That's what nurses are for."

"You don't understand. I didn't call her. I was going to call last night, but then —"

"Wait a minute, wait a minute. Last night? Are you saying your ma died because last night . . . you were with me?"

He didn't answer her. He didn't have to. He just shook his head. No. And then he left.

Outside again, approaching Healy to get his stuff, he had to cut through the line of Georgetown students, a throng of them now, heading into the chapel. It was the mandatory Friday Mass. Without thinking, he joined them.

Inside the church, his eyes failed for the moment it took to adjust to the dim light. Intending only to step out of the way, Terry found himself standing behind another student near the purple curtain of the confessional. He was in the line.

He heard the murmur of the priest behind the curtain, and he wondered, How had this happened? If every move he made was wrong, what of this one? His first impulse was to flee. But he could not trust it. He could trust no impulse if it was his.

He had not been to confession since May, when he'd decided against entering the seminary. He knew he had not caused his mother's death. And he knew he had not blinded Bright. Or deliberately lied to Didi. Or abandoned Nick. Yet moments later, on his knees, curled like a fetus in the warm darkness of the womb of the church, he whispered dryly to the shadowy ear a few inches from his mouth, "Bless me, Father, for I have sinned."

And for the first time ever, he knew, it was true.

✧ 1968 ✧

6

FORTY-TWO YOUNG MEN on their knees, arrayed along the gleaming brass Communion rail. Across an apron of polished marble and up six steps at the high altar itself, a priest on the ceremonial chair, the *cathedra* from which faith and morals were proclaimed and from which the building took its name. The priest was garbed in cassock and collar, not a bishop but a professor of theology and, today, an instructor in the liturgy. The acolytes and servers posted here and there around the sanctuary, and the seminarians themselves, were all dressed in mufti: the ubiquitous black shoes, but also khakis and sport shirts, cord trousers and sweaters, since this was a rehearsal and not the sacrament itself.

They were an impressive-looking group of men, although with their trim haircuts and clean-shaven faces, a not altogether typical one in that year. From appearances they could have been a class of newly commissioned army officers or incoming management trainees at a brokerage house. In fact, they were men who'd worked hard through most of that chaotic decade to root themselves in another age — an age, above all, of order.

Order: the name of the sacrament they were to receive. Order: the word from which the cardinal took his ecclesiastical title of Ordinary. Order: the unifying principle of the architecture of the very building around them, the Cathedral of the Holy Cross, in the South End of Boston. Seminary rituals until now — those mini-ordinations beginning with tonsure, initiating them into a succession of arcane clerical states — had all taken place at the modest chapel at St. John's Seminary, on the far side of Boston. But this ordination to the diaconate would be different, and the massive setting told them so.

They let their eyes drift up the soaring walls to the ribbed, groined vault in the apex of which the late Cardinal O'Connell's red hat hung rotting; to the pointed arches; to the luminous windows and their diffusing filters of colored glass through which common daylight was transformed; to the coarse stonework across which it splashed. What the seminarians saw was an example of the harmony they knew to be the source of all beauty and all truth, the ultimate expression of the laws according to which divine reason had ordered the universe. Orders. The sacrament. The place. The people, the strict geometry of their lifelong relationships not only to authority but to those they would serve, and to each other. The shadowy vault, immense as the night sky, timeless as the ancient silence, efficiently aroused the sacred feeling on which they all depended absolutely now: the Church!

They were forty-two Americans who loved show tunes, jazz, the Beatles, and all kinds of sports. They were fiercey dedicated, even if at an enforced remove, to the politics of peace and civil rights. They knew their Camus and their Flannery O'Connor, their Kazantzakis, their Frantz Fanon even; their Daniel Berrigan and their Camillo Torres. But all that was peripheral now. They had been trained for *this* feeling, conditioned to maintain it — a mystic revelation, the beatitude Thomas wrote of, Saint Augustine's holy intuition, the cloud of unknowing within which all comes clear — the Church!

They had been, in the argot, "formed"; formed every bit as much as the space around them had been — the ribbed, groined vault of their souls. The soon-to-be deacons recognized *themselves* in the Gothic verticalism of Holy Cross, *their* cathedral, a stone emblem — for them, proof! — of God's existence, God's nearness, God's real presence. They'd been taught to believe that the Church was the Body of Christ, and as such it was more real to them at that moment — this was conditioning too — than their own bodies.

"Terence Michael Doyle."

The priest intoned the name with a curling of vowels that hinted at self-mockery; he, for one, could not go on taking this lifeless rehearsal all that seriously.

"*Adsum*," Doyle answered, as if this were the real thing. He stood, entered the gate of the Communion rail, crossed the marble apron, and began to mount the stairs. As tall as ever, still a fine-looking man, he was twenty-six now. He had shed the last vestige of boyishness and carried himself nimbly, with the grace of one who'd learned to move in a sanctuary. When he answered, his voice rang with authority, and as he went up to the altar platform, his affirmation echoed in the dense air overhead. He wore trim-cut corduroy pants and a navy blue cotton windbreaker, clothing that emphasized his leanness. His classmates watched him, as if they would learn now how this part was done.

At the top step, in front of the priest, Doyle went down on his knees again. This is only rehearsal, he told himself, but his hands still shook slightly as he placed them inside the priest's. He thought, despite himself, of his brother Nick kneeling before Gramps in the crypt of this very building years before. Terry Doyle would be a squire now too, but God's.

Father Joe Collins, the cardinal's stand-in, was bald and stout-faced. Sixty years old, his once powerful body had softened and begun to fold down on itself. His cloudy blue eyes contained an aura of resignation, and the faint aroma of whiskey poured off him, as always. But as he squeezed Terry's hands in a way the cardinal never would, he conveyed the strength of his particular affection, and Terry once again felt grateful that this priest had been his spiritual director.

Over the years, Doyle had come to understand that he'd entered the seminary, deciding on the priesthood after all, because, beginning that winter of his mother's death, he'd lost the capacity to believe in himself or trust his own impulses. In the Church he could account for such feelings of unworthiness and, with Father Collins's help, had learned to make the most of them. In relation to Didi and Bright, and even his brother, Terry had felt doomed to failure, but here such an emotion seemed a kind of qualification. "We are broken servants," Father Collins loved to say, "to a broken world."

But now what he said was, "In the presence of God and the Church" — he looked at Terry intently as he recited the prescribed questions without any hint of his former levity — "do you solemnly promise, as a sign of your interior dedication to Christ, to remain celibate for the sake of the Kingdom and in lifelong service to God and mankind?"

"I do," Terry answered, but his mind was blank.

Now Father Collins smiled. "May the Lord help you to persevere in this commitment."

And Terry answered, a bit overly firm, "Amen." Some of his classmates tittered nervously.

Father Collins silenced them with a glance. "And my son, do you solemnly promise respect and obedience to your Ordinary?"

Without having planned to, Terry blurted his answer: "Ordinarily."

And behind him the young men exploded in laughter.

Even Father Collins chuckled, his eyes rolling above his jowly face and collar.

Periodic outbursts of tension-relieving but puerile laughter were a long-standing seminary tradition, but when such a thing occurred in chapel, the men were adept at stifling their reactions quickly. This time, though, the laughter grew, especially once they saw that Father Collins had discreetly joined in. The noise rolled back across the large empty space, swelling in the shadows, and the echoes coming back only made them laugh louder.

It wasn't *that* funny, but the pressure had been building so steadily, and with so little outlet, that it rushed through the small opening of Doyle's wisecrack and became, like air through a penny whistle, something shrill. There was a bitterness in their laughter. They all heard it, they all felt it, they all understood it. Their tension had mounted in the days and hours leading up to this rehearsal, of course, but it had also been steadily climbing in every month of that mad year, the events of which had undercut even their inbred docility.

The year had begun with the turning-point crisis of the Tet offensive in Vietnam, when their attitude of opposition, with Walter Cronkite's, had finally galvanized. Every month since had brought a new shock of disenchantment: McCarthy's unseating of LBJ in New Hampshire, Martin Luther King shot, the King riots, student revolts in Paris and then at Columbia, Bobby shot, the Chicago riot, Humphrey nominated, then Nixon. But for these *ordinandi*, the great shock not of the year, but of their entire time in training for the priesthood was an event few outside Catholicism had found all that surprising: Pope Paul's *Humanae Vitae*, issued only weeks before. The encyclical reasserted the Church's absolute rejection of all forms of birth control save abstinence and rhythm. Despite the arcane *aggiornamento* hoopla of the Vatican Council, and despite the widespread post-Council assumption that the Pill had given the Church an opening it wanted, the pronouncement had slammed the famous window shut on the idea that anything truly fundamental would change. When Soviet tanks rolled into Prague a few days later, many Catholic priests and lay people — and seminarians — thought, perhaps unjustifiably, they knew the feeling.

Respect and obedience for your Ordinary?

Doyle's remark had given efficient, if visceral, expression to the dilemma these men had yet to discuss openly. If the old authoritarian mode still held, what did it mean that they'd been trained in the New Theology? Were confessors expected to enforce Pope Paul's punishing hard line? In the secrecy of the curtained booth, could priests — could *they?* — tell men and women to let conscience be their guide? Wouldn't the cardinal himself do as much?

As the laughter subsided behind Doyle, Father Collins leaned forward to whisper, "Watch that stuff." But there was no rebuke in his voice, and Doyle felt the affection in the way the priest squeezed his hands one last time. Doyle returned to his place and the next man went up. After repeating the run-through half a dozen times, Collins raised his hand to stop the next one. "You get the idea," he said, standing. The *ordinandi* remained kneeling. He scanned their faces, then said, "Lucky for you, Deacs, your Ordinary is no such thing. It takes nothing to make such a vow to him." He turned to go to the altar from which the cardinal would lead the prayers on Saturday. Father Collins bowed at the tabernacle, then turned to face the men again. "At this point, having taken your places inside the sanctuary, you will all prostrate yourselves for the Litany of the Saints. Do we need to practice that?"

The seminarians only looked at him.

"You just stretch out, right forearm under your forehead. Once you're down, be still. Just pretend to be dead. Pretend you hear your friends and loved ones praying over you after you're gone, because, my buckos, that's exactly what's happening. You are dead to the world. If you go to sleep, do yourself a big favor and don't snore. His Eminence will throw his miter at you."

The men looked at each other.

Collins saw someone in the doorway of the sacristy, on the far left side of the sanctuary. He glanced over, and at once he felt a cold wind on the back of his neck. Loughlin. The chancellor. The one man who'd warned him about his drinking. What the hell was he doing here?

Collins pretended to ignore him. "Then, once the litany is complete, you come up to your knees again, and the cardinal will offer the Prayer of Consecration for each of you. And I want you to listen to every word of it, especially the part that says about you, 'May he give the world the witness of a pure conscience. May he imitate your Son, who came not to be served, but to serve . . .'"

As he spoke, Collins was aware that Loughlin had entered the sanctuary, was standing a few feet away, by the cruet table, watching icily. Loughlin was dressed in street clericals, a nicely tailored black suit with slim lapels. Collins considered Loughlin a fop; he was always shooting his French cuffs to show the gold of his Chi-Rho cuff links. At his throat a sliver of red showed below his white collar, the unmistakable mark of the standing in the Church Collins himself would have had if he hadn't blown it with his bending elbow. Loughlin was the man who ran the archdiocese while Cushing was off at bar mitzvahs and bond rallies and picnics for the nuns. As large-hearted and spontaneous and disorganized as Cushing was, Loughlin was that rigid and cold and, well, mean. As he had to be, Collins supposed. Collins knew better than anyone how little of what the Cush started he followed through on.

Out of the side of his eye, Collins noticed the manila folder Loughlin was holding. He found it impossible not to imagine the sheet it held as the official order sending him off at last to the dry-out farm for whiskey priests down in Rhode Island. It was a paranoid thought that the chancellor would serve his summons here, and Collins knew it. But God, the sight of that bastard made him want a drink. He stopped speaking and faced Loughlin, but his eyes went to the cruet table, where the wine would sit sparkling and ready during Mass. It held nothing now except a doily.

"Hello, Monsignor."

"Father Collins," Loughlin said with a bare nod. "Am I interrupting?"

"No, of course not. We're right in the middle of things."

"Then I *am* interrupting."

"We were just finishing up the Litany of the Saints. You know, 'Keep the pope and all the clergy in faithful service . . . Bring all the people together in trust and peace. Lord, hear our prayer.' That stuff." Collins smiled abruptly, unsure why he wanted to make Loughlin think he'd been at the hooch already.

But Loughlin refused to take the bait. He nodded and said quietly, "'Bless those chosen men, and make them holy.'"

"Exactly."

Loughlin glared at Collins. They'd known each other forty years, having knelt side by side in this very sanctuary to be ordained by Cardinal O'Connell. Collins had already been tapped for the Greg in Rome. He was *expected* to become a brilliant theologian, so when he did, no one gave him credit. Loughlin had been universally disliked even then, but he was fastidious and well organized, and already his gift for anticipating the wishes of superiors had set him apart. Collins knew that if Loughlin had not yet forced the pledge on him, it was only because Loughlin knew that Cushing liked the way he poured.

"Since I have interrupted anyway, may I?" Loughlin indicated the line of kneeling men.

"Of course, Monsignor. The lads have waited five years. They're in no hurry." Father Collins sat once more in the *cathedra*, but now there seemed some small presumption in it.

The chancellor turned and took four steps that brought him to the edge of a broad oriental rug. He stopped as if the rug marked a boundary. This prig was all boundaries.

"I'll need only a moment, gentlemen." Loughlin ran the tip of his manicured finger along one edge of the manila folder. "The ceremonies next week are scheduled for eleven o'clock. Vesting will begin at ten-thirty. Prior to that, the sacristy will be reserved for private forum interrogatories. You are to report here at eight-thirty sharp."

"Interrogatories?" Father Collins said from his place behind Loughlin. "We don't require the oath anymore. That went out two years ago."

Loughlin's irritation showed itself in a tightening of the muscles in his face and neck. Clearly he wanted to display no reaction, but his lips went white from pressing against each other. He pointedly did not look toward the fool in the cardinal's chair as he said, "Not the 'Oath Against Modernism.' Instead, an affirmation entitled 'A Solemn Declaration Concerning *Of Human Life*.'" Loughlin's eyes panned across the faces of the men in front of him. *They* were his concern, not Collins. "His Eminence has directed that admission to Major Orders is contingent upon each candidate's individual affirmation."

"Impossible," Collins muttered, but not so openly that Loughlin had to acknowledge him.

Indeed, Loughlin pretended not to have heard. Instead he asked, "Who is head student?"

An impassive Terry Doyle raised his hand.

Loughlin curled his fingers at him.

Doyle felt numb as he got to his feet and crossed the sanctuary.

The monsignor held the manila folder out like a diploma. His eyes burned into Doyle's alone. "Here is the text. You are to acquaint your colleagues with it. Each one is to be prepared to affirm the proposition aloud and to sign one copy, according to canonical form."

Doyle took the folder. He automatically said, "Thank you, Monsignor," and hated himself at once. He returned to his place, but instead of lowering himself to his knees again like the others, he asked, "May we stand, Monsignor?"

Loughlin nodded.

While the men rose noisily to their feet, Doyle opened the folder and glanced quickly at the single page it held. The mark of the cardinal's seal, the crimson hat with its draped and tassled cord framing the cross-bearing shield, was imprinted above a dozen lines of text. But shit, if it wasn't in Latin! "*Auctorita*" was one word that leapt out at him, "*obsequium*" was another.

"Now you may resume —"

"Monsignor!" Doyle blurted. He glanced at Father Collins, whose dead eyes were a warning. But he continued. "Will there be an opportunity for discussion?"

"There has been quite enough discussion."

"But the men may have questions." Doyle looked quickly to his right and left, but no one joined him.

Loughlin spoke with an eerie placidness, a false smile. "The declaration is crystal clear. It is a matter of restoring the confidence of the faithful in the teaching authority of the Church. The confusion must be dispelled. That is the first duty of His Eminence and therefore of his priests and you his candidates." Loughlin lowered the pitch of his voice and slowed his pace as he concluded, "Any hesitation on this matter will be taken as a sign of a disqualifying moral intransigence."

"Would questions indicate hesitation, Monsignor?"

"At this point, in this case, yes. Most assuredly."

Terry realized that he was supposed to shut his mouth now, but he couldn't stop himself. "'Declaration,' you said. 'Affirmation,' you said. But not an oath? This won't be an oath?"

Loughlin stared at him, not answering.

Terry took half a step forward, out of line. "Will we be expected to place our hands on the Bible?"

"What is your name?"

"Terence Doyle."

"Yes, Mr. Doyle. I will hold the Bible for you myself. As head student, you will be the first to make your affirmation, or if you prefer, to swear your oath. Do you have any other questions, Mr. Doyle?"

Still acting, as it seemed to him, involuntarily, Terry now dropped his eyes and answered with a subdued "No, Monsignor." He closed the folder between his hands. He was aware suddenly of the silence of his classmates. It rose as their only reaction into the reaches of the groined vault, where God was.

Caught. When it came to doctrines they knew to be outmoded, those men had honed the skill of slipping through the cracks of interpretation and definition. In all these years no one had called them on it. Once the seminarians were ordained, they too would be untouchable, free to quietly apply what they *really* believed in parishes and Newman Clubs and CYO gatherings — in confessionals where, above all, they intended to be kind. Not like this bastard. Here was a snare they had not seen. They'd stepped into it so blithely, and now it was sprung and each man felt hung upside down by his ankle, and each felt alone.

Doyle heard Monsignor Loughlin's footsteps clacking across the sanctuary, but he could not bring himself to watch him go. Instead, he stared at the smudges his perspiring hands had made on the folder, and that sight made him feel ashamed.

✧

Once, Squire loved bringing flowers to hospitals, but it had been years since he'd made deliveries himself. Cronin's Kerry Bouquet had stores now in six Irish neighborhoods around the city, and each one was a local center of Squire's other activities. He was a busy man.

He carried a paper cone of two dozen long-stem red roses, each one perfect, each one a bloom he'd chosen himself at the market that morning. Approaching a hospital, as he did the Mass. General now, up the narrow West End street a block from the river, he had always been especially aware of how perishable flowers were. Cut flowers, even the freshest ones, were already dead. In hospitals, flowers were rightly taken as a kindness, but to Doyle they were a sign of the death everyone was working so hard to push back. More than once it had occurred to him that, instead of cut flowers, people should bring to the sick pretty cards that said, "For your sake, we spared some roses." But then, hell, the roses would die in the ground. And he'd lose business. His train of thought served to deflect the feelings he had about this fucking hospital where his mother had died.

Doyle was a heavy man now. He was only twenty-five, but his body had the thickness of someone older. His hair had changed color slightly, more brown than red now — or was that a result of its being longer? He wore dark glasses against the bright morning sun. He sauntered with the flowers in the crook of one arm and with his free hand in his trouser pocket. He was dressed in loose-fitting garments, unusual for the time, that flowed around his limbs as he moved. His pleated flannel trousers, oversize cardigan sweater, and soft-collared polo shirt buttoned at the throat were not black exactly, but shades of blue, gray, and green that were close to it. His garb was low key and studied at once, an antistyle more suited to, say, an artist than to a small, if ambitious, businessman.

Doyle picked up his pace as he drew near the looming gray hospital building which, with the metallic curve of windows running its height, looked like the stern of a mammoth ocean liner. He pushed through the revolving doors into the art deco lobby, a glittering space three stories high. Not a ship, he now thought, an airline terminal. A huge painting on the far wall struck him at once, as it always had: a portrait of a dour, Coolidge-era Yankee whose disapproving expression suggested that he foresaw that the likes of Nick Doyle would enter this place as more than delivery boys. Doyle took his sunglasses off and studied the picture for a moment. A pipe was hooked in the man's left hand, a gold chain draped across his vest. His name was prominently etched in the wall below the painting: GEORGE ROBERT WHITE, PATRON, TRUSTEE.

Four couches were arranged in a square below the portrait. On each of two of them sat a lone woman, one sucking on a filter cigarette, the other staring vacantly into the air. The smoker had pulled the standup ashtray close, to hold on to it.

To the left was a long hallway that led to the emergency room. Straight ahead was the main hospital corridor, but, blocking it, a uniformed guard sat at a small table behind a mahogany sign-stand: *Authorized Visitors Only. Observe Visiting Hours. Observe Silence. Children Not Admitted.*

The guard was watching Squire, who nodded, then crossed the lobby toward the information desk in the far right corner. He weaved easily through the sparse traffic of doctors and nurses.

A prim woman, middle-aged but pretty in a tightly wound way, looked up at him as he approached. She wore a beige cashmere sweater and a string of pearls. Doyle's eyes went right to her fingers. In addition to her gold wedding band and discreet diamond, she wore a cameo ring, a pointedly unostentatious ornament. Her flawless nails were painted with clear polish. He noted her blond-gray hair, pulled back from her face in a tidy bun. She smiled at him and the skin around her eyes and mouth broke into a delta of tiny wrinkles. Her self-assurance drew him. A volunteer, some State Street lawyer's wife, no doubt. Mrs. Brahmin was there to help, and now she would be ever so glad to help *him.*

"Hi," he said with such warmth that for an instant the woman seemed to wonder if she knew him. "How are you today?" He shifted the flowers to his other hand, reining the whacky impulse just to hand them to her.

"Very well, thank you," she answered.

And Squire liked it when he saw color rising from the skin at her throat, at those pearls, a blush climbing quickly to her temples.

"May I help you?"

"I hope so." He leaned over the desk. He noticed her legs. Even these ladies were wearing short skirts now. Her calves were sinewy and tanned, and at once he saw her on a tennis court, slender, one long stride to the ball, her brown arm bringing the racket around, an arc of sunlight.

"I'm here to see Tory, Candace Tory." Squire smiled, wanting to hold her eyes an instant longer than was usual, and succeeding. He sensed her breasts shivering inside the illumined fur of her sweater.

She turned to her card file, hooked her finger in the middle, and pulled the first half forward in its tray. With a set of practiced flicks she went through a dozen cards, too quickly for him to see. "No . . . ," she said, then repeated the movement through the same cards. "I'm afraid . . ."

"Really?" Squire leaned closer, letting his haunch settle on the forward edge of her desk.

She adjusted the tray so he could see. "Tippet," she said, "Toomey, Tophet, Tucci. No Tory."

Tucci, G., the card read, and, as he expected, diagonally across it, in red letters, *No Visitors.* Room P504.

"Candace Tory, you say? Perhaps her card is out of order." She flipped a dozen more cards. "No . . . no . . . it's just not here."

"Oh. Well, I'm probably early. She was being admitted today, for an operation tomorrow."

"I don't have her yet. We get the card from Admissions. I don't have her yet. I'm sorry. Perhaps you could —"

"No, I'm sure I'm early. I guess I'm a little anxious." Worry flickered across Doyle's face.

The woman leaned toward him. He could sense the energy in her hand, wanting to touch him?

He stood up. "I'll come back, but . . ."

"What?"

"I'd love it if these flowers could be in her room when she checks in. Could I?"

"Certainly." The woman swung around to point down the main corridor, past the guard. "The flower shop is at the far end of the building. The candy striper takes a cart around every hour. You could leave the flowers with her. Admissions keeps them posted too, as patients come in. Just ask the candy striper to watch the cards for the name of your . . ."

"Friend. She's my oldest friend. She has a tumor."

"I'm sorry."

"So I can just go ahead down there?"

"Of course." The woman turned to catch the guard's eye and gestured at him, an exquisite display of inbred authority.

"Thank you."

"Your friend will be fine, I'm sure. This is a very good hospital, *very* good. A Harvard hospital."

"I know." Squire smiled again, but deliberately remote this time. Only now did he pick up the faint scent of her perfume, and it aroused his sudden wish to see her nude. How cool would she be then? How ready to help?

Just as cool, he decided. Even readier. He imagined her poised and amused, those breasts languid, that hair loose, those thin hands, rings and all, on his shoulders, that unpainted mouth at his ear, whispering, "Very good, *very* good." Balling her would be striking out the pitcher.

"Thanks again."

Breezing past the guard, he winked, as if his purpose here were frivolous. He told himself to bear down. Striking out the pitcher, shit. Balling the teacher, that's what it would be. He nearly laughed, amazed at the tricks his mind could play.

Seconds later he came to the flower shop, which was little more than a partitioned-off corner where two broad corridors intersected. A stainless steel cart in the doorway held four measly arrangements of weary-looking carnations and daisies. Inside the room, on stepped shelves, were several other meager bunches for sale. Just because the people here were sick, did the flowers have to be? The candy striper, a stout young woman of perhaps twenty, stood at a small worktable trimming the stems of daisies, cutting them flat instead of at an angle. Squire resisted the impulse to show her. What a waste, he thought. A real store would make a killing here.

He stuck his head in. "How you doing, hon?"

The girl jumped.

"The lady out front said I should just run these up." He indicated his own paper cone. "The room is P-something. That's —"

"Phillips House, that way."

"Right. Thanks."

He should have known it. Phillips House was the VIP wing. His mother hadn't gotten within a mile of it, but he walled off the old feeling. He headed down the corridor, whistling.

The sterile hospital ambience — the polished linoleum floor, the pale blue walls, the running strip of the wooden gurney guard, the circular neon light fixtures on the ceiling, the unclothed fire extinguishers and the institutional signage — all changed when Doyle crossed the threshold into Phillips House, the lobby of which was the spacious foyer of a pretend mansion. There were wooden floors, broad oriental rugs, a huge fireplace with a black marble mantel, a brass chandelier dominating its center. Portraits hung on the paneled walls on each side of the fireplace.

At a small ebony desk another prim woman sat, her job, no doubt, to welcome wealthy patients with assurances that Phillips House would be like dying at home. Doyle's instinct told him not to even look at this one. He swept past a door marked LADIES VISITING COMMITTEE and found the elevator. Luckily the car was there. He went in, pressed five, and the door closed behind him.

He knew Tucci's room from a distance because of the man in the dark suit sitting in a chair by the door. Doyle recognized him as he approached. The guard would know him in turn.

"How's Mr. Tucci doing?"

The guard looked at Doyle, but otherwise did not react.

"I brought these." Squire pulled back a corner of the wrapping from the roses.

"You can leave them with me."

"I was hoping to say a word —"

"No visitors. You shouldn't even be —"

"Mr. Tucci told me to come. Last time I saw him, he said he wanted me to."

The man stood up and turned to the door. He rapped once.

The door opened quickly, but only partway. A man whom Doyle recognized as Tucci's personal bodyguard showed his face in the narrow opening, then he disappeared. Seconds later the door opened fully to reveal the bald, pasty-faced figure of Guido's son. Behind him Doyle glimpsed the tidy furniture of a sitting room. Tucci's room was not visible, nor were the hospital bed, the tubes, stands, wheeled tables, and metal cabinets Doyle expected to see.

"What do you want?" Frank Tucci's eyes were red, but he asked the question with a snarl.

"I brought these because I knew your father likes them."

Frank stared at the roses. He was about forty now. He had been present for most of the meetings between Squire and his father over the years, always quiet at the old man's elbow, the permanent observer, never a confidant, but a trainee. At some point, Squire had realized it was how Guido protected his son, by making him privy to everything, forcing everyone to see how he regarded Frank. But to Squire, Frank had become like a thick piece of furniture in Tucci's office. He was aware of the way Frank's eyes glazed over whenever Squire described developments in the Irish neighborhoods. He was utterly unlike his father, whose genius lay, Squire eventually understood, in an acute interest in — devotion to, love of — the details of the lives of the people over whom he held sway.

Once, several years before, the three of them had walked along the boardwalk on Revere Beach on a bright but windy May day. When Doyle had handed over that period's shake, the old man had surprised them both by sending Frank home with the envelope as if he were some flunky. Then Tucci had slid an arm inside Squire's. After that, in good weather, the two of them had often walked there, leaving Frank at the house. Squire had hardly dared to think about the strong, forever unarticulated personal feeling that grew between him and old Tucci, each of whom needed something more from the other than the business. Squire understood his own need — the missing father — but not that of Tucci, whose attachment to a young Irishman seemed to come at his own son's expense. Frank had never shown Squire any overt reaction beyond a stolid, morose silence, but it was with a quite open resentment now that he took the flowers. He started to close the door, but Squire put his foot against it. "Your father would want to know I'm out here."

"No. No, he wouldn't."

"Tell him."

"Get the fuck out of here, Doyle." Frank looked at the guard. "Get him out of here, Jerry. What the fuck do I have you sitting out here for?"

The guard responded at once by locking Squire's arm and pulling him away.

Squire could not quite hold his ground. "You've got to tell me how your father is!"

He almost added, He'll be all right, this is a Harvard hospital. For an instant his mind was taken over by an image of that woman at the desk. She was naked, on a bed, her legs together modestly, but the whiteness of her thighs was dazzling.

"Get the fuck away from here, and don't bother me," Frank said. "You get it? Forget coming to Revere. I'll send people to you from now on, you get it? And the vig is going up. Changes, Doyle. You got changes coming."

That's how Tucci is, Squire thought. Dying. Or dead already. Nothing else could account for Frank's spasm of authority. It was what

Squire had come here to learn. It was what Squire had been dreading. The personal grief, yes; despite himself, a bit of it. But more, far more — the prospect of fronting for this asshole, the need to placate him.

Tucci dying. Dead. Also, all these years — his plan would prevail over any sense of loss, over any move Frank made — it was the moment he'd been waiting for.

7

COMING OUT of the cathedral had been like coming out of a movie theater, everyone blinking in the bright light of late morning sunshine, blinded for a moment but still in thrall to the adventure, the romance, or, as in their case, the dread of what they had just beheld.

They moved out of the glare quickly, into the cold shadow of the old iron superstructure of the elevated train. Those tracks had been a Protestant-sponsored blight on the cathedral since early in the century. Soot and noise had ruined the church, and the Irish still held the faded Brahmin establishment responsible. Even these young men were attuned to the primordial feud, taking for granted the special Boston meaning of the chill of that shadow. But today the chill they felt was more Roman than Yankee.

The seminary bus waited in the dead zone between the girders that grew like rusted, leafless trees in the middle of Washington Street. Doyle's classmates milled uncertainly at the curb, reluctant to cross to the bus yet. They clustered in small groups. Some looked toward Doyle, as if he would call them around and explain what Monsignor Loughlin meant.

But what could Doyle say? He held the folder gingerly, as if expecting it to burst into flame.

He caught Jim Adler's eye and raised a finger. Adler came over. His wide-eyed expression said, At your service. His big ears and freckled face kept Adler looking young, and in that crowd where studied world-weariness was a mode, Terry found Jim's boyishness irresistible. As he had previous head students, Adler served as Terry's unofficial factotum, drawing on his considerable gift for ingratiation. The culture of seminary life forbade overt ass kissing of the rector or faculty, but within the pecking order of student seniority, the ethos encouraged it. Terry had begun by finding Adler's eagerness useful, but by now he considered him a friend and confidant.

"It's in Latin, Jimmy." Doyle opened the folder and read, "*In seminarium ab Ordinario . . .*"

"'Ordinarily.' I don't believe you said that."

"Me either." Terry looked at the others, aware that they were watching him. Once on the bus, out of sight of the cathedral, of the monsignor, they would explode. Doyle was not ready to deal with that. "Do me a favor, will you?" Terry handed over the manila folder. "We need to know exactly what this says. Will you bring it to Roger? Ask him to translate it precisely, would you? Then run copies off on the mimeo, get them around to everybody."

"The guys are going to want to know . . ."

"Post a sign at lunch. Meeting at four in the common room. Closed to everybody but our class."

"Then you better not say the common room."

"The music room, then."

"You're not coming back to St. John's with us?"

"I've got an errand to run for the Liturgy Committee."

Adler flipped the folder open, puzzled over the closely typed page, then whistled. "'*De dimissionis.*' Even I know what that means."

"When you get back, go to Monsignor Carey's office for me. Tell him, since we were already downtown, I went over to Campion's for copies of the new rite."

"Yeah, *right*. We already have those."

"We need a couple more, Jimmy. Just tell him, would you? Will you do it all, like a pal?"

"Hey, famous for it, doing what I'm told." Adler dropped his eyes to the arcane text again. "But even I have a line in the sand somewhere, one I won't cross."

Terry laughed. "That's not your line, that's your head."

"Jesus, Terry, this is —"

"Don't jump the gun, Jimmy. Let's see what Roger says it says, exactly. Maybe we can play the Roman game too, like Küng and Rahner do, like the Cush, hiding in the thickets of linguistic ambiguity. The fact that it's in Latin may give us all the out we need." Terry slapped Adler's shoulder, making him feel that, despite Loughlin's air of ultimatum, things were going to be all right. Which was how Doyle often made them all feel.

✧

Terry had once liked going to Campion's, the religious goods store behind Jordan Marsh. It was a mark of how much he had changed, and how little Campion's had, that now he detested the place. With its gaudy plaster statues, its mawkish pictures of the saints, the medals and icons and plastic holy-water fonts and dashboard figurines; with the rosary beads in a hundred colors, the pious pamphlets and the mindless spiritual books, Thomas à Kempis, *Sayings of the Little Flower*, a revolving rack of K of C comics featuring the jailed priest-heroes of the war against atheistic communism — Campion's was a shrine to the Church that was dying.

The salesmen were stooped, effeminate, and old beyond their years, overgrown altar boys. The cash register clerks were talc-ridden sodality ladies. He could not pass those people in the narrow, cluttered aisles, whiffing their too sweet odors, hearing their dentures clack, without the sinking humiliation he'd have felt if they were his own aunts and uncles. He knew very well that, to detached outsiders, to those girls in their September dresses passing in the street, say, this cramped, musty world and *his* world were one and the same. Never mind the Berrigan brothers, Mass Facing the People, or the New Theology. Especially never mind them now.

Terry's liberation from the old Jansenist constraints was relative. Out of a pained impulse to be alone, he'd fabricated an excuse to come here, and so then he'd felt obliged to. Given what had transpired in the sanctuary of the cathedral, Campion's seemed more oppressive than ever. Surely the new encyclical meant just what they'd all first feared, that they'd been kidding themselves, that *this* — the Word become plastic — was the true Church, the One True Church, the Bride of Christ to whom he himself was engaged to be married.

When he noted the dandruff on one clerk's shoulders, he checked his own and was mildly surprised to find them clean.

"There you are!" The familiar voice startled Terry. It was Father Collins. With a sweep of his arm, he took in the rows of books that covered the nearby wall. "Looking in vain for any publication that acknowledges, much less celebrates, what we have accomplished in this decade alone."

"Hello, Father," Terry said calmly, but he could feel his face heating up, as if he'd been caught eyeballing *Playboy* at the drugstore.

"Jimmy Adler told me where you said you'd be."

Terry started: what was Jimmy doing telling Collins? "I told him I need some copies of the revised psalter, but frankly —"

"But frankly, I never thought I'd really find you here. You just had to get the hell out of there, and so did I. I'm glad for the excuse, tracking you down." Father Collins looked around, amazed. "Cherubim and seraphim, all ye holy nuts and bolts. Christ, I haven't been in here in years."

"Get used to it, Father," said Terry, "it's coming back."

The priest shook his head sadly, but before he could reply, one of the salesmen who had so successfully ignored Terry, thinking him a layman, presented himself. "Welcome to Campion's, Father. What can I do for you?"

Father Collins instantly dropped his face to peer over the top of his eyeglasses. "Something on the intact hymen of Mary, please."

"I beg your pardon?"

"In childbirth, how she remained a virgin, biologically speaking, how nothing broke when the baby came out. What do you have?"

"I, that is . . . we have . . ." The salesman glanced at the wall of books, devotions, nosegays. "I'll have to ask Mr. Drew."

"Yes, do."

The salesman shuffled off.

Collins turned his attention to the phalanx of foot-high statues on the counter behind him, each of a baby king, each clothed in silk robes, doll dresses. "God, these things. They still have these things." He lifted the hem of one statue's dress. "This is it, Terry. You know this is it, don't you?"

"What?"

"The Secret of Fatima, what Our Lady revealed, that the Infant of Prague wears no underwear. See?"

Terry burst out laughing. His mentor had just reminded him that the only possible response to this shit must be ridicule. Religion gone wrong is not tragedy but comedy.

Father Collins took Terry's arm, as if now they would move together to the door, but instead they remained where they were, surrounded by odd paraphernalia and books, a stilted pair. "I was hoping you'd have lunch with me, old pal."

"I don't know, Father. I have to —"

"I won't take no for an answer." The priest spoke a bit sharply, time to cut the crap. "I'm going to Dini's, and it's a principle of mine not to eat alone in public if I'm dressed in clericals. Some drunk always wants to hear my confession."

"Your confess —?"

"Right, hear *his* confession. See what I mean? I need you. What do you say?"

"Look, Father, I know what you're up to here. You think I went off half cocked with Monsignor Loughlin."

"No, I don't. You reacted the way I would have. I didn't see that thing coming either. Don't you think I'd have warned you, prepared you?"

"I think you did prepare us. That may be the problem. But —" Terry pulled away, bumping against the golden silk dress of one of the larger statues. What a strange religion, he thought. And he realized that this priest, his friend, his spiritual father, was strange too. "I don't think I'm ready to talk about what Monsignor Loughlin said, if that's what you —"

"Me either. We'll talk the Red Sox. We'll talk Yaz and Lonborg. We'll talk BC basketball. Did you get permission from the rector to help the coach?"

"Yes."

"Good. I told you they'd never turn you down, now that you're almost a deacon. They love a jock. We'll do jock talk, Terry, nice and superficial. My treat. Let's get out of here before that creep comes back with *Mysterium Salutis*."

They left the store. The narrow sidewalk was crowded with office workers in the fold of their day, running to the lunchtime sales. They seemed so full of energy and life, of *humanae vitae*, that Terry wished that his mood would lift. He glanced at Father Collins, whose face had fallen into its habitual benign expression. A passing stranger tipped his hat at him, a woman smiled, and Collins nodded generously at each. He led the way through the crowd, more than ready to shower them all with his affection. Terry, by comparison, felt stingy, and he rebuked himself. The day glittered around him. Sunlight streamed onto the pavement. Here is the main thing, he told himself: human life is good.

The restaurant, a popular fish place on Tremont Street, was crowded. None of those waiting in line objected as the hostess, with her armful of menus, waved the priest and his friend ahead. When they reached the hostess at her podium, she offered her cheek to the priest. A lamp turned on inside her when he kissed her. "Hello, Dolly," he said with a hint of the song, and then he did a little quick-step.

They went to a Naugahyde booth below a splayed fishnet onto which lacquered lobsters, crabs, and starfish were clamped. Terry had barely spread his napkin when a waiter showed up with a martini for Father Collins. He took a quick, ample sip, said "Aaah," and then addressed the waiter with mock sternness. "But what about my young friend?"

The waiter hooked his fingers together and eyed Terry.

"He'll have the same thing," Father Collins said. "Silver bullet."

"No, no."

"Don't be a kid, Terry. Next week you're a deacon. New status, new rules. It'll be legal. We'll just jump the gun a bit."

The chalk-faced waiter leaned down. "It's legal now, sir. If you're eighteen."

"I'll have a beer."

"Bud? Miller?"

"Fine. Bud. Thanks."

How long had it been since he'd uttered those simple words? During his years in the seminary, even *those* years when so much else had changed, he had rarely eaten in a restaurant, driven a car, or spoken to a girl. He had not once left the seminary grounds — that rolling estate across from his own BC — without permission. With his dark windbreaker and button-down shirt, he did not appear all that set aside, but he sensed the waiter sizing him up for a perfect fool. It was a point of view Terry understood. No outsiders were fiercer critics of the defensive, isolating mediocrity of the seminary system than the seminarians themselves. But also they were the only ones with a lively sense of the system's two great virtues: the rare camaraderie it encouraged, and the powerful dependence on God which alone justified the anachronism of the way they lived.

When Terry looked at Father Collins, his eyes had taken on a new luster. Dependence on God? Doyle knew enough to take dependence on booze as a signal too. He knew that his own expression, compared to the priest's freshly lubricated one, would be opaque. They stared at each other for a moment, then Father Collins, letting it go at that, opened his menu.

"I recommend the artichoke."

"Not a feature in Brighton."

"Get it. Take my word."

A few minutes passed before Terry's beer came, and before the waiter took up his position with pencil and pad. Terry asked for scrod and the artichoke. Father Collins ordered only the famous chowder and another drink, but when Terry glanced at him, he ordered the artichoke too. The waiter disappeared again. The priest lifted his martini glass, studied the olive, and said quietly, "The cardinal thinks the great weakness of the modern Catholic Church is the worldliness of the clergy." He sipped his drink. Then he looked at Terry. "But do you know what I think?"

"What?"

"It's the old women."

"The what?"

"Not the literal old women, not them. They make the thing go. No, I mean the old women in cassocks and collars. Like Loughlin. That wannabe grand inquisitor."

Terry had to smile. "Which is he? An old woman or Torquemada?"

"Both. The most dangerous combination."

"Funny thing, Father. I thought *Humanae Vitae* meant that *young* women were the great weakness of the Church. If we could just get rid of them —"

"Now *there's* an idea. You've got a future in this outfit."

"You know what the young women say. It's not the infallibility of the pope they worry about, it's the infallibility of the Pill."

The abruptness with which Father Collins leaned forward banished their frivolity. "It's not an infallible statement," he said gravely. "There is no pretense to infallibility. Nobody claims that for the damn thing."

"Then how can they make it binding in conscience, in confession?"

Collins dropped his eyes. The fresh martini arrived in the nick of time. He stopped the waiter from removing the drained one, to pop its olive into his mouth. Then he snapped the toothpick in half with the thumb and forefinger of one hand. "They can't," he said. "Cush said to me, 'What am I supposed to do, be a cop under people's beds?'"

"Conjugal police."

Collins nodded. "It's impossible. Just impossible. The cardinal knows that better than anyone."

"But that's what he expects *us* to be. Did you see that oath?"

"The one we're not talking about?"

"How does he expect us to sign that?"

"So we *are* talking about it," Collins said.

"Well, how does he?"

The priest looked across the rim of his martini glass and said, "The way professors of a pontifical theologate sign the 'Rejection of the Syllabus of Errors,' which is a summary of everything we teach. The way three generations of priests before you signed the 'Oath Against Modernism,' which is all that the Vatican Council eventually affirmed. By holding your nose, Terry. That's how." He took a careful sip, then lowered his glass. "Which is what I wanted to tell you, what I want you to tell the others. This is just a new dose of the old fish oil. The trick is to swallow it quick. It does nothing except let the dispensing quack pretend he's fixing something. In this case Cicognani, the apostolic delegate whose job is to keep the lid on over here. He's using Loughlin to force Cushing's hand. Loughlin wants the purple shirt, and this is the way to get it, and the Cush can't stop him. Cushing's the one liberal who could do them some damage on this, and that's why Rome has fired this shot across his bow. Cushing's conformity — the best way to show that the American Church has heard the pope speak and will come about. Unfortunately, you guys are the midshipmen on deck doing the saluting. Just a wave of the hand, Terry, that's all. Cushing doesn't buy what's in that declaration, and he doesn't expect you to."

"He expects us to sign it."

"We all sign things, Terry. Hell, it's in Latin. Nobody will notice except those guineas in the Curia, the only ones who can read it."

"I can read it, close enough."

"I warned you about learning Latin too well. Dead language, dead, dead, dead. Now you won't even need it to say Mass."

"What are you telling me, Father? Swear on the Word of God something I don't believe?"

"You don't believe the world was created in seven days either. You don't believe the Red Sea parted for Moses, and you're not sure about the Virgin Birth. But do you debunk any of it? Symbolic language, Terry. We're talking about the truth beyond the literal meaning of the words."

"Which is what?"

"In this case, the order of the Church."

"The order of the Church, Father? It depends on a class of new deacons taking a phony oath?"

"Maybe it does."

"Then things are worse than I thought."

Father Collins dropped his eyes to his hands on the table. In his fidgeting, he had arranged the two sticks of the broken toothpick into a cross, stark against the white tablecloth. "They *are* worse than you thought, Terry. That's my point. What are we supposed to do, jump ship?"

"I appreciate the analogy, Father, but Peter's bark notwithstanding, you and I and my classmates aren't in the same boat, not yet."

"We will be when you make the vow to obey the cardinal. What did you think that commitment means, anyway?"

Terry's fingers itched to hold a cigarette, another out-of-the-question indulgence all these years. He clasped his hands around his beer glass, let its moisture overwhelm his perspiration. "The vow? But the vow, Father, that's an oath, isn't it? How can you point to the gravity of one oath to make the point that another is no big deal? I'm confused, Father. Do we mean what we say or not? Isn't that the question?"

"Come on, Terry. Keep your eye on the ball. The vow is part of a sacrament. This thing Loughlin wants is hazing. One way to think of it is, he has no right, given the moral uncertainty surrounding the question, to ask for absolute fealty. Therefore you have a right to a mental reservation."

"Hey, Father, come on. I'm not a college kid looking to beat the draft."

"What are you, Terry?"

"*You're* asking me that? After hearing my confession twice a month for years?"

"And hearing an oversupply of ambivalence in your voice about your vocation. If you grab this oath business as a last-ditch excuse to bail out, you should at least be aware that that's what you're doing."

"Who's talking about bailing out? As if this is *my* problem. We're talking about *Humanae Vitae*. A problem for the whole Church, you called it. You were the first one to call it a disaster, that first week."

"Before I came to terms with it."

"Well, I haven't done that yet. I'm working on it. I just don't know how I swear on the Bible that I already have."

"Because your word is so precious to you. Because you cannot tell a lie. Who the hell are you, George Washington? It's your only flaw, Mr. Doyle, that perfect virtue of yours."

"Jesus, Father." Terry looked away, horrified to feel a burning behind his eyes. The figures across the restaurant were blurred suddenly. He tried to think of something else, and what popped into his mind was Nick, how his brother would skewer him. "Make like a tree and leave, Charlie," he would say, and when Terry winced, Nick would poke him. "The tree of life, kid. Let's climb it." Terry would answer, "That's what I thought I was doing, so why do I feel like I'm sinking?"

"Now here's my confession," Father Collins said abruptly. "I'm having lunch with you because Loughlin told me to." The priest drained his martini in a gulp and held the glass up until a passing waiter took it. "Loughlin sensed how the boys take their cues from you. He sensed the trouble coming, and he can't have it. And I promise you, the Cush can't have it either. The archdiocese does not need rebellion in the ranks."

"You know better than anyone how far I am from being a rebel."

"Yeah, so were Lucifer's angels. They just thought they were a little better than the others, a little purer. Their word of honor, you know, was a tad more sacred."

"I'm not better than anybody. That's not what I'm saying."

"What are you saying?"

"I'm trying to be on board here, Father."

"Good. That's good."

The waiter brought him his drink. Terry watched the priest's hand shake as he brought it to his mouth, and, to his horror, he found himself thinking, I'm better than you.

"Good," Father Collins said again. He leaned back. "Monsignor Loughlin also told me to tell you not to call any meetings about the oath."

"What?"

"No assemblies, no group discussions. Just distribute copies and leave each man alone to come to terms with his own conscience, in counsel with his confessor, if needs be."

"Like this, you mean."

Father Collins shrugged.

"I don't control whether my classmates have meetings, Father."

"You're just not to call it, that's all. Understand?"

"Yes," he said, then added to himself, Mental reservation: what if I already did?

"Good."

"Anything else?"

"Yes. You've a bright future ahead of yourself, Terry. This thing is temporary. We've been through it before. Hunker down. The wind blows, knocks the Church around. But you know what? It's the wind of the Holy Spirit. Our faith in his guidance means that eventually the truth will out, and *then* you and I will laugh about this little setback. You'll see."

"And meanwhile, the men and women whose lives are wrecked by it? Or whose faith in the Church is? What about them?"

Father Collins's face clouded over, and Terry thought for sure he would get angry now. Yes, that would be next, the revelation that the priest beloved of all was a mean bastard drunk.

But the waiter arrived just then. When he'd placed the artichokes in front of each one, when he'd poured the pungent dressing over the gaping mouth of the crusty flower, he departed.

Terry said, "It looks like a grenade."

"Ready to explode?" Father Collins laughed, and his mood brightened as he lifted his martini. "You've really never had an artichoke?

Reason enough right there not to ordain you. Watch." He set down his drink, flapped his napkin to the side, then tucked its corner into his collar and spread the cloth. Then he removed a leaf of the artichoke, scooped the vinaigrette, and put the tip of the leaf between his teeth. He pulled sharply once, for the meat, then closed his lips on the leaf a second time, to suck it. "Delicious."

Terry imitated him, although without the napkin at his neck. The tiny morsel he coaxed off the end of the leaf *was* delicious, but it surprised him to realize that the nubby tip was all there was to eat. It was a relief to have the complicated novelty of the thistlelike artichoke as a point of concentration.

The two men worked their leaves in silence for some moments.

"Imagine," Father Collins said, "the first guy to eat one of these, huh?"

Imagine, Terry thought instead, the first guy to stand up to the pope. But that was Martin Luther, and if ever there was a man who'd aggrandized himself . . .

The seminarians' up-to-date study of the Reformation had been ecumenical: Luther was sincere and had valid criticisms to make. And it was psychological: Luther was constipated and hated his father. The seminarians were taught not to condemn Luther, but to disdain him.

Terry felt mystified suddenly by how he came to be here, in a public-setting conference with his private confessor, feeling confused and guilty. For what? Hesitating to swear falsely? Only a minute ago, it seemed, he was holding that girl, touching her skin inside her winter clothing at the Lincoln Memorial, his chest full of air, trying to help her remember how to breathe. Over the years, that image had taken over the empty niches in his mind while men around him went on about the proofs of God's existence or the question of whether Christ had really felt pain or only pretended to. If Didi Mullen had presented a classic occasion of sin, what the hell was this?

The rank absurdity of his situation made him laugh out loud as he tore open the core of the artichoke. "Yes," he said, "imagine."

"Watch that part, lad. It's where the name comes from, the heart. Eat that and you choke."

Terry looked up sharply because Father Collins's voice had slipped into a slur. At the corner of his mouth, a ribbon of saliva leaked. His always rheumy eyes were now fully glazed over. The edgy posture in which he customarily held himself had folded. He was smiling serenely, needless to say.

Terry thought of his mother. Her drink was not gin but sherry, with which she had maintained her steady, low-grade buzz. Sherry or beer, like Terry had in front of him now. "When I was a kid," he said, as much to himself as to the priest, "my mother used to make me go to confession when I knew I hadn't done anything wrong. My only sins were the lies I told the priest in the box, so I'd be like the others."

Father Collins reached across the table and clasped Terry's hand. "You know I love you, Terry," he said sadly, "but I have to say your sin was thinking you weren't already like them. And it still is."

"Maybe so, Father." Terry took his hand back and unconsciously wiped his fingers on the napkin. He could not bring himself, after that, to look at his mentor.

The rest of the meal went strangely. They hardly spoke again. Father Collins did not bother to feign interest in the chowder when it came, spooning it over on itself once or twice but never tasting it. Twice more he drained his martini, ate the olive, snapped the toothpick in half, held the torch of his glass up until a waiter replaced it. Meanwhile the fingers of his free hand fussed with the pieces of broken toothpicks, absently arranging them into shapes and figures, boxes and letters and, once, the cross of Jesus again, which, from Terry's vantage, resembled a sword.

Terry, meanwhile, idled with his fish, pretending to eat, aware that other diners increasingly eyed the unsteady priest. Then at last the meal was over, and Terry was mortified when he realized that Father Collins was preparing to leave with no expectation of having to pay.

"What about the check?"

"Not at Dini's," the priest said. "No such thing." He was sober enough to read Terry's reaction: Clerical privilege, no wonder the people hate us. But he was not sober enough to rein in the fierceness with which he leaned across the table. "We do *them* the favor. It brightens the tone of the place, having the dog collar in here. That's why they put us up front. Business, we help business. You'll get the picture soon enough."

But Terry's thoughts, as he looked at the ribbon of spittle on the priest's chin, were: I already have the picture. And: I'm no dog, and neither are you.

On Tremont Street he helped Father Collins into a cab, to bring him back to St. John's, and Terry started to get in too. But the priest refused to allow it. "You'll get into trouble," he said, "if you show up with me."

Terry watched the cab pull away. At the corner of Park Street it swung right, gunning for the golden dome of the State House and then out of sight. But Terry continued staring after it, as if he could see the long arrow of Beacon Street cutting through Back Bay and Kenmore Square, through Brookline and out to Brighton. Unconsciously his eyes rested on the soft greens of the Boston Common, and he allowed himself to slip into a kind of trance of melancholy. He did not move.

One of the things that made Terry Doyle a true Bostonian was the way in which the very geography of the city could serve as the throne of his ruling moods. Nothing had enshrined the ache of his boyhood desire like the sparkling view from Bunker Hill; the sense of marginality that went with seminary life like the location of St. John's on the far edge of the city; and now the feeling, admitted at last, of being weighted down by what he saw from where he stood. The Parker House took over the field of his concentration. Its awning protruded over the pavement. To most of Boston, the old hotel meant the famous dinner rolls, or perhaps the place where Dickens stayed, or the basement Grill Room, Curley's favorite watering hole. But to Doyle, the Parker House meant only Kennedy.

He began to walk toward it and soon was passing the row of storefronts, long since redivided and tenanted, that had served as the 1960 campaign headquarters. His focus went to the curbside spot where he and Didi had briefly met Ted Kennedy, the young, bright-eyed brother who, that night, had been barely older than Terry Doyle was now. The change in Ted's status, more than anything, defined the decade.

Ted Kennedy. Terry could not help but think of him standing at the podium in the sanctuary of St. Patrick's Cathedral a bare three months ago, quoting Bobby: "Each time a man stands up for an ideal, he sends forth a tiny ripple of hope."

Ripples. Doyle was aware of the salty ocean in his throat, and he was waiting for something to breach its surface. How easy to imagine the surviving brother, staggered and afraid, wondering in secret, What will I do now?

Yes, what?

Terry's question, of course. And it told him that, in this navigation, the needle of his inner compass was drawn not toward points of faith, the last words of Jesus, any teaching of the Church — but to Kennedy.

And therefore to Bright. The last time he'd seen McKay was on television, at that funeral, in a pew behind the senator.

At the Parker House, Doyle went through the revolving doors. He crossed the broad lobby toward the stairs in the corner near the elevators. The stairs led to the Grill Room, where Didi had slain the college boys by outchugging them. But also, Doyle remembered, the stairs led to the telephone booths.

"This is a collect call for Neville McKay. My name is Terry Doyle."

He listened to the hollow reverberations as the operator put the call through. The sound made him think again of the ocean. "Ripples" — it was the famous quote from Bobby's South Africa speech — "which build a current that can sweep down the mightiest walls of oppression and resistance . . ."

"Hello?"

". . . a call for Neville McKay . . ."

The person who answered was a woman, and from the cloud in her voice as she asked the operator to repeat, Terry realized she'd been asleep. In panic, he looked at his watch. But it was two in the afternoon. Who would be asleep — ?

"Just a minute."

An eternity passed. Doyle was sure that the muffled sounds he heard were bed linens being tugged at, pillows shuffled. He thought of hanging up, but he'd already given his name.

"Terry?"

"Neville McKay?" The operator was steadily officious. "Will you accept — ?"

"Sure. Terry?"

"Bright? Is that you?"

"Hey, Terry! My man! How you doing?"

"Jeez, Bright, it sounds like I called you a little early."

"What time is it?" The fog was in Bright's voice too, but in fact the happiness in his greeting had dispelled Terry's embarrassment.

"Just after two."

"In daytime?"

"Open the curtains, Bright. Start the coffee."

"Don't shit me, Charlie."

Bright associated the nickname with Charlestown, not Chaplin. Because of the history it implied, Terry liked the name when Bright was the one using it.

"Listen, buddy, I know I've caught you at a bad time."

"Why'd you call me here? How'd you know I wasn't at work? Christ, did you call — ?"

"No, no. I called you there because it's Saturday."

"We work on Saturday in the capital of the Free World."

"Yeah, I noticed. Some work. Look, I need to talk, but if now is a bad time —"

"We can talk. What's up?"

"You've got your friend there."

"She's gone. I mean, she went to the bathroom. Then she'll be in the kitchen. We have our little routine."

"Christ, Bright, you haven't changed."

"Have you?"

"That's what I wanted to talk to you about."

"You know me, Terry. Anytime I get a crack at talking you out of —"

"You're just a PK anticleric. That's your problem."

"Not my problem, my solution."

"Well, I do have a problem. I'm serious."

"What?"

But all at once Terry fell silent. Why in hell was he calling McKay, the one person guaranteed to have no sympathy whatsoever for his situation? Then he remembered why. "I'm at the Parker House."

"Getting laid, I hope."

"No. But I was thinking about our time down here together. About Kennedy." What made us friends, he added to himself.

"The offer stands, Terry. I know I can get you something. We have two new subcommittees coming our way, with staff positions on each."

"Bright, I'm being ordained a deacon next week. A week today."

"I know that. I'm coming, remember? So are the Rev. and Mrs. Bishop. You invited us."

"*You're* coming? All the way from D.C.?"

"I told you I would if I could. It's all arranged. It amazes me, though, what you'll do to get me to come to church. My father is ecstatic. What I will remind you both of, however, is that I'm coming for *you.* I'll even take Communion if it'll embarrass you not to."

"I'm really glad you're coming. And your father. He's agreed to vest and sit in the sanctuary. I saw him in his purple at an interfaith peace service. Cushing was there."

"The war's over, then. What chance does the Pentagon have against Canterbury and Rome?"

"When the cardinal hugged him, your father disappeared."

Bright said, "Aha, back in the fold! All Dad told me was that His Eminence was cordial."

"Cushing *loves* your father. He loves not having to deal with a Brahmin."

"You mean, he loves finally having a bishop of the Episcopal Church he can feel socially superior to."

"Jesus, Bright." Terry leaned back against the wall of the booth. Whoa. Was that true? He could not touch it.

"So what's up, Charlie? You said 'problem.'"

Terry had the feeling that he'd just put his finger in a socket. The rank matter-of-factness of McKay's statement had both made it seem true and made it so outrageous. His problem? It had just become: How do I go on with this conversation? But he had to say something. "Like I said," he began. "I was thinking about Kennedy. Your Kennedy."

"He's the only one left, Terry." Bright's sadness coursed through the phone like a wind.

"I was thinking of his eulogy for Bobby. The ripple of hope and all that. I never asked you — did you help write that?"

"No. Terry, I write his *letters.* To the old ladies in tennis shoes. The speeches are written by the geniuses. That one was Bill Shannon, the *Times* guy, except the Aeschylus, which was Richard Goodwin. The senator had told them what he wanted, though. That speech was his own."

"He's going to be president, Bright. That's what we all thought out here, watching TV. In case you wondered."

"You called me up to talk about Senator Kennedy's political prospects?"

"No."

"Why, then?"

Terry had been absently running a finger along the scratches in the wall of the phone booth. Only now did he read them as words. *Cock sucked? Call Bob at . . .* He closed his eyes. "What Kennedy said about standing up for an ideal?"

"Yeah?"

"Versus, well, the need to sometimes just stay in your seat a little longer, for the greater good. You know what I mean?"

"We all have to eat some of the brown stuff, Terry."

"They want me to eat a big one, Bright. I don't know if I —" He stopped. To hear himself discussing his situation in this way appalled him.

Bright said something.

"What?"

"I wasn't talking to you. Eloise just brought my coffee."

"What a life you have, you bastard."

"Eloise has a sister, Terry. Don't you, El?"

Terry said nothing.

"Charlie?"

"Yes? I'm here."

"God, I'm sorry, Charlie. I'm no help at all, am I?"

"No, none."

"So tell me what the fuck they want."

"No, never mind. It's too complicated. Really, I think I just wanted to touch base . . ."

"Cold feet? Is that what it is? Cold feet is normal if you're on ice, Terry."

"Maybe that's exactly what it is. Maybe that's all it is."

"Do you have somebody up there you can talk to? What about that priest?"

"Father Collins?"

"Yeah."

"Sure. I can talk to him."

They were silent again. Terry began fingering the graffiti once more, the foul words, the profane.

"Because, if you needed to, you could always talk to my father."

"Your dad?"

"You know how much he likes you. He sees you as my one chance."

"I don't know, Bright."

"Just think about it. You're at the Parker House, you said?"

"Yes."

"His office is five minutes away. On Joy Street."

"One doesn't just drop in on the Episcopal Bishop of Massachusetts, Bright."

"*I* would, and so can you. I know that's how he feels. You want me to call him up?"

"No, no. It's helped just talking to you, buddy. I'm glad you're coming up. Where are you staying? With your folks?"

"No." The sound of McKay's voice changed, indicating he'd cupped the phone. "Claudia's. I'll be at Claudia's. You call me, because I can never penetrate that monastic phone system of yours. You still have her number?"

"You *are* a bastard, you know that?" Doyle laughed, hard. *Humanae vitae. Humanae* fucking *vitae*.

A few minutes later he was approaching the subway kiosk at Park Street. Women in short skirts that showed their thighs, or in jeans that clung to their asses, kept cutting him off. Shoppers with large bags from Filene's and Jordan's entered the small building and disappeared in the smooth downward glide of the escalator. He intended to join them.

But then he stopped. He watched the women for a minute, watched them *as* women, their snappy hairdos, their swinging shoulder bags, their clacking high heels, the curves of their flesh — minis everywhere, and loose breasts leaping against cotton T-shirts. Shit, man.

He looked up at the clock on the white spire of the Park Street Church. The sun glinted off the weathervane. The sky beyond was the blue of someone's eye. The clock showed that he had a couple of hours before the class meeting he had called, the meeting he was expressly forbidden to convene.

Kennedy's question: What am I going to do?

He saw a bank of phone booths and now remembered another time he'd slipped into one — at Georgetown, to call Nick when their mother had died. It was out of the question, calling his brother now. But still, he felt the old longing, how he'd never really grown accustomed to life not so much without her, but without him. Nick. Squire. His brother would not remotely understand. But who would?

Instead of heading down to the subway, he cut into the Common and began angling toward Joy Street. It was an uphill trek, but he took it quickly, hardly breathing, allowing himself the barest sidelong glances at the couples here and there on the grass, holding hands, kissing. Sinking, he had felt. He was sinking. Into what? Into sex? Into shame? The feeling was of an old enemy that had him by the ankle and was pulling him down.

The headquarters of the Episcopal Diocese of Massachusetts was half a block up from Beacon Street, in a mansion that was set off from its neighbors by the ecclesiastical flag poking out from the lintel of the second-story bay window. The serenity of the shaded brick façade failed to work its charm on Doyle as he stopped across the street. Beacon Hill was a point around which the city pivoted, but he had rarely crossed into the neighborhood proper. There were no bodies here, no women, only bricks and trim shutters, rooflines, chimneys, and polished brass door knockers. Proud buildings like this lined Monument Square on Bunker Hill, the same bowfronts. But in the Town, otherwise a neighborhood of three-deckers and projects, such buildings always seemed ostentatious, and therefore phony. Here they seemed the height of understatement, completely real.

But what am I going to ask him? What am I going to say? Doyle's questions came quickly. Would crossing this street be disloyal? But Bright's father was a priest. He always wore his collar. He believed in the Real Presence and in the Seal of Confession. In lengthy conversations over leisurely Sunday dinners, Doyle had often heard Father

McKay, now Bishop McKay, describe his own deep longing for reunion with Rome, his respect for the pope's effort to ride the crest of change, his intuitive preference for what some of his own confreres derided as RC Cola.

Bishop McKay was like his son in his wiry, thin handsomeness, although he was smaller. He was like Bright in his high-pitched, rolling laugh and in his kindness. Like Bright, he loved to touch your hand when he was telling a story. But he was unlike Bright in his clipped British accent, his utter lack of cynicism, and, more to the point, his wanting so very much — and saying so — for Terry to be ordained. Ordained by Cushing.

As Doyle crossed Joy Street he told himself, No one at St. John's will ever know.

He went through the spiked wrought-iron fence and up the stairs. Doyle deflected his anxiety by imagining a history of the place, that it had once been home to a Brahmin abolitionist, his poet daughter, and his son, a hero of the Civil War. But had it also perhaps belonged before that to a wealthy merchant whose stock-in-trade included slaves?

It seemed strange to pull open the heavy brass-studded door without ringing a bell first, waiting for a maid, explaining himself. These were offices now. Doyle mustered an air of casual efficiency, entirely counterfeit, as he went in, aware of the house suddenly as a place in which Irish had lived — and to which even now were admitted — only as servants.

Doyle was exquisitely attuned, in other words, to the chaotic implications of what he was doing, turning for help — despite the man's title and High-Church preferences — to a Protestant; turning for help — was this the real disloyalty? — to a black man.

8

THE CONVERTED WAREHOUSE behind the Rancho Diner was a long place-kick off the ramp that led down from the elevated highway, part of the swooping approach to the Mystic River Bridge. The innocuous building was a favorite stopping place for truckers off 95 or Route 1 or the terminus of 93. They could eat at the Rancho, use its showers in back, leave their rigs in the diner lot. Hitching up their pants, blowing their noses with their fingers, they would walk over to Daisy's, as it was known, although no sign identified the door.

This part of Charlestown was called the Flat, and it was hemmed in by the railyards, the MTA tracks, the double-barreled highway, and the river. It was a rough district with dozens of single-story cement-block structures, each with its loading ramp. They were plumbing suppliers and glass wholesalers, a tidy trade-only lumberyard, a scrap-iron dealer, a welding shop, and numerous unstaffed storage buildings. There was nothing to attract the close attention of outsiders, so the Flat was effectively cut off, not only from the rest of the city, but from the hilly neighborhood that abutted it. Patrons could come and go from Daisy's at all hours, and did, and not worry about drawing the notice of anyone inclined to wonder what went on in there. Everybody who had reason to drift through the Flat knew, and, at least now and then, they all went in.

Daisy's was, in the truckers' argot, a joint, a trap, a crib. It was a casino, named not for a voluptuous Irish moll, a figment predictably conjured by roadrunners from out of town, but for the actual flowers that were always on display, sprays and bouquets, cut greens, and especially daisies — all slightly wilted, like Daisy herself would have been if she existed. By the carton and bundle and tubful, blossoms were brought over every few days, the unsold but still piquant stock from the Flower Exchange, near the cathedral. The flowers sat on florist's stands and mesh pillars between banks of slot machines that were arranged in three long aisles. There were flowers against the walls behind the craps, pool, and poker tables. The former warehouse had not been decorated for its new use, so the flowers and the tin artist's lights bouncing indirectly off the whitewashed cement walls gave the place what ambiance it had, cheerful enough and clean. It wasn't Vegas, but neon and cheap plush were not what truckers stopped here for.

The lack of windows meant that the number of players, not the length of shadows, was the accurate indicator of the hour in this realm. Now it was late afternoon, a slow time. Half a dozen men in baseball hats, checkered shirts or green jackets with names stitched on the pockets, and the newly ubiquitous American flag patches on their shoulders were scattered among five times that many slots. The craps and poker tables were vacant, but at one of the two pool tables the room's lone young woman was playing eightball with a man. Periodic bursts of arrhythmic clack-clacking punctured their otherwise rigid silence, indicating a heated contest.

The woman was a striking, out-of-the-bottle blond, her hair short, framing her face like a pouting French movie star's, and if she was as cheap looking as she was pretty, it seemed somehow deliberate. She moved around the table from shot to shot with quick authority, as if completely aware, and in charge, of the impression she was making. She wore tight hip-huggers and a halter that left much of her back bare, not quite up to the job of containing her breasts when she bent over to shoot. Her blue jeans flared at the ankle over a pair of green snakeskin cowboy boots. Her opponent stood back, chalking his stick, frankly enjoying her run for the way it let him watch her. He was a large, well-muscled man, a cigarette permanently at his lip, sending a ribbon of smoke into his squinting left eye. Though it was warm in the room and though, in his mid-twenties, he seemed too old for it, he wore a leather-sleeved high school jacket. *Charlestown*, it read across the back. He was Jackie Mullen.

One end of the game room was taken up by a bar, a long counter but without stools. *Liquor in front*, a bumper sticker posted above the bottle shelf read, *poker in back*. Behind the bar was a large campaign poster, a hazy photograph of a fat-jowled matron in a frilly hat. *Louise Day Hicks for Mayor*; it said. *You Know Where She Stands.*

At the bar two men nursed drinks, one a beer, the other a Coke. The first was wearing the dark blue, shiny-assed trousers of a Boston cop. As a gesture of his customarily minimal but sufficient discretion, his tan poplin jacket was zipped to his throat so that his collar insignia did not show. He wasn't a large man, but his thick neck, strong jaw, big ears, and hair cropped like a Marine's gave him an intimidating air. His jacket also hid the sergeant's stripes on his shirt sleeves. He was Sonny Murtaugh, a Townie — one of several from the City Square precinct house, including a lieutenant, who were the owners of Daisy's, which was why the place was never tipped over.

He spoke in bursts, with punching gestures, but he kept his voice low. "I don't give a shit what that wop bastard said. We keep loansharking and enforcement out of here. This is where the suckers *play.* Everyone can spot Tucci's juice collectors. No fucking way. We keep the system as is or we shut it down." He poked his companion, Squire Doyle, too hard for friendliness, but Doyle did not move for a moment, or react.

Finally he laughed. "You shut this place down, Sonny, and Frank just opens a truckers' joint himself."

"In the Town? Let him try."

"The highway goes north and south, sport. It brushes Somerville and Chelsea. It cuts right through Revere and Everett. All his territory."

Murtaugh shook his head. "We get rigs going south, and in from the west because of the junction. Those are the guys with change. Who goes north? Lobstermen and Christmas tree carriers, frogs and fishermen. Our guys run to Providence, Hartford, and New York. They're the players. Fuck that dago kid."

"That dago kid was at his old man's elbow for twenty years. He's older than you are."

"I can't have those guys in here, Squire. Shit, we're cops. We can't —"

"It's a show of power, Sonny. That's all it is. Transition time. Consolidation. Frank would love for you to challenge him. Now that the old man is dead, he has to move right away to prove he has a pair of big *cojones.* That's all this is. He's showing us and, more to the point, he's showing his own people. I don't take the new rules personally, and neither should you. It doesn't matter how the juice gets collected, and if he ups the ante on you, you can pay it. And don't give me that 'We're cops' bullshit."

"I don't want those greaseball cunts coming in here, acting like this is their fucking operation."

Squire smiled. "But it is, Sonny. You're a franchise holder, and don't forget it. He's the parent corporation. That's the point Frank is making, same thing I'd be doing, a little tickle to remind you. This *is* theirs."

"We pay them to leave it alone. I pay you to keep the sharks and kneecappers out of here."

"From now on, you pay me for the flowers, period."

"I still say fuck him." Murtaugh drained his glass and slammed it on the bar.

Squire pushed his hardly touched Coke a few inches away. "And if the Teamsters put out the word on Daisy's?"

Murtaugh fell silent, taking the point in. Then, abruptly, he went around the bar to the beer tap, drew himself another glass, sucked half of it down, then wiped his mouth with his cupped hand. He looked up at Doyle. "You're awfully fucking philosophical about this, if you ask me. You organized the Irish rackets for these bastards. Now the zips want to run the streets without you."

"It was time, Sonny. Fucking courier service, that's all I've been."

"You're the guy that's made it work. These wops start throwing weight around again, it'll be all hell loose like it was, fucking newspapers, then the feds forced to shine their lights in the corners."

"And cops have to get out of the gaming business."

"Exactly."

"You flatter me, Sonny. We want Frank to succeed, okay? Keep that in mind. We *need* this guy on top of the pile. You want Patriarca taking over Boston? You want Gambino up here? The Tuccis know the tradition. They know how Boston works. Frank knows, and so does Vinnie. They just want to feel like they're in charge, that's all. I say we should help him feel that way."

"But you're out now, as the go-between."

"I just have to find another way to prove my usefulness." Squire smiled. "Don't worry about me."

"What do you have in mind?"

"Couple of things. I'll keep you posted."

"Please do."

Squire looked over at Mullen, who was standing with the tip of his cue at his armpit, watching his sexy opponent line up a bridge shot on the eight.

"On another subject, Sonny . . ." Squire continued staring off toward the pool game, without enthusiasm.

"What."

"I need an exam."

"For who?"

"Not of interest to you, not the department. I need the State Police exam, the entrance test. How do I get it?"

Murtaugh eyed Doyle. "This is another subject?"

"Favor for a friend, you know." Doyle smiled.

"You scared me there for a minute, Squire. I thought you meant for *you*."

The two men laughed.

And while Squire drained his Coke, Murtaugh took a matchbook from a nearby dish, opened it, and wrote a name inside.

"It'll cost you," he said.

Squire pocketed the matchbook without looking at it. "No problem. My friend's father is fixed. This guy will be a good cop."

"Like me, Squire."

"Yeah, Sonny. With any luck."

Doyle slapped Murtaugh's shoulder. They both laughed again.

Mullen was snapping off two fifties from his money clip. He paid the woman, and she reacted by putting her arms around his neck and kissing his cheek. Then, arm in arm, they crossed to the bar.

"Still hustling the suckers, Ginny?" Doyle said.

She left Mullen's side for Squire's. "How about it, honey?"

Squire opened his arm easily, and she fit snugly against him. His fingers dropped into the rear pocket of her jeans, an automatic intimacy. "Ginny, you know I'm too smart to rack up with you."

"Come on, Squire. It's been too long."

Jackie and Sonny caught each other's eyes. Sonny made a show of looking at his watch. "Yeah, about two hours."

She pretended to ignore Murtaugh, but in fact went up on her toes to put her mouth at Squire's ear, to whisper, "If that asshole didn't own the furniture, we wouldn't let him in."

Squire replied by putting his mouth to her ear and blowing softly.

"Thanks for the refill," she said. A joke of theirs.

Squire pressed her ass. "I'll take you on." He clasped her hand and led her to the pool table. At the cue rack he faced her. He put his hands on her hips and pulled her to himself. She smelled of the usual cheap perfume. Her hair, seen this close, was starting to look strawlike from peroxide. Her eyes were caked with blue makeup, with ample hints of coming dark circles visible below them. But by some miracle there was still an essentially unspoiled quality about her.

"I've missed you," she whispered, pushing into him.

"Ginny . . ." Squire backed off a bit. Oddly, he thought of the prim Brahmin lady at the MGH. What, he was at an age to want what he couldn't have? "I'm not playing," he said. "I brought you over here to tell you something. Things are up in the air around here. I want you to watch out for yourself."

"What do you mean?"

"And the other girls too. Tell the girls to keep their eyes open. It's musical chairs upstairs, if you get the picture. Somebody's going to get left out when the music stops. A few weeks, couple of months, a scramble for chairs, Gin. It might get rough. Sonny's the one you have to watch. He'll be covering his own ass. He won't be worrying about you."

Ginny looked back at Murtaugh, who had gone behind the bar to draw a beer for Mullen. "You mean, he's . . ."

"He's all right, but he's not in charge. If somebody was to tip him over, he'd see it coming. He'd have to take his tan coat off and lead the cops in to raid this place himself. He'd be looking to make some easy pinches. That's the point of a cop being in this business — he controls the damage. But somebody would have to fall. A few pothead slot players up from Jersey, maybe, an out-of-town cardsharp —"

"And a couple of teenage hookers."

"Just watch your step, okay?"

Ginny nodded solemnly, the randy mask — her ready and false desire — gone from her face. Doyle had the feeling her eyes were trying to show him something, the helpless child held captive inside that cocky, hard-core body of hers. He knew, though, it was a feeling she was good at planting in men, part of her technique. He had fallen for it once.

She offered him her face. He bent to her, and when they kissed, the tip of her tongue slipped between his lips, her right hand went discreetly to his pants, pressed him there, then moved away, only wanting to confirm his hard-on — the power she thought it gave her.

With his nose in her hair, his mouth at her ear, he whispered, "Don't trust Sonny to protect you. If you get busted, don't try blowing the whistle on him either. Just sit tight. I'll hear about it, and I'll take care of you."

She rested against him, mumbled something he heard as "I love you, Squire."

They parted. Ginny turned to the pool table and started racking the balls, making loud cracks on the felt-covered slate.

Squire returned to the bar. "We got to go, Jackie."

"Oh, come on, Squire, I just got my beer."

"We have a few more stops to make. Drink up." Squire picked up his own glass and raised it at Murtaugh.

"Shit, Coke." Mullen jerked his thumb toward his friend, said to Murtaugh, "Do you believe this guy? Permanent Lent." He swirled his glass and downed the rest of his beer.

Murtaugh put his meaty hand on Doyle's shoulder. "Well, anyways, Squire, come in and play sometime, anytime. Really."

"With *your* dice, Sonny? You kidding?"

"What do you mean? You think the commish'd let me play with crooked dice?"

"But the commish that counts is dead. Isn't that the point?"

"Yeah, I guess it is."

"So be careful. Can you be careful, you and your goons?" Squire was grinning as he said this, but his words had weight.

"Sure, sure. Anyways, don't be scarce, okay?"

"See you around," Squire said, and he left with Mullen following. Jackie was one who always hitched his trousers, going through a door.

Squire drove. For a time neither man spoke as the car rattled through the rutted streets of the warehouse district, but within a few minutes they were back in the neighborhood, heading up Austin Street past the busy stores and taverns to Main Street, the heart of Charlestown.

Mullen was looking sullenly out the window. Finally he said, "Doran's, the Clover, Chi-Chi's . . . Seeing these places . . . it makes me . . . I mean, it really ticks me off."

"What does, Jackie?"

"Having to pull back now, let those fuckers take over here."

"Don't let your spit get in your eyeballs, Jackie."

"No, for real. This shit is driving me crazy. You think I was shooting pool back there? I was listening to you, which is why I lost to Ginny. Her game sucks egg whites."

"I thought you lost because you got your own game of pocket pool going."

"*You* didn't even pick up the stick, just climbed right on her. I'm not sure you should let me watch that shit, Squire. Christ, with Didi pregnant even."

"*Don't* watch, Jackie. Close your fucking eyes."

"And don't listen either, I suppose. I have to fucking eavesdrop to find out that we're walking away from eight years —"

"No we aren't."

Mullen turned in his seat, facing Squire. "What the fuck are we doing, then? What are *you* doing?"

"Keeping the franchise on Main Street, on City Square and Sullivan, our neighborhood. Daisy's is gone, sure, Aladdin's and the Golden Arm. The joints in Somerville, Fields Corner, and Southie, okay. Frank will rope those in too. The book, the sharks, *let* Frank squeeze them. I hate that shit anyway. I hate having to turn markers over to the kneecappers, especially our own guys. Fuck *all* that stuff, who cares? Let Frank run the Dublin Horse Show if he wants. But not here."

"Not the Town?"

"We're not moving off these streets."

"But won't the wop — ?"

"We gave his old man a reason to leave us alone, then we gave him one to need us, *then* we expanded. Bit by bit, Jackie. The old man liked when we connected because we cut him in on everything and kept things smooth. We have to do it again, that's all. Give Frank a new way to need us."

"Like what?"

"I don't know, Jake. That part I don't know yet. The part I know is, the Town stays ours."

Squire slowed for a light, but his eyes swept along — the bakery, a pub called Towne Grille, another called Mehan's, the corner Kresge's, a button shop. Late shoppers took their time, enjoying the balmy afternoon, one of summer's last. Two young mothers pushed their babies along the sidewalk in identical umbrella strollers. Workmen, fresh off the MTA, lunchpails in hand, flag pins stuck in their tweed caps, headed for their tavern, its door open to the bright September air. Ahead on the left stood the pillared, slightly pompous building of the Sullivan Square Savings Bank, where Squire kept his cash accounts for the various Bouquets. For Tucci's tote he used other banks around the city, which he'd be pulling out of now. Things change. But not Charlestown.

A feeling of nostalgia gripped him. Such a golden afternoon, such an air of affection about the people. A huge red-white-and-blue billboard on the wall of the bank, facing the Foodmaster parking lot, read, AMERICA, LOVE IT OR LEAVE IT. And he did love it! This part at least. As he hadn't in years, Squire burst into song. "Oh, Yankee Doodle went to the Town . . ."

Jackie joined in, and they rolled through the local version of the stupid old anthem as they had a million times when they were kids, blasting the rough melody out their open windows, drawing smiles and waves as the car moved slowly up the hill. They grinned at each other. The song, the street, *those* storefronts and bars, the playgrounds and the corner stoops, Old Ironsides, the navy yard, and the school on Bunker Hill — all that had made them friends, would keep them friends forever.

Their song ended. They fell silent.

At City Square, inside the curve of the el, Squire's eyes clicked on the numerous signs in the upper windows of the buildings. He had not seen them before. Apparently they had just been put up, multiple copies of a new campaign poster. Louise Day Hicks, the Southie pudding puss, the gumdrop hat: *You Know Where She Stands.*

After losing the mayor's race a year ago to Kevin White, she was running now for the city council. She'd had no particular clout in Charlestown until the blacks got uppity, but by now she was the Town's fidgety, harebrained aunt as much as Southie's. Her figure was familiar here, smelling of talc, wagging her finger, whining about the priests and nuns who disapproved of her. The school committee wasn't big enough for her anymore. Squire thought her a fool, but he had given her five or six thousand dollars between last year and this, and Ned Cronin had supplied her with his shamrock corsages.

Squire indicated the posters. "Look at that. Christ."

"You don't like Louise? She wants what we want."

Squire shook his head. "The fences stay up around Charlestown only if outsiders don't notice that the fences are there. Louise *dares* the city to come into Southie and change things. You think niggers give a shit about Southie, want in there? No fucking way. But once she makes them feel they *can't* . . ." He shrugged. "We don't want her pulling the same shit over here."

"It's the same with Tucci, right? If he feels he *can't*, then he has to."

"You got it, buddy. Fucking A."

"So how do we — ?"

"I don't know. I'm still working on it."

Their car was heading around the square, under the el, past the police station and courthouse on one side, the short row of storefronts, lawyers' and doctors' offices, on the other. "The point, Jake, is to stay the fuck off Frank's list for now. Head-in-the-trench time, bud. See what I mean? The opposite approach to Louise's. If she was in the rackets, she'd have signs in all the windows. 'Fuck the wops! Come and get me, you dago bastards!' Typical Irish. Typical Southie."

Squire honked and waved at an old woman on the corner, Alice

Mulrooney, one of the altar ladies from his mother's time. She lit up when she saw him. How the mothers loved Squire Doyle.

"Besides, I won't miss hauling my ass out to Revere."

A cool breeze wafted up from the navy yard, and with it the fresh, nostril-cleansing aroma of the sea. All of Squire's senses seemed to quicken when the ocean took over the air like that, and a primrose glow settled on the dying summer day. It was a sensation of complete physical and spiritual awakening, what he loved about life in the Town, and why he'd never leave it.

After easing through the traffic onto Main Street, congested as always because of the post office and the hardware store, Doyle pulled over to the curb near the Irish Rover. End-of-the-day happy noises drifted out from the pub. Half a dozen corner boys, high school kids too young to be inside, were hanging there. They brightened at the sight of Squire, hoping he would wave. But Squire didn't notice. "I want you to go in and tell Bobby to put his end on ice for a while."

"He'll want to know why."

"Tell him I'll be in later, I'll talk to him. But I want the works shut down until further notice. No collections."

"Bobby won't take that from me."

Squire fixed his old friend with a cold stare. "Your job, Jackie, is to make him take it from you. Otherwise, what do you do for me?"

"I keep my fucking mouth shut for you. I don't tell my sister what you do."

Squire reached across and took Mullen's arm in his hand. "Do yourself a big favor. Leave Didi out of this."

Mullen yanked his arm free, wiped his sweaty lip, then opened his door.

"Just tell Bobby old man Tucci is dead. He'll get the picture. Time to take a nap. We want Frank's first move to be in Southie or Somerville, not here. Bobby's smart enough to spark to that. You have to make him think you're smart enough too."

"Fuck you." Mullen got out, slamming the door behind him.

"And Jackie."

"Yeah?" He leaned into the window on his forearms.

"I'm dropping back into the pocket. The flower business. You're going to need something too."

"I'll be all right."

"I'm talking *cover*, asshole. Will you get your hurt feelings off the sidewalk? What, you going to pout now?"

"Look, Squire, you don't have to treat me —"

"We're partners, isn't that it? Through all this shit?"

"Yes." Mullen softened, obviously relieved.

"If you were listening to me with Murtaugh —"

"I was. I heard everything."

"Then you heard me about this." Doyle held up the matchbook. "The exam."

"It's for you, Jackie. We get a copy of the test, then you take it. You ace the fucker, and the next thing you know you're wearing a blue Smokey the Bear."

"Don't shit me, Squire."

"I'm dead serious. With Frank Tucci loose, I'm going to need new kinds of backup. This is something I can't trust with anybody else, Jackie. Just you."

"A fucking cop?"

"Like your old man before he died. But this is *state* cop."

"Chasing speeders on the turnpike?"

"That's not all they do. Think about it."

"I'd never —"

"You got no record. Louise Day Hicks herself will recommend you. Your old man's buddies will. You're a shoe-in. Let the idea roll around in that empty locker of a brain of yours. Besides" — Squire put the car in gear, revved it once — "hell of a pension too. I got to watch out for your old age. After all, you're my Molly's uncle. And pretty soon, my Jack's."

"You're naming him Jack? Really?" Mullen's eyes brightened.

"If it's a boy, Jackie. I want you to be the godfather. So does Didi," he added, which was a lie.

✧

Terry was in the seminary a good two years before Squire and Didi had seen each other alone. It was the night of the day of her father's funeral. Terry had used his grandfather's pull with the cardinal to get special permission to attend the service; he showed up in his impressive black suit and tie. As if in memory of his mother, the old ladies oohed and aahed over Terry, though to Squire he looked forlorn, like a Mennonite preacher or an Orthodox Jew — or one of the assistant undertakers. Squire felt sorry for him, and wanted to spring the guy, break him loose, get him out of there. But from what he could see, Terry lapped the attention up, an Irish muckamuck at last.

At the cemetery in West Roxbury on a cold, battleship-gray winter afternoon, Terry led the prayers of committal, chirping away in Latin as if the words meant something, the police honor guard answering the "*Et cum spiritu tuo*" like the altar boys they had all been. Then Squire watched Terry go to Didi and put his arms around her. She leaned against him and so shook with sobbing that Squire, even on the far side of the hill, with the dispersing crowd and the biting wind between them, felt the stab of her grief. Grief for her father, sure. But also grief for the life she would never have with Terry. Nick saw her feelings clear.

When Didi had rejoined her family, and while other people were returning to their cars, Terry came over to Squire.

"Hey, Nick," he said, hunching into his black topcoat. They faced each other on a low hill up from the tidy road. Their breath came in puffs.

"Sad, Terry, huh?"

"You mean Didi?" They both watched her as she put an arm around her mother. Her brother Jackie was on the old woman's other side. Nick and Terry noticed when he hooked his fingers into Didi's on their mother's shoulder. "Makes me think of Ma."

"Me too."

"But not only Ma," Terry said. "Did you ever wonder what it was . . . ?"

"What?"

"To lose a father."

"We lost a father, Terry. Jesus. Did we ever."

"I mean, to know him first, *then* to lose him."

"No."

"No what?"

"No, I never wondered about that."

"I did. I mean I *do*. Really, Nick."

Squire shrugged. "Maybe that's the difference, then."

"What, between us?"

Squire studied his brother's face, then burst out laughing. "Of course between us. The difference, Charlie. The difference." Squire opened his hands, indicating Terry's black clothing.

Terry looked down at himself. Then his eyes settled on the ground.

"Anyway," Squire said, "we've had Gramps."

"How's he doing?"

"Slowing down, Terry. You should pay a little more attention."

"You know how little freedom I —"

"Can't you call the guy? Why can't you at least phone him?"

Terry looked up at his brother. "I'm not allowed to, Nick."

"When the hell did *we* become the world, the flesh, and the devil?"

Terry laughed. "But not necessarily in that order." He glanced toward Didi, who was just getting into the limousine. "I hate to say it, but I have to get back."

"Before the clock strikes and your black pants turn into a dress again?"

"Exactly."

"I'll drive you."

"I'm going to hop the MTA, Nick. You should go back to the Mullens'. They'll expect you. They'll need you. Say something nice to Didi, would you? She's shaken up." The limo pulled slowly away.

"She never got over you, did she? I got to tell you, Terry, sometimes I think you finally went into the sem just to get out of the corner she had you in."

"I'll tell you the truth, Nick. She thinks that I love her, but that I love God more. When I see her, I feel like a fucking liar."

"Because you don't."

"Love her? Love God?" Terry smiled sadly. "I don't know what love is, buddy." He suddenly clasped his brother by the shoulder. "Except for you, you piece of shit."

Squire nodded somberly. "Yeah. Me too."

They stared at each other, surprised by the strength of what bound them. Instead of a mother and a father, and despite everything — here was the feeling — they had one another.

At the Mullen house on Monument Square, there had been the traditional funeral aftermath: the crowd of neighbors and friends; Tim Mullen's fellow cops; the feed line at the long table laden with cold cuts, brisket, potato salad, and chips; the booze. Didi had downed several Scotches, then disappeared. Squire went upstairs looking for her. He found her in her room, on her bed, crying. He lay down next to her, like a brother. Say something nice, he thought.

All he could think of was how forbidden her lanky body had been all those years, how it had never entered his mind — so that when she turned her streaked face to him and raised an arm for him to enter, he was completely unprepared for how turned on he was.

Something nice: when he opened his mouth to speak, the word on his tongue was his brother's name, and so, quite simply, he closed his mouth again and kissed her. He knew, when she kissed him back, that she too was thinking, Terry. They made love with all those people downstairs, all those cops, her mother, her father unburied still, beside the mound of dirt covered with the flowers Squire had helped lay out.

They fucked with a wildness unlike anything he had experienced before. Was it the forbidden thrill of incest, a kind of adultery? The taboos must have ignited her too, because she kept pounding under him, churning to the rhythm of her own deep, throaty music long after he was ready to begin regretting what they had done. "Dream," she said finally, and then again: "Dream."

When, later, she turned out to be pregnant, there was no question in his mind, any more than in hers, about what to do. Everybody claimed to be just delighted when they announced their intention to marry immediately. Jackie, of course, and even Terry.

Just before the ceremony, Squire had pressed his brother's arm and whispered, "Say something nice."

"Like you did, you bastard," Terry answered affectionately. The truth was that to him, Nick and Didi's marrying seemed the perfect solution. From the pulpit, where he read Saint Paul, what he said was, "'The greatest of these is love.'"

✧

"Hey, sweetie pie," Squire called as he swung through the open door of his grandfather's flower store. Molly had been stacking and unstacking cardboard seedling pots in the corner behind the cash register. She was three now, and her birth had made Squire feel that, yes, he did have the golden touch. He couldn't lose.

When Molly saw her father, she cried out happily. She stalled while getting to her feet, a little momentary arc of triumph, then scampered over to him. Her white shoes slapped the floor. He scooped her up and made her fly; for engine noises, there was her squealing laughter.

"Hi," Didi said, sticking her head out of the back room.

"Should she be out here alone?"

Didi ignored his question, the criticism not so thinly veiled. She had on the blue smock she wore in the store, but it would no longer button closed, her belly was so big, oddly disproportionate to the rest of her body. During this pregnancy, her shape had become even more ostrich-like than the first time. The larger her stomach became, the narrower her shoulders seemed, the smaller her head. Her long neck, once, with her hair, her most alluring feature, now seemed gawkish. It helped not at all that she habitually wore, both in the store and in the kitchen upstairs, bright yellow rubber gloves.

Now she held a trimming knife and two long birds of paradise. Despite the barb in his question and his lack of greeting for *her*, Didi's broad-mouthed face was alight with pleasure. It never failed to make her happy, watching his way with Molly. He was as good a father as he was a grandson.

But her happiness gave way to the other thing. "Your grandfather wants to see you right away. He's upstairs." Didi lifted her hand to her ear to push back an unruly strand of her rich red hair. The blade of the knife blanked her eyes for an instant, giving her the odd look of a *Star Trek* character.

"What's up?" he asked, putting Molly back on the floor, playfully swatting her hugely padded derriere as she waddled back to her corner and her seedling pots.

"Something has Gramps upset. I don't know what."

"What could — ?"

"His Eminence called here. I answered the phone. There was his raspy, barking voice, just like on the radio rosary. He asked for 'my old Ned.' I thought it was somebody pulling a joke. You maybe, or Jackie. I almost said something rude. But it was the cardinal all right. I never knew him to call here, did you?"

"In the old days, he did. Cushing always came by here when he was in the neighborhood. What did he want now?"

Didi shrugged. "I didn't dare ask." She let her right hand rest on the shelf of her belly, the two flower stems dramatically erect. Every move she made lately struck Squire as strange. The woman's uneasiness inside her own body was palpable. "I think he'd been drinking," she added.

"He probably wants some money. He's always hitting people up. Or he wants flowers for some monsignor's funeral. Gratis, natch."

"I don't think so."

"What do you mean?"

"When Gramps took the phone, he listened for a minute, then he said, real shocked like, 'Terry did that? Our Terry?' Then he said, 'Why, that disloyal bastard!'"

"Gramps said that to the cardinal?"

"Yes."

"What the hell did Terry do?"

"I don't know. Gramps said, 'We'll see about that.' He listened some more, then he said, 'Absolutely, Your Eminence. I guarantee it.'"

"What?"

"Then he hung up and went right up the stairs. I went to see what was wrong, and he snapped that it didn't involve me. It was 'a family matter.'" Didi's eyes were at the mercy of an old hurt. "As if I'm still not a member of this family."

"Don't start in on that."

"About an hour ago, Gramps called down. He told me to send you up as soon as you got back."

"Shit," Squire said.

Then Molly, behind him, repeated the word. "Shit, Daddy, shit."

Didi's face darkened. "Out of the mouths of babes."

Squire threw a hand toward the ridiculous flowers sprouting from the vase of her yellow glove on the perch of her stomach. "Do something with those birds, Didi. You look like the Mount of Olives with a TV antenna on top of it, for Christ's sake."

Squire turned his back on her so abruptly that Didi's eyes automatically went to Molly, checking if she'd seen. But Molly, truly her mother's daughter, was only smiling.

When Didi and Squire had married, they'd replaced the tenants in the third-floor flat. Ned had the second floor to himself. It was more cluttered than ever, because he had kept his late daughter's figurines and gewgaws, as if the place were a shrine to her. There were doilies on the backs of the plush furniture and on the tables, copies of Fulton Sheen books and *Catholic Digest*. A dried palm branch arched across the wall behind the crucifix, brushing a cheap oil painting of Flo done from a photograph. The windows were blanketed with double thicknesses of real lace. Squire could never enter those rooms without a burst of wonder that he and his brother had ever lived in them.

The lights were out, and though it wasn't nearly dark yet outside, the living room was deeply shadowed, except for the flickering blue of the television set. Cronin was sitting in the rocker in front of it, his back to Squire, some game show unrolling before him. The parakeet, whose cage sat on top of the forever untouched upright piano, whistled at Squire, alarm.

"Gramps?"

Cronin did not react.

Squire leaned over. "Gramps?"

The old man was asleep, adrift in the country of his dreams. Sixty-eight years old now, his once great crown of white hair had thinned considerably, and his muscled body had gone flaccid. He was always forgetting things, hardly knew the names of lifetime neighbors, was easily angered. In the store Squire cooperated in the fiction that he was still in charge, but customers who struck him wrong, guilty of nothing more, say, than normal indecision in choosing between irises and snapdragons, he simply told to get out. Didi and, occasionally, Squire himself would go after them to apologize.

"Gramps?" He shook him lightly.

Cronin jolted awake. "Wha?" He looked up at his grandson, stupefied. Slowly his memory returned. He grabbed Squire's arm. "That brother of yours has disgraced us."

"What happened?" Squire pulled the hassock over and sat facing his grandfather.

"He led a rebellion against the cardinal. The cardinal wants him out!"

"Calm down, Gramps. One thing at a time."

"He led a meeting. They made demands, just like radicals. Terry disobeyed the pope."

"The pope?" Squire burst out laughing.

"What's funny?"

"Nothing's funny." Jesus Christ, Squire thought, the pope. At Columbia they take on LBJ, in Prague Brezhnev, in Chicago Mayor Daley. But Terry takes on the fucking pope!

"The cardinal wants him to stop, and he won't. He has the whole seminary in an uproar. The cardinal asked me to talk to him. You have to take me over there."

"What demands? What's the issue?"

"That's what I asked."

"What'd the cardinal say?"

"Birth control."

"Oh, brother."

"*Your* brother! TV stations called the cardinal, that's what he's trying to avoid. They said Terry's going on TV, an act of pure defiance, of betrayal!" In his excitement Cronin pushed himself up to stand.

"Gramps, wait."

"The nerve of him, that brazen bastard, who the hell does he think he is?"

Squire forced his grandfather back down into the chair, and with an unprecedented sharpness he ordered, "Be quiet."

Cronin submitted, raising a hand to shield his face, as if expecting Squire to strike him. The gesture stunned Squire, who would never grow accustomed to this man's decline, Squire's Knight, his Lord, his only God.

The old man shook his head, whining, "But wait'll your mother finds out. This will just break her heart."

"What?"

"Your mother. This will —"

"Gramps."

"The disgrace of it, defying the cardinal. She'll —"

"No she won't, Gramps. Ma's not here anymore. You remember."

Squire took his grandfather by the shoulders, his other baby. "Let me worry about this. Let me find out what's going on. Okay?"

"The cardinal asked *me*."

"Gramps, you can. He asked you to talk to Terry and you can. But let me find out first. All right? *I'll* fix it. *Then* you call the cardinal and tell him it's done. Okay?"

"You think you can talk sense into that kid?"

"I know I can. Terry will listen to me." Squire and his born-to-bring-flowers smile. "Doesn't everybody?"

"When you and me used to go down to the Exchange, all the fellows told me what a good kid you was." The old man's face became enlivened with gratitude. "Terry'll listen to you."

"Right," Squire said, afraid all at once that it would someday be like this between himself and Molly.

Downstairs, Didi was just closing up the store. She looked up expectantly when Squire came in.

"Jesus, sweetheart, you won't believe it."

"What?"

"Birth control!" Squire leaned against the cold-storage case and laughed hard, with Molly watching quietly from her corner.

But Didi frowned. "Oh, but that's sad." She waited until her husband looked at her. "Really. Don't you think that's sad?"

"It's pathetic is what it is. *Those* guys in a snit about rubbers and the Pill." He went over to her. "Listen." He took her by the shoulders. "I'm sorry I gave you shit before."

Didi leaned against him.

"Now I have to bomb out to Brighton and talk to Terry. Imagine that. Me, a papal peacekeeper."

"Tonight?"

"Right now. There's a publicity problem. *That's* the cardinal's issue, TV. The last thing he needs, Uncle Walter saying, 'Today's campus riot took place at St. John's Seminary, Boston. Future Catholic priests demanding that, instead of napalm, B-52s should be dropping condoms."

"Nick —"

"I'll be home as soon as I can." He kissed her forehead. She inclined toward him, thinking that now, perhaps, he would gentle her body. But he was careful not to touch her protruding stomach. Even with his mouth shut he could taste her loneliness. When he dared look, he saw that her eyes were closed.

He turned and crossed to Molly, splendid child. He picked her up. She squirmed away but he kissed her, loving her refusal to be compliant. He brought her to her mother, whom he chastely kissed once more. Didi clung to him. Molly twisted between them, working herself free and onto the floor, leaving just the emptiness to bind them.

On his way out he picked up a small shamrock plant, a Kerry Bouquet specialty. "'One always asks, holding a plant' — this is Terry speaking, get it? — 'how the tiny leaves carry their burden of life.'" He laughed, shook his head.

"You shouldn't make fun of him if he's in trouble."

"I could have predicted something like this. The guy doesn't know what he wants. Never has."

"Unlike you."

"As a matter of fact."

"What do *you* want, Nick? That's what I don't know."

Squire smiled. "I want what I have." He saluted the room with the shamrock.

"And what you don't have?"

"I want that too." He wrapped the plant in a square of green tinfoil, deftly bundling it by gathering the four corners in a silver ribbon. "This'll be my calling card. I'll say I've come to offer to do the altar flowers for Charlie's ordination."

"Don't call him that." She was surprised by the sudden edge in her own voice.

Squire looked at her with distaste. "He's my brother. I'll call him what I want."

"Why do you and Gramps need so to have him in the priesthood? You're like your mother would have been if she was alive."

Squire looked slapped. He glared at Didi, and she saw his hatred. He couldn't stand it, the rare times she said what was true. Everybody needed Terry in the priesthood because that was how they would hold on to him. Didi knew this about Nick and his grandfather because she knew it about herself.

She shrugged. "Offering to do the flowers, that's a nice idea."

"I'm a nice person, hon."

Didi laughed, turning away. "It's true, you son of a bitch. You are nice."

✧

Squire drove across Boston, hating rush hour, wondering, as he idled in traffic, how he would do as a diplomat. Everywhere he turned, some wop was sticking his finger in someone's eyeball, and his job was to get their fingers out.

He looked at the other drivers, salesmen going home, cops waving cars through yellow lights, football players practicing on the fields along the river. None of those people knew anything about Guido Tucci, much less his death. If they'd heard of the pope's encyclical, they probably thought it was something cold on a stick. Tucci and Pope Paul, the two posts, Squire thought, of the wire he was walking on.

At numerous intersections along Commonwealth Avenue, college kids pouring out of their classrooms into the streets ignored the lights, as if the rules didn't apply to them. Fucking radicals, fucking peaceniks. He remembered the line from senior year: "College, where false pearls are cast before real swine."

At one corner, a particular girl caught Squire's eye — her tie-dyed T-shirt, her long black hair hanging straight. As she crossed in front of his car, she shifted her books, and he glimpsed an unshaven armpit. Suddenly it was more than he could stand that she had no idea of his existence. He resisted the urge to honk, and instead reached down and snapped on the radio, loud.

"Can't *get* no satisfaction . . . but I try and I try . . ."

She looked his way, startled. Squire raised a forefinger, clicked it once, a minimal salute. And the girl dropped her eyes. I could teach you things, he thought.

Mick Jagger sang with sex in his voice. "Can't *get* no . . ." The way he would have if he'd become a singer. Now Squire wondered, Did they call him Mick because he was Irish?

The light changed. Squire hit the gas, slapping the steering wheel in time to the music as the song built to its conclusion, blaring out into the street.

The entrance to BC was just ahead on the left, but shy of it on the right, hovering over the avenue, was the cardinal's house, a super-rectory set on an obviously artificial and, to Squire's eye, overly landscaped hill. He reached to the dashboard to lower the volume on the radio.

He knew to turn into the next driveway, and recognized the sweeping curves of the private road as it wound past the residence and the chancery and another nondescript building or two before descending into a tidy, fairwaylike valley that seemed miles from the city he'd just left.

The next song to come on was "Sympathy for the Devil." He laughed, but also snapped the radio off.

The road brought him down toward the massive main building of the seminary proper. Twilight had already fallen in this valley, and the Gothic stone hulk loomed eerily, five stories high, row upon row of chaste leaded windows, corner turrets, towers, and arches like out of a fairy tale. Only a cross rising from the peaked center of the roof undercut the impression that this was an asylum, or a setting for a movie about a baron who had no choice but to help the Nazis because they've locked his daughter up in this abandoned old castle.

Squire pulled into a visitors-only parking space near the front door, turned his motor off, and told himself to cool it. For a moment he sat there watching the windows. Lights were on in most of the rooms, but the blinds were drawn. He saw nothing.

Before, when he'd come here, spirited boys in cassocks had swarmed the stairs leading up to the large double oak doors, worthy of a drawbridge, of dwarves to act as porters. But those visits, usually in the company of his grandfather, had been by invitation, on feast days. He was an intruder now, and knew it. Except for the lights in those windows, no human being was in evidence here. It was creepy.

He got out of the car with his wrapped shamrock plant. Instead of going to the door, he walked the length of the building to its corner, from which he had a view of the handball and basketball courts. He had half expected Terry to be out there shooting hoops. All those years ago, how he had been the last to leave the asphalt court behind the high school. How many times, at dusk, had their mother sent Squire out to get him? Squire had always approached the court wondering why his brother seemed so at home shooting baskets alone in the dark, seemed so perfectly himself like that. The sight had always made Squire's heart sink, because his own idea was of the two of them playing. Squire had always hated practicing alone, but not Terry, which was why, eventually, Terry's skill had left Squire's behind. Terry could hit baskets even when it was so dark that Squire needed the snap of the threads to be sure he'd scored.

The seminary courts were deserted, and Squire was relieved. A lone figure out there now could only have evoked the image of the wandering mystic, the hated man who had no place to lay his head, the misunderstood and finally crucified Christ — from whom Squire Doyle had long since claimed his distance.

Why am I nervous? he wondered as he walked back to the pointed arch of the entrance. He mounted the stairs, found a button in the wall beside the door, and pushed it. He pushed it again, then stepped back so they could see him. He nestled the plant in the crook of his left arm like a ball.

Jesus, Terry, he thought, you've buried yourself alive.

After a few minutes, he pushed the button again.

The door opened partway, and he realized someone had been just inside all this time, watching him.

"Yes!" An old man put his head in the opening. His skin was flaked with psoriasis, his eyes seemed twisted, lifeless.

"I'm a visitor. I want to see one of the students."

"No visitors. Come back."

The man's head only now came far enough through the door for Squire to glimpse his Roman collar, the shoulder of his dandruff-layered cassock.

"I'm sorry to bother you, Father. It's a family emergency. I need to see my brother."

"What's that, then?"

"A gift for the altar, a plant." Squire offered it.

The priest shook his head and pulled back. "An emergency? But you bring a plant? You're . . ."

"Terry Doyle, Father. Can I see him?"

"No, no." The name seemed to confirm him in his suspicion. He began closing the door. "You're a reporter."

Squire jammed his foot in the door. "I'm his brother. The cardinal —"

"They're on retreat. They're all on retreat. No visitors."

Squire could easily have pushed the priest aside, claiming authority from Cushing himself. But suddenly he wanted the hell away from here. He'd say to his grandfather, "Retreat, they're on retreat. What trouble can there be if they're on retreat?"

"So when can I see him?"

"Call the rector. Call Monsignor —"

"When can I see —"

"Recreation, tomorrow, after lunch."

Squire pulled his foot back. The door slammed shut, a solid, low-toned *thunk*.

Fuck you, Father. How does Terry survive this shit? But maybe he doesn't. Was that the point?

Squire stared at the oak panels, bile in his throat that he hadn't tasted since being an altar boy. He remembered the monsignor clipping him from behind: "Line up! Line up!"

Doyle balanced the shamrock with one hand, bouncing it slightly, for the heft. Right through the fucking window, that was his thought.

But who was he kidding? No bile of humiliation since the monsignor of his boyhood? What about yesterday? What about Frank? How does Terry take such shit? No, how do I?

He tucked the innocent plant back in his arm and returned to the car. For a long moment he sat at the wheel with the gaudy foil bundle in front of his face. Now what?

The crushed foil reflected light from the windows above him. He studied the sharp green flashes in the dark, thought of them as a meager connection with his brother. His brother shooting hoops, alone, at dusk.

Squire raised his eyes to the windows above him. He felt the loneliness, not only of Terry, but of all the men inside those rooms, and then, just as suddenly, though far more unexpectedly, he felt his own loneliness. He placed the plant on the seat beside him, started the car, put it in gear, and screeched away from that house of the dead.

About a half hour later, he pulled into the long horseshoe driveway in front of the Massachusetts General Hospital. There were twenty minutes remaining in visiting hours. He swung into one of the spaces marked EMERGENCY VEHICLES ONLY and left his car there.

The lobby was far more crowded than it had been in the middle of the previous afternoon. Was it possible so little time had passed since his coming here? Returning to where old Tucci had died the day before released the flood of his anxiety. Squire Doyle was a man without an angle, without a plan. Was that Terry's problem too?

In two separate clusters, men in doctors' coats were conferring with relatives of patients. Other visitors, pulling sweaters on, were heading for the revolving door through which Squire had just come. Children too young to go on the wards had been left in the company of older siblings, and they had taken over the squared couches in the corner. A pair of boys, perhaps seven and nine, were happily rocking the standup ashtray back and forth, and it was inevitable that Squire see them as a version of what he and Terry had been, the Doyle boys. All they'd ever needed was each other.

"Excuse me, thanks," a man said. Squire stepped aside, not realizing he'd been blocking the doorway.

He turned his gaze toward the information desk on the far side of the room. Only when he saw her did he realize how little reason he'd had — wasn't this a different shift? — to expect that she would be here now.

He approached slowly, wanting to savor the sight of her profile before she saw him: her thin nose supporting a naturally perfect brow, her luxuriant hair, part blond, part gray, pulled back to display her ear, the understated single pearl at its lobe. He had remembered best her cheekbones, how color rode them like a memory of the sun.

She lifted her face and turned it fully toward him, smiling with a warmth that made him think, This is how, early in their marriage, she had raised her face when her husband came into the room. If her husband mattered now, why would she be here in the evening?

He was certain she would recognize him.

"Hi," he said, so easily.

"Hello."

Her smile held. In fact, it held an instant too long, so that he began to see it as counterfeit, a Brahmin smile.

Why wasn't she surprised?

He peered at her intently, waiting for her color to deepen, for that ever so slightly spotted hand to flutter to her mouth. Her open mouth.

One place he had pictured her was in the paneled elevator of Phillips House. His erotic fantasy had featured a smooth sequence beginning with his throwing the red switch, the two of them alone, stopped in that elegant box, her so much older, yet bracing her heels and shoulders against the wall, arching her body into a bow, leaving it to him to tear her clothes, her breasts leaping against him, her hair, loose at last, flying back and forth as she kept turning her head, her hair whipping him. The smell of her armpits, the taste of her cunt. Mrs. State Street.

"May I help you."

"I came to see someone."

"Of course, but —" She glanced at her watch, turning her wrist so that he could see the blue veins below the pale skin. "There isn't much time."

She was good. She was pretending not to know him.

"I came to see you."

"What?"

"I brought you this." He put the green-wrapped pot on the desk between them.

She pushed away suddenly, her chair scooting back. "I beg your pardon?"

And then he saw it. She had no idea that he had been here yesterday. She had no idea of having ever seen him before. The charge in their encounter, as dazzling as it was improbable, had been all his. He could feel the heat in his ears, knew that he was blushing. He raised his hands, backing off.

She recovered enough to push the plant a few inches toward him. "Please, take this away."

He shook his head. "It's just a wee piece of the Old Sod," he said with a stagy brogue. "I'm just the delivery boy. I lost the card, Missus, and I'm terrible sorry."

Now she was confused. "Card?"

"It said, 'From your secret admirer.'"

And then he turned and headed for the door. Outside, in the first cool phase of darkness, he laughed aloud. "What an asshole, Doyle!"

Making for his car, he laughed again and shook his head, wishing for Terry, only Terry at last, to throw his arm around. "We're both assholes."

9

Authority which ignores the principle of collegiality does not compel obedience. Terry Doyle was at the blackboard, underscoring each word with chalk, the *squeak squeak* underscoring his exasperation. "That is the essence of our declaration." The sleeve of his tan button-down was white with chalk dust, like the fingers of his right hand.

Doyle's forty-odd classmates stared at the blackboard, not at him. He had become too emotional, too insistently shrill, and whether he knew it or not, there were a number among them whom he had already lost. No one wanted to meet his eyes.

This was a musty basement classroom in a remote wing of the seminary building. The meeting was already two hours old, and they were getting nowhere. They were sitting in the one-armed school chairs that had always constituted the perfect symbol of their degradation. Were they schoolboys or men? The chairs were ordinarily arranged in neatly ordered rows, but during this frustrating session, the space had taken on the look of a storage room, plastic cups and balled paper littering the floor, anarchy in the way they had their legs hooked over the furniture.

One of the few wearing the cassock raised his hand and spoke timidly. "If it is a question of conscience, then we have to find a formulation that respects *everybody's* position."

"That's impossible," someone else called out.

"Then we're screwed," said a third.

"And *that*," Doyle said, "is why we *have* to stick together. *All* of us." He banged the chalk on the board. The stick broke.

The man in the cassock said, "But we've been at this for hours, and we can't —"

"Who says we need a statement at all? This proves we don't."

Doyle met the challenge by banging his fist down on the desk, causing Jimmy Adler's pen to jump on his yellow pad. Adler had been taking notes the whole while.

"We have to issue a statement," Terry said, "something we all agree with. I *know* we can."

"But if we're silent, then we're like Thomas More. 'Our silence,' he said, 'must needs be read ambiguously.'"

Terry leaned back against the blackboard, soiling his shirt further. "That wasn't Thomas More, Mark. That's Robert Bolt."

Adler lifted his gaze. "Can we leave Thomas More out of this? Considering how he wound up?"

Doyle ignored the small bursts of laughter. "That's because he was alone." He pushed off from the chalk ledge to lean over the desk again. "Two points, fellows. Two simple points. One, we do what we do *together*, and the cardinal has to back off. And two, we explain ourselves in a brief statement, because the Church needs us to. All those men and women out there who are waiting for *somebody* to speak up for them."

"They'll never know, Doyle. They'll never know what we've said or what we've done."

"If we release our statement to the press, they will."

A general outburst shook the room as half seconded Doyle and half derided him. Arguments immediately broke out in several clusters. Their tension, weariness, and anger wafted through the air like fumes.

Jimmy Adler exchanged a look with Terry, one that said, I'm with you, bud.

Doyle allowed himself to flow toward Jimmy, as if that brief, consoling expression on his big-eared, freckled face were a swiftly passing log he could grab hold of.

Jimmy put two fingers to his mouth and shrieked a whistle. The commotion stopped.

Gradually the stolid, mute figure of Terry Doyle drew them back. He waited until they were completely still. "I've sought counsel on this with someone in significant authority, someone who knows the whole picture better than we do."

For an instant Terry felt the gentle pressure on his head of Bright's father's hands, and it reassured him. After their hour together in the book-lined study, Terry and Bishop McKay had hesitated at the threshold, a last moment's silence. On an impulse Terry had said, "May I have your blessing?"

"Indeed you may."

Terry had knelt right there in the doorway. It was then, undergoing his first imposition of hands, that he understood about apostolic succession, the passing on of Christ's own healing power, a visceral lesson from a man dismissed by Terry's own Church as standing outside that succession.

"He thinks," Terry was saying now, "that we are absolutely right to stand up to Monsignor Loughlin. His hunch is the cardinal *wants* us to. He thinks we have a chance of helping the cardinal emerge as a spokesman for the American Church on birth control. The cardinal agrees —"

"What 'authority'?" someone demanded.

"I can't say."

"Then let *him* send out a press release, goddamnit!" The seminarian in the cassock came forward, his face purple with anger. "Your adviser is anonymous? Well, we aren't! Why doesn't *he* take on the pope?"

Terry remembered how Bright's father, after blessing him, had drawn him up with both hands. For the first time, Terry had bowed and kissed his ring, and the bishop had squeezed his hands. "You and your classmates have a moment of *kairos* here. You are called to this. The whole Church needs you, not just Rome." And then, leaning closer, bringing the deep umber of his face within inches of Doyle's, Bright's father had added, "*I* need you."

"This guy is a coward if he won't —"

"He's no coward," Terry shot back. "He can't address the issue, because he isn't a Catholic."

"Oh, well, shit."

"Shit?" Terry moved closer to his classmate, his fists clenched. "Shit? Is that what ecumenism means? The other churches have no stake in —"

"A stake for burning heretics. Who are you, Doyle? Martin Luther? Ninety-five Theses? That's what a press release amounts to, and it will get us all kicked out."

Adler had Terry's arm, but Terry calmed himself. Win these guys over, he told himself, make them agree. He said, "Public pressure is our only chance. And it will *help* the cardinal. He can turn to Rome and say, 'See?' But in secret, there's no way he can do anything but back up His Holiness. If we take this on, we *have* to make noise about it." Terry began to walk among his classmates, aware that the reluctance of a few had begun to spread. He touched shoulders and forearms as he moved and spoke. "People will rally to us. Parish priests who feel alone out there will join us."

Two or three in back began drifting toward the door.

"Hey, guys, come on," Terry said.

But others joined them.

The room suddenly reeked of fear and despair, and Terry's anger returned, not at the blindsiding pope but at these, his only friends. "What have all these years been for, if now we can't —"

One of the exiting seminarians, having opened the door, gasped audibly and fell back. On the other side of the threshold, where they'd obviously been listening, were two figures in black cassocks with red piping at the seams and broad red sashes, Monsignors Loughlin and Fenton, the chancellor and the rector. Behind them, even more dramatically outfitted in a crimson cassock and skullcap, a gold pectoral cross stuck in his sash, was stout, crimson-faced Bishop Cowley, the auxiliary.

Doyle waited for them to show some sign of embarrassment, but there was none. The faces of the prelates were like a triple set of radar dishes sweeping across the stunned figures, pointedly avoiding Doyle to settle on the blackboard with its scrawl of interdicted words and phrases.

Monsignor Loughlin, ice in his voice, broke the silence. "Gentlemen," he said. His gold cuff links flashed as he pulled at his sleeve. He was famously proud of his resemblance, especially in that getup, to the acetylene-eyed Fulton J. Sheen, but to Doyle, all he lacked were the steel-rim glasses and a cigarette held aloft in his fingertips to be the very incarnation of a Nazi. "To your rooms," he said, and it struck Terry as strange that he lacked a German accent. "Consider yourselves in *magnum silentium* room restriction until further notice."

The men filed out of the classroom, abject and silent, like prisoners. Doyle was last to go. Great silence? Why then, as he walked past the three priests, was there that ringing in his ears?

The next morning an index card appeared under his door. *Report to me*, it said, above the dread initials *J.F.* Terry opened his door quickly, but no one was there. He crossed the hall, rapped once on Jimmy Adler's door, waited for the grunt from within, then opened it. He remained in the corridor, as the rule required.

Adler was at his desk. The long row of cassock buttons was half undone. Under the formal black garment, his dull white T-shirt seemed shabby.

"Here it is," Terry said, holding up the index card. "I've been drafted."

"Jesus Christ, Terry, be careful, or you might be for real. That's what's waiting for us all out there."

"We'll be okay, Jimmy. We just have to stick together."

"I don't know."

"What do you mean?"

"There was a meeting of some of the guys this morning."

"What?"

"In the second-floor shower room, imagine that?"

"A meeting?"

"Guys who think we should just sign the damn thing."

It alarmed Doyle to see Adler's freckles sink as the tide of color rose in his face.

"How do you know?"

"I was there."

"Why didn't you tell me?"

"What would the point of that have been? You'd just —"

"The point would have been, we'd be together! Shit, Jimmy, we can't start breaking into —"

"You started it. That's what they're saying."

"How? How did I?"

"The press release business. A lot of guys feel like —"

"I can't hassle this now. I've got to get to Fenton's office. But, goddamnit, my only chance was that we're all together."

"Well . . ."

"Why were you at the meeting?"

"I went to see what they're saying. I went for you. Rogers and Graham are taking the oath. So are a few others."

"How many?"

"Maybe a dozen."

"Christ!" Terry slammed his palm against the doorjamb.

"We still have the majority, but . . ."

"But what?"

"Not a majority want the bruhaha."

"The bruhaha comes with the act, Jimmy. We are saying no to the pope."

Adler threw his hands up. "You don't have to convince me. I'm on your side, remember? You'd better go."

"I know, I know . . . It's just . . ." Hurt and disappointment stabbed at Doyle. "Anyway, I'll let you know. Maybe he wants to tell me they're dropping the requirement, to avoid . . ."

Adler was shaking his head.

Terry grinned. "No?"

"Not a chance. Isn't that the nub? These guys don't back down."

"Well, they trained us to be like them."

"You didn't let me finish. They don't back down unless pressed from above. Then they collapse like a house of cards. We are not like them. If we were, we'd eat this shit." Adler stood, went to the threshold, and took Terry's arm, a rare gesture of the physical. "Go get him, tiger. We *are* with you."

A few minutes later, Terry was at the rector's door, knocking briskly.

"Come!"

Terry had trouble turning the doorknob because of the moisture in his palm.

"Come!" the monsignor repeated.

For a moment Doyle thought he would have to pull his hand inside his sleeve, use the material of his cassock to grip the knob. Finally he managed it.

Monsignor Fenton's office was an ascetic cubicle, monastic in feel. By contrast, Father Collins's room always looked like the library annex after an earthquake. This room featured two wooden chairs opposite a small, clean desk that held a telephone, an empty In box, and, centered, the priest's open breviary. Fenton sat with his hands palm-down on either side of the prayer book. He was about fifty, bald and stout. His Roman collar pinched his neck. He sat peering over the tops of his rimless glasses, as he did from the altar when some student coughed too loudly during Mass.

Terry had given himself a rigid set of instructions in how to do this — uncowed politeness — but now it required all his concentration just to get his heavy legs moving inside the tent of his cassock. "You wanted to see me, Monsignor?"

Monsignor Fenton closed his prayer book, but he maintained his stiff upright posture. "Father Collins informs me that you knew full well what you were doing."

"I'm sorry?"

"That he conveyed my order to you in explicit terms."

"What order, Monsignor?"

"Not to call that meeting." Fenton's beefy face belied the impression his monkish room was intended to make. Students took turns serving food at the faculty table, and knew he was a man of undisciplined appetite, although in weekly spiritual conferences he loved to quote Merton. On the wall behind him was a crucifix, on another a portrait of the skeletal Cushing, and on a third of the roly-poly John XXIII, whom he resembled.

"The meeting had already been called when Father Collins —"

"You subsequently convened a second meeting."

"Not a second one. We had adjourned for chapel and dinner, that's all. By then it wasn't up to me."

"You met in secret."

"No." But Terry cut his denial short, tacking. "My job as head student was to bring Monsignor Loughlin's statement before the men, make sure they understood it."

"Not Monsignor Loughlin's statement. Cardinal Cushing's."

"That's an issue, isn't it? We heard that our taking the oath was imposed on the cardinal, that he had no choice."

"Where did you hear that?"

Father Collins had thrown in with these bastards. Why did Terry feel obliged to protect him? He stood mute before the rector.

"I'd like an answer to my question, Mr. Doyle."

"We know that Cardinal O'Boyle in Washington, and the apostolic delegate —"

"You know nothing!" Fenton hissed. "The requirement of this oath is Cardinal Cushing's, do you hear me?"

"In that case, the deacon class would like a meeting with His Eminence to discuss —"

"Out of the question!" The monsignor's left eye seemed to bulge, contorting the side of his face, which he immediately covered with his hand. "And you are not in here to make requests. Is that clear?"

"Yes, Monsignor."

Fenton faced away from Terry, fumbled in his robes for his handkerchief, applied it to his eye for a moment. When he'd regained his composure, he shook his head. "You would insult the cardinal to his face?"

Doyle felt a concentration of heat in the back of his neck. "We'd like a chance to explain to Cardinal Cushing how we feel."

"Feel? How you *feel* is not important."

Such a simple statement, it would be so easy to remember. Doyle recognized it as the perfect summary of all his years here. He said nothing, staring at the red welt swelling on the crown of the rector's left cheekbone.

Fenton slumped back in his chair. "Mr. Doyle." As the cloud of sadness moved in on his anger, his tone changed. "Terry . . . Terry . . . you were the cardinal's *spes gregis.*"

Hope of the flock. Terry felt the heat in his neck spreading to his face. But we aren't a flock, he wanted to say. We aren't sheep.

"You know what you mean to him, what with your grandfather."

"Monsignor, I —"

"No, let me say something. Something simple. Will you let me say it?"

That Monsignor Fenton stopped and waited for an answer confused Terry. Then Terry guessed what was behind his hesitation: the cardinal wanted Ned Cronin's grandson straightened out, not fired. Fenton's notorious readiness to belittle and banish was unaccountably in check, but realizing why only increased the weight on Terry. He said, "Yes."

Fenton nodded. "You've made several mistakes this week. My job is to point them out. Your largest is the mistake of thinking that the issue here is birth control. That is not the main issue of the oath, or even of the encyclical. The issue is whether the Church will continue to tell the truth to its people, the basic truth that life is tragic, it is difficult, that we cannot live on this earth without pain and sorrow. The key to happiness is discipline, *self*-discipline. That's what we teach here. That's *all* we teach."

"And I've learned it. I believe it."

"Yet you prepare to join the chorus of false prophets who tell the people what they want to hear, that there are no consequences to their acts, that they can live for today without a care for tomorrow. Birth control is the perfect symbol of such irresponsibility, and that is why the Church opposes it, and why the Church is right to require its priests to oppose it too."

"But with an oath, Monsignor? Doesn't that imply a breakdown of the trust that priests owe to one another? Our objection is to the oath."

"The breakdown of trust, Terry?" Monsignor Fenton shook his head sadly while leaning to his left to reach into a lower desk drawer. "We trusted you." He pulled out a set of lined yellow pages covered with script. "Yet you betrayed that trust." He dropped the pages dramatically on his desk.

"What is that?"

"The complete record of your inciting to disobedience and to heresy."

"Heresy?" The word hung in the air between them, fetid and musty, like an artifact hauled up from a tomb.

Monsignor Fenton tapped the sheets of paper with a heavy forefinger. Its nail had been chewed. "From the Greek, literally 'a choice,' choosing a doctrine at variance with what the Church holds. What would you call it?"

"I'm not choosing a doctrine." Terry craned over the desk, allowing himself to look at the pages he'd already recognized. He knew the cramped handwriting at once.

"You've chosen to seek counsel with a Protestant minister on a matter of faith and morals?"

"What?"

"You saw him without permission. Reverend McKay."

"Bishop McKay. You mean *Bishop* McKay." Strangely, Terry began to relax. Here was the worst thing that could have happened — speaking of broken trust. The yellow notepad pages were Jimmy's. Only Jimmy knew about his visit to Joy Street. Jimmy Adler, the other Charlestown kid, one of the only men at St. John's remotely like Terry. His closest thing to a friend.

"*Reverend* McKay," Fenton insisted.

"Cardinal Cushing does not hesitate to call him Bishop. Why should you?"

"You don't know what Cardinal —"

"'My fellow bishop,' I believe is how he put it at the ecumenical service at Trinity Church."

Fenton shrugged. "His Eminence is famous for being the liberal ecumenist. Technically, still, he's wrong, but I wouldn't think of correcting him in public. No loyal priest of Boston would embarrass His Eminence."

"Bishop McKay is a personal friend of mine. I went to college with his son."

"You went straight to his office on Beacon Hill after leaving the cathedral. This strategy of orchestrated defiance was his —"

"Wait a minute, wait a minute. You can't say that, Monsignor. You're trying to blame this on Bishop McKay?" Now he saw the priest as a figure less of defensive foolishness than of real menace, an overweight, Deep South sheriff. "You're blaming an 'outside agitator'?" Terry's voice was cold and battering, imprudent and impudent both. He didn't care.

Monsignor Fenton ignored Doyle to make notes in the margin of one of Jimmy's pages.

So be it, Terry thought. "The problem with swearing an oath is *our* problem. My classmates and I have a problem of conscience."

"And the purity of your conscience," Fenton said, violating his clear intention to remain above this, "is more important than preserving the cardinal's room to maneuver, his ability to work behind the scenes to what could be the same end you claim to want. By making a public controversy —"

"The oath is what does that."

"The oath was to be discreet, administered in private, only to satisfy Rome."

"Yes. Private because it's shameful."

"There is no shame in fulfilling our obligation in holy obedience to the Vicar of Christ, a virtue no Protestant divine could be expected —"

"Monsignor, is there no shame in setting your seminarians to spy on one another?" Terry let all his disgust and anger flow into the arm he threw toward the pages on the desk. "Does Jimmy Adler get extra allowance next free day? What'll it be, thirty dimes or thirty quarters?"

"You dare to compare yourself to the betrayed Christ?"

"Monsignor, I never —"

"Silence!"

Doyle's mouth snapped shut. He towered over the rector's desk, hands at his sides, coiled into fists.

The skin of Fenton's face was all veins and splotches now, a mask of swelling conflagration. His eyes refused to blink as he hissed, "You are forbidden to discuss this matter with anyone, do you hear? You are restricted to your room except for meals, chapel exercises, and spiritual direction. You are to examine your conscience carefully, consider your choices as they weigh on the scales of eternity. And you are to present yourself to me Friday, immediately after matins, prepared to recite and sign the ordination affirmation. Now get out of my sight."

Terry moved slowly back from the desk until he was at the door. "Restricted, Monsignor?" he said then. "Does that mean my pastoral work as well? I'm supposed to begin at BC tomorrow. Campus ministry is my deacon-year assignment." Deacon year? What could the future implied in that phrase, once so golden, possibly amount to now?

Monsignor Fenton seemed not to have heard Doyle's question. He stared, as if flaunting his eyelid's refusal to drop.

Terry's mind leapt from the rector's eyes to the image of the eyes of a foul shooter. He saw the open expanse of Roberts Gym, that gleaming stretch of floor, the crisp white nets of those indoor buckets, the glass backboards. Eyes dead on the front lip of the rim. First shot!

Fenton had not said no. Terry turned away thinking, Silence means assent. Fuck him. BC again, and therefore basketball! The smell of wintergreen and sweat, the squeak of sneakers, the feel of the pebbly leather on rosined fingertips. Terry's mind flew to the physical sensations of his sport, leaving his hurt behind, his anger, and also fear.

His job as a deacon would be to hang out in the gym on Wednesdays, a "pastoral presence," imaging Christ among the players. It had been his idea, and once Coach Ryan had embraced it, the BC chaplain had approved instantly. And Monsignor Fenton, just now, had not said no. As he turned the doorknob and pulled, he took complete refuge — Jimmy! — in the idea of the only thing he'd ever been really good at. Second shot!

So he left the rector's office — was this perverse, or miraculous? — feeling relieved. It was the evening of the same day that Squire came with his shamrock plant, and was sent away. Terry was never told of his brother's visit.

The next afternoon, Terry went into the chapel to kneel for a few minutes alone. He was wearing black, but decidedly not a suit. Instead, Levi's cords and a short-sleeve clerical shirt with the little white tab that slid into slots at the collar, marking him as a with-it version of what he'd spent so many years becoming. At BC, he knew, the college kids would think he was already a priest. Usually he loved it.

"Rejoice in the Lord," he began as always, "for he is near." He buried his face in his hands. "O Lord, make haste to help me." His lean, erect body was creased only at the knees. As he automatically recited antiphons that popped into his head — "Lord God, in your saving plan all things are ours, but we are Christ's, and Christ is yours" — he was at the mercy of a strange detachment, wondering if the usual consolation would come to him now. Soon the phrases from the psalter failed him, and in his mind he asked, as if of someone else, "What are you going to do?"

What am *I* going to do? The question hit him as familiar, but not from the psalter or the saints. What am I going to do? Then he recognized the words as those he had attributed to Senator Kennedy after Bobby's death. What am I going to do *now?*

Ted Kennedy: Terry Doyle's unlikely existentialist, his unlikely saint.

He brought his face up out of his hands and, again automatically, his gaze went to the crucifix above him, the gnarled, twisted fist of a body. A lost human life. *Of* human life: how could that phrase have been made to seem so full of death? Looking right at Jesus, he asked his question again. What am I going to do?

No answer.

The faint ticking inside the chapel radiators. The fastidious chirping of some bird outside. The gold light sliding down the chute of rays from the upper windows. A glorious afternoon, the yellow energy of a world outside, its music slipping in through cracks in the wall.

Terry had never felt such a *lack* of consolation so starkly in this place before, and he was trained enough to think, staring at the cross, Now I know better what that means. Pick up your cross.

And then?

Once more automatically, he blessed himself. An empty gesture. Can they really take this from me? From *within* me like this? They could. They were. What he would do, he hadn't a clue. He only knew what he wouldn't do. "No fucking oath," he said, and his lips moved, though he was not one who made a habit of speaking aloud to Jesus. "No fucking lie," he would have said, "to you."

He blessed himself again, a wave of the hand at his face and shoulders, as if before a foul shot. He got up quickly and left.

BC. Roberts Gym. The God Squad. Go Eagles!

Basketball, that's what.

✧

Squire arrived at the gym carrying Molly in one arm. They had crossed Boston singing "Itsy Bitsy Spider," Molly manipulating her fat little fingers in front of her nose, the spider on the spout. Again and again, the spider fell to her lap, *kerplop*, and she made her father start the song over. Heaven.

At stoplights, Squire had leaned his head out the window and sung loudly, putting on display the happiest child in America and her good father. When he'd arrived at the grand Catholic enclave behind the cardinal's residence, he'd let Molly crawl onto his lap, between the steering wheel and his chest. When he'd slowed to ask his question of the first seminarian he saw, the kid reached in to tickle Molly's chin, and didn't think twice about telling Squire where Terry Doyle was.

Molly's eyes opened in wonder as he carried her through the double doors into the gym proper. "Look at that, honey," he said, lifting her higher. Two dozen boys were practicing on several courts around the cavernous arena. Basketballs soared above them like the Ping-Pong balls dancing on air in the parish bingo machine.

"Basketball, Molly."

"Popcorn," Molly said. Her arm shot out.

Squire laughed when he saw it, a better association than bingo. "That's right, sweetheart. Popcorn."

When the scorer's buzzer sounded, Molly covered her ears, burying her face in her father's neck.

Squire moved into the bleachers, a nearly vacant stretch of planks. Only a few students here and there had drifted in to watch. In past years not even they would have been here so early in the season, but this was to be BC's year. Squire sat down, stroking Molly.

At the buzzer, the players had stopped shooting and converged on the bench. Zip Ryan was waiting for them, a ball under one arm, a clipboard in one hand, a whistle between his teeth. A coach you didn't mess with.

On the wall opposite was a huge new banner, gold letters on a dark red background: ALL THE WAY EAGLES 1968.

If there was an air of expectation hanging over this team, it was because of the single player whose head and shoulders protruded from the circle, the colored kid, BC's first seven-footer, Bean Nicolson. Now that he was a sophomore, this giant was supposed to make the big difference.

Squire watched Nicolson, one of only three or four Negroes in the huddle. He wore number 7 on his shirt. Nicolson's face, unlike those of his fellow blacks, was an impassive mask, and across the distance there seemed something sullen in the way he listened to the coach.

Squire put his squirming daughter down on the bench beside him, but kept an arm firmly around her as she immediately tried to throw herself between the bench planks at his feet. "Sit still, honey. Come on." He jostled her roughly as he scanned the gym, the clustered players, the assistant coaches behind them, the team managers collecting loose basketballs in canvas-sided laundry carts, the few other spectators. Then he saw Terry.

His brother sat hunched over his knees on the frontmost spectators' bench, right behind the team, where Red Auerbach would be sitting if this were a Celtics practice. Terry was in black, and only a second glance told Squire it was a priest's shirt he was wearing. He was absently spinning a basketball as he watched the players in the huddle. Terry had never been able to sit on a bench without that pleading air of "Me, Coach. Me!" He had it now, pathetic bastard.

Seeing Terry from behind, at such a distance, Squire felt a blast of insecurity. He wanted to believe that the errand that had brought him here was asinine, but Squire was not indifferent to their grandfather's feelings. Terry had to understand that people were hurting because of him, but how the hell to say so?

His gaze went back to Nicolson. Sportswriters were already comparing the kid to Lew Alcindor. Nicolson too had grown up in Manhattan projects, developed his game in hot-hands shootouts on playgrounds whose hoops lacked nets, and honed it at Power Memorial. If Nicolson had chosen BC instead of UCLA, it was because his mother trusted priests. As a freshman he had set scoring and rebound records. This year, the sports pages agreed, he would lead the team to a coveted slot at the postseason NIT, or even the NCAA championships.

Molly just refused to sit still. Squire picked her up and bounced her on the bench so hard that she looked up at him, shock on her face, before bursting into tears. "Shut up," he hissed. Nothing to do but take her into his arms once more. Molly's crying echoed across the stands. Squire was sure Terry would hear, but he did not look their way.

A few minutes later, before Molly had fully quieted, Zip Ryan finished his talk. The huddle broke up and a few players clapped. Half the team grabbed scrimmage shirts and moved downcourt. Another group, the shorter ones, guards, formed a double line along the far side and began a passing exercise. A third group moved to another corner, where a coach had set up folding chairs, obstacles in a weak-hand dribbling drill.

Nicolson alone did not move away from Ryan. Shit, this is one gawky coon, Squire thought, now that he saw him clearly. His long arms hung, it seemed, to his knees. His burred head was bent forward, leading his upper body in a slouch that conveyed not subservience but brooding unhappiness. His legs were amazingly thin, his white socks rising goofily above his calves.

The coach reached an arm up to the kid's shoulder and leaned into him, talking energetically. Nicolson nodded. Suddenly Ryan swung around, threw an arm toward Terry, and waved him over.

Terry seemed taken aback, and did not move.

The coach barked an order, then grinned for the first time, as if he could use the imperative with Terry Doyle now only as a joke.

Terry joined them, tucking the ball under his arm. He looked out of place on the edge of the court in his priest's getup. The coach put an arm on Terry's shoulder. Terry was taller than the coach, but next to Nicolson he seemed short. And Squire just couldn't get used to seeing his brother in that dog collar.

The coach slapped each young man on the back, pushed him out onto the court. Compared Terry's trousers and shirt, Bean Nicolson's skin was not black but a soft, smoky brown. Terry dribbled the ball easily as he moved. Nicolson trailed him with strides that left the upper part of his body completely immobile. They moved toward the one free basket, and Terry took the white tab from his collar and unfastened the top button. That simply, he stopped looking like a priest and became a coach.

As Nicolson took up a position near the basket, Terry toed the foul line, bounced the ball three times, and drew a bead. He had always been a deadeye foul shooter. At practices he could drop a hundred in a row, and that's what he began to do now. Nicolson took the ball as it fell through the strings and flipped it languidly back to Terry. Quickly Terry sank a dozen shots. The ball never touched the rim. And it was clear that he could keep it up.

Squire smiled to watch him, and he enjoyed sensing the tall colored kid's respect sprout and grow. It showed in the way he notched up the zing with which he passed the ball back. Finally Terry missed. But then he knocked off another string of six or seven baskets. Any hint of Nicolson's resentment was completely gone. Terry took his next pass and snapped it back, moving to trade places with Bean.

From beneath the basket, Terry watched impassively as Nicolson threw three bricks in a row before sinking his first shot. Terry let him sink another, and only then pointed at his feet and spoke casually. Nicolson seemed to ignore whatever the tip was, but after missing another shot, he adjusted his stance. Terry said something else, a word of encouragement, and now Nicolson nodded. A moment later, Terry joined him at the foul line to demonstrate exactly how to place his feet. The kid listened, asked a question, then took up his position again, imitating Terry. He shot. When the ball went in, he grinned and nodded, then resumed the exercise.

Squire saw that Nicolson had a seven-footer's awkwardness at the foul line, an obvious disjointedness that hiccupped the length of his body. The movement began at his feet and calves, but by the time the ball left his fingertips, his upper body and his legs were going in opposite directions. When he had to react in the heat of regular play, a Nicolson could make the moves, even from the outside. But at the foul line, with all that time, the temptation was to think too much, and that was why the pine trees were always lousy foul shooters. The great Nicolson, it was soon apparent, was no exception. If Terry was going to be his tutor, good luck.

"That's your uncle Terry," Squire said at one point, aiming Molly's finger. But they were too far away, and she hardly knew Terry anyway. She pulled her finger back, returned it to her mouth.

Squire stared at Nicolson and thought of all he'd read about him: the Killer Inside the Key, a sure thirty points a game *without* free throws. Bean Nicolson, BC's big chance.

And yes, it gradually dawned on him, what would never be seen in ink. Bean Nicolson was Squire Doyle's big chance as well.

✧

Molly eventually fell asleep in her father's arms while the basketball players worked their drills. Thirty minutes later, the brain-jolting buzzer woke her up and she began to cry. The players, including Nicolson and Terry, converged once more on Ryan at the bench.

Squire stood up with his fussbudget daughter and began drifting down the terrace of the stands. "Molly . . . Molly . . . Molly . . ." He rubbed his face against her shirt, but she only whimpered. He made a game of giant steps out of descending from bench to bench, but to no effect. Still, he did not regret bringing her. Hadn't she efficiently opened the seminary gate for him, and wasn't she maybe about to open a vault? A perfect beard: what could be more harmless than a man with his baby? "Molly . . . Molly . . . Molly."

Terry saw them. He waved happily from his place on the edge of the team huddle. Then he hopped over the players' bench and skipped up several rows to wrap Squire and Molly in a hug. The child's protests did nothing to dampen Terry's delight.

Squire caught Coach Ryan's eye and grimaced: Sorry to interrupt. Ryan glared back meanly, and Squire saw him suddenly as a stooped rodent.

Terry took Molly and carried her down to the floor, to the lowermost bench. Sitting, he began to ride her on his knee, singing, "Pony girl, pony girl." She laughed, bouncing like a rag doll. Terry looked up at his brother in triumph.

The coach went back to haranguing his players, most of whom seemed to take pleasure in being chastised. But not Nicolson, whose face seemed cut from brownstone.

Squire sat next to Terry. "Jeez, bro, I saw you with Bean. You're his Auerbach."

"What are you doing here?" Terry mugged for his niece.

"They told me at St. John's you were over here. What, the team mascot?"

Terry grinned. "Chaplain, Nick. Remember? A true chaplain at last."

"Our Charlie."

"So, what's up?"

"The cardinal called Gramps."

"You're kidding."

Squire reached across for his daughter. Molly did not resist as her father took her.

"What did he say?"

"The Cush? He said you're a pain in the ass."

"Come on, Nick."

"I'm on your side, okay? Let's start with that."

"You don't know —"

"I don't care either. I'm on your fucking side, get it? The question is, how do we get these assholes to lay off? Right, Moll?"

"This is one race you can't fix, Squire."

Squire looked at his brother sharply. "What the hell does that mean?"

"Nothing. An expression."

"You scared me there, a hint of disapproval from my big brother."

"I don't judge you, Nick. Mostly because I don't know what you do."

"Flowers, buddy. A chain of stores now. I'm a fucking flower entrepreneur. But we're supposed to be talking about you."

"What about me?"

"There's an oath, right? And you won't take it because it's bullshit, right? Birth control, right?"

Terry laughed despite himself. "That about sums it up."

Squire put his hand on Terry's arm. "Good for you. Hold your ground."

"That's not what Gramps sent you here to tell me."

At that moment the ballplayers, like a multithroated creature, let out one loud groan. Several threw towels in the air. The coach had just told them to hit the road, the quarter-mile track outside, twenty laps. Ryan stared them down and they scattered, retrieving sweatshirts and warmup jackets, scowling while they balanced on one leg to don sweatpants. A counterfeit protest: if they didn't love to run, this wouldn't be their game.

When Bean Nicolson had zipped up his wine-colored nylon jacket, the coach led him over to where the Doyles were sitting. Bean's hands and wrists protruded from the too short sleeves of the jacket, a Buffalo-haired scarecrow.

"Terry?"

"Hey, Coach." Terry stood, then Squire did, with Molly. "This is my brother, Coach. Nick Doyle, and my niece, Molly Doyle." Terry touched the child's cheek, even as she buried her face in her father's shirt.

The coach nodded without really looking at them. "Terry," he said, "Bean says he'd like it if you could work with him. So would I. What do you think?"

"Gee, Coach, I don't know."

"I thought you said they wanted you hanging out with the team."

"They do. That's if I stick with the campus ministry."

"Well, why wouldn't you?"

Terry couldn't answer, and so Squire said, "There are a couple of other projects that asked for Terry, once he's ordained. They haven't decided yet."

"Is that right?"

"I want to work with you, Coach. And with you, Bean."

"So who do I talk to?" Ryan said. "Father Rafferty?"

"No, I'll take care of it." Terry and the coach shook hands, but Nicolson just walked away, trailing the others out of the gym. Ryan glanced noncommittally at Squire, then turned to go. "Coach?" Terry said.

Ryan looked back.

Terry deftly scooped up a basketball with his foot, a soccer move. He fired a chest pass at the older man. Ryan had to bring his hands up quickly to catch it, and the zing in the pass brought a smile to his face. "It's good to have you back, Terry."

"Thanks, Coach. So close, yet so far away."

"So, if you want to come with us to Madison Square Garden, work it out, okay?"

"Okay."

"And next time, wear sneakers."

"I don't have to dress like this, Coach."

"No, wear the outfit. It'll do the boys good to remember who you are now. Just wear the sneaks." Zip Ryan bounced the ball once, tucked it under his arm, and walked away.

Outside, in the balmy afternoon, Terry led the way to an open stretch of grass that lay between the gym and the sprawling, lime-lined athletic fields where various teams were working out, football players most noticeably, but also pole vaulters and javelin throwers. The basketball team could be seen loping around the cinder track in the distance, the oval between the brackets of the stands.

The brothers sat on a bench while Molly scooted away to chase pigeons. For a few moments the two sat in silence, Squire watching the athletes, Terry his niece. She squealed joyously every time she launched a bird.

"So what the hell, Terry," Squire said at last.

"What do you mean?"

"How are we going to bring the cardinal down from his tree?"

"I didn't know that was our job."

"Gramps is pissed like I've never seen before. He told me you should —"

"Wait a minute, wait a minute," Terry said. "*You* just told me to hold my ground."

"That's right, but —"

"So, why are you moving it under me? I'm not backing down, Nick. I'm not taking the oath."

"That isn't the issue, and you know it."

"Suppose you tell me what the issue is, then."

"The publicity. That's all the cardinal talked to Gramps about. You're going to the newspapers."

"We're making a public statement. We have to."

"And television."

"Look, Nick, our only chance of getting the cardinal to back down is if there's pressure, and you know there will be. There'll be an explosion of support for us. Birth control! Nobody buys what the pope said."

"I do."

"What?"

Squire looked over at Molly scampering on the grass. On the hill in the distance were the crenelated towers of the college buildings, an image of the old Church that even Squire could recognize as such. "If we practiced birth control, that beautiful little girl wouldn't be here." He faced Terry. "Hey, old buddy, I know you've got your reasons for feeling complicated about this stuff. Maybe what happened between me and Didi —"

"That has nothing to do with this."

"I wondered, that's all. We never talked about it. Why is that, Terry?"

"What was to discuss, Nick?"

"Didi was."

"She's a free woman. I was gone. I told you how I felt. You're a free man."

"And that's that?"

"Yes."

"Then you are a cooler cookie than I thought."

"Look, Nick, I didn't second-guess you and Didi. I think you know it made me happy, since you're both . . ."

"We're both what?"

"Special to me."

"But we're the case in point, in this argument you're having. You think it would have been all right for Didi to get an abortion? Or that she should get one for the new baby we're going to have?"

"Nobody's talking about abortion. That's a completely different issue."

"Not in the world it ain't, kiddo. The pope is holding the line. Maybe he's right. You guys live a pretty sheltered life."

"Hey!" Terry stood up angrily. "'Hold my ground' you said. Shit, man."

"Just don't play to the stands, Terry. Make your point, but keep it quiet. That's all I'm telling you. That's all the cardinal —"

"Then I'm *out!*" Terry said. "A nice quiet refusal, a few of us, and we're kicked out so fast our heads spin. I might as well *quit.*"

"Why don't you?"

Terry was too shocked to answer.

"You've never wanted to be a priest. I know that and so do you. Isn't that what's really going on here? You're *looking* to get booted."

After a moment, but softer now, Terry replied, "That's bullshit."

Squire shrugged, conveying a sublime indifference. "All right. Then make it work for yourself. It's one or the other, Terry."

"I'm trying to make it work."

"By humiliating the cardinal?"

"By *helping* him to do what's right."

Squire reached to his shirt pocket for his cigarettes, a confirming display of his essential detachment. He put a cigarette between his lips, where it stayed unlit, bouncing, as he said quietly, "Helping the cardinal do what's right? Who do you think you are?"

"That's the question. *That's* what Gramps sent you over here to ask. I'll tell you who I think I am. I'm Martin Luther, okay? And I'm Martin Luther King."

"Dead meat. Dead, dead meat."

"Don't say that! Don't talk about him like that."

"Which one, the Prod or the coon?"

"Oh, Christ!" Terry whipped away from his brother, and his eyes landed on Molly, sweet Molly whose diaper had come loose and was drooping through her short pants.

"Here." Squire held his cigarette pack in front of Terry. "Have a weed."

Terry laughed. "You trying to get me kicked out?"

"I thought you were allowed to smoke now."

"Next week, after ordination. That's the holdup, Nick. They don't make me a deacon until I walk through one last pile of this shit."

"Go around it, Terry. That's what I do."

The brothers stared at each other. Was it possible they had this in common?

Squire said, "Keep your eye on the rim. Isn't that what you just taught that kid?"

Terry shook his head. "Not the rim. You imagine a spot in the invisible center of the basket. Aim for the rim and that's what you hit. You have to aim at nothing."

Squire grinned winningly. "Hey, what do I know. Birth control, basketball — too complicated for the likes of me, huh? We should just stay on our loading docks and at our toolboxes while you sharpshooters sort this shit out."

Terry took the cigarette, not caring who saw him. "You were always a better lay-up man than me."

"Lay-up. Lay down?"

"Right. Believe it or not, getting laid is exactly the point. A bunch of celibates shouldn't be the ones —"

"Hey, hey, I was kidding."

"Well, I'm not kidding. The pope is dead wrong."

"It doesn't mean diddly, Terry. Nobody cares what the pope —"

"*I* care. To you this is just mush from the pulpit, crap for the women to worry about, but I have to preach this stuff. I'm not preaching mush."

"So don't. Just sign the fucker and preach what you want. They don't care, Terry. Don't you get it? They just want you to let them have the feeling that they're still in charge."

"The people are in charge."

"Whoa!" Squire raised a clenched fist. "Pow-er to the people. Pow-er —"

"Nick, come on."

But Squire went into a mock rain dance. "Pow-er to the people," he chanted, like the Yippies in Chicago two months before. Molly peered back at him from her place in the grass. Terry dropped his cigarette, stepped on it, and waited for him to stop.

Finally Squire looked at him, a wide smile on his face.

Terry said, "There's nothing funny about this."

"It's simple, okay? You think the pope and the cardinal are wrong. Gramps thinks you're wrong. The point is, you guys have to work it out. And right now, *they* got the power. Not 'the people,' Terry. Not you. Your job is to do what you got to do to get the power. That's just fucking life, okay? We all got to play by those rules." Squire backed toward Molly. "'Power to the people,' Terry? You know what that shit gets you? Richard fucking Nixon, that's what."

"Not yet, it hasn't."

Squire laughed again. His brother was an asshole, he forgot. A Humphrey asshole, Humphrey Dumphrey. "There are rules, Terry." Squire had moved far enough away across the grass that he had to shout. "Even for a revolution, there are rules." How ridiculous this was, him lecturing his seminarian brother on the rules. "That's what Gramps sent me to say."

"You tell Gramps —"

"No!" Squire cut him off cold, pointing at him, moving back. "I'm telling Gramps nothing that will hurt him, get it? He's old, Terry. And you haven't been around enough to notice, but he's also cuckoo. I'm not hurting him, and neither should you. That's our job now, protecting the old coot. Suppose you could beat the cardinal down on this, bring all kinds of priests and nuns and liberals and the *Globe* and Walter Cronkite in on your side. The side of what? Honesty and truth, huh? The side of change. Suppose you win. What in hell is it worth if meanwhile that man on Common Street in Charlestown is left with a broken heart?"

"Why don't you help avoid that by explaining to him what I'm trying to do?"

"Because I don't understand it."

"You said you were on my side. My 'fucking side,' you said." Terry thought, First Father Collins, then Jimmy Adler, now this bastard.

Squire shook his head. "Not against Gramps, though."

"You lied to me."

"Let birth control be a problem for people who screw, will you? None of us gives a shit what you people say. So you shouldn't give a shit either. The pope knows this — he's a wop going through the motions.

You're the only guy taking this thing seriously, and it's making you an asshole. What's it to you, I mean really, who uses a rubber or not, who uses the Pill? You're *picking* this fight. You could walk around this thing."

"No, I can't."

"Then fuck you, Charlie."

Their ancient pattern, from the funny to the furious to the futile. The four *f*'s. Fuck you.

Molly, attuned to the shift in the emotional weather, began to cry. Squire went to her, scooped her up, then found a shady patch of grass and lay her down on it. He deftly began changing her diaper, holding her by the ankles, unsnapping her shorts, taking the pins in his mouth, using the dry tail of the dirty diaper to wipe her clean. Like magic, he produced a fresh diaper from his jacket. When he finished, he hoisted her up and went over to a nearby trash can and threw away the soiled cloth.

Terry couldn't watch him without thinking of his teacher, Didi. He could imagine her not only showing Nick how to deal with their baby, but showing him how to love doing it. Didi bent over a changing table, flourishing that pin. Didi ladling stew from a pot. Didi at the cash register in the shop. Didi turning the blanket back. But Terry had never allowed himself to picture her in bed, in his brother's arms. The two of them naked. Making babies. Fucking.

"Hey, Father Coach!"

Bean Nicolson was standing on the path that led from the track up to the gym. Sweat poured off his face, making it shine. Shine, Terry thought. No wonder they call them that, the slick moisture on the skin from slaving in the sun. Bean's warmup jacket was open. His wet shirt clung to his ribs. His stoop was more pronounced than before. If he was a beanpole now, he was a bent one. His teammates trudged wearily past him, heading for the showers.

Bean said, "So, I see you Friday?"

"Monday," Terry answered. "I'll be back on Monday." Terry's wave should have ended the encounter.

But Squire was suddenly at Terry's elbow, holding Molly. "Introduce me," he said.

"What?"

"I want to meet the man. I'm a fan." Squire smiled that smile of his. He was ebullient and pleased, which calmed Molly, but mystified Terry. Did this guy hold his feelings by the fingertips only, that he could so easily shake the hurt of their argument? "I'd like to meet your friend," Squire said. "Do you mind?"

Nicolson stood awkwardly on the edge of the path, unsure whether to leave or stay.

Yes, I do mind, was Terry's thought. But why? All at once he felt the familiar wash of guilt, and he knew for certain that this failure, like all of them, was his fault. Heresy, Monsignor Fenton had said. And Father Collins had accused him of hubris. And now his brother, of disregarding the only people who loved him. Terry raised an arm toward Nicolson, but he thought of Bright McKay. Bright did not think him a heretic, nor did Bright's father. But shit, that's what they were.

"Bean, I want you to meet somebody."

Nicolson did not move.

Squire, then Terry, began slowly closing the distance. Terry smiled wanly. "I want you to meet my niece." And he took Molly's hand. She reached to him, and Squire let her go into Terry's arms. "Molly Doyle." Terry blushed when she hid her face in his neck. "She's shy. She does that . . ." His voice trailed off, not saying, Even to white people. "And her dad." Terry indicated Squire. "My brother."

"Nick Doyle," Squire said, offering his hand. "It's a pleasure to meet you. We're all proud you came to Boston."

"Thanks, Mr. Doyle." Nicolson was just a needy kid. He accepted Squire's affirmation gratefully. After shaking hands with Squire, Nicolson said to Terry, "Father, some of the guys —"

"Hold it, Bean. Hold it. I'm not 'Father,' okay? Not yet anyway. Call me Terry."

"Oh. Oh, yeah. Okay. Well, anyways." Nothing. Nicolson would call him nothing. "We thought you, uh, might come Friday after practice to the Hofbräu."

"The kickoff party? You still do that?"

Nicolson grinned. "The last blast before the season is official."

"Thanks, Bean. Tell the guys thanks. I can't do it, though. No."

"It's against his religion," Squire put in.

"Have fun, Bean." Terry raised his hand, that concluding wave again. "Your last chance to tie one on. Watch out for those Hofbräu schooners. Another reason for making our next session Monday. You'll have the weekend to recover."

Nicolson grinned so innocently it was clear the high life was not his thing. He headed up the path toward Roberts with his gawky, disjointed gait.

"Nice to meet you," Squire called.

But Nicolson seemed not to have heard.

"Christ," Squire said, "inviting the clergy to come drinking. Wild bunch, these Eagles."

The brothers stared after Nicolson in silence. Soon he and the other players had all disappeared into the gym.

Squire said, "Listen, I'm sorry."

"Forget it. Actually, you had a point, and I heard it. I want you to tell Gramps that" — Terry looked helplessly at his brother — "well, that I love him."

"That's your job, bud. But I can do something else." He pressed Terry's arm. "If things wind up . . . you know . . . with you on your ear, I can help."

"On my ear? On my ass is more like it."

"I can get you a job."

"Well, Gramps may not want me."

"I don't mean at the stores, Terry. Hell, you don't want to sell daffodils. I know that much."

"You sell flowers, that's what you said a few minutes ago. But you're not offering me a job in the stores? What do you have in mind for me, Nick?"

The coldness with which Terry asked this question made Squire wonder how much he knew. But then he told himself, Terry knows nothing. Squire shrugged. "You're a War-on-Poverty type. Great Society, all that shit. Right?" When Terry did not respond, he went on. "The new breed city hall, jacket off, sleeves rolled up. You're a Kevin White wet dream."

"And you have pull with the mayor?"

"Not me. I'm just a flower man. But Louise. Kevin owes Louise. And Louise owes me."

"I despise Louise, Nick."

"Doesn't matter. She'd be glad to —"

"No, thanks." Terry looked at his hands, at the slivered welts where his nails had been digging in. "She's a goddamned racist."

"Don't believe everything you read in *Newsweek* about Mrs. Hicks. And don't forget, *she's* what you and I come from."

"No she's not."

Squire shrugged. "I'm just reminding you, you got options."

"So that I'll go quietly? So that I'll quit?"

Squire shook his head sadly. "If you quit, the biddies in the parish are wrecked. If you don't, I guess Gramps is."

"Unless I eat the shit."

"Go *around* the shit, Terry. Go *around*." Squire held his arms out for Molly, taking her back. "I don't want you to quit either. It works for me, Charlie, you being a priest."

"Why is that, Nick?"

Squire shrugged. "Same for me as if Ma were alive. You a priest, I see you on Sundays when you come home for dinner."

"I'm still in the family? When this is over, Nick, I may not be."

"That's what I'd like to avoid."

"Me too. But what the hell, I'm seeing this through the best way I can. I'm not the one who made the encyclical an issue of conscience —"

Squire's eyebrows shot up.

"— of conscience, dammit! They did. I have no choice."

"We all have choices, brother. Keep that in mind. There are consequences too, and not just the ones you expect." Squire glanced at Molly, as if somehow her fate was also tied to this.

Then Terry saw it. Not her fate, but her future as his niece. It was true, his standing in the family was at stake.

"So take good care," Squire concluded. And he walked away, with his daughter perched on his shoulder so that she could stare back at her uncle, blankly.

10

BY FRIDAY the number of men ready to protest the birth control encyclical had dropped to eleven. "The Twelve," Hal Forrester, one of the protesters, cracked as they left St. John's, "if you don't count Judas."

"We have a class full of Judases," Moose Moran, another protester, said. "Right, Terry?"

"What the hell, guys. Everybody makes his own decision."

They fell informally into line, some carrying posters, some carrying stacks of the leaflets they had run off. The posters read *Honesty in the Church, Keep the People in "The People of God," Vox Populi,* and *"Humanae Vitae" Is Not Infallible.*

Each one wore his good black suit and his Roman collar; his shoes were shined; a photographer could find a point of focus in the part of his hair. But they were a dispirited group, and even those who'd sought to layer anxiety with repartee fell silent now that they were out of doors, actually doing it at last. It was late morning of an overcast day.

Terry looked up at the leaden sky. "That's all we need."

But it wasn't raining, and maybe wouldn't.

Other seminarians watched from the bay windows of the library. A group of junior students at work period, leaning on shovels near the statue of Saint Patrick — a bishop standing on a snake — stared openly as Doyle and his classmates trudged up the hill toward the cardinal's residence.

The plan was to form a picket line on the Comm. Ave. side of the mansion, actually the back of the building. Hedges and a low wall stood between the house and the street. Neither the cardinal nor anyone else of importance had rooms on that side, but they were no longer the point. The people passing in the street were the point, anyone who might notice and ask, What are you doing? Reporters were the point. The sidewalk behind the house was public property, so nobody could stop them.

Forrester had proposed reciting the rosary as they walked, but the others had merely groaned. Someone had suggested Psalms, but no one had seconded the motion. So now they moved solemnly but silently at the edge of the grounds, in and out of the chilly, faint shade of huge old elm trees, following the graceful serpentine of the long, sloping asphalt roadway. Some of the seminarians were blank-minded, putting one foot in front of another, a dreamlike procession out of a long subservience, but also out of the closest thing to paradise they would ever know.

To a man, the eleven had found themselves wanting the priesthood more than ever this week — the odd effect, perhaps, of quickened consciences, but also of knowing it might be forfeit now. Tomorrow they would be not deacons but spoiled priests, and their big problem would not be birth control but the U.S. Army draft. But that was tomorrow. This, this was today.

They were coming to the crest of the next hill, an invisible border between their own turf — their turreted, dark-ages building, their ball courts and fields, the wooded corners in which they prayed — and that of the senior clergy staffing archdiocesan offices — the parking lots and the fresh brick, flat-roofed structures, fifties modern, built to look efficient and up-to-date but resembling in the end a soon-to-be-seedy motel complex. Terry could not bring himself to look at the windows, for he knew that to the assistant chancellors, tribunal judges, canon lawyers, and their blue-haired secretaries, he and his fellow protesters — protest*ants* — were Judases and nothing else.

At last, following one more turn in the roadway, the cardinal's house itself came into view, sited majestically at the top of yet another rolling hill, crowning a sweep of broad, open lawn. The vista was punctuated here and there by lone trees, cypresses and poplars. In the valley from which the grassy plain sloped upward were a pair of chipped Roman columns hinting at Old World ruins, since they upheld nothing. The isolated trees and the columns seemed positioned in relation to the cardinal's residence, a deliberate framing of the *palazzo* intended to evoke Tuscany, the Umbrian Hills, the rare country near Assisi. To young, untraveled Boston eyes, it succeeded utterly. Only the futuristic antenna disk plunked on the roof, with its oddly protruding arms aiming, no doubt, at the hills of Rome, undercut the impression that this was a domicile of another era.

As they approached the spot where the roadway would take them past the mansion, Terry could hear a trolley rumbling by — his trolley, what he'd ridden to school each morning years before. But all he could see still was the building itself, the three-story, sand-colored brick façade, the bright balustrade marking the roofline off from the gray sky, the formal portico before the driveway, an entrance fit for *principati.*

Ahead was a statue of Mary, and as they approached it, Terry looked forward to getting that image of compliance behind them. Oh, to be off the grounds, beyond the house, out into Boston, into — here was the feeling — America.

But not so fast.

As they drew abreast of the statue, a cassocked figure stepped out from behind the rampant rhododendron and blocked their way. Father Collins, tired looking, rheumy-eyed as ever, stood with his hand up, less like a cop than a timid pupil. Terry had not seen him since leaving Dini's. "Wait a minute, fellows," he said.

The group stopped. The men holding posters kept them face down. Terry met his eyes directly. "Father, we've thought it through. There's no point in —"

"I'm not here to argue, Terry."

Thirty yards beyond was the point where Cushing's driveway crossed the sidewalk of Comm. Ave. Out there, a group of men and women were peering toward them, perhaps a dozen. And a pair of Boston policemen stood by too. A blue-and-white was blocking the driveway, its lights flashing.

Father Collins opened his hands as if saying *Dominus vobiscum*, an unconscious imitation of the posture of the sculpted Virgin behind him. "We were hoping you'd come in for a minute. That's all."

"We?"

"Me," the priest said, "and the cardinal."

"Cardinal Cushing?"

"No, Stan Musial."

"We weren't expecting —"

"Just a minute, Terry." Father Collins's eyes moved across the group. "What do you say, fellows?"

This was what they'd wanted earlier in the week, but what was the point now? Still, Father Collins was the priest they'd all depended on.

"I don't know, Father."

"Just for a minute," Father Collins said with a note of pleading.

Terry nodded. "Okay." He doubted no more than the priest that the decision was his to make. Father Collins led the way between the pungent shrubs, past Our Lady, to whom not one of the men raised his eyes.

✧

In all those years, they had never been inside that place. The ornate foyer, its polished marble floor and curved staircase sweeping up to the second story, put them in mind of a municipal building or the Museum of Fine Arts. Father Collins pointed to a small room off the entrance. "Do you want to leave your things there?"

The posters, he meant, the leaflets. They did so.

And then, single file, they followed him down the long corridor. Their footsteps echoed on the terrazzo. Oil portraits lined the walls, popes and prelates, expressions fixed in disapproval.

At the far end of the corridor, Father Collins opened a door and stood aside. The men filed past, aware of his whiskey breath, into an opulent dining room. A multitiered Waterford chandelier overhung a long, gleaming table at which Doyle, and then each of his classmates, instinctively picked a chair to stand behind, as if this were the seminary refectory. One broad wall was paneled wood, mirrors, and crystal sconces. The other featured a bank of four ten-foot windows that overlooked the sweeping lawn and O'Connell's Gothic chapel on the hill. The airy vista and the manly dark elegance of the room were countered by its aroma, a stench of cigars, overcooked food, and the generalized odor — altar wine, sacristies, the musty drawers of vesting cases, the mold in old missals — that the seminarians had associated with priests since they were altar boys.

Father Collins did not follow them into the room. For a few minutes nothing happened. Terry stared out the nearest window, wanting to finger his collar, but he felt observed and didn't move. Finally, at a stirring in the doorway, they looked toward it in time to see the startlingly red figure of Cardinal Cushing appear.

He entered the room stiffly, but at a clip, and he was carrying a large white cardboard, holding it gingerly by the merest corner. The men, to their common horror, recognized it as one of their posters.

Cushing was always taller than they expected, thinner and more physically agitated, his hands never settled, his eyes constantly darting about. His pockmarked complexion, sallow gauntness, and crooked teeth always amazed for combining somehow into a rough loveliness. The blue depth of his eyes pulled them in. He seemed in pain. There had been rumors: arthritis, migraines, something with his kidneys.

Doyle and the others could not look at him without feeling a blast of guilt.

"Sit down," Cushing said with no more than his usual gruffness. He remained standing at the head of the table. Collins had come into the room and now hovered in the corner behind the cardinal, like a waiter. Cushing did not speak at first. He centered the poster flat on the table before him. Even upside down, the seminarians could read it: *Honesty in the Church.*

At last he raised his face to look at them. "I got one thing to say to you fellows." Cushing fingered the poster, aligned it with the table edge, before adding quietly, "You're the damnedest . . ." His voice faltered. He glanced out the window. "You're the best damn men I've got." He brought his eyes back. "And I can't afford to lose you." He shook his head. "Not over this birth control, anyways." Then he banged the table with his fist. "I will not have it! Not from you, and not from them! Do you understand me?"

He started, as if realizing only then where he was. He blinked, taking in the sight of several of them individually. "Listen to me. I told Father Collins to bring you in here because I haven't had a chance yet to ask you." He glanced back at Collins. "Did you talk to them?"

"No, Your Eminence."

"Listen, fellows." Cushing sat. His hands moved awkwardly across the table, and Terry recognized fingers itching for a glass. "I'm in the pickle here, and now so are you. We got this thing in common. You got bosses leaning on you, so do I. The difference is, you fellows have one boss who's on your side." He leaned toward them. "Do you hear what I'm telling you? Do you?"

His eye had fallen on Forrester, and so Forrester was the one who said, "Yes, Your Eminence."

"Now listen — are you listening?"

"Yes, Your Eminence."

"I can't have my best men going out onto Commonwealth Avenue and telling the pope he's wrong, because then" — he shrugged — "it's out of my hands." He put his hands together, palms upward, "Like that Allstate ad." He pulled his hands sharply apart. "You fall through. Is that what you fellows want? I send you packing? All these years down the tube? Your vocations lost? All the souls you would of saved? All the young people who'd have found the Lord because of you? Now they never will, and isn't that just so damn sad? And what's worse, when I fire you — and you go out there and talk to those TV snoops, and I *do* fire you — the ordinary laypeople in this archdiocese get the idea that *I* agree with this thing, which as you may have noticed I have not said I do. You guys are about to force my hand. And the result is, people are going to be even more confused. Do you get my point? Wiggle room — that's what I want to leave the laity in this thing, and their confessors too, the room where private conscience rules, which is where birth control belongs. That's what you believe, and that's what I believe. You guys are making it *public*, you see what I'm saying? Do you?"

Moran said, "Yes, yes." The glow of relief on his face was enough to dry the tears he'd nearly shed.

Whatever Cushing was asking for, Moran was ready to grant. So, Terry realized as he looked from face to face, were the others. "But the oath, Your Eminence," Terry said. "The oath is what forced the issue. Not what we're about to do, but what you already did."

Cushing slowly brought his face around. "We haven't done nothing yet." He glanced at Collins. "Right?"

"That's right."

Then Cushing said to Doyle, as if he were the only person in the room, "I'm surprised I have to ask you like this, Terry."

"Your Eminence, you don't have to —"

"I even called up your grandfather."

"I know."

"And you were still marching out there."

"I didn't . . . I mean, I . . ."

"Never mind now. Never mind. Hell, in the old days, I'd have just called the city desk and the newsroom and told the editors to call the bloodhounds off, and that would be that. But this ain't the old days, I guess, huh?"

Recognizing the cardinal's Mr. Blue Collar routine, Terry knew better than to be charmed by it.

Cushing sat back. "The oath, you said. Wasn't that your question?"

"Yes."

"I read it. I read it in Latin. Blazes, Terry, that's the canon lawyers talking, and the Curia and the theologians. I don't know about that stuff."

"But Your Eminence, we can't —"

Cushing brought his fist down on the table again, jolting it, so that every man felt the tremor of his anger. Was he always this erratic? "Let me make my point, will you?"

"I'm sorry."

"Thank you. Thank you very much."

Collins had moved to Cushing's elbow, and Cushing now indicated him with the barest turn of his hand. "Father Collins is my theologian, my *factotum*, my *peritum*, and my all-purpose troubleshooter. Right, Joe?"

"If you say so, Eminence."

"He's my expert on the canons and the *magisterium* and all that *ex cathedra* crap." Cushing reached for the poster he'd carried in and lifted it by the corner. "Who wrote this?"

No one answered.

"Who?"

"I did," Terry said finally.

"Well, that's a damn good motto. When you get my chair, Terry, you can put it on your shield. *Honestas in Ecclesiam.*" He squinted up at Collins. "Right?"

"*Ecclesia.*"

The cardinal's show of counterfeit ignorance struck Terry as sinister, and it struck him that the old man had been faking so much for so long — that down-to-earth gruffness, that irreverence, that liberalism — that he'd lost touch with who he really was.

"Anyway," Cushing said, "the oath is between you fellows, your own souls, and Almighty God, with a little help on the side from Father Collins here. 'Not a bad public, that,' as Thomas More said."

Robert Bolt, Terry thought, as His Eminence surely knew.

Cushing stood and crossed to the door. All eleven seminarians rose at once but remained at their places. "I'm leaving this to you fellows. Father Collins speaks for me, even though" — Cushing shot the priest a look — "I don't know what he's going to say. Private forum between the lads and yourself, right, Father?"

"Indeed so, Your Eminence."

And without a further look at the men, Cushing was through the door and gone. Collins's gaze went to a nearby mirror; in the reflection, he looked the men over. "Have a seat."

They did.

"I'll be in the small dining room across the hall. I want to see you one at a time, starting with you, Moose. And then come in order." He gestured along the line, a counterclockwise swoop, apparently casual, but indicating exactly how he wanted them to present themselves. Doyle would be last.

Beginning with Moran, each man got up, left the dining room, and within a few minutes reappeared at the door just long enough to finger the next. No one returned to his seat, and in a little while Terry was sitting at the huge dark table alone. The chandelier sparkled in the dull morning light. Outside it had begun to drizzle. He imagined taking a light airplane across the rolling lawn, its wheels leaving the ground and just clearing the ruined Roman columns, flying away. Inside his chest he felt a release of pressure, a loosening up, as if he were airborne now, making his escape.

And where would he land? Along the strip of weedy turf between the projects and the piers in Charlestown? On the green apron of Monument Square, across from the high school? At the playground? He saw himself as fifteen or sixteen, in his white Converse high-tops, popping jump shots hour after hour by himself. His closest thing ever to flying, in fact, had been that timeless suspension in the air as his fingers let the ball go so delicately. He saw himself standing in the doorway of the Kerry Bouquet, his mother and grandfather exactly alike in refusing to look at him, his brother smirking, saying "asshole."

"Okay, Terry." Forrester turned away quickly, refusing to make eye contact, to give him a clue. Terry left the room, aware that the poster was still on the table. *Honesty* . . .

The small dining room was small only by comparison with the room he'd just left. Father Collins was sitting at a round table that had chairs for six people. Doyle took the one that was pulled out. The priest had donned a thin purple stole, as for a sacrament. What a strange feeling, to be guarded before this man to whom he'd entrusted his deepest fears.

On the table were a copy of the Bible and a sheet of creased paper that Terry recognized as a copy of the statement he and the others had prepared. Father Collins placed a hand on each and said, "Every man who has preceded you has understood the point I am going to make, and accepted my assurance in this matter."

Terry nodded.

"Cardinal Cushing is asking for your help. It's that simple. He is in a difficult position, and if you really care about changing the Church, instead of merely defying it, you will join him."

"I was ready to do that before. It was only —"

"The oath."

"Yes."

"*That* is the sticking point."

"Yes."

"The only one?"

Suddenly Terry did not know. The only one? What about this feeling squeezing his chest once more? He said inanely, "Monsignor Fenton called us heretics."

"That's nonsense. You know Fenton speaks for no one. Do you think Cardinal Cushing regards you as a heretic? Did you hear what he said?"

"He said we're his best men."

"And do you believe he means it?"

"Yes."

"That's the point, lad. And the cardinal has a special feeling for you. If he were young, you're the man he'd want to be."

"I doubt that, Father."

"It's how I feel."

The affirmation, so surprising, froze Doyle.

"You can forget about the oath, Terry."

"What?"

"You don't have to take it, or sign it."

"How can you — ?"

"That's what I've told each one before you. But I'm speaking under the Seal here. You are to discuss this with no one, not even the other men who just left. And when others ask you, you simply say you won't discuss it. Can you agree to that?"

"Not discuss the encyclical?"

"Only whether you swore to uphold it or not. We all have to discuss the encyclical. We can say what the cardinal has said, that it is a matter best left to the confessor and the penitent."

"Like this."

"Exactly."

Terry saw it now: falling back on the Seal of Confession to avoid confronting the impossible. The solemnized private forum — the perfect venue for sanctioning troubled married couples to ignore the pope, the solution for dissenting seminarians. But if dissent is secret . . . He stopped himself. This was a way out. His buddies had taken it, and now he could.

So say yes, asshole. The command came in the voice of his brother. You've won. Say yes.

But he couldn't. He was simply paralyzed. He stared at Father Collins.

"What's the problem?" Collins asked.

"I have to ask you — does the cardinal know what you are doing here?"

"The cardinal is leaving this to me, which is what I want you to do."

"How do you deal with Monsignor Loughlin about this? He pushed the oath on us. Wasn't he pushed by the nuncio?"

"That's my problem, Terry. Not yours."
"But I need to know, Father."
"Jesus Christ, none of your classmates —"
"Father, the cardinal and the others still expect us to have sworn, don't they?"
"Yes." The priest leaned across the table. "All right, yes. And since you ask, I'll tell you."
"You don't have to," Terry said. "I see it now."
"You see me signing the oath for you."
"Yes."
"Signing your name."
"Yes."
"Forgery."
"Yes."
"And signing my own name, under pain of sin, as solemnizing witness. Is that what you see?"
Honesty in the Church! The words rang inside Doyle as if some Luther had declaimed them. Others lie, he thought, recognizing the real meaning of the new morality, so that I don't have to. Once more he could say nothing.
After a long time, Father Collins pushed back against the stout wood of his chair, never letting up on the gaze with which he'd pinned his now former protégé. As if he had left his body to watch himself do this, he asked in a dead voice, "So you agree, or what?"
And Doyle, similarly, answered entirely from outside himself: "Yes."

✧

The Nail was a tavern in City Square that went back to speakeasy days, and that was part of the reason Packy Nolan felt entitled.
Nolan men had taken shit from nobody, certainly not from short greaser scumbags from across the river. For decades the knuckle draggers who had controlled the flow of booze in Boston had found it possible to deal respectfully with Packy, his father before him, and his grandfather who'd started the place. The Nolans had never quibbled about the covert fees involved in doing business, but they'd never been treated like dogshit before either. And they damn sure wouldn't start now, which was what Packy had told the new wop bagman who'd swaggered in the day before. And hadn't his jaw dropped at Packy's "Fuck your cunt mother too!"
Nolan's grandfather, a carpenter, had kept his table saw in front and served the bootleg hooch in back. In commemoration, the ragged-

toothed disk of a saw blade still hung on the wall behind the bar, although numbers, hands, and works had been added to make it a clock. It had long since stopped running. A variety of old tools were displayed around the blade, including a six-inch nail.

It was early Friday evening. The place was half full of cheesy men who'd done their duty at home — fish sticks and macaroni with the wife and kids — and who now aggressively fisted their beers. The pubsters ignored the ceiling television in the corner, a new color job, because the fights weren't on yet.

Morley Safer, in ill-fitting combat clothing, including a too polished green helmet that jostled as he rattled off sentences into his hand, addressed no one in particular in that tavern, despite the emotional charge in his voice. He was describing the VC tunnels into which GIs had recently begun refusing to crawl, despite orders. Instead, Safer explained without hiding his contempt, U.S. soldiers had taken to tossing grenades into the holes without searching them first for women and children.

Incredible. An incredible coincidence, which one or two of the drinkers at the bar would register later, having heard some of the report after all. Incredible because just then the Nail's large, cloudy plate-glass window had shattered when what they all took to be a rock came crashing through. It bounced into the middle of the wide-planked floor, spinning and hissing — not a rock, they saw then, but a hand grenade of their own, still cooking, emitting steam.

Packy Nolan was behind the bar. When he saw what it was, he hit the floor while others screamed and scattered. Nolan covered his head, but remained cool enough to begin his act of contrition — but also to flash on that wop bastard's face from the day before, a mortal sin, one final act of hatred. Seconds passed as the sound of panicked scurrying was replaced by an eerie silence in which, even from his place behind the cold metal beer kegs against which he'd crushed his cheekbone, could be heard the sputtering hiss of the grenade's unwinding detonation device.

And finally that sound stopped too. An eternity.

"Shit," someone said, "it's a dud."

Nolan got to his wobbly knees, inching upward slowly to bring his head level with the bar, then above it.

Two dozen Irish tough guys were hiding in the corners and under tables, behind benches and the low walls of booths. The grenade lay inert in the center of a well-cleared circle. It had not exploded, and Nolan was among the first to understand that it was not intended to.

The men, when they recovered, were too embarrassed to hang around. No one had exactly thrown himself on the potato masher to save his buddies. No one had scooped it up and hurled it back outside. After an initial burst of relieved chatter, no one much wanted to talk about it either. Fragging, Irish style: the fucking leaden pineapple had shown them up for what they were, Nolan included. By nine o'clock the Nail was nearly empty, so he made the stragglers leave and he shut the place down. Incredible. On a Friday night. Nolan pocketed the grenade and walked up Winthrop Street toward Squire's.

Ned was in his chair, inside the blue glow of the TV, the same Morley Safer documentary blaring away, the chugging of helicopters, the *foop* of mortars, the endless footage of the green jungle carpet. When Squire looked, the screen was filled with a close-up of a GI's haggard face. The camera moved in on his helmet and the hand-scrawled letters *FTA*, which framed a Zippo lighter stuck in the band.

Ned Cronin was holding a can of Narragansett. Next to his chair were four empties. At six, he would go to bed.

"Good night, Gramps."

"Oh!" Cronin jerked in his chair. "I forgot you was up here."

"I just wanted to remind you again about tomorrow. We'll be leaving at eleven. The ceremonies start at noon, but Terry said we should get there early."

Ned took his grandson's hand. "I knew I could count on you."

"I did nothing, Gramps. Terry worked it out himself. He said the cardinal called him and the others in today. That's what the cardinal should of done in the first place. Terry's no rebel, you know that."

"But I knew you could fix it."

Squire's heart sank as he saw once more how lightly his grandfather held to what was real. That fiercely, on the other hand, he squeezed Squire's fingers.

"Terry wanted to obey them, Gramps." As if Cronin saw the issue, or cared about it. "They just had to give him a way to do it."

Cronin nodded vaguely, letting his gaze drift back to the television screen, a fire engulfing a nest of thatched roofs. The old man said, "Cuff Matson told me to watch this in case they show his Ernie."

Squire crossed to the television and changed the channel. "You don't want to watch that crap. Here's *Bonanza*. Watch this."

Cronin did not react. He stared indifferently at the kaleidoscope eye.

"How's your beer?"

"All set," Cronin said.

"Get your sleep when this ends. See you tomorrow. Big day."

"Thanks to you."

Squire kissed his grandfather's head, then went downstairs.

Didi was just coming out of the jakes, wrapping her robe around her. She was so big now that its belt barely fit.

"Christ," Squire said, passing her, "he's giving me the credit."

She cupped his cheek. "You poor dear."

"No, really, this is screwy. Charlie's the one lighting a match to the rest of his life, and the old fart thanks *me.*"

Didi's hair was in curlers, which made her look middle-aged, which was how she felt. "Nicky, when I had Molly, he thanked you for that too. As if the UPS guy —"

"Don't start in on that."

"You brought it up." She went past him to check on Molly.

At that moment the glass in the door downstairs rattled, an urgent knocking.

She looked sharply at him. "Who's that?"

"I don't know."

"They're not supposed to come here."

"Hey, I don't know who it is, all right?"

"Just tell them not here," she said, disappearing into the tiny bedroom, leaving him alone — a specialty of hers — with his resentment.

A moment later, at the foot of the stairs, in the narrow hallway, Squire peered through the foggy glass, but could not make out who it was. At the next knock, he jerked the door open.

"Jesus, Squire, you scared me." A bug-eyed Packy Nolan stood in the circle of light.

"Packy, it's ten o'clock at night."

Instead of answering, Nolan took the grenade out of his windbreaker.

"What the hell is that?"

"A fucking hand grenade, is what."

Squire glanced up the stairs behind him, then went out onto the sidewalk, pulling the door shut. To the left was the large window of the flower shop and, a dozen yards along, its doorway. The pink glow of the fluorescent tubes illuminating the plants and flowers washed into the street, and it was into that light that Doyle and Nolan stepped.

Squire took the thing. He turned it upside down, studied the dime-size hole that had been drilled in the bottom.

"It didn't go off," Packy said.

"I can see that."

"Jesus, it looked like it was going to, though."

"So that was my point, Packy." Squire tossed the grenade back to him. "Now do you get it?"

"I thought you was going to hang on to City Square. I thought you was keeping the Town. That's what Jackie said."

"I'm working on it, Packy. But I told you, for now all bets are off. If Frank Tucci says jump, you say thank you."

"I told his scumbags to fuck off."

"How do you know they were his scumbags?"

"They were these two greasers."

"But *who*, Packy. Figure that first. Always know who you're telling to fuck off." Squire indicated the grenade. "You asked for it, didn't you. These bastards aren't like us. They're killers. But they're stupid. You got to play it smarter than them, that's all."

"What, fork over the juice?"

"For now, sure. Give me some time, will you? That's what Jackie asked you. Now I gotta ask you myself? Old man Tucci's not even buried yet, not until tomorrow. Frank has a tribe of savages who are all maneuvering for a bigger piece of the play now. *They're* his problem, not us. He probably doesn't even know about the fuckers you saw. The discipline is broken down, so anything can happen. You're lucky, Packy, Beantown being what it is, they gave you the warning. So pay attention to it."

"You mean I should pay them?"

"Fucking A, you should pay them. But know who it is, and make sure that they know that you know. Because, sure as hell, the discipline's coming back. And when it does, we come back too."

"We? You got a turd in your pocket?"

Squire smiled. "Papal 'we,' kid. I'm a Catholic, aren't I?" Doyle punched Nolan's shoulder. "Give them what they want, Packy. It's rope. Think of it as rope. We'll get it back. Hey, it's a tug o' war. You got to know when to let the slack out."

Nolan nodded. With a forced jauntiness, he tossed the grenade and caught it. "Meanwhile, I think I'll keep this, as a reminder."

"Of what? The way you threw yourself on it to protect your customers?"

"Yeah. Right."

By the time Squire returned upstairs, Didi was in bed, rolled away from the light. In the old days she always waited for him on her back, but the pregnancy had thrown off her ballast, and not only that. He undressed in silence, turned off the hall light, and slipped into bed. He listened to her breathing and knew she was awake.

After a few minutes of staring into the darkness, he could see the cracks in the ceiling, thought of them, like always, as wounds, the scars on the body of their marriage. Squire Doyle had not wanted them to settle into this, this . . . He hated how let down she was now by everything but babies.

Those cracks in the ceiling, branches of a tree splitting and splitting again, lightning bolts, the tributaries of a river seen from above — they were his rosary, what he moved through at night, waiting for sleep. He was determined not to think of what mattered more, that fuck Tucci. He didn't want that bastard inside his head until he'd figured a way to move.

He followed one particular line in the plaster, thinking of Terry, tracing the crack back through the week, Terry's week, how the wop creakers had finally cut his balls off. And wasn't I the helpful brother, he thought with the self-contempt he felt only at these last moments of the day, under that cracked ceiling of his sad life with Didi. Once it had only been his brother, whose late night, false-sleep breathing had unleashed this kind of loneliness. Now it was her, yet Squire knew that his connection to Didi was nothing compared to what bound him still to Terry.

"Nick?"

"Yeah?"

"Who was it?"

"Nobody. One of the guys."

"Tell them not to come here, would you?"

"I thought you were asleep."

She rolled toward him. The abruptness of her movement, more than her oddly passionless voice, conveyed a depth of anger that surprised him. "How can I sleep with your clippers coming around here?"

"It was Packy Nolan, for Christ's sake. Go to sleep."

"What did Packy want?"

"Go to sleep, will you?"

But now she was up, hauling on her stomach, pushing back against the headboard. "I can't sleep."

Didi was too fucking sharp not to have whiffed the nervousness in the Charlestown air that week, but she was also, Squire knew, bound by her own iron determination to discuss nothing of what involved him or her brother outside the flower stores.

"So what else did Terry say?"

Ah, she would let her frustration spill off into the shallow channel of Terry's trouble. Poor Terry.

"He said it was all over, no problem."

"Just like that?"

"I guess he finally came around. He saw if he got bounced, he'd get drafted and go to Vietnam."

"That's not true. He'd never —"

"It's a factor, got to be. To avoid the draft, Didi, some guys even get married and have a kid, even two."

His remark was followed by a long, deep silence. Finally she said, "If he defied the cardinal, as far as I'm concerned he was right."

Squire stretched for the lamp on the table. He switched it on, then looked at her. "Didi, he was being stupid."

"Saying what's true, you mean?"

"Since when do you believe in birth control?" He reached across to put his hand on her stomach. She covered it with one of her own.

"He wasn't being stupid," she said quietly.

"It's their Church. Either he plays by their rules or folds his hand, one or the other."

"What did you say to get him to go along?"

"Christ, I said nothing."

"You reminded him about your mother, didn't you?"

"The old choke chain, you mean? Terry doesn't need me to remind him that there's a special place in heaven for the mothers of priests. He does that himself."

"You need him in the Church as much as she did."

"Bullshit."

"It's true. That's why you snapped into action this week. You can't stand the idea that he might come out."

Squire withdrew his hand. For a long moment he said nothing. Then he asked, "What does that mean?"

"You'd have to deal with him, Nick. You'd have to take him into account. Terry's not like the rest of us."

"The rest of who?"

"Me, Gramps, Jackie, Steely, Paul, all your puppies up and down Main Street. Everybody on *your* choke chain."

Squire laughed bitterly, throwing his legs off the bed. "Oh Christ, woman, that shows what you know. I'm the one on a chain around here."

"Right."

"You're damn right." He hit the bureau with the palm of his hand, banging it against the wall. Then he whipped around at her. "He *is* like us, don't you see? He thinks he's not, but he is. The Church has him by the balls, just the way —" Tucci, fucking Tucci. Not Didi but Frank Tucci, that prick.

But she was the one coming at him now. She leaned across his pillow. "Just the way who? *Who?* Who's got *you* by the balls, Nick? It sure as hell isn't me."

"Shut up."

"I'll tell you who it is." She pushed closer to his edge of the bed. "It's your dead mother, that's who! Gramps is obsessed with her, and so are you."

"Shut the fuck up."

"I used to think you wanted Terry in the priesthood because you were afraid of losing me. But that isn't it, is it? It's her! You're afraid of losing her. As long as the dream of her son the priest lives, she lives — is that it?"

"Fuck you! Shut up!"

"You've never gotten loose of her. That's why you're no husband!"

"Oh, yeah?" Disgusted, he threw his hand toward her belly. "What's this, the Virgin Birth?"

"It *is* a miracle, considering how often —"

"Not enough fucking? Is that your complaint?"

"No."

"What is it, then?"

But she could not say. Her complaint had to do simply with who he was, with what Charlestown was, with who *she* was. She began to weep, and then found herself saying, "My complaint is our children. Molly, and now . . . We can't bring our children into this. I hate this."

"These are all my people, dammit. The Town is my —"

"Not them. Not the Town. They're not what I mean."

"Say what you mean, then. What do you hate? Who?"

She wiped her cheek and looked up at him. All the ways she could put it, what this awful neighborhood did to its men, what his thin smile hid from everyone but her, how all the others thought her so lucky, such a husband, *not* stubborn, *not* drunk, *not* gone all the time. But they knew nothing of how he could be gone while in the room with you, in the bed. Her friends would say she had no right to what she felt, but she felt it, was all she knew. She felt condemned, except for Molly. Except for Molly, she felt filthy. She could think of only one way to say these things. "I hate you," she said.

Her straightforward statement shocked him. He was Squire Doyle, born to bring flowers, irresistible to everyone. Hadn't he built his life on how they all liked him? Well fuck you, he said inside himself, more out of reflex than feeling. He stepped to the bed, close enough to touch her. The sea of his emotions, so tumultuous only moments before, had turned in an instant to ice.

She had his attention at last, his complete attention.

"Why? Why do you hate me?"

Instead of answering with what she knew he was, a doomed soul if ever there was one, a fraud, a liar, she answered with what he wasn't. "For not being him."

"Who?" His perverse need to make her say it all, out loud, the name, the name he knew best, the first word he'd ever said, the name of what he wasn't, as if news, and not knowledge he carried in his bones.

"Terry."

Squire hit her face with his closed fist. She slumped onto the bed, unconscious.

✧

Squire waited for Didi to come to. He knew better than to apologize, but when he brought her an ice pack, she accepted it. He dressed, and without a word, he left.

An hour later, with Jackie riding shotgun, he was driving across Boston. He said nothing to Didi's brother about what had happened. The night was warm, the car windows were open. At the BU intersections on Comm. Ave., hippie students crossing the street, with their hair and bell bottoms, passed around Doyle's car.

"Faggots," Jackie called toward one knot of jiving kids, but if they heard, they ignored him.

Squire looked across at his friend. "You should let your hair grow, Jackie."

Mullen ran his hand over his close-cropped head. "Missed my chance, boss, because of you."

"How's that?"

"I saw Jerry today. He has me on the list for next week. Baldysour forever."

"So you take the test, then what?"

"First, I pass." Mullen cackled. "Then the academy in Hollis for six weeks. Then they give me my boots, gun, and Smokey the Bear, size seven and a fucking half."

"And badge."
"Fucking A."
"You won't be wearing the dugout coat."
Mullen looked down at his jacket, the battered leather sleeves, the football patch, his name in thread, and the number 61 on the sleeve. "I guess it's about time anyways, huh? That's what Didi says. Your wife gives me shit about this coat every time she sees it, which frankly is a pain in the butt."
"She gives everybody shit," Squire said with such deadly coldness that Jackie looked over at him.
After a moment Mullen said, "Didi'll shit *herself* when she finds out I'm going to be a cop."
"Don't tell her yet. Don't tell anyone until you get the appointment."
"Why?"
"You've got it, Jackie. The skids are greased. But you haven't been talking, have you?" With that coldness again, Squire glanced over as he stopped the car at a light.
"No."
"I don't want noise about it, Jackie. I want you to just ease into the thing, okay?"
"Whatever you say. You're the boss."
"Sounds like you're starting to get into it."
"I am. I have to admit, I am. I just wish . . ." As his voice trailed off, Jackie gave himself over to watching the college kids milling in front of one of their high-rise dormitories.
"Your old man?"
"Yeah. He'd never have fucking believed it. I can't believe it myself. I'll owe you, Squire, if you get me into the troop. I'll *really* owe you."
Squire laughed. "I'm counting on it."
"We'll still be partners, though."
"That's the point, Jake."
By chance Mullen had made eye contact with a passing boy dressed in a fringed leather jacket, long blond hair brushing his shoulders, and a wispy beard — a self-styled Kit Carson. The boy stared back with eloquent sullenness, and Jackie flipped him the bird. The kid looked quickly away, picking up his pace.
"Plus, I get to crack these faggot, long-haired skulls. Wait'll they try that 'Ho, Ho, Ho Chi Minh, NFL is gonna win' shit with me."
"NLF."
"Whatever."

Squire gunned away from the light, and before long had the engine roaring again.

"Where the hell are we going, anyway?"

"Right up here. We'll get a beer."

"Jesus, Squire, we had to come all this way for a beer? I don't want to drink with these BU homos."

"We're in BC country now. Big difference. I got to check a place out I'm thinking of buying into."

"What bullshit. This is me, remember? You're not doing any buying this week."

"There it is, on the left."

Jackie squinted through the windshield as Squire slowed, preparing to swing across traffic. "What? That auto-parts place? I thought you said a beer."

"The bar next door. The Hofbräu."

A large red and black sign bearing that word rode precariously above a dramatically, and falsely, peaked roof. Counterfeit beams and a coat of stucco had been slapped on the two-story brick façade of a large building that might once have housed a car dealership.

"*Ein, zwei, zuffa*," Jackie said. "A beer's a beer." He knew better than to ask what was really up.

As they were leaving the car, each slamming his door in the snap-snap synchrony of all their years together, Squire said, "Leave the jacket."

"What do you — ?"

"Leave your coat."

"If they don't like my Townie coat, fuck them."

"*I* don't like it, Jackie. Leave it." Doyle walked across the sidewalk, toward the bar.

Mullen watched from over the roof of the car. Then he shrugged the coat off and tossed it through the car window.

Inside, the place was pandemonium, a huge hall with dozens of long, picnic-style tables jammed with exuberant college kids. Braless waitresses in T-shirts moved among them with trays of beers.

Jackie leaned close to Doyle. "*The Sound of Music* it ain't."

Against one wall, jerky fragments of black-and-white movie images jumped; a film was being projected above the heads of the carousers. If there was a soundtrack, it was lost in the din of talk, laughter, and the ubiquitous rock 'n' roll. One of the characters on the wall, twice life size, was Humphrey Bogart.

After looking the room over, Squire led the way to the bar, which ran the length of the broadest wall. Marijuana smoke wafted by their nostrils, and it struck Squire that even the straight-arrow BC kids were doing dope these days.

They took up a place near the end of the bar, by a doorway that opened onto the corridor where the restrooms were. Squire ordered up beers for both of them. When they came, he handed Jackie his, saying, "Sip it."

"Like always." Mullen grinned as he gave himself a foam mustache.

Squire had not intended to come here. It had seemed, early in the evening, important not to. He smoked his cigarettes and stared obliquely toward a near corner of the room, where a group of tall boys had pushed three of the long tables together. At those tables were the only blacks in the bar, four or five of them, including Bean.

Jackie had followed his gaze. "Jesus, Squire, look who's here, I mean over there, in the corner."

Squire turned back to the bar, refusing to look. He blew smoke rings toward a nearby rack of silver-lidded beer steins.

"Look, it's Ginny!"

Their lovely Townie kewpie doll, their homegrown masterpiece of ass, Squire's own cushlamochree. Ginny's blond hair, a close-cropped helmet, shone through the haze. There were other girls at the table with the lanky college Joes, but none like her. She was wearing a black turtleneck sweater. The cuff at her neck made it seem long and slender. She wore black jeans too. The color emphasized her leanness and evoked, simultaneously, the lusty anarchy of beatniks and the self-abnegation of nuns. She'd never dressed like that at Daisy's. And except for black lines around her eyes, she wasn't wearing makeup either. So maybe it wasn't her.

Jackie glanced at Squire, who pretended to care less, but Jackie felt the heat of his intensity.

Jackie looked back at her. In that light she resembled Kim Novak in *Vertigo*, the girl who was her own double. Every time she put her cigarette to her mouth, she tossed her head back slightly, just like Ginny did, displaying the soft white delta of skin at her throat, where Mullen had paid her once to put his tongue. Her black sweater showed less of her breasts than, say, the waitresses' T-shirts, but she seemed all the sexier for being less on display, which had never been a trick of Ginny's that Jackie knew of.

Someone cracked a joke, breaking the table up, and Kim Novak leaned into the knot of kids sitting around her. The way she laughed, she kicked a leg out, showing those green snakeskin cowboy boots.

"It *is* her," Mullen said.

All the kids at the table were laughing and hugging, boys and girls both, including Ginny.

"Jesus H. Christ." Jackie was really irked that Squire was ignoring him. "What the fuck is she doing here? And catch that." He poked Doyle. "Catch that!"

The kid next to her, the particular one she had settled herself against, after the more general hugging.

"Goddamnit, Squire. Look!"

"Cool it, Jackie."

"She's with that coon, that tall spade. Look, Squire, Ginny's got her hand on that jig's thigh."

✧

The week that had begun with Tucci's death on Monday ended on Saturday, the morning after the Hofbräu, with Tucci's funeral. Frank was in charge of the arrangements, and, Squire knew, the way the son decided to bury his father would have infuriated the old man.

Outside the community of Boston Italians, Guido Tucci had not been generally well known. Certainly the feds knew of him, and during the early-sixties gang wars his name had brought a shudder to storekeepers in Charlestown, Southie, Winter Hill, and Fields Corner. But Tucci's photograph had never been in the papers, much less on television. His lifelong discretion had assumed a style that set him apart from crime overlords elsewhere. It was as if the mode of the old Boston Puritans had imposed itself on Italians, the way it had on the Irish. Whatever the reason, Guido Tucci had wielded power from behind curtains. He had made himself into a man no one looked at twice on the street — except those who knew.

Yet when it came to his funeral that Saturday in late September, the city of Boston had no choice but to notice. Instead of a Revere parish, he was buried out of St. Leonard's, on Hanover Street in the North End, the church Tucci had baptized his children in, but which he had not entered since leaving the neighborhood twenty years before. Frank had let the word out that he expected everyone to attend, and there wasn't room in the church for them all. Automobiles clogged the narrow streets in the city's oldest section.

Before and after the Requiem Mass, the procession of limos was led by a phalanx of police motorcycles headed up by a squad car in which the commander of Division 1 was riding, the first open display of the family's ties to the cops.

Before taking his own family over to the cathedral for Terry's ordination, Squire Doyle slipped across the bridge, went past the Garden and into the North End to watch. He stood on North Washington Street — where kids had waved at Kennedy eight years before — as the motorcade solemnly crept up the ramp onto the expressway, heading toward Saugus and the Italian cemetery. The thought of Kennedy made him realize all the more how different things would be now, under Frank.

This funeral was Frank's debut, and he was using it to send a message not only to his potential rivals and the city he intended to dominate, but to overlords in other cities. Unlike the old man, he wanted to be noticed. And Squire grasped at once that, for his own purposes, that was good.

It was some days later before he could arrange a meeting. Tucci had efficiently made his point that he was in no hurry to see his father's favorite mick. On impulse, Squire went out to Revere by trolley, as he had in the early days, and it reassured him to arrive so innocuously. Whatever changes Squire had to make in the operation, he intended always to emulate old Tucci in a nurtured anonymity outside his home turf.

He crossed from the trolley circle to the beach. The faded amusement park had just closed down for the season. Only when he saw the bleary-eyed workmen boarding up the game stands and rides did he realize October had come. And sure enough, once he hit the boardwalk, the wind had a new sting in it. He walked slowly northward, an eye on the bright sea. Whitecaps broke across the tossing blue surface, spewing salt spray. Seagulls carved arcs in the air, and far out, a lone tanker made for the horizon. The sight of that ship in its solitude fixed Doyle for a moment. The sea from here was full of a welcome connotation unlike anything he knew from the Mystic piers or the navy yard. It made him think of Guido, who had pressed his arm with unstated affection. He felt an unexpected pang of loss, shocked that the sharp horizon itself could so evoke their intimate meetings on the weathered, splintered boards. Those walks with the old man now loomed, Squire knew, as his main problem with Tucci's son.

At the drooping bungalow, Frank's goons searched him. They let him keep the magazine he'd carried in his coat, and he leafed through it while waiting in a sagging wicker chair on the porch. More than an hour passed. One or the other of the knuckle draggers continually held him in an inexpressive stare. It couldn't have been more clear how dearly Tucci wanted him off his list, but Doyle was unfazed. He slowly flipped the pages of his magazine.

At last he was admitted to the house, to the dark-paneled former dining room that had always served as the office. Frank was in his father's chair, behind the table. He wore a flashy sharkskin suit, a gold collar pin under the tidy knot of his hand-painted tie. Behind him stood another man, unknown to Squire, as Frank himself, never so gaudily dressed, had always stood behind Guido.

"Hello, Frank." Squire went right at him, hand extended. "I'm sorry about your father."

Frank shook hands guardedly. "What do you want?"

"I want to pay my respects."

"Thank you. Now what else?"

"I want to offer you something."

Frank then did what his father never did, not once in eight years: took his eyes off the man he was doing business with to glance back at his lieutenant. Do you believe this punk?

Doyle reached into his coat for the magazine. He dropped it on the table in front of Frank.

Sports Illustrated. Muhammad Ali's grinning face and glistening torso, his gloved hands raised above his head in triumph. But the legend read, CHAMPION OR DRAFT DODGER?

Frank did not look down at it. "What the fuck is this?"

"Page forty-seven," Doyle said.

Tucci did not move for a moment, then he sat forward and flipped the magazine open. After backing and forthing, he found the page.

A large color photograph of a rail-thin Negro dunking a basketball. The headline, NICOLSON LEADS BC INTO THE BIG TIME.

Tucci read the captions and the story down to the end of the page. Then he looked up. "So what?"

"Boston College. Irish Harvard. And soon to be Irish UCLA. A shoe-in for the NCAA this year."

"So fucking what?"

"I can give you their biggest game."

"How so?"

Squire nodded at *Sports Illustrated.* "I own Bean Nicolson."

Frank smiled briefly back at his lieutenant. Yeah, sure.

Doyle took an envelope from his pocket, withdrew a photograph, and dropped it on the table. The picture showed Bean and Squire, Molly in his arms, the tower of a BC building in the background.

Frank looked but did not touch it.

"My brother's one of his coaches," Squire said. My fucking brother, he thought. It wasn't true anymore that Terry was Nicolson's coach. The photo had been taken by a passerby the day Terry went to tell Nicolson he wouldn't be working with him after all. At first Squire had thought Terry had screwed everything up, but then he'd realized that as far as Bean went, it would work better having Terry out of the picture. As for the rest of what Terry had done — Jesus, what an asshole.

The man behind Frank said, "Knowing the kid isn't *owning* him."

Squire removed half a dozen more photos from the envelope and spread them on the table. "These are black-and-white," he said, deadpan.

Bean Nicolson, those mile-long arms and legs, naked, entwined with the arms and legs of a naked white woman. One photo showed her with her face bent to his genitals, another with his face at hers. "Liquor in front," he said, "poker in back."

Another photo had Bean on his knees, fucking her from behind. The woman had her face buried in the sheets, her fists coiled around a bed rail. None of the pictures in which she was paired with the black man showed Ginny's face — which had been Squire's promise to her. But there were several of her alone, lewdly sprawled, various ruttish expressions twisting her eyes and mouth and flaunted tongue.

"Jesus," Tucci said, "it's Rubber Man."

"Rubbers are against God's law, Frank."

Tucci grunted.

"So what's the gig?" the second man asked. "The cunt threatens to say he forced it on her? She doesn't look too unhappy."

"No need of rape charges. She's underage, but we don't need that either. If we had to press, all we say is he was modeling for pornography, which the girl has been known to do. He's in her portfolio now."

"What's a little night baseball? Who gives a shit?"

Doyle looked at him, answering coldly, "BC is a Jesuit school. These pictures would finish him there."

"So one way or the other, you blackmail the fucker, is that it?"

"No." Squire smiled. "Anyone could do that. *You* could. What I do is *rescue* him from blackmail, save his ass. I swear *not* to tell my brother, or the other coaches. I adopt the kid."

"That's right," Tucci said, "I forgot. You're a sweetheart."

Squire shrugged. "I get him helping me out at the Boys' Club in Charlestown. The Jesuits love that. I start giving him pocket money.

Then I make it bonuses, a friendly incentive, for scoring high. Ten bucks, say, for every point over twenty. He starts taking my money for doing what he wants to do anyway, winning. The season goes well. BC gets the tournament bid. By the time of the NCAA, what with the pictures in the background and a history of taking money from me, he has no choice when I tell him it's Burma Shave time. Time to score *under* twenty."

"You'd do that to the guy?"

"Nobody's wise if he comes along. Nobody but him."

Tucci said nothing for a long time. Then, with sudden animation, he exclaimed, "Sweetheart? Shit, you're more of a prick than I thought."

Squire blanked him. "We wait for the heavy game, national television, BC the favorite, high on the Vegas boards. I own the nigger, and I hand him over to you. You set up Jimmy the Greek if you want. After that, all over the country, your selected friends all know who runs Boston. Everything in Boston."

Frank and his lieutenant exchanged another look, not smirking now. The man behind Frank nodded once, and Squire knew he was home again.

✧

A few weeks after Cardinal Cushing ordained his new deacons, Jacqueline Kennedy married a divorced man. The Vatican issued a statement branding her a "public sinner." Cushing replied with a statement of his own: "Leave the poor woman alone!"

Despite his reputation as a liberal, Cushing hated dissent. He would never have done to Rome what his seminarians did to him. But unlike birth control, Jackie's fate was no moral abstraction to him. If the old archbishop had ever loved a woman, he loved her. In the weeks before her marriage to Aristotle Onassis, Jackie had sought him out repeatedly. She knew the rules as well as he did, but, perhaps thinking of his own sister Dolly, who'd married a Jew, Cushing simply could not reassert them. Finally he had told her the very thing he was at that moment chastising his seminarians for: she should follow her conscience. And he promised her that, should anyone deny her Holy Communion, all she had to do was come to him.

When the message came down from the gargoyles in Vatican City that, as the woman's Ordinary, he was solemnly required to condemn the marriage, Cushing thought of the oath he'd made to the dead president. The hell I will! He shut up those wop monsignors by immediately calling a press conference and announcing his retirement — a full two years early.

And when Terry Doyle read of it, he thought back to Cushing's stunning gesture at the ordination ceremony. That event had been, in turn, the most numbing and the most charged experience of his life. His memory had quickly fogged over, but there were certain things he would never forget.

The arrival of his family at the cathedral, for example. It was a few minutes before the ceremony's scheduled start. He had mounted the pulpit for one last look at the Scripture he was to read, the third chapter of Paul's first letter to Timothy: "In the same way, deacons must be respectable men whose word can be trusted. They must be conscientious believers in the mystery of faith. They are to be examined first, and only admitted to serve as deacons if there is nothing against them."

In front of Terry, people were entering the vast church and filing into the pews. It was a child's crying that drew Terry's attention to the arches of the entranceway. Though he'd had no experience of it in such a setting, he knew Molly's wail. He saw them coming in, Molly in Didi's arms, Didi wearing sunglasses, Nick, and Gramps. Terry wished at once that they would take their places far in the rear, but he watched as the knot of his loved ones moved up the nave, driven by his grandfather's K of C need to sit in front.

The figure of his grandfather pierced Terry's heart, the old man bent, walking with a hesitant shuffle, clinging to Nick's arm. Nick himself seemed more erect than ever, a handsome, tall Irishman in his prime, with his brown tweed suit, his dark hair long, brushing his collar. It struck Terry how grown-up and prosperous looking his brother was. The swagger of a Townie punk was gone, replaced by an impressive and appealing air of personal authority, what the old man was leaning on.

Gramps did not recognize the man in the pulpit as his Terry, vested in an alb, amice, and cincture, the white garments priests and deacons wear under their chasubles and dalmatics.

Nick's eyes floated through the space right to Terry's, Nick who never missed a thing. Terry saw the click of recognition in his brother, who then whispered in their grandfather's ear, pointing. And once Gramps saw him, his hand fluttering shyly, Terry felt obliged to go down, which was what ruined everything.

Didi, with Molly in her arms, was wearing sunglasses, as if she were Jackie Kennedy. Terry instinctively took the shades as a signal — but of what? He hugged his grandfather, who squeezed Terry for all the juice of his daughter's dream come true. "Gramps," Terry whispered, "if you want me to get ordained, you'll have to let me go."

When Gramps did, Terry turned to Didi. Molly had squirmed out of her arms and was scooting ahead. Didi and Terry embraced. He felt the bulge of her pregnant belly, was surprised at its firmness. He kissed her cheek, then looked at her, but he couldn't see her eyes. Was she crying?

He reached up and took her glasses off, brushing her cheek as he had once when they were pressed against the cold wall of the Lincoln Memorial. "What's this?"

Not crying. Her left eye was dry as a stone, but the right one was swollen shut, the flesh around it puffy and purple. "What happened to you?" Terry asked.

Didi's good eye was thickly lined with Maybelline, which, juxtaposed to her bruise, seemed ludicrous, like her spike heels holding up her lumpish, swollen body. Didi quickly put her glasses back on, turning away.

But Terry repeated, "What happened, Didi?"

Nick took Terry's arm, squeezing it hard. "She bumped into the door."

Didi nodded. "In the night, in the dark, going to Molly." She forced a smile, glanced toward the altar. "Now can we call you Charlie?"

"Sure," Terry answered, but he locked his eyes on Nick's. "Can I talk to you for a minute?"

They moved down the aisle a few paces, toward the sanctuary, Squire gripping Terry's arm all the while. Terry turned so that his back was to the others. "What did you do to her?"

"You heard Didi."

"Yeah, I heard. But what's the truth?"

"Truth? What is truth? Isn't that the question Jesus asked?"

Terry shook his head. "Not Jesus, Nick. Pilate. Pontius fucking Pilate."

"Mind your own business, Terry."

"You hit her, Nick?" Terry shook his brother's hand off. "You hit your pregnant wife?"

"Look, Terry. She is my wife, okay? The mother of my children. I love Didi. You know that. Do you really think I'd hit her? Is that what you think?" Squire stared at his brother so fiercely that he had to look away.

Terry's gaze went automatically to the ornate crucifix hanging above the altar. Who am I fighting with here? The twisted Christ suddenly seemed an enemy. What is my faith in? Who?

"Terry?"

Terry shook his head. He looked at his brother. "I'm sorry. I take it back. Christ, if I can't believe you, who can I believe?"

"Exactly." Squire was thinking of Nicolson, how he would have to make sure the kid never entrusted himself to this poor, conscience-ridden bastard.

Terry turned and blew a kiss to Didi. He waved at Gramps, who now seemed not to recognize him, then started up the aisle. But Squire grabbed him roughly and hugged him. "I love you, Charlie," he said.

"I love you too, Nick." And for a terrible moment, Terry thought he was going to cry. Instead, he walked quickly away.

In the sanctuary, at the sacristy door, he paused to look out across the church one last time. And it was then he saw the figures of Bright McKay and his mother and father coming in the great door. They looked lost. Bishop McKay wore the distinctive high collar of an Anglican divine, and that was more than enough to set him apart. He carried a small suitcase in which his episcopal vestments would be neatly folded.

Terry nearly started back, but then, would he have to introduce them to his family? He was rescued when one of the seminary professors came in from the vestibule to escort them. Bishop McKay followed the professor to the near side aisle, toward the sacristy, while Mrs. McKay, a large, regal woman whom Terry linked with Coretta Scott King, took Bright's arm. Bright. His eye patch was always a surprise. Terry could never see that patch without his memory slamming open for a second on the image of a man viciously driving his polished shoe into Bright's face, but now Bright's eye called back Didi's. Nick. Squire.

Terry pushed the thought away, hard away. Genius that he was, Bright sensed Terry's distant, brooding presence, and he raised a hand in a cheery wave. Terry waved back, relieved to feel such uncomplicated affection. But then Bright did something that staggered Terry: he clenched his fist and stiffened his arm, turning his wave into a defiant salute.

They put Bishop McKay on a velvet padded chair on the gospel side of the sanctuary, next to Monsignor Loughlin. A plush double prie-dieu stood like a railing in front of them. At the parts of the Mass that called for kneeling, they came forward side by side, their elbows nearly touching, which pleased Terry because he was sure Bishop McKay's presence offended Loughlin.

Through the early prayers and readings, every time Terry found the nerve to look over, the bishop's gaze was fixed upon his prayer book. When the time came for Terry to approach the lectern, he followed the emcee dutifully, then read the passage as if in a trance: ". . . respectable men whose word can be trusted."

He resumed his place in the long line of men kneeling on the lowermost sanctuary step. He watched as acolytes brought the carved oaken cathedra forward, placing it in the center of the top step. Then the two chaplains, one of whom was Father Collins, led Cushing to the chair. Instead of sitting, the cardinal removed his red skullcap and knelt at the chair with his back to the people. That was the *ordinandi*'s cue to prostrate themselves. The cantors began the Litany of the Saints. "Lord have mercy," they sang, and everyone replied, "Lord have mercy." The soft music floated into the dark air. "Holy Mary, Mother of God," the choir sang, and all joined in "Pray for us . . ."

He lay prone on the cold floor surrounded by three dozen others in the same posture, like war protesters pretending to be napalmed Vietnamese.

"Saint Stephen . . . pray for us. Saint Perpetua . . . Felicity . . . Francis . . . pray for us . . . Saint Dominic . . ."

His mind was blank, his chest empty of feeling at last. To lie prostrate at such a time was, ritually, to be dead to the world, but he was dead to everything.

"All holy men and women . . . pray for us."

His head rested on his forearm, and it was a simple matter to move his hand to his mouth, to put his forefinger between his teeth, to bite as savagely as he could.

"Lord be merciful," the sweet-voiced cantors sang. "Lord, save your people . . ."

The pain in his finger awoke his memory, and suddenly he was no longer on the marble sanctuary floor but on the rough wood underlayment of Boston Garden, certain he was dying.

"From all evil . . ."

"Lord, save your people."

"From every death . . ."

A minute later John Kennedy was dead.

"By your death . . ."

"Lord, save your people."

And Martin Luther King was dead, and Bobby. "Is everybody all right?" Bobby's last words rang in Terry's head. The only picture behind his eyelids was that of the bruising black hulk of Daisy Greer cradling the bloody Kennedy on that floor.

"Bless these chosen men and make them holy."

The voices faded above his head, the last notes drifting away and leaving a weighty silence behind. Then movement around him, coughing, the rustle of garments as his classmates came up to their knees, as Cushing put on his skullcap, took his seat, received his miter.

And for an instant Terry thought he might not move, would just stay where he was, a dead man in whose case there was no resurrection. But then he too rose to his knees. And finally his eyes locked on Bishop McKay's.

The bishop's expression was entirely impassive.

I am just pretending, Terry nearly said. I refused the oath. I never took it.

"Most Reverend Father, Holy Mother Church asks you to ordain these men, our brothers, for service as deacons." It was Father Collins speaking, words from an index card.

Cushing asked, "Do you judge them to be worthy?"

"After inquiring among the people of Christ, and upon the recommendation of those concerned with their training, I testify that they have been found worthy."

Terry's eyes remained fixed on Bishop McKay, who seemed more exotic than ever, his Geneva-style, tonguelike collar, his deep purple robes, his ferocious black skin, his unrelenting hard face. It was like looking into the cold stare of the Pantocrator, the Greek Christ whose eyes are famous for following sinners everywhere.

The cardinal was saying, "We rely on the help of the Lord God and our Savior Jesus Christ, and we choose these men, our brothers, for the order of deacon."

The class was cued to say here, "Thanks be to God," and all did but him.

He forced himself to look at Cushing, at Father Collins at his elbow. Both had the hangdog morning droop of drinkers.

This is what I've chosen for myself? He felt a blast of his old ache, the huge ambition he'd felt as a boy looking out on the towers of Boston from Bunker Hill. I'm going to be one of these? Father Collins? Monsignor Loughlin? The most he could ever hope for was to be a Cushing.

Collins took a folder from the nearest server, opened it, and intoned loudly, "Let those who are to be ordained deacon come forward." He paused, but did not look up before saying with a resonance that carried across the packed cathedral, "Terence Cronin Doyle."

This was what they'd rehearsed. He was to approach the cardinal now, insert his folded hands into those of His Eminence, and swear "as a sign of interior dedication to Christ to remain celibate for the sake of the Kingdom, in lifelong service to God," and swear "respect and obedience to you, my Ordinary." Like the others, he knew the words by heart.

Respect? Obey?

Terry came to his feet and brought his steepled hands to a point just below his chin. His finger was bleeding between the second and third knuckles. He was to say "*Adsum*," a last Latin word remaining in the ritual, meaning so much more than "present." Let it be done to me, it meant, according to your Word.

". . . whose word can be trusted . . ."

To have stood was to have come suddenly awake. The fog of stupefaction lifted. To be a Cushing? Suddenly it hit him like the Light of Christ: to be a Cushing, even, was not enough. These men with their hangovers and their lies, their broken hearts — this was the aim of his ambition? To be one of them?

Bishop McKay had still not dropped his eyes, and the feeling was, I cannot move until you do. Peripherally, Terry took in Monsignor Loughlin's mean stare. Its malevolence was like a stink.

Is everybody all right?

The man next to Terry, still on his knees, elbowed him, a blow to Terry's hip. Bishop McKay lowered his eyes to his book. Terry gathered the long white robe clear of his feet, preparing to mount the stairs.

Instead of declaring his intention, the affirmation he'd rehearsed in his mind for six years — "So help me God" — he looked up at the cardinal and shrugged, helpless. He knew what a coward this made him.

"I'm sorry," he said reflexively. Though his words were not loud, they rang out like a shot, carrying back to the congregation. Terry covered his mouth.

The ruddy-faced, wet-eyed Cushing — and here was what Doyle would always remember — nodded as if he understood, as if, after all, he would be doing the same thing.

Terry mounted two steps, but instead of continuing up to the ceremonial level, he faced away and crossed the sanctuary, his heels resounding on the marble floor. He made no effort to muffle them. This sound carried, he was sure, all the way back to his grandfather, to Didi, to Nick. It carried to heaven, where his mother could hear. And it carried to Bright.

Bright and Bright's father would think he was doing this because he was so pure. I cannot tell a lie. Honesty. But Nick would know the deeper truth. Not Nick, but Squire. Squire knew everything. It was not God Terry wanted to believe in, much less the Church, but himself. God and the Church, as they'd turned out, were not enough.

✧ 1975 ✧

11

THE FIRST TIME Terry took Joan into Charlestown was nearly a full year after they married, and several weeks after they moved up from D.C. She had met none of his relatives. If he seemed in no hurry to have her do so, she had not pressed the issue. She was busy, and so was he. Given what happened, both in the city and in the family, the visit turned out to be a classic case of bad timing.

They'd rented a flat on Howland Street in Cambridge, a neighborhood of modest three-deckers near the Somerville line. It was a mixed area, with students and young professors living side by side with families whose fathers were bus drivers and Boston Gas men. But to Terry, their apartment could have been a mansion on Brattle Street, because in the geography of Boston, it was as far from Bunker Hill as their basement efficiency in Georgetown had been. To Joan it didn't matter either way, because with this move, a dream she'd never really dared to have was coming true.

She was an art conservator whose work at the Corcoran on the drawings of painters had given her the makings of a reputation, but nothing to justify what had happened. When they were still in Washington, Terry had come home from the senator's office one day in July. His mood had tipped her off that something was happening, but she was still surprised when, over coffee, he'd said, "You'll never guess what Ted did today."

"What?"

"He called Derek Bok."

"Who?"

"The president of Harvard. He called him up while I was sitting there. It was what he did when I said no."

"No to what, sugar?" Joan smiled, but she felt the tug of her irritation. He had news, and she didn't like his playing it out slowly.

Terry brought his eyes right to hers, her green eyes into which, still, he could so easily fall. Sometimes when he looked at her, she seemed an utter stranger. He forced the marvel on himself again, that she was his. She was wearing a plain brown French T-shirt, a subtle showcase of her small, braless breasts.

"No to going to Boston. He offered me the top job, running the office."

"In Boston?"

"Yes."

"But sugar, that's great. I mean, that he would ask you. You'd be the chief? You said no? My God, why?"

It hadn't occurred to him she'd react so positively, but once more he saw how they were different. He said, "Because I wouldn't go without you."

"Me?" She stared at him for a moment, then got up to go for the coffeepot.

He eyed her as she crossed to and from the stove. She was wearing blue jeans that emphasized her long legs with which, when they had sex, she clamped his waist.

She poured for both of them, replaced the pot, and sat.

"Yes, you," he said.

"Terry, this town is full of couples who —"

"Come and go from each other. Your parents, for example."

"We should have such a good marriage."

Terry arched an eyebrow. "I should join the Foreign Service? You should become a horsewoman?"

"I *am* a horsewoman," she said lightheartedly, but making a point. "And you're a rocket on the launching pad, sugar. You can't say no to Senator Kennedy."

"I didn't. Relax. I didn't say no. I'm taking the job. Back to Beantown."

"Good. Christ, Terry, you had me confused."

"I could happily have never gone back there. Valley of the small potatoes — you know how I feel. But running the shop, speaking for the man — it does put me at a new level." Terry grinned suddenly. "Out from under Bright."

"Bright's your rabbi. Why would you — ?"

"Because even if it's a warm shadow, it's a shadow. Seven years is long enough. From Boston, I'll report directly to Ted."

"So we'll be commuters for a while. That's okay."

"No. I mean, that's what I started to say. You're coming. You'll want to come."

She stiffened.

"The call to Bok. It was Ted's idea, not mine. I told him you couldn't leave the Corcoran, not when you'd just been promoted. He asked me two or three questions, then boom! 'Get me Derek Bok.' And Bok said yes, Joan."

"What do you mean?"

"The Fogg. He said he was sure there'd be something for you at the Fogg. I followed it up. You have an interview Tuesday."

"The Fogg?"

Terry nodded. "Agnes Mognan. I spoke to her."

"Agnes Mognan?"

"Herself. She's heard of you. She's seen your catalogue."

"Jesus, Terry." Joan pulled back. "I like to make my career leaps on my own pony, thank you."

"Fine. Suit yourself. You call Agnes Mognan and tell her you're staying at the Corcoran."

"I didn't say that. I didn't say that."

"Nobody's made any commitments, Joan. That's all I meant."

"Except you. You have, right?"

"Yes. I'm going to Boston."

"With or without me?"

He looked away, recognizing the trap in her question. She was protecting herself, he knew, from how much he needed her. Too fucking much. His only chance of getting her to come, even to Harvard, was if he said he didn't care if she did or not. "Right, with or without you." He looked at her. "It's important, Joan, what Ted has asked me to do. Busing may explode again in Boston. Ted thinks I'm the one to handle things for him if it does. This is my shot."

I *am* important, he was saying, I am a man of the world. Public duty, ambition to serve, and loyalty to Kennedy come before everything, even you. I am a man like your father. I am the man you want. I don't need you, not really. He said it with his eyes, his body, his mouth, but in his heart there was this other thing, the pull of gravity, drawing him down again, hands on his ankles, Boston. Without her, could he do anything there except sink once more into what he really was?

They had met at a Georgetown party. Joan had sensed the difference in him right away. Bison hunters, good old boys, and self-inflated blowhards — she'd grown up in D.C. and had long since had it with the kind of men that came there. When she began to think that he really had no side game, that he was what he seemed, she let her interest show. "Come with me, sugar," she remembered saying as they left the party, "before the bad girls get you."

Many things had smitten Terry, beginning with her offer to light his cigarette. She snapped open a lighter. It was gold, expensive. In that moment of his leaning over it, the lighter seemed to be engraved with the words *This Is Her*.

"Nice lighter," he said.

"Thanks. My first husband gave it to me." He jolted upward with surprise. She said, "We were married for three months. *The Love Boat* meets the *Lusitania*."

"Your first?"

"I call him that, assuming there will be a second. My second will be my last."

Terry loved her refusal to be twittery as they circled each other, her unmistakable air of having fled a past, the defiant elegance with which she'd licked sour cream from her two fingertips, her hard-ass sexual interest.

He'd tested her, because of the South in her voice, by asking about this Jimmy Carter fellow. She lectured him that southern liberals are the only liberals whose politics came at a cost.

"Except the Kennedys," she added. "Theirs have cost them."

"Do you know I work for Ted?"

"Yes, sugar. I know everything about you."

"What about you?" he replied. "I know nothing about you except what's engraved on your lighter."

"Nothing's engraved on my lighter."

"That's what piqued my interest. Tell me what you care about."

"Really? Not what I do?"

"I hope it's the same thing."

She laughed. "Jesus, sugar, where did you *come* from?"

"So tell me."

She shifted, suddenly serious. "I care about the moral delicacy of an artist named Masaccio, whose work changed Leonardo's life, and Michelangelo's, and also mine."

"I know nothing about that. Nothing."

"Don't you have some way to fake me?"

"I wish I even knew what to ask."

"Think of something."

He looked at her, saying nothing.

"No wisecrack? You could ask to see my engravings."

"Actually, I'd love to learn about Masaccio. 'Moral delicacy,' you said. What a thing to say about a painter."

And it struck her then that, of course, she'd used that exact phrase sensing the thing in him.

✧

It *was* busing that worried Kennedy, and it would be Terry's first test. No one needed to spell out the importance of not repeating the events of the previous September. Images of the rowdy Irish holding signs and spouting racist epithets on the nightly news across America were bad for Boston, for civil rights, and, not incidentally, for the senior senator. But as Terry settled into his job in August and began throwing the legendary levers of Kennedy power, he found that, in this instance, they were connected to nothing. As the first day of school approached, children may have been sharpening their pencils, and worried parents may have been attending ad hoc meetings, but Boston's leading citizens were in their holes, and nothing Doyle did, even as the senator's proxy, could get them out.

One afternoon he went up to the cardinal's residence in Brighton. Cushing had been replaced by Umberto Madeiros, a pious, soft-mannered Portuguese-American. His circle of monsignori no longer included Loughlin or Collins, but it was a good bet that the new lineup knew very well who Terence Doyle had been.

When, upon his arrival, Terry was shown into the assistant chancellor's office, he got the picture quickly. The man was about sixty. His name was Morello. Terry came immediately to the point. "If the cardinal's unavailability is personal to me, let's arrange a meeting with my deputy. Senator Kennedy is counting on the cardinal to pick up the flag. We have to get the priests into the streets if —"

"You do not understand the situation His Eminence finds himself in on the busing matter." The monsignor spoke in the measured, stately way of a Vatican functionary. His English seemed acquired. "There is nothing His Eminence can do."

Terry remembered being in this very room years before: *Honesty in the Church*. He stifled a wave of repugnance and launched into a passionate explanation, not of the Church's moral authority or the needs of vulnerable black children, but of Kennedy's personal commitment to a collaboration with Boston's new archbishop.

When Doyle had finished, the monsignor leaned across the polished table and removed his spectacles. "You were not here last year," he said. "You have not been in Boston at all." And Terry wondered, Are they still spying on me?

The monsignor's voice strained with an anger Terry realized only then had nothing to do with him. "You know nothing of what it was like, or will be again. His Eminence went to Gate of Heaven himself. He went to St. Mary's. The people of South Boston and Charlestown cursed him to his face." The monsignor paused. Terry was certain he would say, This is where it ends, what *you* began. But instead he said, "His Eminence is dark-complected, as you know. They called him 'nigger.' Tell that to Senator Kennedy, what his people in this city have become."

A few days later, Terry went up to the State House, heading for one of the broad, opulent offices under the golden dome itself. He was confident that this meeting would be different. Joe Malloy, the Speaker of the House, had been elected rep from West Roxbury in 1960 as one of Jack's guys. Four years ago, when he'd made his move on the gavel, Terry himself had made some of Ted's calls in Joe's behalf, and Malloy knew it. Malloy was wholly owned.

"Hey, Terry," he said, coming out from the small rear office behind his huge desk, his hand extended. "Good to see you, guy."

Malloy was short and overweight. One of the most powerful pols on Beacon Hill, he still impressed as the high school football coach he'd started as. His tie was loose at his throat. The blues of his suit coat and trousers were slightly off.

"Mr. Speaker," Terry said. They shook hands in the middle of the room. Three tall windows offered a view of Boston Common, the shimmering afternoon. On the opposite wall hung oil portraits of a pair of Malloy's bewhiskered predecessors. A glass and mahogany case against another wall held a large model of a China clipper. Malloy eased Doyle toward a leather couch. "Cut the Mr. Speaker crap, Terry. You make me feel like a stranger."

Doyle laughed, having long since learned how this game was played. "Okay, Joe. It's just that you look so good I didn't recognize you."

They sat, Terry on the couch, Joe in a nubby wing chair facing him. A brass-trimmed butler's table stood between them. "Nice suit," Terry said, but Malloy missed the jibe. Terry picked up a strong cigar odor, and then noticed a thin stream of fading smoke that trailed back to the corner room from which Malloy had just come. The door to that room was open. He'd left his cigar behind.

"I'm glad you came by, Terry." Malloy shifted gears, leaning forward, abruptly serious. "Because I can feel the swamp starting to bubble again. We need Ted —"

"No, Joe. No."

"You're going to have to —"

"Hold on, Joe. I came by because the senator expects *you* to be his number one."

"Not on this, Terry. It's going to be just as bad this year. I'm not going to be out front."

"Nobody's talking 'out front.'"

"Here's the thing you got to tell him, Terry. Ted has to call Garrity. That fucking Clover Club judge has pushed too far this time."

"You know the senator can't do that. I already told you what we need, Joe. Your hacks on the street. Holding the line. Your reps all pull in their organizations. Flynn and Butler taking a walk. We're counting on the governor —"

"I can give you the governor. The street is something else."

"We have the governor. Ted knows your people won't ride the buses. We just don't want them on the sidewalk. No mobs. No thugs humping bananas at black kids, Joe. We can't have a rehash of last year."

"Walter Cronkite on A Street?"

"It's not Walter Cronkite we're worried about. It's the kids. We want the kids in school, safe and sound. We want the judge's order carried out."

Malloy sat back, shaking his head. "If I was the senator, I'd think about calling the judge. He could —"

"The senator told me I could count on you, Joe."

"You can." Malloy looked wearily toward the nearby window. "I was just, you know . . . But, what the hell, okay. Behind the scenes, right? I'm not out front on this. But I got a guy who will be."

"Who?"

"To help with the streets. Keep the bad actors off the yams, Southie, the Town. The two hills. Just the fucking guy, Terry."

"Who?"

From the far side of the room, from within the rear office, a voice said, "Me."

A familiar voice, the most familiar voice there was.

Terry looked across as Nick appeared in the doorway behind the Speaker's desk, smiling that smile of his, as if they were easing down the court after a score. He was dressed in his trademark dark clothing, a loose-fitting cardigan, a polo shirt, and well-cut baggy trousers. His hair was long. He looked like a rough-hewn movie actor. He put a cigar to his mouth and drew deeply as he crossed toward them. It was his brother's nonchalance, more than anything, that made Terry angry.

He looked coldly at Malloy. "You've got my brother in your office, Joe? I ask you to call in markers for the senator, and you bring my brother in?"

"Terry, cool it. Squire can —"

"No, Squire can't. What, he'll send his runners around the Town and Southie breaking knees? Saying the senator sent them?"

Nick laughed. "We'd sure as hell never mention Kennedy. You're the only mick left, Charlie, who takes a cue from Ted." He grinned as he reached his brother, and he put his hand out with such openheartedness that Terry had no choice but to take it.

"You're my fucking shadow, Nick. Honest to God."

"I'll wait for you outside," Squire said. Then, to Malloy, "I told you." He shrugged. "You should of called somebody else, Joe."

"You fuck, there is nobody else. As you know."

Squire put the cigar in his teeth and bounced it as he turned and left.

When the door closed, Terry said, with ice in his voice, "Who are you trying to ruin, Malloy? Ted? Me? Or yourself?"

"Look, Terry, you've been in D.C. a long time. Your brother is lord of the fucking manor in the neighborhoods."

"I wanted you to pull together your reps, for Christ's sake. Priests, Joe. Social workers, tavern keepers, the local cops. Who the hell holds your posters for you when you're up for election? Instead, you give me —" Terry stopped, shocked that he'd almost put into words what he knew about his brother.

"But outside the neighborhoods, Terry, hey, that's the beauty of it. He's just another flower salesman. Nobody knows Squire unless he wants them to." A sly grin overspread Malloy's face. "Like Senator Kennedy, for example. I'll lay you odds he's never heard of him. Am I right? I'll bet you've seen to that, eh?"

Terry stood up. "Thanks for nothing, Joe."

"Tell Kennedy if he wants to do something, he should call that fucking judge. Call the fucking buses off, Doyle. That's the way to keep it peaceful. That's the *only* way. You tell Kennedy I said so."

"Don't worry, I will." Terry crossed the room briskly. At the door he looked back. Malloy was still in the wing chair. "One other thing,

Joe. Your suit coat and your pants don't match. What, you get your clothes at Goodwill? Squire doesn't pay you enough?"

Malloy looked at the mismatch of his clothing and shook his head. "Marie's always telling me I'm colorblind." He laughed. "Like the blindfolded lady, right? Like Judge Garrity. I'm colorblind." Malloy, with his half-bald, perspiring head thrown back, was still laughing when Terry went through the door.

Squire was waiting in the gleaming rotunda, leaning back on the marble balustrade, savoring his cigar. Terry went over to him, but before he could speak, Squire said, "You look like someone slapped you."

"You son of a bitch."

"Nice greeting."

"Don't you see what Malloy just did? He used you, you stupid shit, to send a tickle to Kennedy. Through *me*, goddamnit."

Squire nodded. "Teddy's in trouble when jerks like Malloy feel free to flip him the bird."

"But *you're* the bird, Nick. You see what he just did, throwing you in my face. How the hell could you do that to me?"

Squire stared at his brother, not answering.

"Goddamnit, Nick."

"Where the hell have you been, Terry? Why haven't we heard from you? You've been here a month already, right?"

"Not three weeks yet."

"And your new wife. I thought you were going to bring her over. What the hell, Terry. Gramps's feelings are hurt."

"Don't put it off on Gramps."

"All right. *My* feelings are hurt." As Squire said this, his mouth spread, but the grin was not cynical enough to fully undercut the fact that what he'd said was exactly true.

When had hurt feelings last been an issue between them? Terry felt that he'd just walked into the wall of what had first defined them: the younger brother always with an eye out for the older one's interest and approval. But Terry shook that sensation off to stay with what was real. "Malloy wanted to use you to stiff Ted, and as a side bonus, to fuck me up with him. You think Ted Kennedy can afford an association with you, even indirectly?"

"Your worst nightmare, right?"

"One of them, in point of fact."

"Which is why you've been so scarce. Chasing the dream in Washington, so far away."

"Let's put it this way, Nick. I didn't ask to be sent back here."

Squire smiled. "But suddenly Senator Kennedy needs your local connections. What is that thing Tip O'Neill says? 'All politics is criminal'?"

"'Local,' smart-ass," Terry said before realizing he'd been had. So what the hell, he asked his question. "What are you doing with that Italian?"

"Leave it alone, Terry. You fouled out of this game a long time ago. You think you know the score, but you don't have a clue."

"I don't want a clue, Nick."

"I gather that. I fucking gather it."

A pair of nattily dressed pols drew near, engrossed in their own conversation. One, a red-faced man in a seersucker suit, carrying a boater, touched his nose as he crossed in front of Nick, who looked at him. Except for that, there was no exchange, but Terry recognized the salute.

Nick worked his cigar while the two men moved away. Then he lightly slapped his brother's arm. "So what do you say?"

"About?"

"Saturday. You and Joan. Two o'clock. We'll have a cookout."

"*This* Saturday? You kidding me?"

"No matter what happens Wednesday, there's no school on Saturday, no buses, no demonstrations to embarrass you."

Terry shook his head. "I don't think I made my point. The busing thing *is* an issue, but so is your shit with Tucci. I can't have it, Nick. Games like this. I'm back in Boston. I work for Kennedy. I've got the *Boston Globe* tied to my neck. You can't fuck me up."

"Those wiseguys at the *Globe* never heard of me. They cover the Town the same way they cover Southie. No faces. No names. Just Archie, Edith, and Meathead. White racist pigs. Housewives with flabby upper arms. Kids with bad teeth. Boyos in tweed caps. All yelling 'The Town won't go!' You know, typical Irish Catholics. I'm a dumb mick florist, Terry. Relax, will you? And as for Ted, should I give him some dough? Would that help?"

"Fuck you, Nick."

"Just don't lace curtain me, okay? Not in terms of that two-toilet bastard. Who are the fucking Kennedys, Terry? Who was Joe?"

Terry turned, starting away.

But Squire grabbed him. "And I never killed anybody, okay? I never left a girl to drown."

"Oh, Jesus!" Terry pulled free and stalked away from the balustrade toward the broad stairs. But at the top step he stopped again, not knowing why. It was such an old feeling, jerking first this way, then that. When they'd played b-ball, all either ever had to do was bounce the ball away from where he was looking and the other brother was always there. Score!

Nick closed the distance between them.

Terry said, "Are we arguing about Chappaquiddick? Jesus Christ, are we really?"

"Yes. Yes we are." Squire put his hand out. "It's good to see you, brother."

And Terry took it.

✧

Even before leaving Washington, Terry and Joan had formed a habit of watching the late news together. Often it was their first chance to relax, and they sat with drinks in hand while well-coiffed newscasters mouthed their scripts.

But this was Boston, and the images they saw that Friday night silenced them.

Joan had spent all of her time so far at the museum. Her position at the Fogg included teaching a section of a Harvard art history course, and she'd been in a panic about getting ready. But increasingly, like everyone in the city, she too had registered the dark clouds to the south and the north. She'd heard the rumblings and knew vaguely of Terry's work. But she was not prepared, not at all.

They were sitting on the couch, their legs entangled. She took his ankle in her hand and squeezed hard.

The television camera moved in on black children filing off a bus between rows of helmeted, dead-eyed policemen. Under the picture, a voice could be heard: "Yuh muthafuckin' niggers!" The camera cut to a teenage white boy, his mouth twisted, and then to a pasty-faced housewife, and next to her an acne-scarred man whose neck vein could be seen throbbing dangerously: "Yuh muthafuckin' coons! Yuh jungle bunnies!"

Christ, Terry thought, they're putting this stuff on television?

Joan let go of his ankle, pulled her hand away to cover her mouth, as if she were thinking hard. A white baby's face filled the screen. The camera pulled back. The baby, in the canvas throne of her umbrella stroller, was staring at a woman, apparently her mother, who was on her knees reciting the rosary. "What do they want," Joan said with icy detachment, "this Blessed Mother person to overrule Judge Garrity?"

"'This Blessed Mother person'?" Terry said, facing her.

Joan's brow registered the rebuke in his words, which stiffened her face. Her blond hair, cut in a tidy pageboy, offered an image of the perfection that enabled her to meet his stare with an even starker one of her own. "What," she said.

"You make it sound like their religion is the problem."

Joan pointed at the television. "The woman is obviously praying, Terry."

"That's not prayer. It's a crass manipulation of prayer. The fact that they are Irish Catholic is incidental."

"I'm not raising that point. You are."

"'Blessed Mother person' — that's snide and condescending, Joan."

"Since when did you become a defender of that crap?"

Terry faced away, too furious to respond. He was aware that as he became more heated, she became colder. On the television, black children in their ironed shirts and Sunday dresses, a line of them, not ten years old, clutching pencils, marched past the cameras without blinking. Their mute, expressionless bravery awed Terry.

Joan said, "They're babies!"

On either side of these children, blocked by the police, were the gauntlet mobs. The camera zeroed in on an Irish teenager, grunting and hopping, pretending to masturbate a banana. Religious medals flashed at his throat.

"Well, there's a new one," Joan said.

Terry got up and snapped the set off. But Joan was right beside him, just as quickly turning it back on. "You can keep this from Senator Kennedy, but not from me."

"What the hell does that mean?"

Joan pointed at the screen, but still with a lawyerly detachment. "Tell the senator what his people are doing."

"My people, Joan. *My* people. Isn't that what you mean?"

"But why haven't you told him?"

"What makes you think I haven't?"

"He'd *be* here. He'd be on that street there, with those children, helping them. The *black* children. If this was the South, we'd all —"

"Not we, you! You! I wasn't there, remember? Your famous sit-ins at the lunch counters of Williamsburg for the rights of Negroes who were back at campus making your beds every morning in residence halls designed by Thomas Jefferson! Did the civil rights movement ever get William and Mary students to make their own beds?"

"Thomas Jefferson was UVA, not William and Mary."

"Goddamnit, Joan." Now it was Terry pointing at the screen. "Those Charlestown women on their knees with the rosary go down on their knees at work too, making beds in freshman dorms in Harvard Yard, among other places. Believe it or not, they're maids, Joan. Just because they're white doesn't —"

"Terry, listen to yourself. Look what they're doing to those children. You don't agree with them, I know that. But you're tolerating what they are doing. Why haven't you called the senator?"

"I talk to his office three, four times a day."

"Not his office, him." She lowered her voice, emphasizing its lack of affect. "He should be up here. Ted Kennedy. Bobby's brother. One of the few people in America who can talk to both sides."

Terry shook his head. "You're wrong. Those whites won't listen to Ted, and neither will their leaders. The pols, the ward committeemen, the priests, the muckamucks, they've all bailed out. That's what I've spent the last three weeks finding out. On busing, as far as the Irish in Boston are concerned, Ted might as well be Ed Brooke. To them this week, he's worse than Ed Brooke. He's a traitor. That, in fact, is what it's been my job to tell him, which is why he won't talk to me."

"Then what about the black children, Terry? Is he going to let them do this alone? *They're* his people too. Why isn't he here for them?"

"I don't see Senator Brooke coming up from Washington."

"Ed Brooke isn't a Kennedy."

"He's black."

"He isn't a Kennedy," Joan said with stark finality. "Think about it, Terry."

Doyle resented her cool analysis. What gave her the right to such distance? But, of course, he knew. She was born with it. He forced his feelings down, trying to match her tone, saying, "Ted's coming to Boston would make things worse."

"For whom? Him? How could it be worse for those children? If Bright were here —"

"There's the point, Joan. Bright is one of the people who has convinced Kennedy to stay in D.C."

"Well, if Bright could see . . . this." She indicated the screen again, but it had gone blank for a commercial.

He said, "The thing is in flames now, Joan. What's needed is firefighters. Cops. Not Kennedy, and not the pope either. Once the whites see that the court won't back down, they'll stop."

"The senator should be here, in Boston. That's all I'm saying."

"Here? This is Cambridge, Joan."

"Where apparently he *does* have clout."

"Are you talking about your job? Is that what this is about?"

"Derek Bok, but not—" She stopped. "Name one. One of their leaders."

"Ray Flynn."

"But not Ray Flynn?"

Terry shrugged. "These aren't your tribes, Joan. Not your religion."

"But yours. Your tribe. Your religion."

"Sad to say. Yes. Sad to fucking say."

Joan stared at him, then backed away until she reached the door of their bedroom. She turned and went through, closing the door with exquisite control.

He stood looking after her for a long, mystified moment. Then he turned the television off and went into the small kitchen to pour himself a drink. As he brought the glass of diluted whiskey to his mouth, his hand shook. "Jesus," he said aloud. After a stiff belt, he put the glass on the table, then placed his hands, palm down, on either side of it. He pushed. "Jesus Christ, what's happening?"

Later, after undressing in the living room and turning out the lights, he entered the bedroom and slipped into bed beside her. She was on her side, turned away. As he listened to her breathing, his eye began to scan the ceiling, looking for cracks. An old feeling of sadness choked him.

"Terry?"

He thought at first he'd imagined the sound, so much did he long to hear it.

"Sugar, I'm sorry." Her voice was barely more than a whisper. She'd spoken without moving.

"I'm sorry too, Joan. But mostly what I am is ashamed."

Joan was silent, then she turned halfway toward him, so that they were alike in lying on their backs, staring into the void above. "But for the wrong reason, Terry. You're ashamed because it's Charlestown, when you should be ashamed that you're not doing anything."

"Don't start again."

"Well, don't be ashamed because it's Charlestown. That has nothing to do with you."

"You think." The talk was making Terry lightheaded, as if he were floating in the vacuum of darkness, the vault of time. Was this twenty years ago, the room with the slanted ceiling? Was this Nick next to him? Nick was the one who'd always made him feel both too emotional and too passive. Now it was her.

But Nick. "How do you feel about tomorrow?" he asked abruptly. "I mean, now."

"You mean, can I go to your family's house without being snide and condescending?"

"I guess so, yes."

"Don't worry."

Terry grunted, half to himself.

"Just don't be ashamed of the wrong thing, Terry. There's nothing wrong with where you come from, and there's nothing wrong with having left it behind. That's all something else."

"So tomorrow we'll just be like . . . tourists, huh? Wonderfully detached anthropologists." He elbowed her as once, seeking recovery, he would have Nick. "In quest of the cult of 'this Blessed Mother person.'"

Joan put her hand on his thigh. "Your mother's house, sugar. That's enough. I wish I could have known her."

Terry was instantly aware of sharing no such wish. What a nightmare, the idea of introducing Joan to his apron-sucking mother. As always, the thought of her filled him with sadness, and so he pushed it away. He took Joan's hand and brought his face close to hers. "Rattle the headboard?" An old phrase of hers; the joke always was how odd it sounded coming from him.

"Not tonight."

"I didn't think so."

They kissed lightly and rolled apart, as was their habit. A few minutes later Terry said softly, "You'll like my brother."

She did not hear him.

"Everybody likes my brother."

12

ALMOST SIXTEEN YEARS to the day after Guido Tucci and Deebo McCarthy took their fateful stroll down to Mystic Wharf on the far side of Charlestown, Tucci's son and Squire Doyle retraced it. McCarthy had suggested the heart of the Town for his meeting out of an inbred caution, but now, all these years later, Doyle had a more pragmatic reason for wanting Frank Tucci to see the Charlestown waterfront up close.

Still, thinking of that other meeting, Doyle was capable of indulging an admittedly twisted Irish nostalgia. Few in Charlestown had ever forgotten how far short McCarthy's caution had fallen that day in 1959, or how his failure to read an enemy had changed things in Boston. Old Tucci's shocking murder of the mick chieftain had given Squire Doyle's life, for one, its untouted shape and meaning.

Frank, the year after his father's death, had moved from Revere to a big house in Weston. With a discretion and swiftness that had surprised Doyle, he had solidified his hold on his father's organization, and expanded it. His grip was as iron-fisted as the old man's had ever been. Even the Patriarcas had found it prudent to give him room, and ultimately had formed an effective alliance with him that had deterred the Gambinos from moving into New England.

It was noontime Saturday, and though a bank of dark clouds blocked the sun, the sky was bright. The wind had picked up and feathered Squire's hair as he held Tucci's door for him. The car wasn't a limo, but Frank, unlike his father, always rode in the back seat.

"Hello, Mr. Tucci," Squire said.

They shook hands. Tucci was wearing a trimly cut double-breasted suit that evoked the Via Veneto. Gold flashed at his wrist and at his collar. His shoes were tassled. He carried a soft leather man's handbag, a true Italian dandy who didn't want his wallet ruining the line of his Armani. His appearance contrasted with the dark informality — that cardigan, that polo shirt, those loose trousers — of Squire's clothing. Except in the flower business, where it served his purposes to be a figure, and except in the Town, Squire had made himself more invisible than ever, and his way of dressing was part of that. Frank, on the other hand, cut a swath in Boston: judges, cops, and newsguys knew him. The pols openly took his money. Squire knew that Tucci wanted it both ways.

"Thanks for coming over," Squire said. "You'll like the view from out here."

Frank hooked the loop of his leather handbag around his wrist. The bag, hardly larger than an envelope, swung at his hand as they walked along.

The man who'd ridden in front with Tucci's driver had fallen into step several dozen yards behind them. Squire had seen him many times, hovering near Frank, and had long ago recognized him as one of the thugs at Boston Garden the day Kennedy came, an event Squire made it a point not to call to mind. Sometimes he could not help it, though. The shoe was in his face, there it was.

Doyle and Tucci set out along the edge of the ball field nestled between the projects on one side and Terminal Street with its storage buildings on the other. Neighborhood softball teams were playing their end-of-the-season championship, and knots of spectators lined the field. A set of stands was full. Even as the air had turned blustery, mothers still pushed strollers and old ladies leaned on the arms of granddaughters, as old men on the arms of other old men stood watching the boys at play. All bright, Irish faces.

Those people knew very well who Squire was, and though they did not know Tucci, they were savvy enough to sense his importance. As the men walked along, other Townies nodded at Squire. If he sensed tension in some of their faces, or saw signs of the urge to speak to him, he knew it was about the busing bullshit. They were parents who were keeping their children home from school, or brothers of guys on the police force who hated both sides, or their houses overlooked the corners where teenagers hung, acting more and more like juvenile delinquents. They would all want a word with him, advice or help. Goddamn busing. Everywhere he went in the Town, he saw how crazy it was making people.

At the railing of the backwater inlet, on one side of Mystic Wharf, they stopped. Doyle faced back toward Boston. Tucci did likewise.

They leaned against the railing, both pretending to look at the view, the ballplayers, the hill in the distance, the monument. In fact, they were each noting Tucci's bodyguard, who had hung back, and was now hunched over cupped hands to light a cigarette. To be certain they were not followed was the real point of this stagy stroll.

"City on a Hill," Squire said. "Fucking city is killing us."

"What do you mean?"

"Busing. The judge. The niggers. Fucking killing us."

"Oh, yeah," Tucci replied, but with a dullness meant to show that he didn't care about busing.

Squire hadn't meant to bring it up, but looking back at the city had made him feel its violation fresh. Now that he thought about it, he realized he was discharging the useless energy of his anticipation of Terry's coming visit. Fucking Terry, and his wife.

But Tucci — Squire forced himself to concentrate — was the brother that mattered now. This asshole, Squire thought, is more my brother than Terry is. And this asshole carries a purse.

Squire faced around toward Mystic Wharf and aimed a finger toward the sprawling, crane-dominated commerical dock, fronting on the deep-water channel. Charlestown had beat Southie out for these new piers, and Quincy too, the government making up for shutting down the navy yard. This was the new heart of Boston Harbor, where container ships tied up. "That's what I asked you down here to see." Squire was pointing at the new crane that dwarfed the buildings in Everett and Chelsea beyond — a bridge-shaped, automated offloader six stories high. Its two legs rode on parallel sets of railroad tracks that ran two hundred yards along the water's edge. Its hoisting mechanism yawned, empty now, dangling from the crane-bridge like the claws of a hovering bird of prey.

"It's big," Tucci said.

"There are only two cranes like that on the eastern seaboard. We got this one thanks to a guy named Kennedy who remembers that his brother got his start in Charlestown."

"You fucking Irish."

"Yeah, how about that. In the year it's been here, shipping into and out of Boston doubled, and will again even sooner, but Charlestown still gets screwed. This crane practically operates without longshoremen. Instead of jobs, what the Town got is a caravan of heavy trucks rattling through Sullivan Square. Sea-Land trucks, you've seen them. The containers go right on the flatbed."

"Yeah, I've seen them."

"People see them go by, now they say, Fuck Kennedy. First these trucks, then the buses." Squire snorted.

Tucci stared at the crane, saying nothing.

Squire thought of Deebo McCarthy, twitching on this pavement with a knife in his gut. Did Frank even know how close they were to the very place? Probably not. What was Deebo's death to him?

"So why the fuck am I here? To get wet when it rains?" Even against blue sky, dark clouds were massing.

"I'll show you." Squire led the way across to Terminal Street, past a pair of potbellied men in baseball hats and nylon jackets who'd been fishing and were now packing up their gear. As Doyle and Tucci approached the fenced-off dock area, an airliner just taking off from Logan soared into the sky above them, its engines screeching. Squire pointed at it, Frank looked. Squire scanned the road behind them, the warehouses in the distance, the storage yards and the pier ahead, all quiet. He took Tucci's arm and picked up the pace, heading for an innocuous gate in the high fence. A padlock dangled from its slot, but when Squire tugged it once firmly, the hook fell open. He pushed the gate and they went through.

Once inside the yards, with the gate closed behind them, the men stood for a moment, taking in the sight of metal massed like the granite blocks of which the monument was built: the boxcar-size containers on one side, some on truck beds and some stacked three or four high, as tall as buildings; and on the other, on the waterfront itself, the massive crane. The dark glass of the cockpit control booth at the top of the nearest leg was like an eye staring out over the harbor, toward the hills of Everett. The crane, like everything else, was shut down. The black mushroom-shaped bollards on which a ship's lines would be secured were naked. The pier was empty of men. Nothing was moving.

"This way," Squire said.

He led along a wall of sealed cargo containers to a narrow, ad hoc aisle that ran between the rows. It was like entering a maze, and with a single turn they were surrounded by the metal walls. Squire approached a particular container without hesitating, and he threw a latch. One side of a set of double doors popped open. Squire pulled it and drew back, revealing the cavernous dark interior of an empty container.

"Come on in," he said.

Frank followed him into the box, ducking, though at eight feet it was two and a half feet higher than his head. Opening his arms, Squire turned slowly. "Forty feet by eight feet by eight and a half." He slapped the flat of his hand against the nearby wall, jolting the air. "Two thousand of these babies offloaded in Charlestown every month last year. Four thousand a month next year, packed with everything from reed bathmats to sacks of coffee beans to mahogany furniture to Datsun muffler pipes to —"

"To your flower bulbs?"

"Yes. Dutch tulips. Daffodils. Hyacinths. Narcissus. Hardy bulbs, bred in ice-skating country, just right for tough New England weather. My wholesale bulb business gets bigger every year." He slapped the wall again. "I have four of these guys coming in over the next three weeks. I could sell eight. People are just catching on to bulbs. After dormancy, all they need is dirt, water, and rising temperatures, and poof! The glories of spring in your own back yard, in your windowbox. Bulbs. It's what made me see these fuckers." And once more Squire banged the wall. "Hear it?"

"What?"

Only using his knuckles now, he struck the metal again.

Tucci shook his head.

"It's hollow, Mr. Tucci. The walls of these containers are a double thickness of aluminum bolted together onto I-beams." He pointed out the ribs of the containers. "Twenty-four I-beams per container. Along each I-beam runs a hollow cavity. Here, see?" Squire knocked the metal, off the beam, then on it. The sound displayed the difference. "Each beam can take four and a half keys of packaged powder."

"Ten pounds?"

"That's right, each beam. Two hundred and forty pounds if you used every beam, which you probably —"

"Jesus Christ." Tucci put his little handbag under one arm, then ran his hand along the corrugated metal.

"Two or three special containers a week, Mr. Tucci, with these wall panels rigged to pop off. That would more than double Masio's *monthly* take at Logan — but over here you have no customs, no narcs."

"How do you know what Masio's take at Logan is?"

"I didn't read it somewhere?"

Tucci stared at Doyle. "You hold out on me, Doyle. You do it all the time."

Squire smiled that smile. "I'm showing you the future, Mr. Tucci. Two million of these containers entered the U.S. last year. Next year, four. The year after that, eight. The days of smuggling dope in suitcases in the holds of airplanes are over. There are too many of these things for the government to deal with, and even if they could, the whole point of shipping cargo like this is *not* to open them. These containers wind up everywhere, so port of entry means nothing anymore. The worst the narcs could do is spot checks, but with these mothers, even that isn't simple. There's no on-site customs here, and in this yard, not even the government can unload one of these containers, which is the first thing they'd have to do to check these walls. So they'd need trucks. They'd need an inspection site. They'd need crews. They *could* get all of that up now and then, but by the time they did, I'd know it."

"How?"

Squire went on as if he had not heard Tucci's question. "And it would be a simple matter to keep our special, one-in-a-thousand gift box on board the ship for delivery another day. Even if customs snagged one, whose name would be on it? Not yours."

"And it wouldn't be tulip bulbs."

"You can bet on that."

"An arrangement like this . . ." Tucci stopped, intensifying his stare. "I'd have to coordinate with people in New York."

"I assume that."

"They would expect me to have total control."

"You'd have that."

"And this would change your participation."

"Not much. I'm still only interested in the Town. I'd be your guy on this dock. That's all."

"So what has to happen?"

Squire looked out. The rain was just starting to fall, and with it the patter of drops hitting the metal container began, a surge of resonating noise inside the thing, like the warning clicks of a Geiger counter. Squire said, "Someone has to make the deal with the shipping company in Rotterdam. It should be you. I can introduce you to a guy from my Dutch bulb business."

"What about that other fellow?"

"Who?"

"Moran."

Squire missed a beat as he scrambled inwardly — away from a cliff was the feeling. "Moran?" He shrugged. "Quincy is not in the picture."

"The shipyard there is slated to get a crane like this."

Squire smiled. This fucker was good. "Not this year. Probably not next. If Quincy lands a crane, it'll be —"

"Moran runs the action at the shipyard. Unless I'm mistaken, your

Dutch friends had a meeting with Moran in Amsterdam. They flew him over."

"And you say *I* hold out on *you*," Squire said. "Lots of people go to Amsterdam, Mr. Tucci."

"Venlo, I should of said." Tucci paused for effect. "He had his meeting in the town of Venlo."

Doyle faced away to watch the rain fall. Jerry Moran, the fucker.

From deep in the container, from well behind Doyle, Tucci's voice resonated gravely, each word weighing more than before. "I'm not going to compete with Moran. Understand? When I go to New York with this, they'll ask me who else is on the square, and I'll have to say no one. Do you hear me?"

"Yes. I'm sure I can —"

"So kill him."

Doyle immediately faced Tucci, knowing how everything depended on the Italian's seeing his eyes at such a moment, their clarity and resolve. "That's not how I operate. I don't even own a gun."

Tucci surprised Doyle by flinging his handbag at him, that effete item of wop fashion. But instead of soft leather, it was the bulk of steel that hit Doyle's chest, and as he caught the bag, he realized what was inside. It was not a wallet but a holster.

"Now you have one. Use it."

Deebo, Squire thought. Here was the difference between Frank Tucci and old Guido. Frank uses one mick to kill another.

"I didn't hear you, Doyle."

"All right, Mr. Tucci. Whatever you say." The two men stared at each other for a long time.

Finally Tucci walked to the edge of the container, to a place next to Squire. They stood shoulder to shoulder, watching the rain collect in puddles. That close to Tucci, Squire's size bulked. But he had the feeling he was the only one of the two who knew how much bigger he was than the Italian.

Tucci was content to stand in silence for some moments before asking, "When?"

"By this time tomorrow. Jerry Moran is no friend of mine."

"You didn't answer my other question, before."

"What."

"About customs. Jumping this place, if they did. How you'd know ahead of time."

Squire laughed. "Mr. Tucci, they're all micks. Customs, FBI, DEA, the State Police Task Force — they're all my people. Your people are in the olive oil business. Mine are cops. Of course I'll know."

"That's what makes some of my friends nervous about you."

"Good," Squire said quickly, twirling the leather bag, the dead weight of it. "I like folks to be nervous about me." Then he flashed that born-to-bring-flowers smile of his. "Everyone but you."

Tucci's eyes lingered noncommittally on Doyle's bright face. Then he looked out at the rain. He turned his suit collar up. "Christ, I hate to get this suit wet."

Squire knew what he was being ordered to do, but now he did not hesitate. He took his large sweater off and draped it around Tucci's shoulders. Tucci tugged it closer, as if he had expected this, and started to go.

"One more thing, Mr. Tucci." Squire's hands were still on his shoulders, holding him. Tucci stiffened. "None of the coke stays in the Town. That rule holds."

Tucci stepped away and faced him. "You're the boss, Squire."

Doyle held up the leather bag. "Is this loaded?"

"I loaded it myself."

"Thinking you might need it here?"

Tucci stared at him for a moment, then said, "After you use it, ditch it. I'm trusting you to get rid of it."

"Don't worry, Mr. Tucci." Squire smiled. "But maybe I'll keep the bag. I don't have one this nice."

Tucci continued to stare a moment longer, then ducked out into the passing storm, cut quickly across to the turn in the maze of containers and was gone. Squire stayed where he was, listening as the roar of another airplane overwhelmed the drumming rain on the metal box.

✧

At the end of that Georgetown party where they'd first met, Joan and Terry had found themselves at the door together. She'd been the one to offer him a lift, which he accepted, as if he did not have his own car parked farther down the same block. He found himself in the passenger seat of a churning Austin-Healey, in British racing green, the top down, though it was January. The low-slung headlights split the night. Joan's profile was backlit by the illuminated marble walls of the Kennedy Center. As the car whipped past Watergate, and as he saw her face outlined against the shimmering Lincoln Memorial, for once the sight of that Ionic temple did not make him think of Didi.

After that, Terry had often pictured Joan barreling down Pennsylvania Avenue from the Corcoran, beyond the White House. From the west parapet of the Capitol, where he usually waited, he could spot her half a mile away. When her car disappeared into the fold of trees just below, he would take off full tilt for the other side, to be there when she pulled up. The sports car fit her like an item of apparel, and her face was never more its vibrant self than when framed by the short, desert-colored feathers of her windblown hair. When the car stopped, her hair always fell instantly into place.

When he married Joan Littel, he married the Healey too. He grew accustomed to himself as a man who rode shotgun, although not on that Saturday in Boston. He would drive because this was his town, and his return. By the time they left the house, the noontime showers had passed, and though the streets were still wet and the sky cluttered, there was no question of not folding back the top.

Terry gunned down the length of Memorial Drive, along Cambridge Parkway, and up onto a new sleek bridge that took them from Cambridge into the Town, above the rail yards and the Flat. Terry repeatedly slapped the wooden knob of the gearshift, clutching, revving the engine, going home. The new bridge meant that Charlestown wasn't Charlestown anymore, but that was all right. Terry Doyle wasn't Terry Doyle either.

At the grubby projects, the three-square-block, whites-only housing complex that served as the Town's west wall, Terry slowed the car. His eyes went by chance to a particular window in the nearest building, and he saw the pale face of a child staring out at them. As the child dropped from sight, Terry glanced at Joan. She had seen it too, and he felt her pang for the tyke, whose misery was quickly conveyed by the sagging chain-link fences and yellowed undershirts flapping on a clothesline. Terry said, "You should have seen the tenements those projects replaced. Toilets in the back yard, right behind the prison where Sacco and Vanzetti died."

"Really?" Joan said, but with a flat, noncommittal voice.

"There used to be a Flying Horse gas station on the corner."

Vacant lots separated lone storefronts, several of which were bars: Pat's, O'Grady's. Their doors were open, offering glimpses of permanently shadowed interiors. He sensed her registering the sudden stink of stale beer, and he said, "The true Celtic Twilight."

He turned onto Main Street, squealing rubber. Marked by stanchions of the el, the street jogged right a few blocks along, into City

Square. A large, pillared bank building anchored one corner; on another were the courthouse and the police station.

Joan pointed at the courthouse and Terry said, "The site of the original settlement of Boston, John Winthrop's —"

"Look, Terry. What's that?"

On the top floor of the courthouse, letters blanked out each of the row of windows, spelling out the word NEVER!

"Well, *I* never," Joan said.

Terry felt a bolt of anger, but channeled it into his driving, taking the next corner too fast. On Warren Street he continued to accelerate most of the way to St. Mary's, where he swung right again. He could have climbed this hill blind.

He turned onto Monument Square, their first view of the great obelisk. "Bunker Hill," he said, slowing. "The hallowed American shrine, 'degraded now,' as the *Globe* so eloquently put it this morning, 'by misguided and self-appointed defenders of the notorious high school.' *Le voilà.*"

The high school rose ahead, dominating the northwest corner of the square, the same old granite hulk. A single glimpse called the place fully to mind, because what his eyes went to were the seven false columns embedded in the façade above the otherwise undistinguished entrance. Eventually those columns — like the stucco-and-beam Tudor façades on Sullivan Square taverns and the marbleized Con-Tact paper on kitchen counters and the wire-propped shamrocks that his grandfather fashioned — symbolized all that he'd wanted to leave behind. No matter that, much later, he had taken the Gothic turrets of Boston College, the reforms of Vatican II, and the high-mindedness of the Kennedys as absolutely authentic.

The bone-white flagpole flew nothing but its ropes. The multiple windows had always been filthy, but the view they offered had nevertheless drawn his constant gaze. He remembered being yanked back from the rooftops of the city by the clang of the period bell. He remembered crowds surging in the corridors, locker doors slamming, the pungent stale air pouring off the bodies of kids who should have been his friends.

FUCK THE TPF, read one sign that the wind had plastered against a fence. POWDER KEG FOREVER! read another. Terry slowed almost to a stop. "Imagine going to war over that sad place."

"What year were you?"

"Nineteen sixty." He pointed to a row of dreary brick houses down the block. "When I was a kid, we thought those places were mansions, but Jesus." What dumps they seemed now, with flaking shutters, sagging bay windows, decked with hand-lettered signs. *Never! Resist! Go Townies!*

Terry stopped the car without pulling over. His memory supplied a set of tastes and aromas: cabbage, talc, stale tea, egg salad, the smell of Borkham Riff tobacco. Once he'd loved everything about life inside those houses. Now the houses themselves seemed utterly grief stricken.

"Look at those signs," Joan said.

But Terry's eyes were drawn by boys coming out of the variety store where he too had gone, though in his day for Pez and finger-size wax bottles of red, green, or orange sugar water. Three kids, no four, moved onto the sidewalk like heavy machines. They wore caps and sneakers and trousers about to be outgrown and identical school jackets, the white leather sleeves, red bodies, football emblems on their breasts. Linemen. The sports car had drawn their attention.

Terry put the car in gear and turned the corner, past the high school, away from the boys. They took the next turn easily, onto the fourth side of the square, the front of the park. "I want to show you something." He pulled over, shut the engine off, opened his door, and, before Joan could react, went around to her door. He held his hand out. "Close your eyes."

"What?"

"Close your eyes. I want to surprise you."

"No way."

"Come on, Joan. Really." He took her hand and pulled gently. She swung her legs out and stood. "Close them," he said.

She was wearing a trim tweed jacket over her jeans and sweater. "You're asking me to trust you, is that it?"

"Exactly."

She slipped her arm inside his and closed her eyes. She allowed him to lead her across the street and onto the stairs that led up into the park. "Watch it here," he said.

"How can I watch it if my eyes are closed?" She laughed and leaned into him.

"There are maybe twenty stairs going up. Twenty-five. Careful here, it curves. And a railing is on your right now, if you want."

She squeezed against him. "Who needs a railing? But you better get me there. Three minutes of trusting and I start to feel dizzy."

"I've noticed."

"What is this, Outward Bound?"

"Just a bit further . . . across here . . . just a little further."

"Terry, really . . . this is . . ."

"We're almost there." He had taken her to the base of the stone monument, and now he turned her so that she stood with her back to it, at the bench to which he had always gone. "Now," he said. "Now open."

She did, and her mind reeled at what she saw. Muscular clouds of the passing rain marched across the sky, but her eyes went right to the spine of the strange city, Oz, at her feet. "Oh, it's close!"

"Ain't it beautiful?"

"But it's . . . it's . . ." She hesitated, then saw what made the view strange. "It's reversed!" The familiar Custom House and State Street Bank were in the foreground, a switch with the gleaming Hancock tower. "The skyline is backwards from here."

"Maybe it's backwards from Cambridge," he said, but he was moved by her readiness to lose her breath to a view he loved. "This is where I used to come as a kid. Boston seemed so close from here. Everything seemed possible."

"Everything *was* possible, sugar." She leaned against him once more.

"I love this city."

"But you moved away. You love it as something you can't have."

Terry laughed. "Which is *why* I love it. I only love what I can't have."

"But you have me."

"The exception that proves the rule?"

"And since that's what I am, I give this to you." She tossed her free arm at the skyline. "I let you have it, finally."

"'All of this I lay before you.'"

"What?"

"The Devil, to Jesus, when he took him up the mountain and showed him the world. A temptation."

"Well, when you get to be Jesus, you can start worrying about it. Meanwhile, the city's yours."

His gaze went back to the side wall of the high school. NEVER! he read. The Irish Nazis. For a moment that wall seemed to be falling toward him, but that was an effect of the clouds soaring by behind.

"If I want it."

"Yes, if you want it."

Joan set off down the steps toward the car. He lit a cigarette, cupping the match against the harbor breeze, inhaling deeply but tasting nothing. Then he followed.

What he saw, over the lip of the hill, stopped him. The four boys from the variety store were in, and on, the Healey, one in each seat, the others lounging on the fenders. Joan had stopped dead where she had registered the sight, and now she turned toward Terry. He skipped down the stairs. "Wait here," he said, passing her.

But she didn't. She followed closely behind, as far as the curb. As he crossed the street toward the car, she cried after him, "Call the police!"

What, the TPF?

He put his weed between his lips, grinning at the boys as if glad to see them. Do this like a coach, he told himself. "What say, guys? Pretty nice wheels, huh?"

"Brit piece of shit," the boy in the driver's seat said, and he sent a wad of spit shooting past Terry's feet. A trail of saliva fell across the side of the car. The others laughed.

"Brit? Don't you know what this is? Austin-Healey, see there?" When the punks turned to look at the medallion on the steering wheel, Doyle sensed his power. They are children, he told himself. "Healey is as Irish as we are. Healey owns the company. The Irish are very proud of this car. That's why most of the models you see are green."

The two on the fenders exchanged a wary glance, but the boy at the wheel, with a malevolent eye, said, "We was going to go for a ride." Earlier Terry had made them for linemen, but this kid had the confidence of a ball carrier. There was something familiar about the way his close-cropped head rode on his shoulders, like a pumpkin on a board.

"I'd love to let you go for a ride, but I'm not insured for it."

"You're insured for theft, aren't you?" The boy on the rear fender grinned at the others.

Terry held out his cigarette pack. "Have a smoke, fellows. Let it go at that."

"Give us the key, mister. This car don't belong in Charlestown. We'll take it out for you."

"You going to loop it?"

"You know about looping?"

"Yeah, I know about it." Terry leaned toward the driver and read the name on his jacket. "'Boss.' What are you boss of? The Town bullshit factory?"

The boy on the rear fender pulled his hand from his pocket, producing a switchblade. He flicked it open. "Hey, O'Keefe, the bullshit factory. How did this jerkoff know?" The boy buried the blade in the folds of the automobile top, teasing it, but not puncturing the canvas yet.

Terry ignored the knife. O'Keefe? The name was what, without knowing it, he'd been hoping for. He opened the driver's door. "Get out of the car, kids, before you have a problem you don't want."

"Fuck you, mister." The boy with the knife jerked forward. "This fucking car belongs to a friend of ours. He asked us to watch it for him."

"That so? Was he going to pay you to make sure nobody cut a hole in the top?"

"Yeah, I guess he was."

"Twenty bucks?" Doyle read the kid's name. "Twenty bucks, Jimbo?"

"Thirty. I think he said thirty." Jimbo pulled the knife free of the canvas, and he fingered the blade.

Terry looked at the driver, O'Keefe. That stump of a neck, and now with that name, what Doyle saw was not a pumpkin but a helmet banging against the knees of an enemy tackle. Keefe O'Keefe, All-City fullback, '58 and '59. Terry shook his head. "Does Keefe O'Keefe know that his son hangs out with a two-bit, penny-ante extortionist? Not to mention your mother. The Lindy O'Keefe I know would have you by that cauliflower ear and out of here by now."

Boss O'Keefe seemed to shrink into the leather. The years dropped away until he was ten, maybe five. Terry made one last offer of a cigarette, which now the kid took. Terry lit it for him. The boy winced at the rough French smoke and stared at it.

Terry turned to the others. "Put the knife away, Jimbo, before you cut yourself."

"Where's my twenty bucks?"

"Is that what I tell *your* mother?"

"You don't know my mother."

"I don't?"

"Anyways, you said twenty bucks."

"Me? That was your *friend*. What *I'm* saying, Jimbo, and I'm saying it to you, Boss, and to you" — he read their names — "Chuck and Chris, is that if you beat it now, I won't tell your mothers what you tried to do here."

"Hey." Boss swung his legs out of the car. "If you would of said before you was a Townie. We just never saw the fucking car before."

The others followed O'Keefe in backing away. One waved at Joan, to let her know they'd been aware of her throughout. "Hiya, doll!"

They curled into a knot and sauntered up the sidewalk. Joan joined Terry, watching them. "Well. Good old boys, even here."

"They're just kids. They don't know if they're coming or going."

"Meanwhile, they've got knives."

Terry shrugged sadly. She crossed to the far side of the car. He got in, started the engine, pulled into the street and away from the monument. Joan looked up at it, but saw instead the oddly slanted telephone poles just there, the tangle of wires — the sort of machine mess that was rarely seen anymore elsewhere in the city.

13

TERRY WENT RIGHT on Winthrop Street, onto a downhill slope. Ahead was the tidy Common with its Civil War statue. Terry stopped on Adams Street to say something about the Town as an abolitionist stronghold. Before he could begin, the car was suddenly bumped from behind.

Joan yelped, a breach of her composure which, as much as the jolt, brought her anger up. She whipped around. A battered tank of a car — a Buick, an Oldsmobile, something — had slammed into them.

Two men sat grinning. Joan's eyes went to the tiny figure on their dashboard, one of those creepy religious statues. On the snout of the hood, a red and blue metal plate had been wired to the grill, a Confederate flag.

Terry got out of the car, then she did. He was more rigidly in control than ever, but she was ready to explode. Like a pair of adjusters they checked for damage, bending over the sleek rear of the car. In the four years Joan had owned it, the Healey had never been so much as dented, and to her horror now, she felt pressure building behind her eyes. But despite the disparity in the bulk of the two cars, and because the Healey's bumper had been mounted high to meet import specs, the force of the collision had gone harmlessly into the steel designed to take it. Neither vehicle showed damage.

The Buick driver leaned out the window. "Sorry about that!" Then his companion appeared out the other side. Each wore a tweed cap above a happy flushed face. "Yeah, we're sorry."

In Virginia, that they were drunk would have increased the air of menace, but here their condition defused it. Civil rights marches at bus terminals and rural courthouses were a lifetime ago, and the gutsy, sandaled art history major who'd thrown herself into them so boldly seemed another person altogether. Joan told herself that these two men who'd so startled her were buffoons like the schoolboys had been.

Terry called across to her, "Let's go, Joan. Back in the car."

At the wheel again, Terry jumped the light and squealed into a turn. "I'll show you the loop," he said, hitting the gas. He wanted her to think the rushing engine and the recklessness were reflections of his mental state, but in fact he was so inwardly composed that he was afraid to show her. "The idea was to dare the cops to chase you."

The car shot up the street, past the blurred rectangles of windows, doors, and slanted storefronts. Joan looked back once, quickly, to be sure the bloated car with the plastic Jesus had not followed.

Just shy of Sullivan Square, before looping back on Bunker Hill Street, Terry forced a grin. "So what do you think so far, of my hometown?"

"What can I say?"

"John Harvard lived here."

"What?"

"Honest to God. Your guy, John Harvard, one of the first Townies."

"Did he loop the loop?" she asked. All at once, Joan laughed heartily. Terry joined her. They threw their heads back into the wind.

This was the street Terry had used a million times, coming and going from the basketball court. On his bike, to ease the burden of the hill, he'd hook onto the rear door straps of Edison trucks and haul along behind without the driver seeing him. Now he was a driver with no need of eyes. Unlike other parts of Charlestown, a version of this stretch between the playground and the monument was still duplicated somewhere inside him. Even blind, he could tick off Dick Ballard's house, Tom Foley's, Sean Nutley's, and then Mary Ellen Guiney's. She was the first girl he'd ever looked at *as* a girl, and at her door, at the crest of the hill, instinctively he shifted, the way, as a boy, he'd let go of the truck just there, to coast. The momentum brought him into Monument Square again, the completed loop. "And no arrest!" he yelped in triumph, and he honked three times, according to the old rubric.

Terry took the downhill slope out of the square fast, angling right, to the Common again. His eyes went automatically the full length of the block to the large brown clapboard three-decker that dominated the next corner. Kerry Bouquet had a bright new sign, and the display windows were twice as large as when Terry had last been here.

He exhaled a whistle.

"What?"

"That's it." They slowed down. The windows were gaily filled with flowers and foliage, and on the sidewalk potted mums were tiered, bright yellows, the glitter of aluminum foil. On the second and third floors of the house, impressive corner bay windows rode above the street and the Common beyond like twin bridges above the deck of a ship.

Terry pointed to the other windows. "They have air conditioners."

The lace curtains in the bay windows struck Joan, the Irish cliché of them. The house had a surprising dignity, but she could not see it as having anything to do with her husband; that is, with her. As much to deflect the complicated feelings as because it struck her then, she pointed to a school building on the far side of the Common. "What's that?"

"St. Mary's, the parish school." It too was closed, but someone had draped its fence with a long banner made of several bedsheets pinned together. *Rally at City Hall*, it read, *Monday at 11. Resist!*

"Resist," Joan repeated dully. "As if this were France."

Terry turned back toward the store. The place looked good, a prosperous island of happiness. His heart flew to the bay window on the second floor, what had been his mother's room. He half expected her to appear, staring down at the green sports car, her hand jumping to her mouth when she recognized him. He felt the old sadness, and wanted to turn to Joan and say, If I have anything to give you, it comes from her.

"It looks okay," he said, "doesn't it?"

"Yes, sugar. It looks nice."

At the corner Terry stopped the car. He looked left, up the hill toward Monument Square again. Every street in this part of Charlestown led to the obelisk. On the next corner, just shy of the square, was a proud Victorian mansion with a mansard roof, a carriage house, and a large yard that ran down to the narrow alley, Monument Court, that separated the place from Kerry Bouquet. It was one of the finest houses in the Town, built by a Yankee merchant just before the famine wave of immigration overtook Boston — and the Irish overtook Charlestown — more than a century before. By Terry's time, the mansion had long served as the convent for the two dozen nuns who staffed St. Mary's school. The carriage house had become a storage barn for disused pieces of school furniture. Terry had grown up regarding it as a privilege to live half a block from the nuns. His first association with the wealth such a grand and well-maintained house implied had been with the Church.

But now his eyes were drawn to something else entirely, an object hanging from a jury-rigged beam projecting from the peaked eave of the carriage house. The beam was, effectively, a gallows. Dangling from it, twisting gently, was a dark-suited human figure, head in a noose, bent at its broken neck. Its shoes were perhaps a dozen feet above the sidewalk.

The car was not moving, yet Doyle's impulse was to throw an arm across his wife's chest, to protect her in the crash. Crash? What he wanted was to throw his arm over her eyes so she wouldn't see the fucking thing.

He touched the gas to pull through the intersection, to the curb by the flower shop. He pulled on the brake, opened his door, and got out. He walked up the incline in the middle of the street, his eyes fast upon the effigy. The figure had no face, just a white sack unevenly stuffed. With rags? Drawing nearer, he saw a rough sign pinned to the chest. *This Judge Loved Niggers*, he read. And a tag attached to the figure's ankle added, *WAG*. W. Arthur Garrity.

He might have insisted to Joan that nothing could have shocked him more than this, but then Terry saw something else. The suit in which the effigy had been dressed was made of plain black flannel. The trouser cuffs were thick. The middle of three buttons on the coat was missing, and so were both buttons on the right sleeve. It was the suit he'd worn himself, *his* suit, when he'd first entered the seminary.

He went to the large double doors of the carriage house. Buildings like this along Brattle Street in Cambridge had been quainted up, and such doors, if they survived at all, did so as decoration. But these doors were unrenovated, badly in need of paint and new hinges. When Terry kicked them, the doors bounced. The quartet of cloudy glass oblongs rattled in their frames. Chunks of dried putty flew.

Moments later, a small pedestrian door on the side opened. Joan had to crane back to see as a young man in a tattered tweed jacket stepped out onto the sidewalk. He cradled in the angle of his arm what she took at first to be a pipe wrench, but then recognized as some kind of gun.

Terry saw it too, and froze.

The man was tall, gaunt, and icily calm, as if he'd stepped into the street to watch the color change in Joan's face.

A car approached quietly from the square. Joan glanced at the driver, but as he passed he was staring straight ahead. Once beyond them, he sped up, was gone. Terry had yet to move, and Joan, since she could not see his face, was unsure of him. "Terry," she said, despising the weakness in her voice, the fear. He ignored her, and so did the man with the gun.

The weight of the moment shifted as the large double doors swung open, apparently by themselves, revealing a swept garage room with a couch and two old wing chairs on one side and a long library table on the other. In each of two corners stood a flag on its staff, an eagle-tipped spear. One was the red-white-and-blue, the other the Irish green-and-gold. The table held stacks of folders and pamphlets. In the middle of the room was a card table at which four young men had been seated, but now they were standing, still startled, at their chairs. This table was littered with playing cards, poker chips, a pile of dollar bills, and a small forest of beer bottles. The men were dressed in blue jeans, sweatshirts, sneakers, or work boots. Two wore caps. A cigarette stuck to the lips of one.

A fifth man stepped out from behind one of the double doors, and from behind the other, like the star showing himself only once the stage is set, came a policeman.

Joan felt the pressure in her chest break. The sight of the blue uniform, the shiny buttons, the badge — what a relief! She almost cried out to him, and in fact involuntarily pointed at the man on the sidewalk with the gun. But they were not looking at her. They were looking at Terry.

"Hey, Charlie," the policeman said. "Long time no see."

Charlie? Had he called Terry Charlie?

"Hello, Jackie."

Even in those two meager words there was something in Terry's voice Joan had never heard before — not defiance, but a kind of hollowness, the sound of a stone which, dropped in a well, finally hits not water but other stones. She was so far outside the scene unfolding before her that she might have been watching a movie.

The policeman was grinning at Terry.

Terry said, "You joined the state cops. I heard that."

"You heard right."

Terry gestured at the others. "So what are you doing here with these —"

"These are my deputies, Charlie. Right, fellas?" Mullen laughed. "The Charlestown Marshals, to be precise."

Joan couldn't take her eyes off him, his size, his cocky fluidity, the brightness in his face that she recognized as slight drunkenness.

"You're a disgrace, Jackie," Terry said.

Mullen laughed again. "To who? You? I got news for you, Charlie. We're winning. We're protecting our neighborhood. Right, fellas?"

"Jackie, Jesus Christ, what are you talking about? With a lynching? You're a cop."

"I don't appear in public. The boys —"

"'Our neighborhood'? You said 'our neighborhood'? Our neighborhood stood for something decent. Not cops meeting behind closed doors with thugs."

The man with the gun, a sawed-off shotgun, stepped forward. "Who the fuck do you — ?"

"Back off, Brownie," Mullen said sharply.

Terry pointed at the man, as Joan had done, and said to Mullen, "You're a cop and you let a weapon like that in sight of the monument? You're protecting the neighborhood? Is that what the Marshals are, punks with shotguns?"

Joan rose in her seat. She wanted to warn Terry, to dampen his fierceness. His authority had cut through the alcohol buzz of the clubhouse, seizing their attention, but the men looked dangerous.

Terry stepped toward Mullen, a fist raised. "Tell him to put the gun away, Jackie."

Mullen jerked his thumb at the man, who glowered as he turned and reentered the side door, closing it. The stairs there led up to a loft.

"Do the nuns let you use this place?"

A question that made no sense to Joan.

But Mullen laughed hard. "Goddamn, Charlie, you *have* been gone, haven't you? The convent's sold. This isn't the Sisters' anymore. This place is Squire's, Charlie. This *and* the convent building. Squire lives on the corner now." Mullen pointed toward the old mansion. Then he let his arm sweep to the boys behind him. "Say hello to Squire's brother, fellas. Except he doesn't even know where Squire lives."

"Doesn't know shit from a shingle," one of the others said with unconvincing toughness.

Terry made a show of looking them over. "These are kids, Jackie. You could have made a difference to them. You still could. Somebody's going to get killed over here before this thing is over."

"That's probably true, Charlie." Mullen leaned in on Terry. "You still work for Kennedy?"

"Yes."

Mullen poked Terry's chest. "Then you tell the senator that. *You* tell the *Globe* and your fucking federal judge. You be our messenger. 'Somebody's going to get killed.' Fucking A, Charlie. Fucking A."

"Yeah," one of the men said, "the next nigger that comes into the Town."

"Even if it's a second grader?"

"A spade's a spade, Charlie. We didn't start this, did we, fellas?" Mullen turned for his echo of "Fuck no"s, but now his friends weren't looking at him. The eyes of the card players had gone to a point in the street beyond.

Terry sensed it before Jackie did, but Terry was slow to turn. He was the last to see Nick. The first had been Joan. She had glimpsed him in the rear-view mirror as he'd come out of the flower shop and loped up the slight incline to a point behind the car that seemed prearranged, so centered in the mirror was he. Though they'd never met, she knew him at once, the hairline and the chin, the large eyebrows, the loose, athlete's posture, the walk with a hand sunk into his pocket, purposeful but unhurried. With his other hand he held a wrapped plant, a lavender cone in the cradle of his arm. From the way he carried himself, he might almost have been her husband.

"Hello, Terry." The calm in Terry's brother's voice made Joan realize how shrill the exchanges up till now had been.

He looked toward her. Their eyes did not come close to meeting in the small circle of the mirror. He had no idea she'd been studying him. "And this must be Joan."

He disappeared from the mirror, then came up beside the car. She looked up at him.

He smiled warmly. "Do you know who I am?"

"You're Nick."

"I finally get to meet you." He half bowed, and she had no idea how to respond.

Squire gestured at the others, spoke from where he stood, and quickly the large doors of the carriage house were closed, with Mullen and the Marshals shut up once more inside. Terry and Squire faced each other from opposite sides of the sports car, Joan small between them.

"What's going on here, Nick?"

Squire shook his head sadly, glancing up at the dangling effigy. "I'm sorry you came upon it this way, before I could explain. I can see why you're upset." His voice was higher than Terry's, his Boston accent sharper, but those differences were small, and Joan realized for the first time that her husband had consciously worked to lower his voice and round out his way of pronouncing vowels. The brother's calmness, and the contrast with Terry's furious agitation, made her think for a bizarre moment that this was Terry's father, not his younger sibling. His arrival would make all that had just happened seem like the roughhousing of maladjusted children.

But these two men had no father. Joan knew what a wall that lack had erected in Terry, what she had yet to get through. Now she sensed that that wall stood between the brothers too.

"You own the carriage house now?" Terry said. "You let them use it?"

"I do, yes." Squire looked down at Joan, as if she were the one to whom he owed this explanation. Already, and implicitly, he was conveying a basic self-acceptance that she had never sensed in Terry. "It's a way to keep the lid on. This is bad, you could say grotesque, even." He meant the effigy. "But at least it's not a human being. These kids would be out of control if Jackie wasn't riding them. Now they're a club." He looked up at Terry. "You remember how we like a nice club in the Town. But let's drop this nonsense. You didn't come over here to —"

"Jackie Mullen is playing with fire in there. And he wouldn't do it unless you gave him the matches."

"Relax, Terry. Jackie's been assigned over here by Community Affairs. As a local guy, he can help keep the peace. Don't be so thick."

"His punk had a sawed-off shotgun just now."

"There's no pin in that gun, Terry. We let Brownie carry it so he won't get something that shoots." Squire shifted the plant to his other arm, with no more thought for it than a delivery man would have had. He was all patience now, patience with the juvenile delinquents, patience with his forever uptight brother.

"The Marshals are a safety valve, don't you see? We're a step ahead of violence over here, no thanks to the Boston cops, or to the court, or to the mayor, or for that matter to the liberals who keep urging us to be peaceful. What do they expect, we should get these sixteen-year-olds to hold hands and sing 'We Shall Overcome'? It's *their* high school that's been hijacked. That is point number one." Squire looked at Joan again, seeming to expect a signal of her support.

He said, "These kids are pissed off, and I don't blame them. Jackie has them organized into squads 'protecting the Town,' when what they'd really like to do is storm over to the Berry and burn crosses up and down Blue Hill Ave. Instead, they patrol Old Ironsides and Bunker Hill. Where's the harm? Playing with fire? Colored people have torched whole cities with less provocation than we've had. All we do is yell at buses and lynch dummies. The kids are right to string up

Garrity. He's punishing the Irish for embarrassing his good friend and yours, Kennedy. The kids know what we all know — we're being screwed." Squire paused. When Terry did not react, he added, "I would expect you to understand, and give some clue to Kennedy."

Terry exchanged a glance with Joan: Everybody wants me to talk to Ted. He said, "What I understand, Nick, is that children are being terrorized."

"Yes, *our* children. So what if they hang out in the carriage house drinking beer and saying 'Fuck the judge!' I say it too. Fuck the judge!" To Joan he said, "Excuse me."

"I've heard the word before." It hit Joan at once — what a strange statement with which to introduce herself.

"I'm surprised," Squire said.

"Don't be." There was an explicit daring in her voice.

And with an air of display, she brought her legs together, her close-fitting jeans emphasizing her slender thighs. Squire sensed that she was aware of his abrupt interest in her body. She would take it as a victory, and he would let her.

She never lowered her eyes from his. He knew a warning flag when it was waved in his face. And he understood now that his brother's built-in uneasiness had wrapped itself around her. Terry's marriage had him in over his head. Squire liked her.

"Joan," he said with unforced sincerity, "I'm sorry this is how we finally meet. You are very welcome here, and I want you to see our good side." He flashed a smile. "We've all been wanting Terry to bring you over."

"That wasn't my impression, frankly. I wrote your grandfather last year, and then again when we were moving up here. He never answered."

"Letters are not in Gramps's bag of tricks, Joan. But I wasn't thinking of him." Squire looked forlorn. "He's in his own world. I was thinking of myself and Didi, and of our kids. Come on. Let's go up to the house."

Terry hooked his thumb back toward the flower store, the old house. "I want to check in with Gramps."

Squire turned toward his brother. "He lives with me, Terry. You think I'd move without him?"

The brothers held each other's eyes for a long, hard moment. Finally Terry, like an older brother yielding authority, said, "Okay, kid. Lead the way."

They left the hanging effigy and the carriage house behind. Joan drove up to the corner and pulled to the curb while the men followed on foot.

"You might want to put the top up," Squire said to her.

Joan gave Terry an anxious look.

Squire saw it and laughed. "Because of the rain," he said, "not the kids. It might rain again."

"The car's okay here, Joan," Terry said. They both pulled the canvas top up. "In front of Nick's house we're safe." He glanced at his brother. "Joan has a serious commitment to her car."

"I like a serious commitment."

When Joan joined him on the sidewalk, Squire surprised her by crooking his free elbow at her. "Madam? Allow me." He was an Irish tenant suddenly, receiving the lady from the big house. "Welcome to our wee abode."

Joan put her hand inside Nick's arm, surprised at how natural it seemed to do so. Who is this man? As she walked in step with him, she looked over at Terry, who faced away.

The Victorian house dominated the corner near the crest of the hill, just below tidy Monument Square. Joan and Squire took the stairs up to the house like dance partners.

The door was framed by leaded glass side panels. The doorbell was a knob, which Squire pulled. He opened the door, pulling the bell again.

Joan hung back to wait for Terry, drawing a plastic bag out of her purse and handing it to him. They heard the thud of footsteps and the squeals of children. Two boys and a girl appeared, swirling around Squire, with a chorus of "Daddy! Daddy!" that seemed remarkably unstaged.

One child, the smallest but stoutest one, a somewhat pasty-faced boy, clung to Squire's leg. The other boy grabbed on, crying, "Troll! Troll!"

"Oh, you got me!" Squire reached out to put the wrapped plant on a hall table, then rubbed the child's head. "But look who's here, kids. Your Uncle Terry!"

Only the girl said, "Hi, Uncle Terry."

Terry hugged her, then knelt on the polished wood floor of the foyer. He opened the bag and emptied it of a dozen different wind-up toys, all animals of various colors. He cranked each, and soon they were scurrying in chaotic circles at everyone's feet. The children hopped with delight.

As Terry straightened up, his brother stooped to play. One boy, then the other, pushed at Squire as he laughed like a kid, sending first a dinosaur on its way, then a croc.

Joan winked at Terry.

A woman appeared across the foyer, beside an ornately carved bench below a tall gilded mirror. She was large, older than Joan, dressed in flowing white pants, a white Mexican wedding shirt, and sandals. Next to her a spiraling staircase drew Joan's eyes up to a glittering brass and crystal chandelier. On a stand beside the staircase was a French bouquet. The woman seemed too composed, and her setting too elegant, to have anything to do with the horseplay at the door.

Squire began extricating himself, but the children were not stopping. The older boy wrestled his sister down. "Jackie," the girl cried. "Stop it, Jackie!"

The boy went limp, pinning her with dead weight as the last of the animals wound down. The children became still.

"Hello," the woman said, walking toward Joan. She stepped around the children, her hand extended. "I'm the mommy troll."

"Hi," said Joan uncertainly.

"Also known as Deirdre. Didi." She turned to Terry and very simply opened her arms. "Hi, doll. Where the hell have you been?"

Terry said, "We'd have brought you flowers, but —"

"I know, I know." Didi winked at Joan from inside Terry's arms. "He was my first boyfriend," she said. "His flowers ruined me. So I had to marry into the family." She had a long face, a too prominent nose and chin, overly styled red hair, yet there was something surprisingly attractive about her, particularly in white as she was, like a figure from an art magazine.

Joan surprised herself by picking up the remark. "Well, he's my last boyfriend — and he *never* brings me flowers."

"I spare them for your sake," Terry said.

As Didi stepped back, Joan slid her arm inside Terry's. "But you're my last beau, aren't you, sugar?"

"You're from the South?" Didi blurted. "Nobody ever told me you're from the South."

Joan mugged, "Look away, Dixieland."

Didi moved to Joan's other side. "Oh, we're going to like you. Aren't we, kids? And here are the trolls. Say hello, you little monsters."

"Hi," the smallest said, the only one to look up. He was a freckle-faced charmer, about five, with a head full of red curls. His thumb dove into his mouth.

"Get up, Jackie," the girl said to the older boy.

"No!" the boy said, too loudly.

Joan and Terry retreated a step.

"Ease off, Jackie," Squire said, bending to take the boy's elbow.

"No!"

"Game's over, Jackie." Squire took both his arms, pulling him up.

"Goddamnit, let go of me!"

"Jackie —"

"No, goddamnit! Goddamnit!"

Such defiant rage in a boy of perhaps seven made Joan look again at the flaccid body, the pinched asymmetry of his face, eyes askew, nose wedge-shaped, mouth curled, skin aflame. He was in the grip of a merciless emotional derangement. He was retarded.

Joan glanced at Terry, whose eyes widened, which only made Joan angry: Why don't I know about this?

Didi joined Squire in holding Jackie, who continued to scream and flail his arms.

Joan felt a crushing claustrophobia, the only way panic ever overtook her. But the boy's parents, embracing him jointly, controlling him, responded with complete calm. Didi softly repeated his name, "Jackie, Jackie, Jackie," a mantra, all the while rubbing his back, while Squire closed him in the full circle of his arms, firmly and tenderly.

In a minute the storm passed. The boy relaxed between the woman in white clothes and the man in dark. The three were still.

Joan was surprised to realize that she herself was leaning against Terry, inside his arm. What, she wondered, had this scene to do with the snarling, anti-busing mob at Charlestown High School? She wanted to apologize to Didi and Nick for witnessing what was far too intimate — not their son's outburst, but the unfettered kindness with which they'd soothed him.

When at last Didi stepped back from Jackie and opened her arms to the other two children, they each took a place at her side, near the beautiful French bouquet. Didi said, "Kids, this is your Aunt Joan."

Joan nearly gasped to hear herself referred to in that way. Before she could respond, yet another child appeared from the hallway beyond the staircase, a barefoot two-year-old in a T-shirt and diaper, clutching a fistful of Cheerios. Behind her came a young woman holding a wailing infant.

"Ah, good. Good!" Didi clapped her hands, then threw them wide. "The holy family. We're all here now. Thanks, Teresa." She took the baby and nuzzled him. The young woman withdrew with the trained deference of a mother's helper. Squire stood with an arm around Jackie and an eye on the others. The expression on his face was what struck Joan most, the vivid love.

Didi invited Joan and Terry to follow her into the kitchen. The kids dropped back to wind up the toys as the adults trooped toward the rear of the house, past a spacious living room with floor-to-ceiling windows and a satiny grand piano, and an oval library the walls of which were lined with books. Joan glimpsed a rolling ladder, which emphasized the height of the ceiling.

The doorway at the end of the foyer led into a narrow corridor that twisted around into a pantry, and then into a large, cheerful kitchen which, with its bright appliances, crisp white Scandinavian cabinets, stainless steel sink, and Marimekko curtains, suggested *Architectural Digest*. This was the house of a wealthy family. Not Charlestown, Joan thought, but Georgetown.

Didi handed the baby back to her helper, saying as she did, "This is Teresa, who keeps me sane. Don't you, Teresa?"

"You call this sane?" Squire said happily, bringing up the rear. "How about a drink?"

"I'd like to see Gramps," Terry said.

"And I'd like to meet him." Joan was still at Terry's side.

Squire studied them for a moment before saying, "Sure, sure."

Didi moved to a counter spread with tomatoes, and began slicing.

Joan said, "I'll come back and help."

Didi smiled, reached for a nearby glass of wine, and raised it toward Joan before sipping.

Squire led them to the staircase. "There's an elevator in back," he said, "but maybe you'd like to see the house." They climbed all the way to the fifth floor. The entire place had been restored: the rosewood banisters, the oval stained-glass windows, the plaster moldings on the walls and ceilings. The staircase was carpeted with a long runner, an oriental with threads that sparkled in the illumination of the skylight. The higher they climbed, the more light there was.

At a landing, Joan leaned to Terry and whispered, "You said they lived above the flower store. Who *are* these people?"

"Good question," he replied, but so coldly her next thought was, Who are you?

At the top of the stairs, without pausing for breath, Squire knocked softly on a closed door. "This is his apartment."

There was a muffled word. Squire pushed the door open. They entered a cozy sitting room with slanted ceilings meeting in a peak. A television in the corner was tuned to a baseball game, but the volume was off. In the other corner, on an oval table, sat a stunning flowering plant. Because the blossom was black, it took Joan a moment to realize it was an orchid.

An old man was sitting in a wheelchair, staring blankly at the TV screen. He was cradling something inside his folded arms. He looked over.

Terry took Joan's hand, and they moved forward together. "Hello, Gramps," he said.

The old man smiled. "Hiya, Terry," he said casually, as if they'd last seen each other the night before.

"This is my wife, Joan."

The old man looked at her. The bright flecks in his eyes made him seem youthful. He leaned forward in his chair, as if, for a lady, he would stand. But he did not.

Once his eyes met hers, Joan saw their essential disorientation. "Hello, Mr. Cronin."

"Nice to meet Terry's wife," he said. "I want you to meet mine." He opened his arms to reveal a framed photograph of a pretty young woman. "This is Nell."

Terry saw that it was not Nell, but Flo, his mother. Not Cronin's wife, but daughter. Strangely, he felt a wash of gratitude that Joan did not know.

Joan leaned in front of Terry to kiss the old man on the silver crown of his head.

✧

A few minutes later, Joan found Didi in the dining room, another spacious room, with rich blue drapes at the windows, wood-paneled walls, silver candlesticks, mirrors, yet another bouquet giving off a lively scent. The table was set for eight, with stoneware and pewter. At two of the places were highchairs.

Entering, Joan said, "Terry and Nick are going to sit with their grandfather for a little while." Joan had a hand at her breast, pressing, as if short of breath.

Didi was placing napkins. "You're surprised?"

"I didn't know he was . . ."

"Terry hasn't told you much, has he?"

Before she answered, Joan noticed an impressionist painting above the mantel, an original work that seemed vaguely familiar. Joan drew closer to study it while Didi continued with the napkins.

"This is Manseau," Joan said.
"Yes. No one's ever known to say that before."
In the painting, three half-naked women idled in a shadowy grove, a waterfall spilling behind them against the sharp blue sky.
"The Nabis," Joan said.
"What?"
Joan faced her. "The Nabis. Manseau was a minor member of that school. Followers of Gauguin."
"I didn't know that." Didi laughed. "I just like it."
"Where did you get it, if you don't mind my asking?"
"At a place on Newbury Street."
"Vose?"
"Yes. How did you know?"
"Not that many galleries in Boston handle paintings like this."
"Oh, I just like the way the colors in the sky match my drapes."
Joan eyed Didi carefully, then smiled. "Right. Since you're a woman of no erudition or taste."
Didi laughed again. "Now you've got it. Would you like some wine?"
"Sure."
Didi moved to a side table that held an open bottle. She poured two glasses. "Red okay?"
She pulled chairs back from the table, and they sat. Joan settled in, surprised at how comfortable she felt, and how, all at once, relaxed.
Didi raised her glass. "Here's to you two, you and Terry."
The women sipped.
After a long time Joan said, "Your children are beautiful."
"Thank you."
"They keep you busy."
Didi shrugged. "As you can tell, birth control was Terry's issue, not mine."
"What?"
"He didn't tell you about his famous stand on birth control?" Didi said. "Against the cardinal, what made him leave."
Joan shook her head. "No, no. He didn't. He never . . ." Her voice drifted off. She had no idea what to say.
Didi drained her glass. "School," she said, pouring again, "is where I knew Terry."
"He told me."
Didi smiled. "Those were the days."
"You were Terry's girlfriend first? Before Nick, I mean."

"Quite a pair, those two. Very different, very different."

"How?"

"I can't speak for Terry now, but back then . . . he was hard, but he thought he was soft. Nick is just the opposite. Soft, but he thinks he's hard. So do a lot of other people — think Nick's hard, I mean."

"The kids in your garage."

"For some."

"I don't think of Terry as hard."

"He was supposed to be a priest," Didi said.

"I know."

"Oh, so he *did* tell you."

"Some of it."

"Not about the cardinal and *Humanae Vitae?*"

"The cardinal and what?"

Didi smiled. "You're not a Catholic."

"I was raised Episcopalian."

"The Tory party at prayer." Didi smiled.

Then Joan did too. "We believe in one God — at most."

"And you know about art." Didi glanced at the painting above the fireplace. "'Nabis,' you said."

"Yes. It's the Hebrew word for 'prophet.'"

"Profit? Like in money?"

"Like in Jeremiah."

Didi laughed. "It *should* be money for what that dealer charged. I didn't want the thing *that* bad, but Nick insisted." She swallowed some wine, then reached to a silver box for a cigarette. She offered it to Joan, who accepted and produced her gold lighter from her purse. Didi tapped her cigarette on the table, like a man, then leaned across for a light. When she exhaled, leaning back, she said, "They were Jews too."

"Who?"

"The art dealers."

"The Voses? They aren't Jewish."

"They acted like it. Real Jews about that price." Didi stared at Joan as if daring her to express her disapproval. But Joan was impassive. Didi made a show then of the pleasure she took in her cigarette. "You know, they make you quit the weed now when you're pregnant. As if being an elephant wasn't bad enough."

"You quit smoking while you were pregnant?"

"The last one, yes. As if that will make Jerry perfect. When we started out, I assumed all our kids would be perfect." Didi actually stopped to inhale and blow a set of smoke rings, one small circle penetrating a larger pair. "But they aren't, of course," she added, with no need to mention Jackie by name. Looking directly at Joan, she said, "Our children are not perfect because I'm not perfect, and neither is Nick."

To back away, Joan said, "Well, your house certainly is. Your home is beautiful."

"Thank you."

"Your husband is a florist?"

Didi laughed. "Jesus, why don't you be direct or something. I mean, come right out and ask how much he makes a year, how we can afford the Kitchen Aid or my closetful of Ultrasuede or the" — she threw a hand toward the painting — "Manseau."

"That wasn't what I meant at all. I was thinking of the flowers everywhere, which are so beautiful. That was my point."

Didi took an exceptionally deliberate sip of her wine. "Well, I misunderstood, then. But I won't say I'm sorry. Yes, he *is* a florist. But more to the point of all this" — she looked around the room, but with a hint of weariness, as if she knew now that the sum of beautiful things is not happiness — "Nick is an importer. We still run the shop on the corner, in his old house, and there are other Kerry Bouquets around town, but mostly now it's Kerry Imports, bulbs from Holland and cut flowers too, wholesale distribution all over New England, that sort of thing." There was an exasperation in Didi's answer, as if she'd had to justify their affluence often.

All at once Joan's question wasn't about Terry's brother, but about this woman, whose self-assertion was the last thing Joan expected. "You," she said, "I'd love to know more about you."

"So would I," Squire said, breezing into the room. "Didi is the riddle of Bunker Hill." He circled the table to stand by his wife, touching her cheek with the back of his fingers. Didi inclined her face ever so slightly toward him.

"What's the riddle?" Joan asked.

"How can she still be so beautiful after all I've dragged her through?"

Didi slapped Squire's thigh, a friendly swat. "You can't kid a kidder, big guy," she said, rising. "The leg of lamb is butterflied, ready for the grill. Get the fire going, will you?"

Didi left the dining room with her glass. Instead of following, Squire reached for a cigarette. He spied Joan's lighter. "May I?"

"Certainly." She picked it up and handed it to him.

After using it, he studied the lighter appreciatively. "Someone gave this to you."

"Yes." Joan was surprised to feel warmth in her cheeks, and she was sure from the intent way he looked at her that he saw them redden.

"Terry?"

"No."

"I didn't think so. It's nice," he said, and he held it out to her. When he put the lighter in her hand, his fingers rested in her palm for a long second. And Joan felt the heat in her face climb to her ears.

She looked down to put the lighter back into her purse.

"If you don't mind my saying so, I never pictured the woman with Terry as so glamorous."

Joan looked up. "Don't be fooled by my false eyelashes, Nick."

"Call me Squire. Everyone calls me Squire."

"Not Terry."

"Terry's our straight arrow. No curves in Terry. As I am sure you know. Nothing warped. Nothing bent."

Joan recognized the invitation to join in the condescension, to say something disloyal. She never would. But she couldn't help thinking, Curves make a man interesting, and yes, my husband lacks them utterly.

Squire brought his face down toward her, close enough that she could smell his cologne. She resisted the impulse to back away, just to see what he was doing. If he could play, so could she.

He said, "Your eyelashes are real." And then he made no effort to disguise it when he dropped his gaze to her breasts: Also real. He straightened. "I have to start a fire," he said, and walked off.

What a jerk, she thought. But when she brought her cigarette to her mouth, her hand shook.

✧

At dinner all was chaos for as long as the children remained. Jackie in particular kept things stirred up with loud demands, punctuated by "goddamnit"s and china-rattling blows to the table.

Finally Teresa herded the children away, leaving the adults. Didi and Squire sat at opposite ends of the long table, Joan and Terry faced each other on the sides. All smoked cigarettes and sipped coffee.

"Didi, that was great," Joan said. "I loved the salad especially."

"Julia Child. I never miss her."

Joan stared, uncomprehending.

"On television."

"Oh." Joan glanced across at Terry. By now everything seemed wrong, and even a compliment was doomed to underscore how different they were.

Terry was rimming his cigarette in the ashtray. Joan sensed his sadness.

Didi piped up, "So tell us about *you.*"

Her interest seemed genuine, but Joan could not think what to say.

Didi supplied, "Your father's a diplomat?"

"Foreign Service, yes."

"So you grew up everywhere. That must have been exciting."

"He has served in Washington a lot, so we kept our ties."

"In Virginia."

"Yes."

Squire asked, "Did they approve?"

Joan and Terry exchanged a look before Terry burst out laughing. "Christ, Nick, why not ask something personal?"

"Approve of Terry, you mean?" Joan asked steadily.

"Yes," Squire answered. "Your marriage to Terry. Did your parents approve?"

"Of course they did. Why wouldn't they? He's not black."

Squire, still with that smile, said, "Given your rebellious history, you mean?"

"Given the modern era."

"So they were at your wedding?" Didi asked.

"No. They were in San José. We decided not to wait." Joan looked at Terry. "Right?"

"Right."

"San Jose, California?" Didi asked.

"Costa Rica. Where my dad is posted."

"Oh." Didi grimaced. "What an ignoramus — or is it ignora*ma?*" She took a hefty swallow of wine, then looked out the window. "I wonder if it'll rain again?"

A silence fell, and no one broke it for such a long time that it became a powerful revelation of their condition. Joan was desperate to think of something to say, but she couldn't.

When Squire spoke, it did not surprise her, when she brought her eyes up, that he was looking right at her. Which was doubly strange, given what he'd said.

"What?" Joan said. "I'm sorry, what?"

"I just wondered what you'll tell the senator." Only then did he bring his eyes around to Terry. "Your briefing on your reconnaissance trip to Charlestown."

"That's not what this is, Nick. You invited us, remember?"

"But isn't that your job now? Isn't that why Kennedy — ?"

Terry abruptly raised his hand, cutting his brother off. "Don't push this, Nick."

"But what are you going to tell him?"

"Maybe that it looks like lynching is making a comeback. What next, burning crosses?"

"Lynching?" Squire said. "Hanging a straw dummy beats hanging a person." He looked over at Joan. "Wouldn't you say? Where in Virginia are you from, Joan, anyway?"

"What prompts the question, Nick? Lynching?" Joan smashed her cigarette.

"I guess so, yes."

Determined to keep things light, Joan turned to Didi. "Does he ask whatever pops into his mind?"

Didi nodded, her wine glass hooked in the bridge of her hands. She seemed tipsy now, and exhausted. She said, "He's bad."

"Lynchburg," Squire said. "Didn't I hear someplace you're from Lynchburg?"

"In point of fact, Warrenton."

"But near Lynchburg, right? Horse country? FFV and all that?"

Joan's look toward Terry said, Is that what you tell him?

But Terry was watching the smoke curl around the tip of his cigarette. He said quietly, "I want the effigy down, Nick."

"Hey, Terry, it's not my thing. I agree it's ugly, but . . ."

"You're saying it was the wiseguys who lynched the thing, not you?"

"Yes. That is what I'm saying."

"How'd they get my suit, then? They've got the judge in my suit."

Joan blurted, "Your suit?"

"Yes, my suit."

Squire opened his hands. "It must have been in the boxes, in the garage."

"Right. Sure. I guess this *has* been reconnaissance, Nick. And what I'll report is that it's worse over here than they think."

"Good, Terry. You tell them that. And don't forget, when you tell them about the kids lost in the firing range, remember this — some of them are your nieces and nephews."

"I remember."

"Well, you don't act like it."

Terry pushed away from the table.

Joan felt embarrassed for him, the defeat she saw in his face.

"We'd better be going," he said. He reached to Didi. She met his hand with hers. "Thanks, Didi. This was great."

"You're coming back though, right?"

"Yes. Sure, Didi." Terry stood and crossed to her, to kiss her forehead. "Thanks for taking such good care of Ned."

"Don't mention it, Charlie."

Terry laughed at her use of his old nickname and kissed her again. She got up, but unsteadily.

Squire stood, but he remained at the table as Joan, Terry, and Didi moved into the foyer.

Joan turned back toward the dining room, remembering her lighter. She stopped in the threshold just as Nick, with his back to her, picked the lighter up. He studied it for a minute, then put it into his pocket.

Joan felt the blood rush to her face once more, as if she herself had just been caught in an act of theft. The boldness of the man.

As he turned toward her, she looked away. She wanted to go right over and slap his face, but also, something made her skin tingle, like dirty movies had at frat house parties. She moved into the foyer again.

At the door, Nick and Terry shook hands stiffly. Then Nick faced Joan. "So anyway, welcome to Boston," he said. "Don't believe what you read." He kissed her cheek, but his left hand went to her waist, inside her jacket. His finger found the hem of her sweater and, for an instant, rested on the bare skin of the curve above her hip.

"What?" she blurted, meaning, You touched me there?

His eyes twinkled. "I said, Your eyelashes, I'd swear they're real."

Joan stared at him. You're really his brother? You're really going to keep my gold lighter?

By not making an issue of the theft, she realized suddenly that she was his accessory, and then she thought, My God, he wanted me to see him take it. He wanted to see what I would do. She took Terry's arm, holding on to him all the way down the stairs. On the sidewalk, she leaned against him and whispered, "Get me out of here."

"Not yet," he said. "Not just yet."

At the car, they pushed the canvas top back. Terry said, "You drive. Let it coast back, with me."

Terry walked down the hill to the carriage house. The large double doors were still closed, but he could hear the boys inside. Joan edged the car toward the curb cut, as if they'd planned it.

He hopped onto the green hood and stretched to his full height, just able to reach the black pretend corpse. He pulled it loose, then turned and dropped the lifeless dummy into the car, behind the seats.

Joan revved the engine, wanting out. But Terry remained on the hood, looking across at the large sign again: *Rally at City Hall. Monday at 11. Resist!* Yes, he thought, resist.

He hopped down and got in. Joan popped the clutch and the car shot forward. But just as abruptly, she had to hit the brakes, because right in their path at the crest of the hill stood Squire.

He wore that smile of his.

She thought, Now here comes my lighter.

But no. He was holding the plant sheathed in a cone of lavender paper. He moved quickly toward them, to Joan's side of the car. "We forgot to give you your presents. This is especially for you, Joan." He had unpinned the paper and was now folding it back. The plant featured a graceful set of leafy stalks a foot high, out of the center of which had sprouted a stunning pair of purple-veined black orchids. It was like the plant in Gramps's room, only more beautiful. The flower's liplike petals opened around deep red wounds from which the stigma-tipped ovary styles protruded. Other petals, hoods, overlapped the pistils. "I grew it for you."

The flower shimmered before her. She felt the color coming into her face again, that color. Tiny beads of water glistened on the petals. The plant seemed to move toward her slightly, because of him.

The colors went, now that she really looked, from deep red to purple to cobalt, never quite — like his clothing — all the way to black. The black faces of the frightened children she had seen on television passed through her, and then these faces, here. The boys at the high school, the drunks in their mammoth, crude car, the glum Marshals in the grotto of their carriage house. All their disappointment and all their fear went through her. On impulse she said, "Did you ever hear of Saint Roch?"

"What?"

"A dark holy man pictured in medieval chapels. From his wooden staff a black flower miraculously sprouted."

"Like this?" Squire brightened.

"The flower was black because Saint Roch nursed victims of the plague."

"Jesus," Squire said, "the plague!" But he was grinning. He looked for Terry's eye: What's with this broad? But Terry was staring at his own hands.

Squire offered the plant again. "It's rare. Not miraculous, maybe, but rare. The black trillium. Soil moist, but never wet. A cool room, but lots of light. Okay?" He lowered the plant to her hands. Even the paper wrapping the pot, once her fingers touched it, seemed delicate. He had not used the kitsch foil wrapping she associated with cheap florists.

But she corrected herself. That he was a cheap florist was her former prejudice. He was anything but. "Thank you," she said.

He bowed. Then he held up a small envelope. He opened it and produced a small flower. It was green and white, delicate, lovely. "Remember these?" he said to Terry, reaching across. "I make them now."

Terry took it numbly. A shamrock boutonniere, pin and all. Squire tossed his head at the crushed black heap in the seat well. "I'm sorry about that."

"Right," Terry said. He held up the shamrock. "Thanks, Nick." And to Joan, "Let's go."

Joan held the orchid toward Terry. His distaste was undisguised, but she gave him no choice. He took it onto his lap. She put the car in gear, then hit the gas, thinking, Still no gold lighter.

Without Terry's having to tell her, she knew to take the next left.

"And left again, at the corner," he said as they approached Main.

"I know." She sped into City Square, past the precinct house, toward the bridge across the river that marked the Charlestown boundary.

"Stop," he said. "Stop here!"

She did, just short of the bridge. Ahead, on the left, was the congested Italian neighborhood, yet another hill, another spire. But he pointed the other way, toward North Station. "That's Boston Garden. I've told you about it, where Bright lost his eye." He held up the orchid. "An earlier gift from the fabulous Doyle brothers."

He got out of the car, put the orchid on the pavement, and took the dummy out of the well, spreading it on the back of the car. Joan got out and came around beside him. He unfastened the buttons of the out-of-fashion black suit, its narrow lapels and cuffed trousers. He methodically removed the stuffing from the corpse, letting the rags and bunched newspapers fly in the wind. Then he pinned the shamrock to the lapel of the suit. He folded the jacket and rolled the trousers around the shirt cardboard on which someone had written the obscene epitaph. He stood up with the bundled suit.

Joan slipped a hand inside his arm. "I can't believe they used a suit of yours."

"Fuck the judge. Fuck Charlie."

"Why did they call you that?"

"An old nickname."

"Because of Charlestown?"

"Because of this," he indicated the suit. "Charlie Chaplin. You wouldn't get it. There's a lot you wouldn't get."

"Oh, Terry." She squeezed his arm, rested her head against him.

"Joan, I . . ."

Each wanted to find the other. But despite the way their bodies pressed together, there was a sea between them. He pulled away, turning to heave the suit into the filthy harbor water, toward Old Ironsides. They watched it slowly sink in sewage. The feeling was, they watched *him* sink.

His eyes drifted up to the rigging of the ancient ship, all those crosses, and then to the white spire of Paul Revere's church. When he looked, finally, at Joan, his sadness had been replaced by anger. "Saint Roch? Jesus Christ, you're telling him about some fucking saint? Saint Roch?"

Anger, she felt it cleanly, at her, as if he'd tracked this strange route her emotions had just taken.

He bolted away, circled the car, and got in on the driver's side, slamming the door. He pressed the ignition button so hard she saw his thumb go white.

"Get in," he ordered.

She did, but only after picking up the orchid plant.

He said, "I'm going back to the apartment to pack some things. Then I want you to drive me to Logan. I'm going to D.C."

"To see Bright?"

"To see the senator."

"Oh, Terry." She put the plant on the floor between her legs and leaned across the gearshift to him, an assertive move of the kind she'd once regularly made in that car. She put her mouth on his and kissed him. "Not tonight."

"I have to go. I want him up here Monday. It's what you wanted, isn't it?"

"But now I see how much more complicated —"

"Fuck complicated, Joan. You were right the first time."

She kissed him again, thinking: Not "fuck complicated," love; fuck *me*. It was a phrase she could not use with her good, straight husband, a man — yes — without curves. She felt wholly turned on, and refused to think why.

"Hey," he said, coming up for air, "it's only Washington. I'll be back tomorrow. Monday at the latest."

"I'll be waiting, sugar." It relieved her when he laughed and squeezed her hard. He began to pull away, but she held him. "What does he do — really?"

"Nick? I don't ask. My brother has a lot of irons and a lot of fires."

"What does that mean?"

"I don't talk about this, okay?" He turned back to the wheel, and soon he had the motor roaring, the wind hard in their faces. Talk was impossible, and she was glad.

She was glad, also, to have him behind the wheel for the ride back to Cambridge. She needed to think, to sort out what had just happened.

Also, if Terry was driving, she could hold the fragile orchid carefully, out of the wind, away from her husband. This is so direct, she thought, so obvious. Yet Terry, poor Terry, hadn't a clue. She stared at the blooms all the way up the river, thinking that not even in Georgia O'Keeffe had a flower ever seemed so erotic. "Black trillium," she said aloud, words lost in the wind. "Black trillium."

14

Even before waking, Terry heard the unmistakable sounds, the frantic pulse of two breathers out of synch with each other, the rail of a bedstead thumping against the other side of the plasterboard wall at his head. The noise was a bank of rough clouds that floated into his dream, warning of a storm, filling him with fragmentary sensations: a knee touching his ribs, another knee pressing his opposite thigh, a hand pushing against his chest, then withdrawing, then down again on his heart; his own hand cupping a languorous breast, a nipple in the sweet spot of his palm; music, particular music, a driving rhythm, spurts of blood bubbling the sea between his legs. His thumbs were in the waistband of underwear. His grooved fingers were digging into some moist cavity of flesh . . .

He opened his eyes.

A curtain above him lifted in the warm morning breeze. He forced his mind first outside that window, toward the sounds of light traffic drifting in from Independence Avenue, the chirping of birds, branches and leaves rustling, the complacent noise of a September morning on Capitol Hill.

"Oh . . . oh . . . Bright . . . here! . . . here! . . . hon! . . . hon!"

The woman's throaty whisper carried through the wall. Terry pictured her, the black sheen of her skin, her breasts swaying as she straddled Bright, her head bent above him, brushing his face with the soft wire of her Afro . . .

Not Afro. Not black. The woman Doyle had met last night was white. She was short, had brown hair, wore a loose-fitting summer dress, was pretty and happy looking, like a nurse or teacher. She had a dramatically crooked tooth, and when she smiled, Terry had found himself worried about her, what it had been like to grow up in a family that could not get those teeth fixed. Her name was Suzie. She was with Bright when he'd met Terry at the airport, and the three of them had gone for dinner to the '89 in Georgetown, and then to Mister Charlie's. She was a funny kid, and Terry liked her, but her presence had made it impossible to talk to Bright. They'd had a lot to drink, and carried on as a raucous trio, but when they had returned to the apartment, Terry had stepped aside like the knowing roommate he used to be.

Now he was cold. He had slept in his underwear, beneath a yellowed sheet that was now twisted at his waist. He was wet with perspiration, and the breeze at the window was what chilled him. The sofa cushions had gapped beneath his spine. The arm cushion bunched under his head was damp.

Sound contortions continued at his ear, the low male notes of a moan hammering a woman's whine; the bed sent its vibrations into the wall. "You! . . . you! . . . you!" Bright's voice seemed ignited and unfamiliar, though Terry had heard his friend in the throes of orgasm before. He knew that McKay always called his lovers "you" at such moments, to avoid the risk of a wrong name. He had recommended the method back in the days of Terry's initiation into the rituals of D.C.'s frenzied bison hunt, but Terry had never succeeded as a hunter. After his years in the seminary — "prick on ice," Bright had called it — Terry knew he had forever lost several steps to his friend. He was secretly in awe of the way Bright had reinvented himself in Washington. Bright had encouraged Terry to do the same, but McKay had seemed supremely detached from the effect of his smoldering personality. It was Bright who'd introduced Terry to raunchy French cigarettes; the defiant angle at which those stubby weeds rode on the perch of Bright's lips had been a vivid first lesson that some blatant affectations can succeed. How Terry had loved walking into Mister Charlie's or the Cellar Door with him, as if with Richard Wright or Jimmy Baldwin, a black man back from Paris. Terry was his Camus. In addition to his rakish eye patch and loose-limbed strut, Bright wore an aura of sexual readiness. His entrance charged the air of pubs and coffee joints. Girls lifted their heads, whites as often as blacks, and each boy knew at once that his plans for the evening were at risk.

The girl with Bright was now letting out a restrained but shrill cry, seemingly of pain, animal sacrifice. Her discomfort, more than the sounds of ecstasy that had led up to it, made Terry feel like an eavesdropper. He closed his eyes and threw an arm over his exposed ear. He imagined he was in bed with Joan, and once more she was rolling away from him, disappointed. How long had it been since she had cried out like that?

Instead of arousal, the physical sensation that dragged him out of the last wispy shadow of sleep was a poignant sadness in his chest, the familiar void of deflation with which he had begun most of the days of his life, and still did. Leaving the Church, moving to D.C., joining Kennedy, marrying Joan, moving back to Boston — nothing had altered the deep feeling of unconnectedness that he associated with this aftermath of waking. It was only worse now that mornings meant the naked woman at his side shared such a feeling.

Miles Davis blowing "Someday My Prince Will Come" was Terry's notice that they were getting up. There were plumbing sounds and voices, but the music overrode most of it. Bright had become an extravagant man, and his sound system reflected it, with speakers in all four rooms of the apartment. The cassette deck and tuner were, of course, in the bedroom. Music from the footlocker-size speakers at each end of the couch jolted Terry, even though the trumpet elegy was plaintive and turned low.

Terry threw the sheet aside and was pulling on his cord trousers as Suzie walked into the room wearing a bronze slip, which heightened the white of her skin, displaying her body more than covering it.

"Knock, knock," she said.

"Who's there?" Terry asked, though he knew she'd only been announcing herself.

She smiled, and once more the sight of her crooked front tooth made him want to reassure her. The slip shimmered though, and, no doubt because he'd just heard her going over the top, she seemed far sexier than she had last night. He stood to buckle his pants, which seemed foolish suddenly, given the ease with which she presented her near-nakedness.

"Marmalade," she answered.

"Marmalade who?"

"Everyone but Daddy." With a grin and a pointed twitch of her ass, she went by Terry into the kitchen, saying, "Need that coffee."

While she worked the coffeepot, Terry went to the bedroom door and stuck his head in. Bright, naked, was just coming out of the bathroom. It was a shock to see him without his eye patch. His left eyelid was shrunken into the socket, wrinkled like a walnut.

"Good morning," Bright said. He smiled warmly. "I forgot you were here."

"I thought you might have." Terry pointed toward the bathroom. "May I?"

"Sure." Bright took a brown velour robe from a hook and put it on as Terry went by him into the bathroom. His shaving kit was not on the toilet tank shelf where he'd left it, and it took a moment to spot the black case on the narrow sill by the small window beyond the shower. As he stood before the toilet, urinating, his gaze went again to the white porcelain tank lid, only now he saw a remnant line of white powder separating a Gillette Blue Blade and a red plastic cocktail straw.

Terry flushed the toilet and went back into the bedroom. Bright was sitting on the edge of the ruined bed, listening to Miles. His eye patch was on again.

"You've gone uptown on me," Terry said.

"Huh?"

"Your nose candy." Terry glanced back toward the john. "Is that smart, buddy?"

"Terence, Terence. What in the fucking world are you talking about?"

"The cocaine, Bright."

"Oh, the cloud walk." Bright grinned. "You want?"

"No."

"Hey, let the air out of the ball, what do you say? It's not my shit, man, it's Suzie's."

"Hers? You're kidding."

Bright raised his palms. "She seem too Wonder Bread for you? Too white?"

"Too white? What does that have to do with it?"

"Niggers are the cokeheads, isn't that why you immediately — ?"

"Bright, fuck you. It's your bathroom."

"Time out!" McKay made a T with his hands. "Time out! Time out! Talk about controlled substance! You! Your control! Ease off, Terry, really. You're wound as tight as a watch, have been since the airport."

"Since the airport, I've been wanting to talk to you. I'm not down here on vacation."

"So talk."

Doyle looked across at the door just as Suzie appeared in it, her hands closed around a steaming mug. She said, "Coffee's ready. You guys help yourselves while I do my thing in the potty." She leaned against the doorjamb, hooking her legs in a stagy but still seductive pose. She remained languidly in the threshold, a perfectly turned leg in the way, as the men passed her. Her toenails were painted a deep purplish red. Terry was unprepared for the directness of her look as he went by, sensing a challenge in it, or an invitation. The sharp aroma of the coffee alerted him also to the distinct scent of sex rising from her. She bowed as he stepped over her leg, a playful bit of courtliness, the main effect of which was to give him a staggering glimpse of her breasts.

In the kitchen, next to a golden, uncurtained window, were a café table and two chairs. A bud vase held one exquisite silk rose. Bright poured their coffee. They lit up, each staring for a moment at his own goatshit Gauloise, each picking a flake of tobacco off his tongue.

Miles Davis had moved even further into the realm of melancholy with a bluesy "When You Wish upon a Star."

"Who'd have thunk it," Bright said. "Walt Disney, a soul brother."

Terry's eyes drifted to the window, and out. Several blocks away, looking like the backdrop of a news broadcast, was the Capitol dome above a line of trees and rooftops, its whiteness stark against the blue sky. "What was that 'nigger' shit, Bright?"

"Gut reaction. I thought you'd jumped the track."

"Me?"

"Hey, come on, Terry. You. You're exempt?"

"With you, yes. Or so I thought. I was surprised at the coke — okay, I'm a stiff. And I assumed it was yours. But hell, what does that have to do with your being black? That wasn't in my mind. I can't believe we're talking about this."

"Really? After what's happened this week?"

"You mean in Boston?"

"Of course I mean in Boston. Isn't that what's got you down here?"

"Yes. But Boston is something apart. You and me, we're . . ." Terry's voice sank into a swamp of grief and guilt as he thought, Bright knows. He knows about the lynched effigy.

McKay sipped his coffee in silence.

"It's bad," Terry said. "Worse than you think. Something awful is going to happen."

"Something awful *is* happening, bro."

Terry leaned across the small table, claiming full possession of his friend's good eye. "Black children are going to get killed in Boston."

"Bureau reports say the police are doing the job."

"Bright, listen to me. Every day two thousand white people surround the high school in Charlestown, and another two thousand do it in Southie, and every day they get a little bolder. The president has told them he agrees with them. The mayor sends them the same message, groaning about the court order. Their state reps and city councilors lead them in their jungle bunny chants. The cardinal hasn't been heard from, the priests lead the rosaries in the streets, and the cops whom the Bureau praises are the brothers of the Southie and Townie racists. The whites in the Town call themselves the Powderkeg."

Bright surprised Terry by smiling. "*There's* the powder to worry about."

The line threw Terry, for he recognized it as a stiff-arm, the kind of fending off he himself had been doing for weeks. They both knew where talk like this would lead. "Since everybody in charge is invisible, ambivalent, or on their side, the people in Charlestown and Southie are drawing the wrong conclusion. They think they can win this thing. They think if they're just a little nastier, a little louder, a little bit more physical —"

"Terry, cool it. You're —"

"I guarantee you, kids are going to die unless somebody has the balls to stand up and tell these people to stop, tell them that they're wrong, and that they're going to lose."

"Somebody?"

"The senator."

Bright snuffed his cigarette, then immediately reached for another. "We've been through that."

"I know, but that was weeks ago."

"Staff meets every day on this thing. Are you kidding? We're on top of it, and you —"

"*I'm* there. I was in Charlestown yesterday. I'm telling you something you don't know. Staff meetings? What about the senator? Who's briefing him on this?"

"I am."

"Why won't you listen?"

"They fucking hate Ted already, that's why. They won't listen to him. They know his position on busing, not ambivalent at all, buddy. I've written the damn speeches."

"And you wrote what he said when he blasted Ford."

"You're damn right I did."

"Very brave of both of you. The battle of Pennsylvania Avenue. As long as Ted Kennedy stays down here, the Irish in Boston, who are his first people, assume they're winning. Nobody gives a shit what you write for him to say if he's stuck in the Senate. He's ducking like everybody else, but in his case, he ducks just by not being there. I'm not asking you to get him to win the saps over at this point, but to stand with the black children, that's all. Nobody is standing with the children, Bright. *Your* children. I can't believe I'm having to argue this with you."

"Because I'm a black man."

"Yes."

"Shit, bro, listen to yourself." Bright held up his fist, turned it, eyed it. "That's the most important thing about me? What if they were one-eyed children instead of black children? Would you still assume my special burden? You know me since 1960, Terry. Fifteen fucking years. And what *else* have I been all this time? What else besides black and one-eyed?"

"With Kennedy."

"Right. You and I in a blizzard at Jack's inauguration. I fell in love with him, Terry. First Jack, then Bobby. Now Ted. The Kennedys is what I believe in. Why can't that be the main thing with me, the way it is with Ted's other staff? Why can't I look you in one of your two good eyes and say, 'No fucking way Ted goes to Boston this week,' the way they would? No fucking way Ted stands up in front of those animals in Southie. You weren't in L.A., buddy. I was. I stopped being black when Bobby died at my feet. I became the color Kennedy, okay? The kitchen in the Ambassador. Dealey Plaza. That's enough. Some of us are left with one fucking simple idea — keep the man alive. Keep him away from the mad haters. Somebody's going to die? That's what your gut tells you? Okay. I hear you. But not Ted. You got it? Not Ted Kennedy."

"Some child, then."

Bright shook his head sadly.

"Everything we love fails, Bright. That's what I can't stand. I'm talking about my own people here. *They've* failed. My Church failed."

"And now I did."

"It's Ted I'm thinking of. I believe the Kennedy thing too. Boston needs him. That's what I came here to say. And if saying it to you is pointless, then I want to say it to him."

Bright shook his head.

Terry stared at his old friend, feeling anger mount in his throat. He pressed his cigarette out in the white porcelain ashtray. Everything was white in this room. "You know something, Bright," Doyle said. "I think you're full of shit. No more Dealey Plazas? Come off it. You've decided busing is a loser. The staff thinks busing is a loser. No more losers for Ted, isn't that what you guys are really saying?"

"That isn't it, no." Bright was cool. "This week belongs to the cops, Doyle. That's all."

Doyle. That was Bright's boss-name for him, a little tickle to remind him who was in charge.

"The cops? I saw a cop yesterday standing guard over a lynched effigy of Garrity. The sign on the dummy corpse said, *This Judge Loved Niggers*. It looked like Mississippi, Bright."

"At least it was an effigy."

"That's what Squire said. The cop was an old friend of yours too."

"How is Jackie?" Bright's hand went to his eye.

"He's in it. So is Squire."

"Figures. Tell your brother I still love every bone in his head."

Terry was incapable of making the shift into repartee. He sat there red-faced, at the limit of his articulateness, and he asked himself for the millionth time, Why am I in politics?

"Hey, sweetheart," Suzie said from the kitchen door. Bright swung toward her just as she sent his wallet arching into his lap. She was wearing the same dress from the night before, white polka dots on blue, and a large leather bag was hooked on her shoulder. Except for her crooked tooth, she looked like a woman from a *New Yorker* ad, prettiness more than beauty, the barest hint of the sexual restlessness Terry had sensed before. He liked the flaw in her smile because of its suggestion that wholesome perfection was far from the entire story here. As if to prove it, she said casually, "I dusted that line of yours and put your bag back in the drawer."

Having opened his wallet, Bright ignored her.

But Terry said quietly, "I thought you said it was hers."

Still McKay remained focused on his money. Terry saw a thick wad of bills, and when Bright counted out three of them, he realized they were hundreds. Bright held the money up.

She came into the kitchen. As she took the bills, she leaned to Bright and kissed him with a luscious wet mouth. The money disappeared into her bag.

The sharp scent of her perfume hit Terry.

Bright touched her ass absently. "See you next week?"

"Sure, honey. But through Yolanda, okay? She'll kill me if you call direct again." She gave Terry a parting sweet smile. "Knock, knock," she said as she walked away.

"Who's there?" Terry asked.

"The little old lady," she answered with a flip of her shoulder bag, and then she was gone. A moment later they heard the apartment door open and close.

Terry looked at Bright. "The little old lady who?"

Bright nodded ruefully. "You betcha."

"Do I believe my eyes? Bright McKay pays?"

"Take it from me, pal. It's better in every way. You get fucked without getting fucked."

"And the coke that wasn't yours?"

"Maybe that's none of your business, Terry. I really can do quite handsomely without high-almighty moral judgment from you."

"Yeah, you're doing fine."

"What has your nose out of joint, Terry? That she's white? All the coon hookers in this city, I have the nerve to go salt and pepper?"

"Nerve? From what I see, your nerve went up your nose. I need your help about Boston. That's where *my* nose is, and yes, it's out of joint. I want you to take me to Ted right now. Let *him* decide if he should come back with me. My job is to keep the senator in touch with his hometown. It's what he pays me for. And by the way" — he nodded at McKay's fat wallet — "he doesn't pay me like that."

"You have to decide, Terry. Are you here about my bad habits, or are you here about Charlestown High?"

"Charlestown High."

"I'll never let Ted go there. Neither will Kenny. They'll kill him."

"All right. Then Government Center. There's a rally tomorrow. They want to flip the bird at the federal judge and the U.S. Constitution, the Irish daring anybody to stand up and tell them they're wrong. Ted's the last one left who can. He'll be safe. Compared to Bunker Hill, Government Center is easy to secure. The Bureau's right there, and so is District 1. Plus, it's neutral turf, or almost neutral. Ted will have the advantage, because the protesters are coming to the building named for Jack."

Bright turned his face away, then sat immobile in the flood of morning light. Terry could no longer see his good eye, but from under the black leather oval covering his bad one, a thin line of moisture had appeared. The secretions from that eye were not tears, and not tied to emotional responses. Terry knew this. But still the sight shook him, and he saw suddenly the absurdity of his badgering this man on the subject of race.

"He'll go," Bright said at last.

"If he won't, then he should get out of public life."

"It just makes me sad, that shit like this always comes down to a Kennedy."

"But Bright, *that's* why we love them."

✧

Sunday morning, and Harvard Yard was quiet. He stood in the center of the large grassy quadrangle and watched as an occasional student crossed it on the way to Widener Library. Pigeons swooped within the canopy of trees. A pair of girls in sweat clothes walked their bicycles along a cinder path from Sever Hall.

Squire checked his watch again, then looked up at the sharp, white spire of the Harvard church, a classic brick-and-pillar version of the Yankee house of worship standing on village greens everywhere in New England. A man of Squire Doyle's background could not see one of those spires without feeling the stab of exclusion. Yet that church was what had brought him here. He was waiting for the service to finish. Their worship took forever; if the Romans had been Protestant, they'd have talked Jesus to death instead of crucifying him.

To be certain she was in there, as her neighbor had told him, he'd have slipped into the rear of the church. But it seemed, what, disrespectful? not allowed? Everywhere he went that morning, he was breaking rules. He had broken a rule in Quincy, to which he had driven three hours before, and now he thought of it again.

Hough's Neck, an old Irish neighborhood on a peninsula jutting out from Quincy proper into Boston Harbor, was crowded with modest frame houses that had been built for the skilled workers at the shipyard during its Great War expansion. After World War II the yard had been cut back, and Quincy had never prospered again. But the Neck was still proud, and the houses were neat. The rich who'd built their "cottages" along the shore in towns to the south had found a workers' neighborhood easy to resist, and so even the houses on choice sites facing the water were saltboxes and Capes separated by mere ribbons of carefully tended grass. Far out on the peninsula, where Jerry Moran's house stood in a row with several others, the view to the south was of the open ocean, and to the north of the next peninsula up, which was Southie. In the far distance stood the Boston skyline.

Approaching Moran's seaside house, Squire drove slowly to muffle the sound of his car. Moran had tripled the size of his lot by buying his neighbors' houses and demolishing them. His own place he had expanded with a pair of pseudo-modern wings that featured flat roofs, flagstone siding bound with stained cedar beams, large plate-glass windows, and sliders. But the original tract house with its asphalt shingles, narrow windows, and peaked roof was unaltered. On the street side, most of the yard had been paved, and now three Cadillacs were parked inside the low stone wall. Squire pulled in alongside.

He went to the front door and rang the bell, which chimed loudly enough to scatter seagulls from the roof. When Moran's wife answered, Squire greeted her by name, Maeve. She told him that Jerry was down on the rocks, collecting mussels before the tide came back in.

In street shoes, Doyle had to hop gingerly as he crossed the boulders toward the stooped figure in the distance. The blue sea shimmered behind him. Moran was at the very tip of the peninsula, where the water from Quincy Bay washed into the open harbor. Moran was twenty years Squire's senior, but from afar, in his work boots, lank hooded sweatshirt, and baseball cap, he looked like a roustabout, vigorous and strong. He held a bucket in one hand, a garden claw in the other. He saw Squire coming, and he straightened up to meet him.

"Hey, Jerry," Squire said.

"Hello, friend. What brings you down here on a beautiful Sunday morning?" There was more than a hint of the harp in Moran's voice still, though he'd come from Ireland as a child.

Squire smiled, closing the distance, one eye always on his footing. "Would you believe me if I said I was looking for a new church to go to?"

"Sure I would."

"But would I believe you when you said so?"

Squire took up a position atop an adjacent boulder. Moran put the claw in his bucket. They reached across the rocky chasm to shake hands.

"How's your grandfather?"

"Holding his own, Jerry."

"I want you to tell him I miss him. The K of C council meetings ain't the same without him."

"Ned misses the Knights." Squire looked down at the bucket of mussels. "You don't eat those things, do you? From that sewer?"

Moran eyed the black shellfish. There was a note of uncertainty in his voice as he said, "Course I eat them. This is ocean water here." He looked up sharply. "The pollution stops the other side of Southie, Squire. Between Southie and Charlestown, which is where shit belongs."

Squire laughed. "I've missed you, Jer."

"You should get down to Quincy more."

"I hear things are good."

Moran shrugged. "Depends on who you're talking to. Who would *you* be talking to, Squire?"

"Frank."

"I thought that might be it. You still carrying his water?"

"He's slightly pissed, Jerry."

"Fuck him. Quincy is out, Squire. Tucci gives us nothing. You're in Boston, you got no choice. This is another world down here. We got other choices."

"Tucci gives us the umbrella, Jerry. All of us. Just because it isn't raining this morning doesn't mean we don't need it."

"I don't need it."

"You do."

"I've talked to Sciabba. He's my umbrella now."

"You're joking."

"Why not? We're as close to Providence here as we are to Revere."

"You stupid fuck. Tucci can't let Sciabba move north. No wonder he's ripped. You went to Sciabba behind Frank's back? Behind mine?"

"This isn't about you, Squire."

"You took a trip to Holland too, Jerry. You've been traveling."

"Who said I went to Holland?"

"Town name of Venlo, wasn't it?"

Moran stared at Squire, unable to answer. Absently, he took the claw out of his bucket again.

"Holland makes the business mine, Jerry. As I'm sure you knew it would. Who'd you meet with, Nouwen?"

"He and I agreed we'd have to bring you in."

"Jerry, I'm surprised at you. Really surprised. The point of a franchise system is control. We're all in one business. We can't have competition inside the company. That's Frank's point, and it's mine also."

"Squire, we *can* take control back from Tucci, don't you get it? We don't have to run our shit through him. A lot of fellows think you're too soft."

"How soft am I, Jerry?"

"I mean soft with Frank. You don't challenge him. You don't fight for our —"

"So you will, is that it? You'll be the mick they deal with?"

"Tucci can't take on Sciabba. Not direct."

"That's right. He can't. He does it indirect, by getting rid of you."

Moran looked coldly at Doyle, unafraid. "That's why you're here."

"Yes."

"Another order from Tucci."

"It's me you've crossed, Jerry."

"I was going to bring you in, once we had it set."

"I know you were. But things don't work that way, Jerry."

Moran faced away, toward the open sea, closing his eyes into the wind. "So what'll be? Like Deebo? You got a boat coming for me?" He opened his eyes and pointed to a lobster boat two or three hundred yards out. It was white, small, bobbing in the swells as it moved from pot to pot. "Thinking of Deebo, the Irish used to stick together, Squire. That's what you stood for when you started out."

"I still do."

"Which is why you've come to kill me?"

"I've come to tell you to get the fuck out of Boston, Jerry. Move to Florida, today. Empty your safe. Call your kids. Tell them you're retired. Put Maeve and her poodles in one of your Caddies and get out. You do that and I'll deal with Frank for you. I'll get him to lift the curse. That's what sticking together means in this case."

"I can't."

"Then I'll kill you, Jerry."

Moran turned back to Squire. He held his bucket up in front of Squire's face. "And you say I'm the one who eats sewage?" The bucket fell and the mussels scattered at Squire's feet. But the older man held the claw. "Go ahead," he said in a dead voice, devoid of bravado.

Squire shook his head. "If I did it now, Jerry, I'd have to do Maeve too. She saw me. Besides, I want you to think about what I said. You have today. I'm giving you today. It's Sunday."

"Fuck you, Squire."

Squire turned away. When Moran did not bring the steel claw down on the back of his head, Squire knew that his grandfather's K of C chum would leave. Squire hopped to the next boulder, and to the next, and to the next.

Back at Moran's house, Maeve had been watching him from behind the curtain of one of the narrow windows. Squire waved as he got into his car. He made a quick U-turn, gunning it.

✧

The minister was the first one to appear at the blue door of Memorial Church, which, Squire recalled, was what Protestants did when services were over. Lovely sermon, Reverend. Fine message.

He was watching from his perch halfway up the stairs of Widener Library. After the clergyman's white surplice and cassock, the first thing Squire noticed about him was that he was black. "Perfect," he said aloud.

He had no trouble picking her out from the line of worshipers as they took the steps down, out of the church portico, dispersing into the alternating light and shadow of the burnished maple-leaf tent of the Yard. Joan was wearing a bright green dress and white, high-heeled shoes. She was carrying a straw hat with a white ribbon; in her other hand she carried a purse. From the distance, Squire admired the way she walked, heading off alone with long, self-affirming strides. His eyes went naturally to the movement of her thighs under the loose fabric of her dress, and he could sense the fine-toned pull of her muscles. As his gaze lagged in her wake, he sensed that this woman was not trying for effect, had no idea of being watched. Suddenly he thought of another woman, from years before, the prim lady at the MGH. Had they fucked or not?

He set out after Joan, past empty bike racks, wire trash baskets, jogging at first, with the brio of an undergraduate. He left the pavement for the oatmeal path between the brick and, yes, ivy-covered buildings, the gap into which she had disappeared. By the time he saw her again she was beyond the gate, at Quincy Street. From one Quincy to another. He began to jog again, and caught up on the far side of the street. He fell into step with her as she started up the broad, formal stairs of a large Harvard building.

"Hello, Joan."

Looking up, seeing who it was, she fell back, entirely startled. "My God, what are you doing here?"

They faced each other on the staircase. He put his closed hand forward, upending it like a magician, and he opened it — poof! "You forgot your lighter. You left it at our house."

Joan stared at the gold oblong. "Not exactly," she said, looking him in the eye. "You took it."

"Oh?"

"You took it from the table. I saw you."

Instead of replying, he only looked at her.

"Do you always take what you want?"

"Only when I'm sure I won't get caught."

"But I told you, I saw you."

Squire smiled. "That's not what I mean, I guess, by 'caught.'"

His eyes never left hers. Finally she asked, "What do you do, Nick?"

"I sell flowers."

"No, I mean really. Who are you?"

"You like the orchid?"
"Yes."
He shrugged. "I'm Saint Roch, then."
"You're bold, is what you are."
"Does that scare you?"
"No." Though this was true, it was also true that, inwardly, she was trembling. When had she felt so intrigued by a man, or less in control of herself in meeting one? Terry's brother? She couldn't get over it.
"I know you're not afraid," he said. "I admire that, and I like it."
She took her lighter back and dropped it in her purse.
"Solid gold, Joan."
"More than you usually shoplift?"
"Who gave it to you?"
"None of your business."
"A man with taste. And money." Squire bowed slightly, as if describing himself.
At that moment, a pair of Asian tourists presented themselves on the sidewalk at the foot of the stairs, two men. One was consulting a guidebook, the other grinned up at Squire. "The museum is open?"
Squire had not realized that's what the building was. With its massive windows and ivy, he'd taken it for a dorm or another library.
"No," Joan answered. "I'm sorry. The museum is closed on Sunday."
The tourists moved on.
"But you were going in," Squire said.
"I work here. With Terry out of town, I was going to clear up some things at my desk."
"Would you show me around? Is that allowed?"
"What?"
"I've heard of the Fogg. I've never been in it."
"I'm sorry. I couldn't."
"Are you afraid I'll take something?"
"No. No, I'm not afraid of that." She looked at her watch.
"You're an expert on something."
"Drawings. Of the Italian Renaissance."
"Do they have that?"
Joan smiled. "A fair representation. Fra Diamante, Botticelli, Ferrari . . ."
Squire shrugged with exaggerated self-effacement.

"You've heard of Michelangelo?"

"I think I have."

"We have a wonderful collection of his presentation drawings."

"Which are?"

"What he'd have shown his client, the elaborate design, multiple drawings, for a sarcophagus, for example."

"Nice."

"You'd really like to see it?"

"Sure. You kidding?"

"Okay." Joan turned. Instead of going the rest of the way up the stairs to the main doors, she took the path around to the side of the building. Over her shoulder she said, "If we run into the guard, you'll be my graduate assistant."

"Gladly," he said, following.

"Not that you look like a student."

Squire turned up the collar of his dark green polo shirt. "Now?"

But she ignored him. At the staff door, she applied her key. When it clicked, he helped her pull it open, and they went in. There was a long, narrow corridor, then another door that they pushed through. Squire followed her through a dark foyer into a brightly illuminated stone courtyard that made him think, unexpectedly, of a monastery. A more informed eye would have recognized the surrounding portico with its Romanesque arches, the balcony ringing the second level, and the marble casements at the third as belonging to the style of an Italian villa, not a cloister. There was the overhanging lip of an orange-tiled roof, but above that the courtyard was covered with glass, which filtered the morning light, making it seem unnatural.

"Wow," he said, turning slowly, taking it in. His voice echoed.

"Come on. I'll show you Michelangelo." She pronounced the name with a short *i*, like *mick*.

Joan's shoes clacked on the slate floor as she crossed toward one corner of the courtyard and disappeared in the shadows of the portico. Squire followed, though he'd have preferred to linger in the bright hall. They went up a narrow, turning staircase to the second floor, then down a corridor, away from the courtyard, and into a small, windowless gallery so dark it was impossible to see.

Joan said, "Wait here a moment." When she had gone, Squire had the feeling someone else was in the room with him. He was sure of it. A large figure was standing against the wall a dozen yards in front of him.

Suddenly the room filled with light. The ceiling here was entirely glass too, but instead of being open to the sky, light bulbs were hidden behind the smoky glass. Joan had turned them on.

The figure in front of Squire was a statue, a naked man ten or twelve feet tall. His face was twisted back, one arm was wrenched behind, the other was across his breast, tugging at a cord that bound him. With his contorted face, he was a man in agony of some kind, so real the thing was hard to look at. His penis, flaccid and defeated, was at the level of Squire's eye.

He looked away. On the walls to the right and left were ornately framed drawings and prints, all showing human figures, men and women both, seated on thrones or in clouds, robes draping them casually or leaving them half naked. One drawing seemed familiar: it showed Mary holding Jesus, and even before Joan returned and told him, he recognized it as a sketch for the *Pietà*.

"What do you think?" she asked from behind him.

"I'm amazed. Nobody ever told me they had Michelangelo in Boston. Of course, it figures it would be over here."

"What do you mean?"

"What the hell, Harvard." He shrugged. "It's one way a wop can go to Harvard — by being Michelangelo."

"That's a parochial reaction, if you don't mind my saying so."

"True." He laughed. "I'm of the parochial school."

"That's an act, Nick. A routine of yours, and it's wasted on me. I've seen your house. I've seen the Manseau in your dining room."

"Didi's in charge of that stuff. Now this" — he approached the statue — "would look great in our entrance hall."

"It's a plaster cast. Not original. You wouldn't tolerate it."

"How true." He drew close enough to read the plate on the pedestal. "*The Dying Slave*. Jesus, he really nailed the guy, didn't he?"

"Yes."

Joan came and stood beside Doyle. They regarded the sculpture in silence. Finally he said quietly, "Would you tell me about it?"

"We have this, even if it is a cast, because Michelangelo was a sculptor, a carver of marble statues. All his drawing and painting imitated the roundness of sculpture."

"Who has the original?"

"The Louvre. This is paired with a second statue, *The Rebellious Slave*."

"That's the one I'd like to see."

"Come here then," she said, walking to a long glass cabinet that lined one wall of the room. A dozen drawings were displayed. "This is the tomb of Julius II, as Michelangelo designed it. Here . . . and . . . here we see his drawings of the slaves. One dying . . . see? And one rebelling."

Squire studied the drawings. Statues of various figures, some standing, some seated, were posted around the elaborate door of a tomb. Of the dozen drawings, three, no four, featured the pair of slaves. The second slave was looking up from his bonds, defiance in his face.

Joan said, "When he'd carved the slaves, they were never placed at the tomb. We don't know why."

"Maybe the kings were —"

Joan's head jolted. Was he kidding? "Pope, Nick. Julius II was a pope."

Squire stared at one of the drawings impassively, but the color rushing into his skin showed his embarrassment.

"These statues turned up in Paris, because of Richelieu probably. After 1789, the French celebrated them as symbols of the revolution. Especially *The Rebellious Slave*, naturally. Look at it. I wish you could see that statue, the original. It vibrates with energy, with life. Like *David* or *Moses*. The wonder is that it does not speak."

"Saying 'I refuse.'" He looked at her. "Saying 'I resist.'"

If she caught his reference, she would not show it. Her face was lit with admiration for the statue. "*Terribilità* is the word Michelangelo's contemporaries used for this. The sublime, we would say."

Squire turned back to the plaster cast. "This one is dying because he gave up."

"I don't know if that's the case."

"I can feel it."

"To be alive is to rebel, is that what you believe?"

Squire laughed. "If I was a slave, maybe. Before this busing shit in the Town, what was there to rebel against? My life was simple. Still is, really. My work, my family, my neighbors . . ." He opened his hands toward her, as if what he was saying were the most natural thing in the world. "And now you."

"Me?" Joan put her hand on her breast, mugging, Scarlett O'Hara. "Little old me? My goodness, I'm just too honored for words." She laughed.

But he stared at her, right through the pose of her snappy derision.

The color in her face became ashen. She turned and walked toward the door, the noise of her heels resounding in the gallery. He watched her body, wasp-hipped, the motion of her legs and ass under her dress, the line of her underpants.

He stayed where he was until the light went off again. All of Michelangelo's presentation sketches, and even the slave behind him, ceased to exist. Then he joined her in the corridor. "'The guard,' you said. Where's the guard?"

Joan looked around, listening. "The other wing, probably. The basement. There are two, but it's a big place."

Joan started for the stairwell they had come up, but he saw off to his left what he was looking for, a thing to stop her with. At the far end of the corridor that ran along the balcony overlooking the courtyard stood another massive statue. This one was black and dramatically set off by a sequence of frames: the doorway of the room it was in, the line of pillars and arches, and the Gothic vaulting of the ambulatory leading to it. A woman. Nude.

"What's that?"

Joan stopped and looked where he was pointing. "Aristide Maillol," she answered. "A bronze."

"Your field?"

"No. France. This century."

"Can we look?" Without waiting for an answer, Squire started walking. Here, along the balcony, with the light washing in from the courtyard, the floor was not slate but antique tiles, uneven underfoot.

"This could be Venice or something," he said.

"Have you been to Europe?"

"I have business now and again, but only in Holland. Not a big art country."

"Van Gogh. Rembrandt."

"Sidewalk Sam. Hey, what can I say? My interest is flowers. Dutch tulips. Bulbs."

She did not reply.

He said, "Our footsteps echo so loudly because, in this part anyway, no one else is here. Like that tree in the forest."

"Which tree?"

"But the museum is empty, right? Except for us and the guards someplace."

"I guess so. There could be somebody in the offices upstairs, but probably not on a Sunday."

"I thought Sundays were like big days for museums."

"Not Harvard." She spoke ironically. "This art isn't for the public. This art is for us."

"Hey, privileges of the elite."

"Believe it or not, it's an issue for some of us. We're trying to —"

"I could get used to this." Squire began to waltz ahead of her with his arms outstretched, a graceful dance of circles.

Despite herself, Joan smiled.

Unlike the dark gallery of the Michelangelo, the room in which the Maillol stood was illuminated by a skylight, and the statue was positioned to take advantage of it: a female figure eight feet tall, arms clutching a bronze towel behind, chest thrust forward, a heaviness in the breasts and thighs, the round rise of her abdomen, a looseness of the parted lips which alone made her seem to be offering herself.

He said, "Now I see why the slave is dying."

Joan circled around behind the statue, making a show, perhaps, of her expertise. She said, "Don't you see how static she is, how detached? Where is the energy we saw in Michelangelo?"

"She seems pretty content with herself, I guess." Doyle stretched to his full height. "Except for those lips. Look how they're parted. Did you notice that?" He began to reach a finger up to the statue's face.

"Don't," Joan said.

He looked at her. "Don't what?"

"Don't touch."

He held his position, his finger a few inches from the bather's lips.

"It's a rule," she said.

"Like, don't steal?"

"Yes. Because your skin has oil in it. The oil marks the bronze imperceptibly, but nevertheless."

Squire withdrew his hand and slowly began to circle around the statue, his eyes on Joan. They were surrounded by impressionist works — Renoir's *Seated Bather* on one wall, Pissarro's *Montmartre* on another — and a second piece of sculpture, an exquisite small naked dancer by Degas. Women's bodies, glowing in the love of the men who'd made them.

He moved silently, because in this room the floor was covered with a flat-gray carpet. The huge bronze loomed between them, an abstraction of the female form, an abstraction also of negritude. A glistening black curve, the line of the buttock, disappeared in the hollow of the small of the woman's arching back.

Joan studied Terry's brother as he came toward her, a mystified chill running through her. If he'd been a Michelangelo come to life, she'd have felt this very sense of inevitability. Why has it taken so long?

When he was next to her, he brought his finger to within inches of her lips. She thought he was going to ask permission, but what he said was "*Terribilità.* Is that how you say it?"

"Yes."

He put his finger between her teeth then, and she bit him until she tasted blood.

They pressed their bodies together. When they kissed, their tongues fought each other. As they sank to the floor, she pulled her face away. "I can't."

"We'll hear the guard if he comes."

"I can't," she repeated.

"Why not?" he answered, with a freedom that gathered her up, releasing her for the sexual urge. Quickly he was on her. She pulled at his clothing as frantically as he pulled at hers.

Once she almost called him Terry, and then realized it. The thought of her husband — of how the feel of this man's weight was both like Terry's and entirely different — did not check her passion, but made it seem the fulfillment of promises Terry's body had made, but never kept.

Squire was massaging her with his fingers. "Oh," she said as she became still more aroused. "Oh." She took his face firmly between her hands and made him look into her eyes. "What is this?" she whispered.

"Sex," he said.

"Oh, Nick." She hugged his neck as he continued touching her with his fingers. She was coming. Coming.

Yet, in her mind, he was hurting her with what his expertise implied. He was an awful man, awful. She knew it, yet blanked it out. "God . . ." This approaching storm of sensation, could it be hers? Who cares? she asked as it lifted her. It's wrong, she told herself. Wrong. She didn't care. She gave herself over to the swelling sea of her body.

"Oh stop!" she cried.

She pushed him up. He resisted, but she forced him halfway off her, out of her. "I'm not wearing my diaphragm," she said with a gasp.

"It doesn't matter." He was so calm, indifferent even to their witnesses, the paintings and statues surrounding them, a man who did not care if it was blasphemy, holding one of these goddesses in his arms. "Let it go, Joan," he said quietly.

"No," she said, "I can't." She pushed against him, but knew, of course, it was futile to do so. He did not take no for an answer. Wasn't that clear from the start? Wasn't that what drew her in? How had she let this happen? She was aware of his hands pinning hers, of her head whipping back and forth, a wild gesture of refusal. Any other man she'd ever known, she could have closed out right then. But he knew exactly where the opening was, not just between her legs, but between what she wanted and what she didn't want at all. He pushed into it, the genius, the bastard, the fuck. "No," she said again, while her body opened to him.

15

TAILLIGHTS FLASHED on the gleaming, sand-colored surface of the tile ceiling as the automobiles ahead hit their brakes. Traffic slowed suddenly, all the way back from the point where the Sumner Tunnel emptied into the maze of downtown Boston.

"Shit," the driver said, but under his breath so that only Terry heard him, and not the two passengers in back. When Terry glanced back, the senator was going over his speech, pencil in hand, marking pages Terry himself had given him. Bright rolled his one good eye, a self-mocking bit of Stepin Fetchit. Facing forward, Terry watched the tunnel ceiling again. Up ahead it was awash in red, as if the tile had cracked and was leaking, not harbor water — here was his strange thought — but blood.

Along the right side of the roadway was a narrow catwalk, separated by a railing. As the traffic slowed nearly to a stop, Terry leaned out his window toward a tunnel cop standing by his booth. The cop held a walkie-talkie. "What's up?"

"Big crowd the JFK Building. Protest march."

Now when Terry glanced rearward again, Senator Kennedy was looking right at him. "Is that us?"

"Yes."

A cloud moved across Kennedy's face, settling there. The traffic continued inching past the cop, leaving him behind. Terry saw it when, stooping, the cop had recognized the senator, and had put his handset to his face. That single gesture, to Terry's surprise, pulled the cord on an inner alarm. His stomach lurched, the emotional equivalent of a fire whistle, and it became his complete purpose to get that alarm suppressed again, for himself and for Ted. He touched the driver's elbow.

"When we get out of the tunnel, go right on Endicott Street. We'll come up on the building from the North Station side."

"Right."

The four sat with eyes fixed on the red lights of the tunnel ceiling; when traffic opened up ahead, the red would disappear. It never did. Cars crawled along, braking all the way. Kennedy, after lighting one of his putrid cigarillos, turned back to his speech, three pages inside the black binder, five minutes' worth, maybe six. When Terry had handed the binder to him at National Airport, Kennedy had opened it, flicked the pages, and said, "This is it?"

They'd been standing in the VIP lounge at Eastern.

"Four hundred words, Senator," Terry had said. "Gettysburg was less than three hundred."

Kennedy had looked up sharply. "At a graveyard."

"To the people you'll be talking to, that's what Boston is, the site of a battle with no winners, only losers. A speech can change what people think and do, and what they feel. Sometimes a speech has to."

"The Gettysburg Address, huh?"

"Why not?"

Ted Kennedy had found Bright's eye then, and to Terry's chagrin they had laughed — laughed, he knew, at him. He had broken the great rule, invoking Lincoln. In their speeches they could do that, but never, never in their talk among themselves.

Now, from his corner in the rear seat, under his cone of light, Senator Kennedy said in a detached voice, "They're going to hate me for this."

"They already hate you," Bright said.

Terry whipped around. "No, no, they don't. That's ridiculous. These people love you, Senator. That's the point. That's why you have to be the one telling them —"

"That they're wrong."

"That's not the main point. You're reminding them what being Irish means, how the doors open in this country, how the last thing we want is to be a closed door for someone else."

"The Irish *open* doors." Kennedy snorted, elbowing McKay. "Irish doormen."

"In fact, Senator, that's exactly right. Your family has opened doors for —"

"But on busing they are wrong. That's what I've come to tell them. Tell them to their red Irish noses. They're dead wrong."

Terry was afraid suddenly that Kennedy's mocking, angry tone meant he wouldn't do it. The cloud in Kennedy's face, Terry realized now, was fear.

"Yes, Senator. That's what you're saying."

"Because no one else will say it except the *Globe*, Anne Cabot Wyman, Thomas Winship, William O. Taylor — Boston WASPs."

"That's right."

Kennedy closed the folder. "Just wanted to make sure I knew what I was doing. Jesus Christ." He looked away from Doyle, pretending to find something of interest in the grimy tile wall of Sumner Tunnel. He inhaled deeply on his cigarillo. A moment later he said softly, "I wanted to see David, but we won't be up here long enough. Ethel said he's not doing so great."

"We set him up in the office," Terry said. "He and a couple of other Harvard kids come over twice a week. I'll keep my eye on him."

"I'm going to tell his mother that. Keep Bright posted, will you."

"Yes, sir."

A few moments later, their car came out into the sunlight. The car swung right, past Martignetti's, onto the border street of the North End, leaving the bulk of traffic creeping onto expressway ramps. They shot into the Italian neighborhood, past a barber shop, a row of stoop-fronted tenements, and a butcher shop with lamb and pig carcasses hung to drip above the sidewalk, blood again.

Two blocks along, Endicott Street wedged into North Washington, and at the next intersection stood Boston Garden. Terry felt Bright's hand on his shoulder. "Jumpers. Remember?"

"Christ, yes," Terry said. "All those bobby sox."

Bright said to Kennedy, "Terry and I massed an army of kids here for your brother, election eve."

"Big difference, his hometown rally and mine."

Bright poked Terry again. "Where are the flowers?"

Bright's touch, and that awful reference, made Terry feel coldly certain that he'd made a terrible mistake in forcing these men here — like the mistake he'd made years before.

They passed Boston Garden and crossed onto the sloping back side of Beacon Hill. At Cambridge Street traffic snarled again, backing up from the demonstration three blocks away. When the car stopped, Senator Kennedy opened his door. "Let's do this," he said. And he got out.

Terry took the radio mouthpiece from its clip on the dash and handed it to the driver. "Call Hazzard. Tell him the senator's on foot. They can pick us up as we go by the building."

A moment later, Doyle and McKay were striding along beside Kennedy, one on each side. That block of Cambridge Street, between the boxy Saltonstall Building and the brute concrete of the Lindemann Mental Health Center, was clogged with honking automobiles, drivers craning out their windows to see what the fucking holdup was. Blue lights flashed up ahead, but police vehicles were stuck in traffic too.

"Hey, Teddy!" one driver called. "Tell them to get it moving."

The senator ignored him, and others in cars and on foot whose heads turned in recognition as he passed.

The rally had already begun on the vast brick plaza in front of City Hall, beyond the towering JFK Building. Though they could hear echoes of the amplification, roaring applause, hoots and cheers, neither Kennedy nor his aides could see the crowd yet.

At the next corner they crossed the wide street quickly, skipping between the shiny bumpers of stalled cars. Three tall men in blue suits, English shoes, and silk ties, they moved crisply. Only the fact that one of them was black — a black man with an eye patch — would have set them apart from other lunchtime big-shots up from State Street, except that one of the two whites had the most familiar face and hair in America.

A particularly loud roar went up from the crowd ahead, and it rolled back at them, echoing through the canyon of government buildings. Another block to the JFK Building itself, to connect with Hazzard. Terry worried that Kennedy wouldn't wait for the security men. He was afraid to show how afraid he was, which made him seem so brave. He'd been adamant: no police escort from the airport, no motorcycles, no uniforms, no obvious bodyguards. The rendezvous with Hazzard should have been simple, but Terry hadn't anticipated this fucking traffic.

Bright reached around Kennedy to nudge Terry. "There's your man."

Hazzard? Perry?

Terry checked the faces of the men they were passing, but McKay was pointing to a bronze bust on a stone pillar surrounded by benches in the center of a tidy park by the Bowdoin subway stop. Cushing, the beak of his nose, the jutting longshoreman's chin, the sunken cheeks. The eyes of the sculpture were dead, but otherwise, it was him. Cardinal Cushing at the foot of Bowdoin Street, where Jack had lived. Who had thought to put him there?

"Dear Jack . . ." The old prelate's words at Kennedy's bier, the bent head, the spotted, gaunt hand on the coffin. Terry felt the breath catch in his throat.

The three men had slowed and were looking at the bust. Terry said, "If he was still here, Senator, you wouldn't need to be."

"Not true. He'd have had me up here before this. You were right." With his closest aides, Kennedy felt free to be withholding, but now he looked at Terry Doyle with what, between them, was a rare directness. "I wish I'd come up sooner. Thank you."

"I hope it goes well, Senator."

Kennedy held up the black binder. "'Four score and seven years ago.'" He laughed suddenly, his great, infectious, releasing laughter. What freedom the man had to laugh at himself. He slapped Doyle's shoulder with the binder, and then led the way.

Passing the JFK Building, Terry saw Mike Hazzard, Joe Perry, and four or five others slipping in ahead of and behind the senator. Terry knew there would be others, Kennedy's personal Secret Service, but instead of relieving him, the sight of the bodyguards made Doyle afraid, really afraid, for the first time. The noise of the crowd had fallen off, which mystified Terry until, turning the last corner, they saw the plaza at last. He had expected a few hundred people, but the vast space was jammed with thousands. They were listening to a single speaker who was standing on a platform near the entrance to City Hall. A huge banner had been hoisted behind it: ROAR! NEVER! Kennedy would have to walk through the crowd to address them, which, Terry saw at once, would be a disaster. He expected the senator to turn on him with, Why did you bring me in on this side? Who advanced this?

But Kennedy, having seen what he had to do, was only doing it. He walked directly into the narrow aisle that a few cops were maintaining with sawhorse barricades. It ran through the heart of the throng to the platform, narrowing further all the way. For a moment, Kennedy was ahead of Hazzard and Perry, who roughly pushed people aside to get in front again.

"We're white," the man on the platform was bellowing, "and we want our rights!"

The crowd cheered and hooted.

The man was familiar to Terry — a tavern keeper or a City Square merchant, someone he had seen at church years ago. Terry had nearly to run to keep up with Kennedy. Bright had fallen back.

"We are white!" the man intoned again, a mantra with which to end a speech. The crowd responded, "And we want our rights!"

Terry felt a heightened perceptiveness as he moved through the crowd, as if he were taking in everything that fell within the range of his senses. Youths in Charlestown High dugout jackets, the white sleeves and red bodies, were posted at the ends of rows along the aisles. They wore armbands stenciled *CM,* Charlestown Marshals — the kids from the convent carriage house on Bunker Hill, Nick's garage.

"It's fucking Kennedy!" one of the kids yelled.

And then someone else repeated, even more loudly, "Fucking Kennedy!" Pronounced *fooking,* the phrase was repeated and repeated again as the people turned. The exclamation rolled back through the crowd.

Later Kennedy would laugh and say, "How did they know?" But not now.

"Nigger lover Kennedy!"

Where was Bright?

For a moment Terry's attention left the senator, who had pushed ahead. Where the hell was Bright? Who had advanced this? Christ, Jesus Christ, what have I done? Doyle looked and looked, but his friend was gone. Along the aisle down which they'd come, police were standing with outstretched arms, holding back the crowd.

Now came a surge against which those cops nearest to Terry were powerless, and the crowd spilled into the aisle, breaking the wooden sawhorses and closing off the Kennedy group's way out.

"Get Kennedy!" one of the nearby Townies cried, and Terry recognized him as the kid who'd toyed with Joan's car, putting his knife in the folds of the canvas top. The crowd pushed the boy from behind, right into Terry, who reacted instinctively by punching him in the face. The boy fell.

Hazzard and Perry were on Terry then, each with an arm around Ted. They were pushing through the crowd, back the way they'd come, through the vestige of the aisle. Terry turned and went ahead, swinging his fists, landing punches in the faces of everyone in his way.

"Don't hurt them!" he heard someone say. To his amazement, he realized it was the senator.

"Fuck Kennedy! Fuck Kennedy!" Red faces twisted around those words.

Don't hurt them? Terry Doyle would always remember that order for what it said about Kennedy, and for what it said about himself, because, as he pushed viciously through the crowd, he *wanted* to hurt them. They were would-be Oswalds and Sirhans. But like him, they were Irish. Like them, he wanted to kill.

✧

Because Hazzard and Perry knew what they were doing, also because they were lucky and because a flying squad of cops arrived to open a way through the crowd, Senator Kennedy, with Terry Doyle beside him, made it safely back to the JFK Building. They rushed through the heavy plate-glass doors that the building's guards had held open for them, and for a moment the large marble foyer felt like sanctuary.

This was Jack's building, the federal government's building, the FBI's — not some ambivalent mayor's building, not Boston's.

The mob had followed Kennedy, pushing against the hastily formed line of cops who were standing them off now outside the doors. The guards had the doors locked.

"Fucking Kennedy!" Even through the glass their curses carried. "Fuck Garrity, the Kennedy judge! Fuck the *Globe*!"

Terry slowly turned away from the faces in the glass, unable to stand the sight of people he was sure he knew. To his surprise, he realized that he had been craning his head back across his shoulder, and that he had his arms around the senator, and so did Joe Perry. They had pressed Kennedy against the marble wall, shielding him. Kennedy was limp. His face was completely pale, except for an ugly blotch of red on his left cheek where someone or something had hit him. His suit coat was ripped at the shoulder seam. But his eyes were clear and cold, absolutely focused. "Where's Neville?" he asked.

"Neville?"

"McKay."

Bright! Terry looked back toward the door just in time to see the surge of energy cresting through the crowd, the hundreds of people who had mobbed the entrance. Those in front were being forced against the glass, at the mercy of those behind, who were pushing, pushing, until . . .

The huge plate-glass window beside the doorway proper shattered in an explosion. Shards of glass flew everywhere, and the noise was deafening, like a mortar shell. Was this Vietnam? The first row of people stormed through, and Terry thought, Now we die. Now the last Kennedy dies.

Then, suddenly, it was over.

The mob was stopped by what it had done. The people froze, all staring in horror at Kennedy.

Here and there, those bloodied by shards were crying, and some woman was shrieking "Help! Help!" But compared to the previous noise, the glass-strewn foyer, even open as it was now to the outside, was quiet. Doyle had no memory of having moved from his place with Kennedy by the wall, but now he was standing, as if alone, in the center of the space from which others had scattered. He stared at the stunned faces in front of him, the faces of mothers, fathers, and teenagers, faces like those he'd held the paten for at the Communion rail of St. Mary's, and like those he'd seen turned to the sun on the benches of Bunker Hill. Faces like those he'd waved at and kissed all his pointless life.

The crowd on the plaza had fallen back, away from the building. Those inside, near him, twenty or thirty people, the ones who'd been pushed from behind and whose momentum had carried them into this other realm, had not moved. They had not meant to do this.

Is everybody all right?

"Go home," Terry said.

They did not move.

Terry looked back for the senator and saw Mike Hazzard, holding a pistol now, as he pushed Senator Kennedy through the door of one of the elevators.

For an instant Terry's eyes and Kennedy's locked together, and Terry saw clearly the pure terror in the man, and its meaning. The source of Kennedy's strength as a champion had turned against him. First Joe Malloy, then Squire, and now Irish children, Kennedy's children. They all felt free to say it: Fuck Ted! Why had it taken this long for Doyle to see it, that Kennedy was finished? Even now, Kennedy was being hauled back down into the muck of his own origins by people who'd never escaped it, never wanted to.

For Terry Doyle the moment was an exact replay of his having looked at Cushing years before and realized, Not for me. Only now, at last, it was Kennedy; the dream of being Kennedy was not enough. They may have you, Ted — the monster hands, hauling down — but they haven't got me!

The door of the elevator slid closed, taking the senator away. Physically safe, but finished. Kennedy was not Kennedy anymore.

Terry turned toward the mob, his old neighbors, assassins after all. "Go home!" he ordered loudly. He began shoving against those nearest him, a pair of Charlestown Marshals. "Go home!" He jolted the boys, pushing them back with the stainless steel of his oldest feeling, pushing back against everything that wanted to hold him down, to keep him from fulfilling the ambition that had become the core of his very self. "Go home!"

The people scrambled away, stumbling out through the jagged opening in the wall where glass had been. Terry Doyle ordered them out — and they went. He would never be one of them again.

At last he thought of Bright. Bright, where are you?

He went outside. Cops were using their sticks to push people back toward City Hall. They swung at anyone within range. One cop brought his club down on the head of a Townie. Terry heard the dull *thunk* of the hickory, and without thinking he grabbed the cop's arm. "Jesus Christ, you'll kill him!"

The cop raised his stick again, but now above Terry's head. Terry fell back, and the stick, swooping down with full force, just missed him. Another bursting red Irish face, all the madness of what was happening had collected in the policeman, who swung again, insane.

Terry pushed away. Instead of going with the crowd, he moved toward the low wall that separated the municipal plaza from the tree-lined apron that ran alongside the Kennedy Building toward Congress Street. The wall was low enough to offer government workers, when the world was not ending, a place to eat their lunches. Terry hopped onto it and turned to scan the crowd from there. Where are you?

Worry for Bright choked him. But then he remembered that the night before, when he'd called to tell her, so proudly, that Kennedy had agreed to come, Joan had said she would be here too. Jesus Christ, Joan! What if these animals — these Irish — hurt her?

✧

Squire Doyle had watched everything from the place he'd taken across Tremont Street, in the shadow of the great arch of the curving brick Crescent Building. Government Center terrain was a long, gentle slope taking the city from its hill down to the sea. Squire had a sweeping vantage of the entire scene, from the new Druid temple of City Hall to the glass-and-concrete upended shoebox of the JFK.

The Crescent Building had cut off access between the courthouse at Pemberton Square and the government offices; the broad, through-the-building archway was the architect's solution, centered on an open-air escalator that carried pedestrians down the last notch of Beacon Hill into the brick expanse of the plaza. Ordinarily tourists, secretaries, stenographers, court workers, and jurors used the thoroughfare, but the moving stairs had been mostly vacant since the demonstration started.

What few passersby had gone through would have had no reason to notice Squire Doyle. He was dressed in the dark, loose-fitting but well-made trousers, shirt, and sweater that set him apart only slightly, and his position between the escalator and the side door of a Shawmut Bank branch was discreet. With him was Jackie Mullen, but not in uniform. Mullen was dressed like a Townie dock worker, in sweatshirt, overalls, and ankle-high work boots. His jaunty tweed cap completed the image. He resembled dozens or hundreds of the demonstrators, which served his purpose. He was one of a number of state cops in plain clothes, but he violated his own costume with the handset of the police radio he was holding to his ear.

Because they had seen the frantic ebb and flow of the crowd, but also because, with the radio, Mullen had monitored the panicked police alarms, they had been aware of the threat to Kennedy. The commotion at the entrance to the JFK Building had been calmed, but word of what had happened had passed through the mob. Even from across Tremont Street Mullen and Doyle could hear the triumphant shouts: "We got Kennedy!" Kids had put on football helmets and were brandishing pipes. "Fuck the judge! Fuck Kennedy! Don't fuck with Southie!"

Mullen touched Squire's sleeve. "He's all right. They took him through the basement, out the service entrance on Congress Street. He's on his way to Logan." Mullen lowered the radio.

"Whose idea was the football helmets?"

"Those aren't our guys. They're from Southie."

"White and red? Shit, Jackie. I thought you had them under control."

"Hey, Squire, if Kennedy shows his puss here, it serves him right. What a stupid-ass thing to do."

"I thought the point was, we *want* Kennedy. Isn't that it, Jackie? We have a grievance, and we want it heard. We want to win these guys over. Or was all this a way to come downtown to say Fuck you."

Mullen shrugged. "The folks are pissed off. I don't blame them. Kennedy was just going to wag his finger in their faces, as you know better than me."

"Because of Terry?"

"The greatest finger-wagger of them all," Mullen said.

"I encouraged Terry to get Kennedy here if he could. I'm amazed he was able to do it. I didn't think Ted Kennedy had the balls." Squire faced his friend. "And I didn't think Townies, including our punks, were looking to kill the bastard."

"Shit, Squire, don't blame this —"

"Forget it. Like you said, he's gone. Christ." Doyle turned back toward the throng, which was suddenly dispersing, as if the rank meaning of what had nearly happened had spontaneously dawned on thirty-five hundred people. Rowdies continued to hurl epithets and fists into the air, but the chalk-faced men and women around them moved in a subdued mass out into the surrounding sidewalks and streets.

At the edge of his vision, off to his left, Squire saw a dark form glide by like a mote. He turned his head fully to look and saw Joan, the upper half of her.

She was riding the escalator from Pemberton Square down to the Tremont Street sidewalk. He could have lobbed a basketball at her, she was that close. Her long neck was hidden by her black turtleneck, and he knew why at once: the mark of a poppy blossom that he had left on her throat.

She was staring straight ahead at the unraveling demonstration. She would have no idea that the rambling punks, now in clusters of three and four, were nothing compared to the just-passed danger of the mob. Watching her smooth descent, Squire saw a flash of the scene from the day before, her colorful underpants bunched at the base of that statue, what he had found himself staring at when, at last, he'd opened his eyes.

She might as well have been asleep, so unaware was she that he was looking at her. He regretted not telling her how she'd made him feel. Would she have been complimented, he wondered, to know how confused she'd left him when, afterward and so abruptly, she'd made him go? Usually he was the one who wanted out, and her urgency had impressed him almost as much as the shock of his feelings for her.

He took one step toward her, and as if she had registered the consequent movement of air, she turned toward him, a backward glance, as the escalator continued carrying her down and away.

"Hey, isn't that—?" Mullen checked his question when he saw Squire's face, connecting it to hers, the look between them. Squire seemed timid, that was the first clue. And the woman — surely it was Terry's wife from the other day — seemed made of stone.

Even before Joan reached ground level, she was moving, with her eyes fixed on Squire. Mullen began instinctively to back away, aware as he watched her leave the stairs and come forward that she did not see him. By the time she reached Squire, Mullen was safely on the fringe of the crowd, still watching.

Joan stopped a few feet short of Squire, whose face showed nothing.

"Do you feel better, Nick?"

"Feel better?"

"Now that you've fucked your brother. Wasn't that the point of fucking me?"

Squire smiled. "Gee, it sure felt like you, just you."

"It will never happen again. Do you understand that?"

"I wouldn't want it either, sweetheart. Not that it wasn't great."

"You got what you wanted, as usual."

"Are you afraid I'll tell? Is that it?"

"No. That would ruin it for you. I see that. But if you ever did tell Terry, it would destroy him — not because of me doing it, but because of you. You may not know this, but he loves you. He loves you, you bastard."

Squire said nothing.

"Get out of his life. Stay away from us. Do you hear me?"

Still Squire only stared at her mutely.

She stepped closer. "I'll tell you something else. If you ever did tell him, I'd —"

He seemed as hard as she, as close to an extreme. But he mistook for reluctance the pause during which she allowed weight to accumulate on her statement. Without meaning to, he yielded something when he indicated curiosity by raising an eyebrow. You'd what, sweetheart?

"— kill you," she said.

✧

Only moments had passed with Terry standing on the ledge of the masonry wall near the JFK Building. Now he saw Joan pushing through the crowd. She had seen him first, and when his eyes fell on her she waved, but there was doom in the gesture, not joy. He thought that was because of the scene she'd found herself in. He hopped down from the wall but remained by it, waiting for her.

She ran across the last stretch of the brick pavement. With none of the composure he'd thought of as her absolute possession, she threw herself on him. He took her weight without budging.

She held him as she rarely had before, and he misunderstood entirely. "They didn't get him," he said. "He got away."

"Who?"

"The senator. They would have killed him, but they didn't. He's safe. He's gone. It's Bright I just can't find."

"What?"

"Bright disappeared. I don't know what happened to him." Even as he spoke, with his mouth and nose at her hair, his hands tight on her slim hips, Terry began scanning the plaza again. Most of the crowd, heading off toward the Common or thronging the subway stop, had their backs to him. Even so, it was such a simple matter seeing them all as white.

"Christ," Terry said then, "look who's here."

As Squire passed the tag ends of the crowd, coming through them, the men and women gave way for him ever so slightly, and Terry recognized his brother's power. And at that moment it was only a relief to do so. Mullen came up behind, but it was only his brother whom Terry saw.

"Nick, Nick — I can't find Bright."

Squire had once searched for ways to get his brother to need him. He'd imagined Terry capsizing out in the harbor channel and waving desperately from the upturned hull of a dinghy. He'd imagined him getting stuck in the narrow storm pipe below the navy yard, pulling him out by his heels. He'd even imagined him asking for a job after he left the seminary. But the wish to help his brother had died with the expectation that he ever would. Besides, he was now thinking of Joan.

She had not released Terry.

"I can't find Bright!"

"What happened?"

"We were with Kennedy. When the mob pushed in on Ted, Bright disappeared. I saw him shoving back, same as I was, but then —"

"Then?" Squire was what, making him spell it out?

Terry shrugged helplessly, then looked down at Joan, still in his arms. He turned her toward his brother. "Look who's here," he said again.

Joan continued leaning against Terry. She knew how important it was to look at his brother, to speak his name. She raised her face. "Hello, Nick." But her eyes fell on the other one, the man she recognized as the leader of the gang who'd hung the effigy. His lips were parted and turned up in a half sneer — the smirk, she realized, of his knowledge. How did this creep know? Her former strength, the will with which she'd just confronted Nick, had evaporated. She simply could not keep track of herself. Who was she now? What would she become? Everything in front of Joan blurred as she thought of Nick and this lout discussing her. It would amaze her later that she had not, right then, simply ceased to exist.

"Hi, Joan," Squire said. "We meet again."

"Help me find him, Nick. It's my fault if something happened."

Squire raised a hand at Mullen. "Check it out, Jackie."

"What do you mean?" Jackie said.

"Your radio. Call your dispatcher. Have him call the precinct."

Mullen produced the walkie-talkie from inside his jacket.

"Incidents involving Negro males . . ." Squire swept the scene with one arm. "How many Negro males are down here today?"

"Negro male," Terry put in, "with an eye patch."

Mullen brought the handset to his face, turning away. A moment later he swung back to them. "District One," he said. "They just brought him in."

The station house was on the far side of the JFK Building, and they were there in minutes, only to find the entrance closed off by a barricade of paddy wagons parked bumper to bumper along the curb. The sidewalk was blocked by wooden barriers, inside of which a number of agitated uniformed and plainclothes police were milling. Terry tried to lead the way in, but a cop challenged him. He stepped aside for Mullen, who held up his credentials folder. Terry and Joan and, last, Squire, followed Mullen through. At the window cubicle inside the entrance, Terry pushed Mullen aside and demanded of the desk sergeant, "We're looking for Neville McKay."

Jackie leaned back, his badge against the glass. "A nigger with an eye patch."

The cop swiveled away from the window to confer with others. He came back. "He's still in booking. We're not —"

"Booking!" Terry yelled against the glass. "McKay is Senator Kennedy's AA! What do you mean, 'booking'?"

"Just what I said, Mac. The man is being charged —"

"He was protecting Kennedy," Terry screamed. "What the Boston Police clearly were not doing."

"That so?" The cop's indifference was amplified by the metal grate through which his voice came. "You say his name is McKay? He didn't give us a name. He didn't mention Kennedy."

"*I'm* mentioning him. You arrested the one black on City Hall plaza? Out of five thousand people, the only black? What is this, Mississippi?"

The sergeant stood up. He pointed toward the entrance, speaking now to Mullen. "Get him out of here before —"

"Hold it, Sarge," Mullen said, "hold it."

But Squire pushed Mullen aside, and his brother too, stepping to the window, grinning like a bettor at the track. He put his mouth against the grate and said softly, "I want to see Lieutenant O'Brien. Tell

Chuck O'Brien that Squire's out here. Tell him he's got a problem that Squire wants to help with."

The desk officer shrugged, then crossed to a nearby door.

Two cops at a metal desk beyond had been watching, and one of them raised a forefinger at Squire, who nodded.

The sergeant returned with the lieutenant following, a Red Auerbach look-alike whose most impressive feature was the cigar in his mouth. He opened the cubicle door and waited as Squire walked over to him. They spoke quietly for a full minute.

Then Squire turned to Terry. "They didn't know who he was. They'll bring him up."

"No. I want to see him now. I want to see where they have him."

"Look, Terry, you've got to let these guys play it the way —"

"*No* way, Nick."

"What are you here for? To make a scene, or to help your friend?"

"Make a scene? Me? After what your assholes have pulled? You talk to *me?* Goddamn you, you've done this before."

"What?"

"Thrown Bright to wolves, *your* wolves. Or have you forgotten? Are you happy with your Charlestown Marshals now? Or were they supposed to *kill* the senator? Why is Bright McKay under arrest and not you? Tell me that, Nick, will you?"

Squire said, "Get yourself under control, Charlie."

Terry turned to the lieutenant. "Take me to McKay."

The lieutenant said, "We don't have a name."

"The one-eyed nigger, Lieutenant. Take me to your one-eyed nigger."

The cop looked at Squire, who shook his head in apology. "This is my brother."

"The spoiled priest?"

"That's right," Terry said coldly. "And also director of Senator Kennedy's Boston office."

Lieutenant O'Brien took the cigar from his mouth and tapped it with marked defiance, so that the ash fell at Terry's feet. He reached behind the door, to an invisible hook, for a ring of keys. "All right. Come with me. Just you."

Joan grabbed Terry's arm. "No. Take me too. Don't leave me here. Not with *him*."

"Lady, believe me, you don't —"

"I'm not staying here."

O'Brien rolled his eyes at Squire.

Squire said, "I've got checks to write, folks." He backed toward the exit, grinning. Joan alone refused to look at him. He added with a mocking flourish, "Besides, I'm out of my element."

"I'm coming too," Mullen said.

Lieutenant O'Brien winked at him. "Still on the payroll, Jackie?"

Mullen stopped, an emphatic interruption. "What payroll?"

"Why, the governor's. Who else's?"

"And you, Lieutenant?" They looked at each other out of similar, pug-shaped faces, joined by mutual expressions of contempt. "I'll be sure to tell Captain Harris what a great job you're doing." Mullen followed Squire out.

O'Brien led the way through an adjacent steel door. It opened on a starkly lit set of cement stairs that led down to a cinder-block corridor. At another heavy door he pressed a button, and while waiting to be buzzed through, he said, "The bear cage."

The door opened on yet a narrower section of corridor, which was marked by a row of barred cell doors. Despite the furious outbreak on the plaza and the shattered wall of glass at the Kennedy Building, the holding cells were mostly vacant. Vagrants and drunks, but not Powderkeg rowdies, stood bleary-eyed at the bars as Terry, Joan, and O'Brien passed.

In a cell at the end of the corridor was a lone figure in dark trousers and a white shirt. The man had folded himself into a corner on the floor next to a lidless steel toilet bowl.

"Bright?"

McKay brought his head up from his knees. His shirt was soiled and torn. His tie was gone, and so was his suit coat. He had been holding a handkerchief against his brow. When he pulled it away, a red gash could be seen on his forehead above his good eye.

Terry said, "Why hasn't that wound been treated?"

O'Brien passed his hand across his own face, as if shooing a fly.

Bright got to his feet and went to the bars. He spoke haltingly, through swollen lips. "I'd get a doctor, they said, when I signed a statement admitting I resisted."

"When you told us your name," O'Brien corrected.

"What difference does his name make?"

"That wound is deep," Joan said.

"It's not even bleeding," the cop answered.

Bright held out the red cloth in his hand.

Terry passed his own handkerchief through the bars. "Get him out of there."

O'Brien unlocked the door and pulled it open. "Why didn't you say who you were?"

Coming out of the cell, Bright put his face in the cop's. Its bruises and welts and the high color of his flushed brown skin were more visible now. "Because every time I opened my mouth, one of you motherfuckers hit me. So then I decided to just shut up and see how far you bastards would go."

"And how far was that?" O'Brien asked.

Bright looked at Terry. "Do you have a pen, a pad?"

"Yes."

"Take these numbers down." Bright waited while Terry pulled his pen out. Then he dictated a series of three- and four-digit numbers, a set of ten of them perhaps. Badge numbers. When he'd finished he turned to O'Brien.

"Your word against theirs, Mr. McKay," the cop said.

"Right. And against the doctor who sees me now. Against these two witnesses. In civil rights law, that's plenty."

It wasn't, as Bright knew. And Terry knew it too. He admired his friend's defiance, especially when he saw the policeman falter, which was all Bright hoped for.

"We offered treatment," O'Brien said. "You refused to sign a waiver."

"Bullshit. I saw what you wanted me to sign. There's no question of a medical waiver. This is one nigger who reads, Lieutenant." Bright turned to Terry and Joan. "Can you get me out of here?"

Terry led the way down the corridor, past the other cells. One prisoner hissed, "Fucking coon!"

The door buzzed open even before they reached it.

On the street outside, Bright stopped. In the sunlight, the beating his face had taken was even more evident. One side of his jaw was badly swollen, and the skin on his lips was raw. He touched the fresh handkerchief to his head.

Joan went up on her toes to look at the wound. "We've got to get you down to MGH."

Bright did not move, and neither did Terry. They were alike in looking up at the surrounding buildings, the distant City Hall. They had the air of men who'd just survived a car wreck.

Finally Terry put an arm around each of them, but it was to McKay that he spoke. "Do you see what I see?"

"This fucking city?"

"I hate it as much as you do."

Bright looked at him. "No. You don't."

But Terry was still scanning the buildings, as if seeing them for the first time. A new idea was taking form in his mind. He said, "I'd like to show this town. Christ, I'd like to show it."

"Show it what?"

"Something it's never seen before." Terry looked at Bright. "I'd like to show it you and me."

"Terry —"

"No, listen. You and me, Bright. We should make a move on Boston. Let's take it on."

"For Ted?"

"For us!" Terry squeezed Bright and Joan both. "Christ, what a fool I've been." Doyle thought of that bench on top of Bunker Hill, how he'd longed for Boston to know of his existence. He said, "I thought that by *serving* — Kennedy; before him; the Church — but *serving* isn't it at all." The strength of his new idea, whatever it was, seemed all the strength he needed. "That's over," he said. "I don't want to serve Boston."

"I get it," Bright said. "You want to *own* it."

"Yes!" Terry laughed out loud, and he hugged them again, in the thrill of his recognition. "It's what I've always wanted."

✧

That night Joan took the black trillium into the bathroom and put it on the shelf by the tub. Nick's words hung in her mind: "The soil moist, but never wet." She plugged the tub and let the water run until it was full. Then she put the pot into the water, submerging the plant halfway up the stem. She took a pair of clippers and snipped the blossom. She put it between her hands, her own personal flower of the plague, and crushed it, what Terry had known to do immediately with his lapel flower. Now she knew too.

Then she undressed and put on her striped pajamas. She went into the living room. Nearly an hour before, after the news with its scenes of the mobs assaulting Kennedy, the film showing the shattered glass, Terry had told her he wasn't ready for bed. He'd remained in front of the television. Now Johnny Carson, wearing a beanie and shoulder pads, was impersonating President Ford playing golf.

Joan said, "I thought you might come in."

"You still awake?"

She watched him from behind, his broad, unmoving body. Women all over America going to bed without their husbands. No wonder

Johnny Carson's laughs were always sly, as if he knew very well what was layered beneath his silliness, all his innuendo, all the prancing beauties, all of Ed McMahon's cracks about sex — and all the simultaneous, secret shuddering with loneliness, the going to sleep in shifts, the nightly ritual of not touching. We will not be such people, she told herself. We simply won't.

She stood with one foot in back of the other, like a dancer. She looked at the glass on the floor beside his chair, drained again, and she thought perhaps he was drunk. Drinking and television — he would not become one of those men whose forest-size need to believe and to do is cut down to such stumps. He simply wouldn't. His will — she hoped this was so — was a match for hers. They only had to find each other again.

"Then wake me up when you come in, would you?" She hesitated, then added, "I'd like to make love."

Terry turned in the chair to look at her.

"I'm just very full of feelings, Terry. After today. I don't want to be alone."

He got up to turn the television off. When he faced her, she was gone.

In the bedroom she was waiting for him with her pajamas off, the sheet covering her. The only light was on the table beside the bed, and when he came in he turned it off and sat next to her. Through the sheet he touched her breast, gently, admiringly, then turned away to undress.

Pulling the sheet back carefully, he lay down beside her. They embraced with a tentativeness that had been unknown when they'd begun as lovers, but that had become customary between them. His passion began to mount. To his surprise, she was way ahead of him. They kissed more deeply, wrapping their arms and legs together. His fingers found her clitoris, but when she arched up at him impatiently, he pushed one finger into her vagina, to moisten it, as she'd instructed once.

And then he stopped.

"You've forgotten your diaphragm," he whispered.

"No. No, I haven't."

"It isn't in you. I don't feel it."

"I don't want it, not tonight." She put her face on his, pushed her tongue into his mouth, rolled onto him.

"Not after today," she said. "Nothing between us."

"You want —?"

"You! I want you! Come in me!"

Amazed and dizzy, he touched her face. "Joan." He felt knocked down, as if that were why he was lying here. "I love you."

They turned so that she was underneath. When he pushed inside her, she feared that he would thank her. She sensed his relief, easily imagining it as that of a man allowed at last to breathe. It was no surprise when he began, while coming, to say "God, God," or that he seemed to mean it as a kind of prayer. It was no surprise, even, that the display of his gut piety did not offend her.

The surprise, still, was the certainty of her knowledge — more than intuition, an absolute sensation of blood and flesh, what she'd have dismissed in someone else as *female* piety — that she was already pregnant.

And the surprise was, also, the efficient calculation with which she was managing — "Yes, darling, *there*" — to adjust herself, and also him, to this unbearable situation. How she wanted to undo the day before, but she never could. How she wanted this child to be his. Her only hope was in his never, ever knowing. That was the heart of her ambition now, and always would be. The heart of her will, and of her love.

Her self-possession was a wonder to her, that she could do this, keeping from him what she knew. Something was alive in her, and something was dead. Black trillium.

"Oh, yes," she said. "Oh, sugar."

"Joan. My Joan."

Her sweet, weak husband was feeling saved. She was damned.

✧ 1984 ✧

16

THE TRAIN RATTLED along the elevated tracks forty feet above Washington Street, entering the long, curving stretch south of the cathedral where the steel wheels began their ungodly screech. Terry Doyle stared out the window across the rooftops of the indifferent South End. He did not look like an Orange Line rider, but neither did the others in the seats and aisle of the single train car, and ordinarily they weren't. A well-groomed collection, dressed in suits and polished shoes, the few women in suits and heels, they looked like what they were, bankers and developers, city, state, and federal officials, presidents of companies. The less nattily dressed were reporters and the few low-level functionaries needed to hold doors, but even they were in suits and ties.

The knees and shoulders of those who were seated jounced with the jerky movement, and those standing rode the car with the necessary loose-jointedness of surfboarders. Doyle was one of these. He was still slim and tall, but he was forty-one now, vaguely stoop-shouldered. The skin around his mouth was creased, and his eyes were glazed with a hint of burdened weariness. His hair was thinner, showing gray. His clothing drew no special attention to itself, but in fact his blue suit and white shirt were handmade, perfectly fitted. The knot of his red tie rode above a gold collar pin. He was not the oldest of those on the subway car, not the wealthiest nor most powerful, but there was in everything about him, except perhaps those too moist eyes, the air of a man to whom the others were subordinate. He was the vice president of the Hammond Company now, an old Boston real estate management firm, which under him, in the Kevin White boom years, had become a major developer.

Old Hammond would retire soon, and Doyle was slated to succeed him as president, a discreet Irish takeover of yet another corner of the Yankee realm. BC guys had arrived, not just as pols, like their fathers and grandfathers, but as the businessmen who had the knack for riding this, the city's first big kanaka wave. Lately, it seemed, they were in on every deal, not just the renaissance of the city, but the reinvention of it, and that was why they were on this subway car. Nobody believed in the old prejudices anymore, or in the old limits either. From their predecessors, the Irish comers had learned to believe only in money.

The thin light of a spring morning washed the grid of dirty streets onto which Doyle looked. It was a mild day in April, but the scene below was meant for winter. Storefront windows were covered with splintered plywood. Here and there burned-out row houses, open to the weather, broke the line of dark rooftops. He glimpsed derelicts hunched in ill-fitting coats along a blank wall, early birds for the Pine Street soup line, and quickly looked away.

The train slowed as it veered west, and the noise became more piercing. Dover Street, Savoy, Waltham, Union Park — as the train clicked the distance off, Doyle's eye followed each South End street north to the point where it ended in the wall of the rail embankment three blocks away. The old Penn Central right of way, already a gash between two neighborhoods, had been widened in the sixties into a wasteland of cleared earth on which I-95 had been slated to make its run through Boston. Thousands of homes and businesses had been demolished, and one of the inner city's few manufacturing belts had been destroyed. The jobs lost had staggered the South End and lower Roxbury, and the all but impassable physical barrier had quickly drained both neighborhoods of vitality. Residents had denounced the highway scheme, and in 1970 Governor Sargent killed it, but the isolating gash remained. Cambridge-based urban planners had dubbed it the Southwest Corridor, but Roxbury preachers called it the Berlin Wall. Now, from downtown all the way out the five miles to Forest Hills, the rail line was bordered by wide, weed-ridden margins of moonscape, a savage and seemingly permanent no man's land, Boston's finest method yet for keeping people in their place.

But a miracle was about to happen in the South End and lower Roxbury, and on this midmorning train ride he and these others, like so many Gabriels, had come to announce it. The boom that had caused seventeen major skyscrapers to go up in ten years had generated more money than anyone in the weary old town had ever dreamed of, and it showed every sign of doing so indefinitely. As of this winter, a new mayor had been elected expressly to bring some of the money back to the neighborhoods. Beginning here, which was, in Irish Boston, the miracle.

A *lot* of money. Terry Doyle, as one of the men who'd been making it, had some idea how much. Private money and public, HUD and Model Cities grants, Interstate Transfer and Mass Transit funds; under Title 23 alone, six hundred million dollars had been appropriated to relocate the Orange Line from Washington Street to the Southwest Corridor, stimulating a whole complex of other projects, the latest of which they would unveil today.

Tom Lacey, head of the MBTA, leaned in on Doyle, and Terry became aware of the man's warm, sour breath. Lacey pointed out the window at the dark hulk of the cathedral, which seemed close enough to toss a line to. It had all the grace of an oil tanker run aground. The classic rose window was just above eye level, a massive gray disk enmeshed in wire screening. It and the granite façade were filthy, black with soot. Pigeons roosted on every ledge, in each nook and cranny, cutting the soot with the acid of their shit.

Lacey had said something.

"What? I can't hear."

"My point exactly." Lacey cupped his mouth. "When Cardinal Cushing was buried from there, we suppressed service on this line for three hours, out of respect, because of this racket. We did it for Curley too."

"I know about the noise. I've been inside." Terry thought of the ordination ceremony nearly two decades before, his own melodramatic take on Adam stalking out of Eden. He thought of the K of C ceremony even earlier, where Gramps had dubbed him Charlie. The old man had died in 1979, a blank-eyed ghost who didn't even know Squire. Terry winked at Lacey. "These trains have done a job on that place over the years."

"Wasn't that the point?" Lacey said. Both men laughed, a draft of the old amused bitterness. The Irish loved to tell themselves that the Brahmins had put the el here to ruin their grand cathedral.

Doyle said, "The truth is, Tom, the cathedral was always an ugly rock pile."

"Well, this fucking noise is another reason to move the line to the Corridor. The protesters are numbskulls."

"What protesters?"

"Never mind about that." Lacey slapped Doyle's shoulder. "If Curley was here, he'd claim it was called Orange for the Protestants who built it."

Doyle laughed. "You going to quote Curley in your speech, Tommy?"

"God, no."

Doyle's eyes lingered on Holy Cross, bereft on that mean-hearted street, and he was ambushed by a feeling of loss. The cathedral, the Church itself, the first life he'd chosen — all of it lost. A familiar taste came into his mouth, a surge of nausea, the old insistent wish that his empty faith was the Church's failure, not his.

Moments later the ribbed mansard roof and twin cupolas of Dudley station came into view. Dudley was the hub of one end of Roxbury, a bus terminal and the site of a courthouse, a library, and what remained of a retail center. The car stopped with a jolt and the doors hissed open. MBTA policemen awaited them on the platform, keeping others back. "Not in service," they barked. "No one boards."

Duke of Dudley, read the scrawl on the station wall. *Mandela '84.* What advertising signs there were seemed less posted than abandoned. The platform was littered with debris. A wire trash basket lay on its side, and the wall behind was charred, partially burned through, leaving a thin sliver open to the gray sky.

An MBTA bus was waiting at the sidewalk. The group filed on, pretending no interest in the dreary, overshadowed square. In fact, they were all instantly aware that across the street, on the plaza in front of the branch library, a crowd of blacks was hemmed in by police. *Don't Abandon Dudley!* read one sign. *Ask the People!* read another. The big shots refused to look across at the demonstration. Instead their eyes went, as they were supposed to, toward a bunting-draped branch of the Commonwealth Bank. In its main window was a crisply lettered poster: *Commonwealth Bank and the Roxbury Planning Council Salute the Southwest Corridor Improvement Project.*

Soon the bus was loaded and heading out behind a pair of motorcycles, through the congested, blighted streets ringing the train station overhead. Doyle took up his position in front of the bus, aware of the cold stares of the people on the sidewalk. No matter what you did in this fucking town, somebody said no. Especially if what you did was try to help.

A few minutes later the bus broke out of the maze of narrow streets around Dudley, into the surprisingly open plain of cleared land. The bus picked up speed as traffic fell off. Instead of grim, dilapidated rooming houses, tenements, and pawnshops, the streets here were bordered by fields of waist-high weeds and mounded gravel.

Doyle gestured at the stretch of land to the south. "Eighteen acres, ladies and gentlemen, parcel twenty-two. The future site of Madison Park Townhouses, one hundred twenty units. Model Cities–funded; the Hammond Company, developer; Phillips and Phillips, architects; Commonwealth Bank, financing." He fell silent as the bus moved deeper into the leveled Corridor, turning onto Ruggles Street, where the view opened on seventy acres stretching out on all sides. "Jesus," one of the passengers said, Harry Clapp, a mall mogul from New Jersey, "hell of a lot of open land for an inner city."

Doyle pointed. "More housing was flattened here than anywhere, because this was to be the site of the cloverleaf joining I-95 and the Innerbelt. The most devastated area, but now the richest opportunity, more than Hammond can handle, Harry." Doyle grinned suddenly. "Which is why you get your shot in Beantown."

Clapp snorted.

Doyle tapped the window. "We have key pieces in place already. There, for example, in the stretch running to the foot of the hill, is where we site the new campus high school. Beyond it, a post office and the community college. Two or three thousand kids, a retailers' bonanza, Harry."

The man next to Clapp elbowed him, and several others exchanged remarks, inaudible but obvious: retailers' *nightmare*, more like it, all those unleashed black boys, their boom boxes, basketball shoes, the old hit and run.

The bus plunged into the eerie, wide-open valley. Along its center ran the Penn Central tracks, and at one end a massive construction site straddled the trench along which the new Orange Line was being laid.

"The new Ruggles station," Doyle said, "to replace Dudley as the local hub." A pair of cranes towered over cement trucks, framing structures, and scaffolding. "The parcel to the west, parcel nineteen, is for the new Water Resources headquarters, but the governor hasn't inked it yet, last we heard, right Joe?"

"You asking me, Terry?" Joe Turino, seated three rows back, opened his hands helplessly. "You know Beacon Hill as well as I do."

Doyle laughed good-naturedly. "Which is why we're glad to have private interest in Ruggles Center." He swept his arm around, facing forward. The savage clearance had spared a pair of churches, St. Francis de Sales, Catholic, and on Tremont Street St. Cyprian's, Anglican — the West Indian church of which Bright McKay's father had been rector years before. Hard against that church, a platform had been built and dressed with bunting for this occasion. Bright was there, and so, Doyle saw, was the large crowd it had been Bright's job to deliver. On one side, a small knot of people held signs — more protesters — but here too they'd been isolated by police.

"And here we come," Doyle said as the bus slowed, "to Ruggles, the new heart of lower Roxbury, a mixed-use twenty-acre site of office, retail, housing, manufacturing, institutional, and hotel development." He paused, then added wryly, "Depending on you bastards, of course."

They laughed.

The bus slowed even more. A reggae band on the platform churned out languid, hip music, its every member swaying in soulful hats and army-surplus coats, horns at their faces, guitars at their groins. The crowd, perhaps two hundred people, seated on folding chairs, was neatly integrated. The blacks among them seemed to be moving with the music; the whites sat stiff and nervous, having either ventured across the tracks from Northeastern University or been bused out here from jobs at City Hall.

Among the black protesters in back, Joe Grant, the long-time South End agitator in his trademark dashiki and sunglasses, was brandishing a well-worn sign: *Stop Urban Removal!* Other signs read *Deeds Not Weeds!* and *People Not Promises!* Terry felt a bolt of the old anger. The fools, didn't they know they'd won?

He saw Bright standing off to the side of the platform, near the flag-draped church steps that served now as stairs to the stage. His eye patch, as always, was what Terry fixed upon first. With Bright were Senator Kennedy, Mayor Flynn, and a man whom Doyle did not know, which was what attracted his attention. The man was short compared to Kennedy, Flynn, and McKay, and he wore a flashy dark fedora while the others were hatless. Something else struck Doyle about him, he didn't know what. But it didn't matter.

The bus door snapped open and Doyle faced his charges. "On behalf of the Southwest Corridor Working Committee and the Community Development Corporation, welcome to the future of Boston."

✧

Bright's first position at the Commonwealth Bank had been with Community Affairs. Naturally, a black face in the window. But he'd insinuated himself into the counting rooms. Power over the movement of money was what mattered; it had enabled him, for one thing, to do this.

"You pulled it off, man." Terry pressed his friend's shoulder, affection and pride. McKay had just managed a stunning presentation, and shortly afterward, the ceremony had ended. "Your old man should be here."

Bright glanced over at the church. "Me, bringing back St. Cyp's."

"Bringing back a lot of things."

With Doyle, he looked wistfully around at the scarred, empty expanse. "It was so fucking lively here once."

"It will be again."

"Think so?" Bright grinned, then added, "Let's see what these folks do. Our letter of agreement commits to nothing until the anchor drops. Joe Grant thinks it's all just cover for getting black people off the Orange Line, which is what it will be if—"

"We've got Madison Park, the campus high, Roxbury Community College, and Northeastern. And you know I'll get the office building nailed down."

"MWRA is balking, Terry. The governor—"

"Bright, come on. We're doing it, man. Four careful years. One step at a time. We're doing it."

"You're right. Christ, you're right." Bright slapped one hand into another and surveyed the scene again, swiveling his head in that odd way of his. "We'll bring back this whole fucking area. My old man wouldn't believe it. Me."

On the platform, aides were folding up the display boards, *Dudley Square Reborn*, *Ruggles Street Returns*. The crowd was dispersing. Some drifted into St. Cyprian's, where the coffee was. Others headed to their cars. The VIPs were getting back on their bus. Flynn was gone, but not Ted Kennedy. Reporters had gathered at the platform in a tight circle around him, including the film crew Bright had hired. Without notes, Kennedy was enumerating the titles of the U.S. Code from which the funds he'd just announced were coming. Since his failed 1980 presidential campaign and his failed marriage, Kennedy had become corpulent, a man flirting with obesity. His rough-and-tumble life showed in his face, the uneven blotches of pink and red on his cheeks and neck, the veins in his nose. Yet there he was, citing appropriations and authorizations, many of which he'd sponsored, his voice clear, his mind sharp, a man entirely focused on what had brought him here. "And twenty percent of all moneys contracted," he said firmly, "to be expended on minority-owned enterprises. That's the law." He pointed across at the protesters. "Somebody go over and tell Joe Grant that."

Kennedy's young aide took his elbow and began to move him toward the car. But the senator glanced across at McKay and Doyle. He pulled himself free and came over, and in an abrupt shift of mood hollered, "Look at you two, a couple of new-age tycoons, doing well by doing good."

"Not that good," Terry said automatically.

"Not that *well*," Bright added.

"Not what I hear," Kennedy said, fixing McKay with a stagy look. "Not what I hear at all. How'd you bring the bank around? I heard that Van Buren pitched the governor. How'd you sell him?"

Bright smiled. "I promised him something from you, Senator."

"Oh, great. What?"

"That he wouldn't have to go to your clambake."

Kennedy laughed, too raucously. Then he said, more quietly, "Seriously, how'd you get Van Buren to sign on?"

It was a question of Terry's too. Ruggles Street was well inside the bank's redline. None of the other Boston banks had committed themselves, even to the point of letters of intent.

Bright shook his head. "My secret."

"Even to me?" Kennedy produced a cigarillo and faced Terry, who from an old habit produced a light. He used Joan's gold lighter, which she had given him when she'd quit smoking. After the senator got his smoke going, Terry lit his own cigarette, prompting Kennedy to poke him. "We're the last two left, Terry, who do this."

"Don't you enjoy it more for that?"

"Yeah," Kennedy said, as if just realizing it. "Yeah, I do." Kennedy laughed again, more jarringly than before. There was something manic about him suddenly. He threw an arm around each of them. "I miss you guys. I want you to come down to Florida for Easter. What do you say?"

Terry started to decline, but before he could, Ted blurted, "Bring Joan, bring Max." He turned to McKay. "Bring whatshername. Are you still with whatshername?" More raucous laughter.

Doyle and McKay exchanged a glance. Reporters hovered nearby, watching. McKay raised a finger at the film crew to stop. It was not like Ted Kennedy to shed his crafted, stately demeanor so quickly, and in the open. It was as if he'd been drinking already, but apparently he hadn't.

His aide had him now and began pulling him toward his car. "Call the office," Kennedy said. "Let them know about Florida, when you're coming."

"Thank you, Senator," McKay said, "but I'm also calling you about Amory."

"Oh good, I liked that guy." Then Kennedy turned and went to his car, leaving his two former aides to watch as the new young one held the car door open.

"Jesus," Terry said, "he's burning it at both ends, isn't he?"

"But oh, what a lovely light. One way or another, Terry, the candle goes out."

Doyle did not comment until the car was gone. Then he looked at Bright. "Who's Amory?"

"Our new partner." McKay pointed at the man in the fedora. He was sitting by himself at the end of the row of chairs, the last person still seated, a tan raincoat folded over his arm. He was reading the fancy brochure, the cornucopia that would follow up and down the Southwest Corridor once Ruggles took off.

Bright said, "He's almost signed up."

"For what?"

"The showpiece, Ruggles Center."

"What do you mean? *I'm* Ruggles Center. Ruggles Center is Hammond's."

"I know. But I heard Hammond is shy about thirty million dollars."

"Which Amory has?"

"Not all of it. But he's collatoralized at the bank. He gives me the bubble I need to float to the surface in. I've already run the numbers past Van Buren."

"*He's* your secret? And I've never heard of him?"

"He's from out of town. This is his first Beantown deal. Come on, I'll introduce you."

Following McKay, Doyle eyed the man carefully. He sensed now that Amory had only been pretending to read the brochure, and that his flinch of surprise at their approach was also counterfeit.

"Victor," McKay said emphatically, "here's Terry Doyle."

The man stood and removed his hat, exposing his baldness, a gesture intended to ingratiate, but it only underscored an impression of phoniness. His thin hair was neatly combed up from a part at his left ear. The strands pasted across his skull were a sad hint of how he fancied himself. A green boutonniere was pinned to the sewn-over buttonhole on the lapel of his coat. Eagerly, he put his hand out.

"How are you?" Doyle asked. "Neville tells me you're interested in our Center."

"I am indeed."

"Glad to hear it. Retail, office, and restaurant, eight hundred thousand square feet —"we're going to build a beautiful building."

Amory waved the brochure. "I can see that. Thirty stories tall. Very impressive." The man had a slight, vaguely familiar accent.

"Where are you from, if I may ask?"

"I'm from Naples. I just flew in this morning."

"Naples?"

"Florida. Naples, Florida. I build condos."

Bright touched Terry's sleeve. "Along the water, high-rises, Naples, Marco Island, and Fort Myers."

"With?"

"With iron beams, cinder block, and stucco. Nice marble also."

"With *whom?*"

Amory shrugged. "Just my brothers and me. A modest outfit. We're looking to expand up north."

"Ruggles Center will be held close, Mr. Amory. Hammond welcomes investors, but on this we retain title."

"That's the kind of deal we want, limited partnership, since we're new here. Although, point of fact, all three of us were born in Beverly. Our mother moved to Florida when we were kids."

Beverly, Beverly Farms, North Shore Brahmin — that was what his accent evoked. Victor Amory, spun out of an old Boston family, looking to return.

"Coming home," Amory said.

"Me too." Bright pointed at St. Cyp's. "My father was rector of this church. I was a teenager here, long time passing."

Was McKay shifting focus here? What was going on? "Amory . . . Amory," Terry said casually. "Cleveland Amory. North Shore?"

The man didn't miss a beat. "My mother left after a messy divorce. My father's people are total strangers to me."

"Maybe you can rediscover them."

"Perhaps." He grinned oddly and put his hat back on. "I must be off. Thanks, Neville, for the nice meeting with Senator Kennedy. One of my brothers and I gave him a wad in 'eighty. None of us could stand that Jimmy Carter, 'I'll never lie to you' bullshit. Ted's a guy who lives in the real world with the rest of us. I guess he didn't know it was me, though, huh?"

"I'll make sure he knows the next time, Victor."

"He's the last liberal. We're liberals, me and my brothers. That's another reason they're going to like this project. You can only build so many winter love nests for rich Jews, right?"

Instead of answering that, McKay let his smile stretch. Then he said, "I'll lay out your terms for Terry. We'll be in touch later. If you want to use an office while you're in town —"

"I got offices, thanks. Just leave word for me at the Ritz. I'll get back to you." He and McKay shook hands, then Amory turned to Doyle.

As they shook, Terry said, "I was admiring your lapel flower."

"Oh, this. It's shamrocks, a little bunch of shamrocks in with this lacy stuff."

"A sprig of baby's breath."

"Nifty, huh?"

Terry recognized the thin green wire, a single supporting strand wound around each of the dozen clover stems, keeping it upright even after it had wilted, a delicate creation but impossible to make money with. Now that he saw the thing, Terry's question was, Why the hell didn't I see it before?

"Welcome to Irish Boston, right?" Amory's face was distended as he looked down at his lapel.

"Where'd you get it?"

"The Ritz," he said. "The flower shop at the Ritz."

"Really?" Terry said with surprising calm. He gave no sign of what he was thinking: This lying fucker. Did Squire know he would see me? Was the kitsch boutonniere a message of some kind, or in the word Squire would use, a tickle?

✧

Three things he loved above all: his wife and his son and a view of the city of Boston. He welcomed the return of spring because it was their custom, when the weather made it possible, to go together to the river before dinner, Joan and Terry jogging, and Max riding along on his bike. They lived off Brattle Street now, on Sparks, two blocks from the Charles, and it was a simple matter to get to the jogging path, which they followed, always the same way, along the stretch of Harvard, down the Cambridge side two miles to the curve around which the magnificent view appeared — to Terry, always like magic. It was a reverse of the view that had transfixed him from Bunker Hill as a kid. Indeed, the monument was a feature of it, standing like a sentry among the sweeping girders of the Mystic River Bridge. Not a sentry, an upright needle, because it still pricked him, his eye always moving away from the obelisk to the rich green skyline.

He headed for that point, aware of Joan pounding along beside him, and of Max gunning ahead. Max was eight, a sunny, blond child whose exuberance never served him better than on that bike, which was also, at various times, a motorcycle, a stallion, a dolphin, and the space shuttle *Freedom.* He was a true child of *E.T.* The sight of Max up ahead usually soothed Terry, but not this afternoon. Despite the presence of his wife and son, he kept returning in his mind to the awful moment with Bright. They'd returned to Bright's office on the thirtieth floor of the Commonwealth Bank Building downtown. Terry had stood facing the floor-to-ceiling window of his friend's posh office, looking out over the Back Bay, watching a blue tourist trolley wend its way toward the bar on Beacon Street that inspired *Cheers.*

"So what's the problem?"

And why hadn't Terry just come right out and told him? But he knew. One thing about which he'd never been direct with Bright McKay, the only thing, was Squire.

So Terry had answered obliquely, "What do we really know about this guy?"

"We know he's ready to put two million dollars cash into the deal, cash that's already been transferred into his account in our bank. I know it's there. And on the strength of it, Van Buren is ready to approve our loan to Amory for twenty million, and we have a verified letter of intent from his bank in Naples worth another twenty. That's forty-two million dollars for Ruggles Center. That's what we know."

"I heard all that the first time, Bright."

"And you think it's more likely we'll make a major-tenant deal with the governor? Requiring a bond that the legislature has to approve? Requiring several hundred state-hack micks to move their offices to deepest, darkest Roxbury?"

Terry turned back to the room to face Bright. "Don't make the issue micks, all right?"

"Victor Amory makes the Massachusetts Water Resources Authority *and* the State House irrelevant. Suddenly we don't need them to pull this thing together, which is damned lucky. Micks aren't the issue? What the fuck is?"

"Amory."

"What are you worried about," Bright said, "that he has Japs behind him?"

"No. Not Japs."

"Hey, the guy has made a killing in Florida real estate. It happens. He's worth two hundred mil, easy. He's in business with his brothers."

"I heard him say so. Brothers."

The old friends stared at each other then, neither willing to take it further. Bright was standing at his desk, which was an expanse of smoked glass large enough to land airplanes on. Fastidious McKay. On the wall behind the desk was a shelf holding photographs of his father in cope and miter, of his stately mother, and of Martin Luther King.

On another wall were large photographs of John Kennedy and Bobby Kennedy, a young Bright McKay posed with each. Brothers.

After a long time Bright said coldly, "This guy is the dealmaker for Ruggles Center, Terry. Ruggles Center is the dealmaker for the whole fucking Southwest Corridor. The Southwest Corridor brings Roxbury and Jamaica Plain back from the dead. Whatever your problem is, get over it."

He wanted to, but he couldn't. He hadn't. Now he was jogging along a path with the glistening river on one side, eight-man sculls scooting across its surface like waterbugs. Joan was on his other side. He glanced over at her.

She was wearing a pale blue windbreaker and dark blue nylon shorts. Her sinewy legs were still tanned from their February vacation in St. Barts. On her feet she wore only shoe liners with her running shoes, and her bare ankles always gave her the look of a marathoner. Her hair was pulled back in a red railroad kerchief. She was forty-two years old. Time was touching her kindly.

She seemed unaware of him. The black foam pads of her Walkman sealed her ears; Puccini, she often said self-mockingly, was what kept her running. Joan habitually withdrew into a shell when she ran, an exertion in solitude, which was not altogether unlike what she did during sex. The limits of their physical expression had long since ceased to be a source of disappointment for either; their proximity was enough when they were running, and a mutual, if introverted, somewhat passionless expertise satisfied the needs they brought to bed.

Joan's eyes were fixed on a point ahead, but in her trance, he knew, she was not actually seeing anything — not Max on his bike and not the tops of the downtown buildings just coming into view. She loved running for the way it blanked her mind, she said. He loved running for the focus it brought to his.

The differences between them, in other words, had become more sharply drawn over the years. She'd been successful at Harvard, where she was now a tenured associate professor and the curator of prints at the Fogg. Terry, for his part, had become busy in the mode of men like him. They grew apart. Terry assumed that she was as chilled by their marriage as he, but also he knew that whatever disappointment she felt had been assuaged, to put it mildly, by his beginning to bring in real money. What bound them still — and in this weren't they like every couple they knew? — was their child.

They came to their bridge and took it, to head upriver on the business-school side. But halfway across Terry reached over to her. "Stop," he said.

She didn't hear him. When he took her arm, she looked around in alarm.

"Can we stop here a minute?"

"What?" She lifted an earphone pad.

"I need to talk to you."

Only then did she stop running, and he did too. He sensed her impatience at this violation not only of their routine but of the running ethic itself. It mattered to her, not cooling down. She craned to look past him. "Max is getting too far ahead."

The boy was on the far bank, with the white cupolas and weathervanes of the sham colonial Harvard Business School behind him. Traffic was whizzing along on Storrow Drive, but he was back from it, safely pedaling up the dusty cinder path between two broad swaths of grass.

"He's fine," Terry said. "When he sees we've slowed up, he'll wait."

"We haven't slowed up. We've stopped."

"I wanted to show you something from here."

He took her shoulder and turned her toward the view of Boston. She shut off her tape player and dropped the headset to her neck. A film of perspiration decked her upper lip and brow.

"There, see the BU buildings? The ed school and the dorms?"

"Yes."

"Right there in that gap is where our Ruggles Street building will be, three times higher than the BU buildings, a mile farther back, but it will show up as huge from here. The first major jump in the skyline away from downtown. It's going to happen. Boston will never be the same."

"That's great, Terry." She pressed his arm.

She thought he was good at what he did. She didn't know that any fool could make money in this market, although her pride was spot-on this time, since the market did not stretch to Roxbury. "If we succeed at Ruggles Street, Joan, if we show that investment pays off there, then Roxbury Crossing and Jackson Square are next. The new Orange Line will tie the city together. It'll make everything different. That Corridor has given us a once-in-a-century chance to heal this city's worst wound. And Joan" — he turned to her, took her shoulders in his hands, wanting to press his feelings into her — "we're doing it. We're really doing it."

"But something's wrong. I can tell."

He turned again to the bridge railing, brushing a weathered bronze plaque that was unobtrusively attached to the concrete pillar there. His gaze went to the downtown skyline. What he loved most about the view from here was the way the modest profile of Beacon Hill, with its terraced brick houses, its trees, the Gothic spire of the Advent Church, and the gleaming gold sphere of the Bulfinch State House — how it all refused to yield center place to the towers behind. Two of the shining skyscrapers that loomed above the oldest part of the city were deals of his, Dewey Square and One Beacon. If they were beautiful to him — and with their razor-sharp edges, glass-and-steel surfaces fitted with Swiss-watch precision, they were — it was because in the very shape of that skyline they did not obliterate the past, but grew out of it. He not only loved the city, but believed in it. Except for this one nagging, goddamned doubt.

"What?"

He looked left a notch, to Bunker Hill. That fucking monument. "There *is* something wrong, something I wanted to ask you about." He swiveled around, looking at her, then glancing upriver for Max, who, still on his bike, was leaning on a bench, looking back at them. Terry waved. And Max, patient, respectful, waved back. Terry said to Joan, "Bright has brought in a partner I wonder about. I'm trying to decide whether to push my misgivings or not."

"What makes you wonder?"

"The guy is a sleaze. I can smell it."

Joan laughed. "Sugar, I thought they were all sleazes over there."

"Said like a Cambridge yuppie."

"I wish." She touched his cheek fondly. "We're not young enough to be yuppies."

"This guy's name is Amory. He claims to be from Beverly, but he doesn't know any local Amorys. He says they don't know him."

"That doesn't make him a sleaze."

"He never heard of Cleveland Amory. Wouldn't he know — ?"

"Cleveland Amory, Grover Cleveland. Christ, Terry, if Bright trusts him, what's — ?"

"Bright only sees one thing, Joan. Making this deal. He doesn't care."

"That can't be true."

Terry looked again at the bronze plaque in front of him, and rather than fight with her, he seized on it as something to read. The raised green letters were barely legible: IN MEMORIAM, QUENTIN COMPSON.

"What the hell is this?" he asked.

Joan ran her fingers lightly over the worn metal. "Some literature professor must have put it here."

"I don't get it."

"*The Sound and the Fury*, Sugar. Quentin came to Harvard. He jumped from a bridge. Don't you remember?"

"Oh, Christ, you Harvard people!"

"Don't, Terry."

"Then don't give me shit about whether this guy is a sleaze, even if he *is* an Amory. Or about Boston not being Onomatopoeia County, whatever the hell it was."

"Yoknapatawpha."

In another context, he'd have loved such a cocky show of his wife's trap of a mind, how it let go of nothing. But at that instant her erudition fueled his anger, which flared now, to his surprise as much as hers. "I'm talking about Boston, not Mississippi! Boston! Do you hear me?"

"Yes. So does all of Cambridge."

"Fuck Cambridge!"

"Terry —"

"I think the man is a sleaze, Joan, because I think he's involved with Squire."

Joan's shock — not surprise — registered in the jolt of her face and a quite dramatic backward movement. She leaned against the bridge with a false casualness, to steady herself. "What makes you think that?"

"I guess . . ." He was suddenly vague, the way he was after too many drinks. "I always have an eye over my shoulder, looking for that bastard."

Me too, Joan said, but to herself. Because of her, they had arranged their lives so as to see him as little as possible. In fact, Joan had not laid eyes on Nick since their grandfather's funeral five years before. Terry knew — he must have known — of her repugnance, but he had no idea what sparked it. "Look over your shoulder, Terry," Joan said stiffly. "No one's there."

"But he is there." Terry spoke with such an absence of inflection that it frightened her. She was sorry that he could see the blush that seared her skin from her throat to her forehead. What did he know?

"When I met Amory this morning, he was wearing one of those shamrock things."

"What?"

"You remember, the Kerry Bouquet shamrock, what Squire gave me when he gave you that black orchid years ago."

Black trillium. She could not believe that flower was being referred to. Confusion and dread filled her, emotions she simply had to flee. Without meaning it to, her tone became mocking. "A boutonniere? You're talking about a boutonniere?"

"A shamrock boutonniere. My grandfather's invention. Squire's the only other one who's ever made them. They're foolish things that only last a few hours. Even on St. Patrick's Day, they've never made it out of Charlestown. Amory said he bought it at the Ritz, which is ridiculous. Imagine, shit like that at the Ritz."

"Not even the Ritz is the Ritz anymore. They might sell —"

"If I'm right," he said coolly, "it means the money Amory is offering us isn't his. Nick would be a go-between. The money would be from the mob."

He had never mentioned any of this to her; so much unmentioned between them. Their secrets about his brother — hers above all — had grown like tumors inside the body of their love. "Terry, just leave this alone. Why throw open a door into a place you don't want to go?"

"That's what I'm telling you. The door opened in front of me, on its own, this morning."

"Then close it." She had. He could. She turned and began to run. Her mind flew to the day two or three years ago when she had bumped into Didi at the new Neiman Marcus at Copley Place. Amid the gleaming brass and marble, Didi came up to her and said, "Mrs. Livingstone, I presume?" Joan was nonplused, and Didi used that against her. "You don't know who I am."

"Of course I do."

Each woman shifted her shopping bag to shake hands.

Joan said, "How are you?"

"Well. Very well. But you were going to call after Gramps's funeral. You never called. I called you, but you never answered me."

"Didi, I'm sorry, but I —"

"You don't have to explain. I know everything."

Joan's heart sank. She stared at Didi, who was still grinning. She wore a beige linen dress and a silk cravat; she looked like a restaurant hostess.

"Everything?"

"Why you won't see us. Why you won't let Terry near us."

"Why?"

"Because of Squire," Didi said with supreme matter-of-factness. "Because of what he does. You disapprove."

"I disapprove?"

"Yes. Of him. Of us."

Joan backed away from her, blanching with relief. "I disapprove of you?" She began to laugh then, a release from panic, even as she turned and moved away as quickly as she could. "I'm late," she said. "I'm sorry, but I'm late." She'd almost broken into a run, thinking, She doesn't know. Didi doesn't know.

Now she *was* running. Terry watched her leave the bridge and turn upriver, toward the business school. His gaze went ahead of her, to the classic stadium and the gabled Victorian boathouse. He saw the scullers in sweatshirts hauling their pencil-thin boat onto the dock, their workout over. The boathouse, the adjacent graceful bridge, the river itself, all glowed crimson in the setting sun, a Thomas Eakins scene so beautiful it hurt Doyle's eyes to look.

Against the sunlight, framed by the arching brick bridge behind, he found the small, golden figure of his son. Max was still at that bench, resting his bike, but staring back hard, worried now at what had kept his parents. Doyle began running too, toward his son, letting the current of his love flow on ahead.

✧

Of all the rooms in the house, theirs was the one devoid of "touches," but pointedly so. The house had been built by Artemas Ward, one of George Washington's generals, and he'd made the second-floor parlor its grandest room. Joan and Terry had made it their bedroom.

An enormously high ceiling crowned the full wall of windows, which were actually four sets of French doors opening onto a narrow wrought-iron balcony and overlooking the sweep of garden. The property was bordered by a ten-foot-high serpentine brick wall worthy of Monticello, and it gave the garden a perfect frame. The flower beds and shrubs were laid out around, and the ribbons of grass were centered on, a masterpiece oak. The tree had reputedly been planted by Ward, but it was known in this decade as Max's Ladder, because it so lent itself to climbing. Its branches undulated toward each corner of the garden, and reached high above the house toward the unbroken sky. When the wind brought its leaves forward, they brushed the glass of the bedroom windows with a gentle sound of wooing.

The garden, the tree, the wall of windows — Joan had wanted nothing in the room that would detract from the world it gave them. That was why she'd had it done in white, entirely white. The carpet was white, as was the ornately trimmed mantel over the fireplace on the east wall. The pieces of Design Research furniture in one corner

— Formica-topped bureau and writing table, canvas-backed chair — were white, and so was the large, unornamented platform bed against the west wall, with its Parsons table bedstands and architect's lamps. The pillows and linens and puffy down comforter were white. Joan's thought had been to create a vacuum in the room that would draw the color of the garden in. In the winter, black and gray and green, the skeletal oak against the pewter sky, rising from a carefully nurtured grid of boxwoods and sculpted spruce. In the spring, summer, and autumn, a movable feast, beds of rotating crops of annuals and perennials, all colors, but red and yellow especially, from the self-renewing roses which, to her surprise, had brought her husband to his knees in all weather, a gardener, rose grower, flower man at last.

At night, even when they did not draw the blinds across — there was no question of lacking privacy, since no one had a view of their home — the garden outside ceased to exist. Then the room became Shakerlike and austere. Except on moonlit nights, the pitch darkness outside clashed with the light inside, transforming the wall of windows into a black mirror in which Terry often watched his wife taking off her clothes. Floodlights on the ceiling splashed ovals on the walls that held nothing — a relief for Joan from the Fogg, where the walls were everything. The only exception in the bedroom was a barely lit, small oil painting over the mantel, a portrait of Joan holding Max when he was a baby. It had been commissioned by her father.

Terry was at the window, using it for a mirror, fussing with his black tie. He said, "Ted asked us to come to Florida for Easter."

Joan, in her slip, was sitting on the bed, putting on her stockings. They were dressing for a gala benefit at the symphony, the kind of thing they did two or three nights a week.

"You saw Ted?"

"At Ruggles today. Bright leaned on him, and he came."

"Do you want to go?"

"Not really. Florida. Ugh."

"It's warm."

"Do you know something, Joan?" Terry paused, then went on casually, as if caring nothing for this. "The economy of Florida makes more off drugs than agriculture, including citrus. Did you know that?"

"No." Joan sat up. His back was to her. She waited for him to find her in the black glass, but he didn't. "Why do you say that?"

"It's interesting. That's all. If there were other kids Max's age . . ."

"What do you mean?"

"At Palm Beach. I wish Max could somehow . . ."

"Know who the Kennedys were?"

"I guess so. There." He patted his finished bow tie and turned toward her. "How do I look?"

"Bond. James Bond."

He watched as she hiked her slip to fasten the stocking to her garter. He saw her thighs, the flash of her underpants. Once such a move would have seemed provocative, but he knew, for her, there was no question of display. Her toned, brown arms and legs, her breasts, her perfect ankles — she took her sexiness for granted, but it could still stir him. Often, before dawn, they would turn wordlessly to each other and make love. It had come to say everything about their marriage that, at such moments, they said nothing. There too, as it were, Joan wore her headset. Whatever the music of lovemaking was to her, she kept it to herself. For Terry, the moment of climax was always a moment of escape from what he hated in himself, and the truth was that he too experienced it as exquisitely isolating. A mutual solitude. Whenever he would look, her eyes would be closed.

Joan stood and walked briskly to the bathroom, but she stopped in the doorway and looked back at him. "What is it?" she asked. "What's bothering you?"

"Nothing."

"As usual."

"What does that mean?"

"With you, Terry, it's always nothing. Nothing is what bothers you."

"Look, Joan, I tried telling you before, and you wouldn't stop running."

"I'm not running now."

"Amory and my brother, that's what's bothering me. Okay?"

"I've been thinking about it. Can't you just back out of the deal? Let Bright handle it."

"Hammond is the developer. Not Commonwealth Bank. *Me.*"

"But if Bright's in charge of financing —"

"Nick. I have to deal with Nick."

"Leave him alone. Stay away from him."

Terry shrugged. "He's my brother, Joan. He sent me a signal with the fucking shamrock."

"He's no good."

Terry stared at her. "After all these years of refusing to have anything to do with him, you finally put it into words."

"Don't make it seem like the issue is my being a snob. I didn't notice you beating any path to Charlestown. Your brother is a bad man, and you know it."

"How do *you* know it?"

Joan just stood there, the curves of her body backlit by the bathroom glare.

"Well?"

"I know it," Joan said, "because of the effect he has on you."

"Which means?"

"Nothing. Never mind."

"No, answer me. Please."

"He makes you weak, Terry." Joan went into the bathroom and closed the door, hardly breathing. What she'd said was true, but only half true. Nick was the reason, also, that when she leaned close to the mirror, the eyes into which she looked were stone cold dead.

✧

At the glittering Symphony Hall reception, Joan and Terry moved through the crowd, drawing glances. They were one of Boston's golden couples, a new embodiment of the old Athenian ideal, Art and Commerce hand in hand.

As Terry greeted his friends, the tuxedoed men who looked like less handsome versions of himself, he knew he was doing what, in this town, he was never meant to do. The bankers were there, the pols, the Brahmins, the Harvard rich. And when they saw him, their eyes flicked; each one hoped for a nod.

"Hey, bro," a familiar voice said from behind. Terry turned. Bright, in his tuxedo, leaned across Terry to kiss Joan. "God, you are so lovely," he said, but as he did, he pulled into their circle the tall, thin woman who was with him, a brown-skinned model with a neck like Nefertiti, a face for launching ships, the most beautiful woman in the room. That Bright.

While Joan and his date greeted each other, Bright, aware of the envy in the eyes of the men around them, leaned to Terry and whispered, "Don't you just fucking love this?"

Terry nodded and laughed, but his feelings differed from those of Bright, for whom it seemed to matter not at all that choices they had made meant their women loved them most in settings like this.

Terry wanted to say something like, You, buddy, with yet another bimbo; me with a wife I smite only in black tie. But he shook the feeling off in favor of the other thing, the triumph he and Bright had in common. "Fucking A, brother," he said, and he realized how much he *did* love it. He was king of the hill in Boston now. If he felt hands on his ankles once again, hauling him down — that shamrock! — he knew that this time he would kick free no matter whose face he hit.

He looked at his old friend's one eye: Except yours, he thought. Then he looked at both of Joan's: No matter what you think of me.

17

THE MOVIE about Kennedy included scenes of his inauguration, spirals of snow gusting up a deserted Pennsylvania Avenue, the faces of Negro workers sweeping the stands, puffs of steam coming out of their mouths, then the president letting the word go forth. The camera moved in on him, a young man with no hat or overcoat, while behind him sat Eisenhower, bundled up like a nursing home porch-sitter. "The torch has been passed to a new generation of Americans, tempered by war, disciplined by a hard and bitter peace, proud of our ancient heritage" — as the camera cut to flames shooting out of an oil drum, where an old black man was stooped over it for warmth, a transistor radio to his ear.

The movie had been showing out here at the Kennedy Library for five or six years now, but he'd never seen it, and he was not prepared for his reaction. He'd always said he could take Kennedy or leave him, no big deal, but here he was, feeling tears come to his eyes as he watched the pictures flitting by: Kennedy in white tie and tails, with his piece-of-ass, bare-shouldered wife; Kennedy with binoculars, a missile breaking the surface of the ocean; bombers; black kids getting hit by cops; Kennedy on Cape Cod with his little girl, his sailboat; his speeches; Krushchev; the Berlin Wall; Lyndon Johnson and *Air Force One*.

Squire was not ready for the freeze-frame shot of the shadow of that airplane, falling on the runway at what the narrator said was Dallas, like a grainy, out-of-focus crucifix, for Christ's sake. Kennedy was dead again, and the screen went blank, and silence thickened in the theater. He realized his cheeks were wet. Squire Doyle was not a mick who'd spent the past twenty years weeping over what was lost with JFK. He'd had no impulse, even, to come over here, the Kennedy Lourdes. It had surprised him when Mullen, saying the feds had agreed to his proposal, said also that this was where they wanted to meet.

He did not like the feeling of being blindsided. As the lights came up, he was glad to be sitting alone, and now that it was over, the slick movie, frankly, made him angry.

The tourist ladies were digging for their Kleenex packs. The men were blinking, adjusting their nylon-mesh baseball caps, hitching their beltless pants, feigning coughs. There were perhaps two hundred people in the theater. They got to their feet, a subdued group, shuffling sideways to the ends of their rows, into the aisles and filing out. Squire remained where he was, in a seat in the middle of the fifth row, watching the others leave, feeling not at all superior. Americans, he thought. We're all lost sheep.

This was August 1983, eight months before Bright and Terry's Southwest Corridor Improvement Project kickoff. Also to the point, this was six months *after* a Washington meeting in an office on that same Pennsylvania Avenue at which the head of the Criminal Division of the Justice Department, the chief of criminal investigations for the IRS, and the associate director of the FBI for drug enforcement agreed on a new strategy. Highly publicized street sweeps in cities across the country, in which tens of thousands of drug dealers were arrested, were having a more disruptive effect on the police and the courts than on the drug trade. The national net of secret electronic surveillance of Mafia meeting places was snagging well-known, ruthless, but only low- and mid-level gangsters. The real leaders of La Cosa Nostra had learned to insulate themselves even from their own operations. The FBI's extensive bugging and eavesdropping simply were not getting them. Like the massive border interdiction efforts of the 1970s, the switch in the early eighties to prosecutions based on RICO statutes was turning out not to be enough.

But to the savvy longarms, an alternative strategy suggested itself, a bold reversal in which drugs were not targeted so much as the money drugs produced. Since the explosion of demand for product began a decade earlier, the drug trade had been generating many times more profits than criminal enterprise ever had before, annual amounts in the billions of dollars. That success was giving the otherwise immune heads of the crime organizations their biggest problem, and it gave law enforcement an unprecedented opportunity. The overlords kept their distance from street trade, but not from money. The whole point was money, and that was the key.

Drug producers in Colombia and other countries, who controlled their governments and dominated their national economies, could impudently accumulate and spend vast quantities of tainted cash, but not so the distributors in the United States, with its regulated financial system. Vast drug profits were useless to Americans until they could somehow be made to appear legitimate. The days were past when a series of duffel-bag cash deposits into phony accounts at neighborhood banks would do, partly because a 1982 revision of the Bank Secrecy Act had tightened bank reporting obligations, and partly because the $10,000 deposit figure that triggered a bank's Currency Transaction Report fell so far short of the amounts the top drug traffickers now had to legitimize. Large city couriers — in the argot, "smurfs" — who brought such bundled cash to teller windows at numerous banks found themselves at it all the time, yet still failed to keep up with the cash flowing in. A new laundering system was needed. When Squire Doyle had positioned himself to provide it, he let Frank Tucci know, offering once again a service Tucci needed and could not otherwise obtain. Doyle knew that Tucci had never trusted him, but this time the prize would seem worth it. And hadn't Doyle proved himself in all these years? All these years since Causeway Street? All these years, yes, since Kennedy? Kennedys don't get mad; he thought of Bobby and, to himself, he laughed. We get even. Frank Tucci was not the only one whom Squire Doyle had notified.

Despite his earlier reservations, Doyle realized, as the last of the tourists drifted from the theater, that the library was a good place for the meeting. No wops. No fucking wops anywhere at this St. Jack by the Sea. He heard locks being snapped on the rear doors, from outside. When he looked around, there were three other men sitting in seats widely separated from one another in the otherwise empty auditorium. All were staring at him. Three familiar faces, three Irishmen, with two of whom, over the years, he'd done lesser pieces of business, just enough to keep afloat: Colin Joyce, the head of the New England Organized Crime Strike Force, and Joseph Farrell, the assistant special agent in charge of the Boston FBI office. Farrell's legs were stretched out on the seat in front of him.

"Well, well, Mr. Doyle," Farrell said. "We hear you're in the banking business now. You've bought yourself a bank."

Squire stared back at him. "A little one. I'm a small businessman."

"The Sullivan Square Savings Bank in Charlestown."

"Where I've kept receipts from my flower stores for years. It was a bargain. The bank was going under."

"Because Schrafft's is going out of business next month, and Domino Sugar is sure to close up its waterfront depot shortly after. Schrafft's and Domino have kept their payroll accounts at Sullivan all these years. You got a bargain because what's that one-room bank without those payrolls?"

"I'm a sentimental guy."

"Nobody put a value on a long history of big money moving through such a little bank. Interesting, huh? Nobody but you."

"Interesting, yes."

"Even interesting little banks need big partners downtown these days." Special Agent Farrell studied one of his flashy black-and-white wingtips, turning his foot this way and that. "Are you ready to get married?"

"Let's say I'm ready for a little action on the side." Squire grinned. "I'm already married. Very happily." Squire let his eyes drift across the vacant plush seats to the third Irishman, the deputy chief of the State Police's Office of Special Investigations, John P. Mullen. "Right, Lieutenant?"

"Right," he answered. Jackie.

✧

Not long after the meeting at the Kennedy Library, Squire went into a bar alone. The smoke, the throbbing jukebox, the crush of bodies — but the bodies were different. The place was full of men in blue jeans and T-shirts that clung to worked-over curves, pecs and biceps, also buttocks. The short hair struck him, the smooth tanned skin, the stench of cologne. The men looked like models.

Buddies was a no-announcement, blanked-window gay bar on Huntington Avenue, across from Copley Place, the mall where Ralph Lauren sold his underwear. It wasn't only the dress of the clientele that set Buddies apart from pubs in the Town. Mirrors covered the walls and the ceiling, and at every corner light pulsed from blue neon tubes in synch with the music. Day-Glo bulletin boards listed wines and exotic coffee drinks. As Squire made his way toward the bar, he thought of raucous clubs he'd passed in P-town, but these men were not drag queens. They did not look all that queer. They were dressed with casual flamboyance, but it was easy to imagine them in Lauren's idea of cordovans and gray flannel. He'd been told that Buddies habitués were affluent Boston comers, businessmen and professionals, but still —

To reach the bar, he had to move through knots of hand-holders and easy flirts, whisperers and laughers, men draped over each other. But Doyle was past master at stifling repugnance, letting nothing show of what he felt. Though he was older than the men into whose midst he moved; though his body was softer, if larger; though he wore his loose-fitting, distinctive, but decidedly unchic dark sweater over non-descript dark trousers, he found it possible to move among the homosexuals as if he were one of them. Inhibited? No, just reserved, cool. A marvel of self-possession. At the bar, he pushed between groups and ordered a Diet Coke, which the bartender served with a nonchalance that said lots of guys were off the hard stuff these days.

Doyle stood aside with a preoccupied air intended to discourage advances, and it was true that he was looking for someone. After a few minutes he left the bar and walked easily through the crowd, aware of all the double images, the mirrors everywhere, how the men kept snagging their own eyes, stealing glimpses of their own good looks. On the far side of the next room, a subdued enclave where paired-off men sat talking at small round tables along the walls, Doyle saw him. He was at one of the tables with a young friend, but the mirrored wall made them seem a pair of twins. Focusing on the one, Doyle still saw two men with black skin, two men with gaunt features, two men with the telltale eyepatches, two men with head-back, vigorous laughs and cigarettes.

"Honor Bright," Doyle said.

McKay looked up, disoriented in the haze of his own smoke. It amused Doyle that his brother's old friend did not recognize him. Bright was dressed in chinos, polished loafers, no socks, a yellow Izod shirt that contrasted dramatically with the deep color of his arms. He wore a gold Rolex watch and a thin gold chain at his throat.

"It's Nick," Squire said, putting his hand out.

McKay reacted at once, an overly effusive greeting that made Doyle instantly aware that he'd had a lot to drink. If he was embarrassed to be identified here, he did not show it.

"Jesus, Mary, and Squire!" He was on his feet, slapping Doyle's shoulder, his face charged by an apparently heartfelt, joyous recognition. Their handshake was as overlong as it was warm, and Doyle realized that Bright's show of familiar affection was succeeding, as it was intended to, in undercutting the confidence of the well-built, tanned young white man opposite him at the table.

Before Bright turned to introduce him, the man got up. "I need a freshener," he said, raising his glass. And he went away.

Bright watched the young man go, and when he slapped a buddy's ass, Bright's face clouded over briefly. "Well, shit, Squire," he said, gesturing at the chair, "have a seat."

"I guess I better — before someone else does." Squire laughed. "It's obviously a privilege." The mirrored wall, the sensation of sitting next to himself, made Squire dizzy.

"My animal magnetism," Bright said. "That's what draws them."

"Or maybe it's that they think you're Sammy Davis Jr." Doyle grinned.

But Bright stiffened. "What are you doing here?"

"Is that your standard icebreaker?"

Bright only looked at him, awaiting an answer.

"I came to see you."

"But here? Surely you could have found me at the bank. You know where I work."

"Yes."

"Then am I right to assume our encounter comes wrapped in a little message?" Bright said. "Same old Squire."

Squire sipped his Coke, watching Bright put a match to one of his fat cigarettes. "You still smoking those things?"

Bright waved the match out. "How's Didi?"

"I forgot you knew her."

"I knew her before you did."

Squire shook his head. "Shit you say. I grew up with Didi."

Bright shrugged. "What I should have said was, I knew her before I knew you. She worked with us in 'sixty. Hell of a worker, a great girl."

"In the Town, Didi could be a grandmother."

"Whoa! Jump back! That means —"

"Yeah. Me too. Imagine that?" The bittersweet pleasure of the passage of time. For a moment it joined them, and it felt as if they'd been friends.

But then Bright adjusted his forever stilted glance so it went to the mirror. Doyle followed, and they made eye contact through the reflection. "So, what did you want?" Bright asked.

"Moving right to the point." To Squire the encounter seemed unreal, an effect of the strange men around them, of the mirror, of the blue light, of the eye patch. The odd angle at which McKay had to hold his head made him seem suspicious.

And McKay's voice was indeed laced with ice when he said, "Unless you wanted to talk about rimming, fisting, water games, or HIV."

"No."

"So?"

"Banking. I wanted to talk to you about banking." Squire paused, but Bright only waited. "I own a bank now. Or rather, I own a company that owns a bank."

"I used to hear more about you, Squire. I assumed you weren't doing so well lately. I guess I was wrong."

"Always looking to diversify. Isn't that good business?"

"Which bank?"

"Sullivan Square Savings Bank."

"Never heard of it."

"It's in Charlestown, near Everett."

"Well, no fucking wonder I never heard of it. I thought Charlestown seceded from Boston when they let niggers cross City Hall plaza without a flagpole up their ass."

"Come on, McKay. Don't start that shit."

"You still haven't said what you want."

They were still looking at each other through the mirror, as if they could not talk any other way. Little Richard's "Good Golly, Miss Molly" was on the jukebox now, and the frenzy of the blue light's pulse had jumped, and with it the mood of the bar. It seemed to Squire that he and Bright were in their own private bubble. Indeed, for all that those around them cared, they were. Squire said, "A client of mine needs to move some money. I'd like to move it through you."

"I'm in PR, Squire. I'm a VP for Community Affairs. Not in the counting room. But surely you know that about me, if you know that I come here."

"I know that you've been trying to get into the real estate end of the bank. For obvious reasons they like to keep you out front. But I also know that you deal with Van Buren and Hayes all the time, either one of whom could approve the arrangement I want to propose, and either one of whom would be thrilled to share the credit with you for the fees my client would be paying. Shall I speak directly?"

"Please."

"My depositor needs a bank that's set up to make wire transfers out of the country."

"As in, to the Cayman Islands? Or to Panama?"

"Switzerland, as a matter of fact."

"How traditional. Why? Closer to Italy? Shall I guess the rest? You need a bank official who's willing to oversee these transfers without observing the federal reporting regulations."

Squire raised his eyebrows, and with his fingers he made a pair of Nixon V-for-victory signs. "That would be illegal, Bright." He smiled, and both men turned, as if on cue, away from the mirror to look at each other. Squire continued, "That's the beauty of what I'm proposing. Sullivan Square Savings Bank, the receptor institution, carries the legal burden of currency reporting. We take care of that. When we send funds on to Commonwealth Bank, there is no legal requirement on you to report anything. No federal statute regulates wire transfers."

"That can't be true."

"Check it out. Financial institutions are required to retain records of wire transfers out of the country in excess of ten thousand dollars, but there is no reporting to authorities required. And there is no definition in the code of what 'record keeping' means. Nothing says it has to be accessible. Tell Van Buren to have his lawyers check it out."

"And I suppose you're anticipating sums in excess of ten thousand."

"Eventually, the high six figures a day. Of which Commonwealth will receive its usual one percent handling fee and the benefits attached to accounts maintained in the millions of dollars. Other fees to be negotiated."

"Why would your depositor maintain accounts with us if all he wants is a pass-through?"

"Because he'll be bringing money back from Switzerland as well as sending it over."

"It comes back clean."

"Of course." Squire flashed his born-to-bring-flowers smile. "The way it starts."

"And *when* it starts at Sullivan Square, the bank owned by the company you own — your name is on the charter?"

"No."

Bright nodded. "And *when* it starts at Sullivan Square, of course the CTRs will be filed with the proper authorities?"

"Does it matter to you, Bright, how I answer that?"

"Yes."

"Because you'd have to answer Van Buren."

"Yes. If I were to speak to him."

"Then the answer is, Of course. We will file everything just the way we should."

"And the enterprise generating this largess is?"

"Real estate. Florida real estate. My client has made a killing on the west coast down there. He banks in Switzerland because he has international partners who insist on it. Paranoid Latin Americans, you know. He'll be happy to meet you. He'll be happy to meet Van Buren, if you like. I have the impression he'll be looking to invest around here. Maybe in Boston proper, even. Isn't pushing local investment an area of yours, Bright? Isn't that *mainly* what you do?"

Bright used the cinder edge of his cigarette to flatten the ashes in the ashtray, then to cut canals in them.

Squire added with quiet emphasis, "It's legal, Bright. Check it out. For you and Commonwealth Bank, it would be entirely legal."

"And for you?"

Squire answered by sipping his Diet Coke.

Now McKay did raise his face, and his eye went right to Doyle's, no mirror, no reflection. "Does Terry know?"

"About this?" Squire indicated, with a first show of distaste, the nearby patrons.

Bright laughed. "This isn't secret, Squire. That man you just snickered toward is a partner at Choate, Hall and Stewart. That other guy is on the governor's senior staff. You thought what, you would blackmail me? I have nothing to hide."

"So Terry knows you're gay?"

Bright did not answer.

"I thought you guys were still friends."

"We are," Bright said, but he was unable, despite an old resolve, to keep from feeling shame. "What I meant was, Does Terry know you're approaching me?"

Squire shook his head. "Terry doesn't have the elbows for shit like this. You remember how weak he was under the boards. Besides, I don't see Terry all that much. I assumed you knew that."

"I did. I guess I did."

"I would assume also that your oldest friend would know about you — if you have nothing to hide, that is."

Not shame now, but hatred was what Bright felt. He could not speak.

"How's my brother doing? How's that fancy wife of his? How's that nephew of mine?"

"They're good. They're fine." Bright's hand trembled enough so that both noticed it as he lit another cigarette. He sat staring at the match for a long moment, a deliberate contemplation.

Then he stood up abruptly. Everything had fallen from his face except a look of deep anguish. A line of moisture glistened at the edge of his eye patch, but his good eye was dry. He dropped his fresh cigarette onto the floor and crushed it with his shoe. "The answer is no. Nothing doing."

Squire took another sip of his Coke. "Okay. That's fine. I was just asking." Now he stood, and he pressed Bright's shoulder firmly, pushing him down again. "You sit. I'm the one who leaves, remember?"

Bright adjusted his eye patch to wipe his cheek, lifting the black oval momentarily, giving Squire a glimpse of the walnut socket he did not want to see. Then Bright looked up at him. "You're the same son of a bitch you've always been."

Squire opened his hands. "Hey, I just wanted to help build the new Boston. Isn't that what you call it?"

"How does it make you feel, you bastard? The shit you do?"

With relief, Doyle realized only then that he had this sucker hooked. It would take a while to reel him in, but he had him. And McKay knew it too, which was why he was angry. Squire said, "Can I answer your question like a mick, with a question of my own? Can I?"

Terry's old friend let his stunned half gaze slide into the mirror again, where Squire met him and asked, "Why do they call it 'gay'? I've never understood that. You're all obviously unhappy. Why 'gay'?"

✧

Terry Doyle's drive into Boston took him across the Charles at the bridge by Soldiers Field and then down Storrow Drive along the broadening stretch of the river, past BU and Back Bay. It was the morning after the gala at Symphony Hall, the day after the ceremony at Ruggles Square. A night rain had drenched the road, but the day had broken free of weather already, and now, at the rush hour, the clean chill of a New England spring had cleared the air. Tires hissed on the wet pavement, but the commuters drove as fast as ever, bunched slot cars. Doyle's mind was always blank on the way in to work, and sometimes he arrived at his garage downtown with no memory of having driven there. This morning was no different — except for the hole in his throat, the morbid, sick feeling that he had not shaken since waking up for good at three-thirty.

He made a split-second decision to get off Storrow Drive at Arlington Street, as if the pain in his chest were a tail he could shake. He cut right onto the ramp that would take him through the absolute worst of downtown traffic, around the Common and into the maze of colonial-era cow paths. But also, first, it would take him past the Ritz-Carlton, which sat on the edge of Back Bay like a disapproving dowager.

As if he'd arranged for it ahead of time, a parking space was open across from the hotel, a Back Bay miracle that made the impulse behind this detour seem preordained. The spot was on Arlington, at the head of Newbury Street; after pulling into it he realized that from that vantage he could see both entrances to the Ritz. Was he a genius or what?

He shut his engine off and sat there for some moments, the traffic passing on one side, the dewy lawns of the Public Garden on the other. Doyle drove a Volvo. Joan's old Healey they kept garaged in Somerville, and soon enough she would have it out again. But for his purpose that morning, the dull gray, all too Cambridge sedan was perfect.

He got out, crossed to Newbury Street, and walked briskly to the door. The doorman touched his hat, as if Doyle were staying there. At the bank of lobby phones, he picked one up and asked for Victor Amory. The operator said "Surely," and seconds later the room was ringing. Now what?

When he heard the upswinging inflection of Amory's hello, he hung up. The receiver handle was moist, and only then did he notice his perspiring palms. What was he doing? Taking this one step at a time, that's what. He crossed the lobby to the flower shop. A lady in a pink smock over a tan cashmere twin set of the sort Joan favored was spraying mist onto the banked flowers.

"Good morning," Doyle said, swinging in. "I was hoping for something for my lapel."

"Good day, sir. Certainly, sir. Right here." She put her copper mister down and crossed to the cooler. "These lovely bluebells . . ."

"No, no. I was hoping for . . ." He craned his neck to look past her.

"A small iris, perhaps?" She pointed with a hand so bejeweled Doyle wondered why she had to work.

"No. Shamrocks."

"I'm sorry?"

"Shamrocks, in a sprig of baby's breath."

"I've never seen that."

"You don't sell shamrock boutonnieres?"

"No. I rather doubt that shamrocks —"

"You're sure you didn't sell —"

Her prim smile cut him off. "Not shamrocks. Ever. Of any kind. We don't sell novelties."

"Of course you don't. Foolish of me. Thanks anyway."

On the way out of the lobby, he cursed himself for calling Amory's room, alerting him. He wasn't good at this. A fool. He was a fool. He glanced back at the flower shop, expecting the woman to be watching him. But she had gone back to spraying blossoms.

He waited for the doorman to turn away before crossing Arlington, back to his car. He got in and closed his door quietly, and realized that precaution was foolish too. This whole thing was foolish.

He waited an hour, smoking, listening to *Morning Pro Musica*, Mozart and Bach, their greatest hits. He observed every person who entered the hotel — no Squire; and who left it — no Amory. For most of that time, he kept at bay a sense of the absurd figure he'd become, but eventually a feeling of claustrophobia closed on him. The car interior began to seem small and airless. He imagined Joan sitting next to him, exuding disdain in her cashmere, her drawn-back blond hair: We don't sell novelties. But Joan had, in fact, encouraged him to think that at the Ritz they would. Why?

No sooner had the stain of his suspicion spread to touch his wife than Victor Amory appeared, barreling through the revolving door. Dressed in the fedora and the tan raincoat he'd had on his arm yesterday, he held a black carry-on bag in one hand. When the doorman reached for it, Amory veered away, heading up Newbury Street away from the cab stand, which told Doyle he didn't need the car. He got out and began to follow. He maintained the half-block separation they'd started with.

Often, when he had serious thinking to do, Terry hit the sidewalk, wandering aimlessly, as if hoping to get lost. He could pass shop windows, cut through crowds, and cross busy intersections without altering the self-assured pace before which others gave way, his mind working the whole time. In his brain he was making brilliant moves, square to square, against his friends who were enemies, yielding a pawn to Killian at the BRA, castling Zimmerman, trading Hammond's interest in the Fan Pier for Marty's redundant piece of Park Square, always, always, where to find money, how to keep it, money the queen, money the king, money the everything. The development game in boom times was less Monopoly than gilded chess, but Doyle constantly had boards on every side, a dozen opponents at once, bomb-rigged master's clocks running on every move, and the miracle was, he kept making them. What he never had was time to separate out in his mind the reasons for his instinctive choices, how two or four moves ahead he knew, he knew. He never had time, either, to answer his largest question, why his trade — which after all *was* a game of building blocks, buying and selling, borrowing and dealing — could feel so dangerous. Now and then a desperate need to think about it took him out of his office, out of the building on Liberty Square, as if the sidewalk itself would answer him if only he trod enough of it.

But now he was moving automatically, not thinking. Block after block of Newbury Street went by, the chic stores and galleries, the ultimate cafés, bowfront windows shimmering with paintings, vases, sepia lithographs — but it all passed in a blur. The field of his concentration was entirely taken over by the bobbing, distant figure, like a hypnotist's charm, of Victor Amory.

Clarendon, Dartmouth, Exeter, Fairfield — how those Yankees had hoped to wake up English if they only named enough streets for Brit manor houses. At Hereford Street Amory turned left. By the time Doyle caught sight of him again, he had crossed Boylston and stopped. He had put his suitcase down on the sidewalk, and stood there shaking his arms, an indication of the weight he was carrying. Doyle stalled in the open alcove of a fire station, then set off again when Amory did.

At the next corner, at the Cheri movie complex, he turned right onto a side street. Doyle reached the corner in time to see, to his amazement, Amory mounting the stairs of the least conspicuous Catholic church in Boston, St. Cecelia's. It was a towerless brick of a church, built at the turn of the century for Irish servants of the prim householders of Back Bay. Amory took the stairs warily, as if he knew that, long ago, his kind had gone there only to demand to see the pastor, to dispose of their outrageously pregnant maids. He pushed against the large wooden door and it swung slowly open. He glanced toward the street once, perhaps seeing Doyle, perhaps not. Then, without taking off his hat, he disappeared inside the church.

Doyle was out of moves. He remained outside, dispirited and confused, not realizing that the decision to stop was also a move. He crossed the street and stood in the arched doorway of one of the row houses. He lit a cigarette and watched the church entrance, soon finding himself fatigued. This peculiar thing with Amory, with Bright — with Joan — was less than a day old, yet the distrust it implied seemed now very familiar, and his sudden weariness made him feel that it had been years since he'd had a good night's sleep.

St. Cecelia's, the servants' church. He counted the steps. He traced the outline of the door, the ribs of the sooty window above. To the right of the entrance was the sign announcing Mass and confession times, and below the schedule was the line REV. JAMES ADLER, PASTOR.

Jimmy Adler! Doyle hadn't thought of him in years, the kid who'd pulled him through the tunnel of the seminary. Jimmy Adler, freckle-faced, forever grinning, always at Terry's door with a word of cheer, affection, gossip, a joke. To Doyle's dismay, when he thought of Adler now it was as a child, a boy, and then he realized it was as *his* child. Jimmy. Staring at Adler's name in the space before that impossible ecclesiastical word "Pastor" was like looking at a mirage, a fact without past or future.

But Jimmy Adler had betrayed him, and wasn't it so like Terry Doyle to draw that up from the well of his memory last? Adler's careful notes on Terry's heresy, sitting on the rector's desk, evidence that Doyle had conspired with Protestants, Bright's father, that he had refused to take an oath, that he had lied in confession because he could not think of a sin.

Jimmy, you bastard. And this is what they give you. Doyle thought of their favorite play, *A Man for All Seasons,* More's response to his betrayer: To lose one's soul not for the whole world, but for Wales, Rich?

But for St. Cecelia's, Jim?

The church door opened. Doyle tossed his cigarette aside, ready to move. Victor Amory came down the stairs quickly, looking neither right nor left, and he headed back the way he'd come. Amory's hands swung nervously at his sides, conveying an urge to escape. Amory's hands were empty. He'd left his suitcase in the church.

Without realizing it, Doyle had built his previous perception of the man around that piece of luggage, as the day before he had done so around a ridiculous knot of clover on his lapel. Only now, with its disappearance, did the suitcase's importance come to the fore. The suitcase was what he'd followed. Amory would return now to the Ritz, Doyle was sure of it. Instead of following, Doyle watched him round the corner and vanish behind the theater.

Now what? Enter St. Cecelia's? Confront Jimmy Adler? How have you done it to me again?

Doyle remained where he was, stymied. Seconds passed, or minutes. Perhaps an hour. The church door opened once more. A man appeared and Terry knew him at once. Not Jimmy Adler but Didi's brother, Jackie Mullen. He took the stairs at a clip, gingerly carrying Amory's suitcase.

Doyle began to move. Mullen headed up the sidewalk toward Massachusetts Avenue, going fast. Doyle began to run. Half a block up the street, Mullen stopped at a parked automobile, a dark green Plymouth. Vacant. He opened the passenger door and tossed the suitcase in, closed the door, then hopped quickly around to the driver's side. Doyle ran faster, pouring it on like a jock doing wind sprints. Mullen got into the car without glancing back, while Doyle scrambled along the sidewalk in the cold shadow of low-class brick houses. His shoes echoed on the pavement. His suit coat flapped up at his elbows.

Mullen had the engine going and was edging away from the curb when Doyle reached the car, on the passenger's side. He slapped the steel once, then lunged at the door handle. The car was still moving. He opened the door and jumped in, hitting the suitcase.

Only then did Mullen react. He slammed the brakes, jolting the car to a stop, and reached to his belt for a weapon.

"It's me, Charlie!" Doyle screamed. "It's me!"

Mullen leveled a gun at him. "Jesus Christ, what the fuck are you doing?"

"Jackie, Jackie, come on." Doyle flapped his hands apart.

Mullen grabbed at the suitcase, which blocked the seat between them. "What the *fuck* are you doing? Christ, Terry. Jesus Christ!"

"You too, Jackie!" The adrenaline kept Doyle going. "What are *you* doing?" He reached for the zipper on the suitcase and pulled it. The black leather flap fell open, exposing only a corner, but, because of what he saw, exposing enough. Bills. Banded stacks of money.

"Fuck!" Mullen slapped his gun against Doyle's head, knocking him back. He closed the zipper, yanked the suitcase free, and threw it into the back seat.

A radio speaker attached to the dashboard crackled to life: "Seven-one, Haymarket Square." The voice was simultaneously gruff and blasé. "Seven-one, OP relief. Check. Seven-one." The police radio fell silent. The message had meant nothing.

Jackie's lips twisted once more around the same words. "You fuck! What are you doing?"

"What are *you* doing, Jackie?" The pain in Doyle's head seemed to focus him.

"Blowing your fucking head off, that's what." Mullen pushed the barrel of his gun against Doyle's cheek. He seemed insane, his eyes jittering. "Who else is here?" He pushed the steel snout harder. "Where's Squire?"

Squire? Terry recognized Mullen's fear without understanding it. He moved his eyes toward the money, then back to Jackie. "He'll be right along. Want to wait?"

"No!"

Mullen looked wildly around. The street appeared to be deserted. He grabbed Doyle's coat and hauled him across his own body, forcing an exchange of seats. "Drive. You drive!"

Terry got the car into gear and pulled away. Mullen continued pointing the gun at him, but his eyes were on the street now, behind, ahead, everywhere.

Terry said calmly, "Squire will be following us, Jackie. He and I are together in this. He knows where I am."

"Oh yeah? Where the fuck are you? Huh? Where?"

"With you, Jackie." The street ended at Mass. Ave. "Which way?"

"Turn left. Turn left, goddamnit! Down to Symphony Hall and turn right. Over to the Fenway."

"Jackie, you've got to —"

"And shut the fuck up. Do you hear me, shut up!"

Doyle did.

Mullen regained control of himself, like a stoical maniac, but he continued looking back, expecting to be followed. He put his gun on the seat, the barrel pointed at Doyle, but he kept his hand on it. At various corners he barked directions, and Doyle obeyed, executing a series of random, sudden turns in the maze of streets around Northeastern University. Once, when the dashboard radio came to life again, Mullen kicked it, then snapped it off. They made two complete circuits of the elliptical Fens parkway. At one point, Mullen ordered Doyle to drive into the parking lot of the Museum of Fine Arts, but when he realized there was a guard booth, he told him to keep going, onto Ruggles Street. For an awful moment, Doyle thought Mullen's manic orders would bring them over to Ruggles Square, and the symmetry of that seemed perverse, an ominous climax. The thing was to be able to keep driving, to get Jackie talking. Doyle turned onto Huntington Avenue, heading for the hospitals.

"Why don't you tell me what's going on, Jackie?"

"You don't know?"

"No."

"I thought Squire knew everything." He kept looking around. "That's the fucking feeling you're giving me. Shit."

"He knows everything. But I don't."

"When did you start working with him?"

"When he brought Amory into my deal."

"*Your* deal? I didn't know you were part of that."

"What'd you think?"

"McKay. I thought it was McKay's deal."

"Well, McKay and I are partners."

"So you know about that?"

"Yes."

"Shit," Mullen said, then fell silent.

Doyle continued driving along Huntington. After a block or two he said, "So it's Squire, Amory, and McKay." He paused, then added, almost absently, "And Tucci's money behind Amory." Doyle slowed the car for a red light, then stopped. "It's all a laundry operation."

"So what is your part in it?"

"I brought McKay in."

"Funny . . ."

"Why?"

"McKay acted like he really did not want you to know. I heard him say that."

"You know Squire. He likes to keep his players guessing."

Once more Mullen looked back, to see who was there.

Doyle said, "What happened, Jackie? You turned against your old buddy? You turned honest? A good cop after all?"

Mullen faced Doyle with dismay and surprise, and then a dark look came over his face. "I'm not the one who turned, Terry. Squire is." He leaned across the seat, suddenly hopeful. "Did you know this? Squire is working with the feds. He's setting us all up. You too."

"Not me."

"Your friend, then. Squire's been wearing a wire from the start."

"A wire?"

"For the feds. That's what I'm telling you. He's a walking tape recorder, and the game's up tomorrow."

"When he tapes Tucci."

"Yes. They're all meeting."

Terry indicated with his eyes the suitcase in back. "You just sold him out, isn't that it? If he's wired for meetings with Amory and Tucci — you just told them."

"Amory, Tucci, and your friend McKay. He's going to be there too." He pressed Doyle's arm. "You should rethink this shit, same as I did."

The light changed then, and once more Terry began to drive, relieved to do so. Yes. Rethink. Think. Rethink again. Jackie was no longer interested in giving him directions, so where Huntington Avenue intersected the Riverway at an overpass, Doyle turned, heading back to the Fenway, toward Boston.

In his mind he could not get past the impossibility of Mullen's position. Caught in the act of his mortal betrayal, Jackie was now going to have to kill the man who'd caught him. Me. He has to kill me.

The road wound along the weed-ridden Muddy River, the border at that point between Boston and Brookline. The curves broke right and left through woods and stretches of overgrown grass. The trees smelled fresh, but there were sweet, rotting odors in the air. The road came to a rise where, for a moment, the view ahead featured the tops of the Hancock and Prudential buildings, the light scaffolds and layered rooflines of Fenway Park. Terry felt he saw the city very clearly, but the road dropped and he lost it.

Mullen lifted his gun. "I don't know what I'm going to do with you."

"Help me understand how it looks from your side, Jackie. You've been in bed with Squire all these years. He's married to your sister. His kids are like yours. Why'd you turn on him? Why are you doing this? I thought Squire always took care of you."

"Bullshit, Charlie, bullshit! I'm the one who's taken care of *him*. I've covered his ass the whole way. Every time they put him on the wanted list, I cooked a deal for him. I set him up with the Bureau in the first place."

"So he's been feeding the FBI information on Tucci right along?"

"Not Tucci. His operation, the mid-level guys, shit that hardly counted. Never Tucci himself until now. That's the point. This is stupid. This is taking on God, and you don't do that. Squire's lost his fucking mind, and my fingerprints are all over this. I had to protect myself."

"You mean, in case Tucci scores. You're covered either way, is that it?"

"I'm in the fucking middle, don't you see that? If the feds succeed, they don't stop with Tucci. For them, the point of this thing is to blow open the *network*, not just Tucci but what Tucci hides behind, Commonwealth Bank — which is why they'll want McKay. And the State Police. The feds love turning over the rocks of the State Police to see what crawls out."

"You."

"You got it. If the feds win, I go to jail with Tucci. If Tucci wins —"

"He kills you."

"Unless." Jackie shrugged. This.

"So you've put money on the mob instead of on Squire."

"He doesn't give a rat's fart about me. Nothing matters to him but scoring on Tucci. That's all that's ever mattered."

"I thought he came to terms with that."

"Never. He has no heart, your brother. None. Not for me. Not for you. Not for Didi. Not for nobody. You should know that best of all." Mullen waved his pistol, the perfect emblem of his superiority. Yet he seemed more uneasy than the stoical Doyle, increasingly crazed. The weapon was in plain view of other motorists, and because of that, Doyle turned down a deserted side street that ran behind Fenway Park. Warehouses rose on one side, the bleachers wall on the other.

"Where you going?"

"We don't want to be in traffic, Jackie."

Mullen's agitation increased. He looked wildly about for signs of an ambush. "You shouldn't be with Squire. Not you, of all people."

"What do you mean?" Doyle pulled the car over and stopped. In a few weeks the Sox would be in town, and this street would be packed. But now it was completely deserted.

Mullen put his face in front of Terry's. "Ask your wife," he said.

"My wife has nothing to do with this," Doyle said coldly.

"Just ask her what she thinks about your brother." It was Mullen's red-eyed leer, more than the lewd insistence of his words, that set off the charge, exploding inside Doyle. His right hand shot into Mullen's face, slamming his skull back against the rear-view mirror, the mount of which snapped in two, bouncing Mullen's head forward again. Once more Doyle hit him.

Mullen dropped the gun. Doyle grabbed it and began to beat him with it. Mullen fell back against the door, blood spurting from his head, one hand raised as a shield, the other scratching behind for the door handle. He got the door open and fell out backwards.

Doyle went after him onto the pavement, pounding the butt of the gun against Mullen's head until his body curled into a fist.

Finally he stopped. His breath came in gasps. His eyes burned as if lye had been thrown in them. He moved back until he bumped into the automobile. The solid steel against one hand, the steel weapon in the other — the thick immutability of steel, of the solid pavement beneath his feet, brought him back to what was real. He looked up, away from Mullen to the sky above, the moving clouds, the play of sunlight and shadow against the uneven roof edge of the adjacent green wall of Fenway Park.

Mullen raised an arm to look up at him. "What are you going to do to me?"

Instead of answering, Doyle reached into the car, first for the keys, then for the suitcase. Bringing it out, he nudged Mullen. "How much is this?"

"A hundred thousand. It's supposed to be a hundred thousand."

"And you betrayed Squire — why? Because he doesn't love you?"

"Take it. You can have it."

"Of course I'll take it."

"But don't tell Squire, Charlie. Please, Charlie."

"What about Bright?" he asked. "What's supposed to happen to him?"

"That's right." Mullen grabbed at the thought, as if McKay would save him. "If Squire gets his way, the feds indict your friend."

"And if you got yours, he'd just get his head blown off, along with Squire. Tucci blows away his betrayer and the only witness, right? Am I right? Same old story, huh, Jackie? Bright gets his eye kicked out again, either way."

"He's just there, that's all. In the target range."

"Has Squire been wired in his meetings with Bright up to now?"

"Yes, but he hasn't handed anything over to the feds yet. Squire controls the tapes as a way of staying in charge."

"So the Bureau doesn't have Bright yet? Dealing with Squire?"

"No evidence. But after tomorrow, once Squire gets Tucci —"

"What are the feds giving Squire in return?"

"A free ride. Boston. Whatever the fuck he wants. They'll have plugged the biggest mob money-laundering gig in the country. They'll have sent a message to every bank that winks at drug money. They want this bad."

"Where's the meeting?"

"Wait a minute." Jackie sat up, wiping the blood from his face, staring helplessly at Doyle. "Why don't you know all this? I thought you said you were in on this."

"Where's the meeting?"

"I don't know." Mullen pulled at Doyle's leg. "Christ, Terry, please."

"What? Don't tell on you?"

"Don't, don't."

"Don't tell Squire? Listen to yourself. I could have told you it would end like this, you stupid shit."

"Give me my gun back at least."

"If I thought you'd use it on yourself, I would."

Doyle pocketed the gun. He hoisted the suitcase by its strap, turned, and walked away.

"Ask your wife!" Mullen cried one last time.

Terry let those words in, but only so far. "Here are your car keys," he said. Then he flipped them up over the lip of a rancid Dumpster.

A few minutes later, having cut across the edge of the newly turned community garden plots on the apron of the stagnant Fens, and having hurried down Boylston to Mass. Ave., Doyle headed out onto the Harvard Bridge. He was going into Cambridge, toward Harvard and the Fogg, despite his infinite desire to go the other way, warn Bright, murder Squire, do anything but act upon Jackie Mullen's self-serving, vicious dare.

For once, he was indifferent to the view of Boston, the golden dome, the brick hill, the glass skyline that he and his friends had planned into being. The season's first sailboats had broken out across the river basin. He saw the white blades against the blue water and bluer sky, but the sight did not tug at his heart or put him in mind of all that he had been deprived of.

Halfway across the bridge, he stopped. A cast-iron manhole cover in the sidewalk had caught his eye. He'd seen it a thousand times, jogging here. MIT kids had painted it lavender and drawn a pair of arrows out from it on the cement, sign of the male organism doubled. He looked behind and ahead; no pedestrians were approaching. Passing motorists weren't giving him a second look. He knelt, put his forefinger in the crowbar hole, and pulled. A second mighty jolt freed the lid, and it came up. One of the traditional Townie capers in early April was stealing the much larger DPW manhole covers, then selling them to boaters at the navy yard for use as mooring mushrooms. He had never done it himself, but he had noticed.

This iron lid covered a small well that held knots of electrical wiring, switches and patches for the streetlight system on the bridge. He unhooked the shoulder strap of the suitcase and pulled one end through the hole in the iron lid, tied it back to the bag, which he then opened. He took the gun from his pocket and put it in with the money. The fucking money.

He zipped the case closed again. He made sure all the zippers were fastened. Then, with an abrupt lunge upward, a power press, he picked up the suitcase and the lid together and threw them over the railing. It took two or three seconds for the thing to hit the surface and sink. When the water splashed, droplets caught the sun and flashed, and he realized how pitilessly the morning light illuminated every failure.

He turned and walked quickly off the bridge, reversing himself to go away from Cambridge, from his wife, back into Boston, not to his brother, but to Bright.

18

JACKIE DOYLE was fifteen years old now. He attended a special school in Quincy, and every afternoon the school van arrived to drop him off, not at the big house up the hill, but at the flower store. Squire had turned the second floor of the old building into his offices, but he always made a point to be down in the store when his son came lurching through the door like the happy puppy he mostly was.

"Dad," Jackie cried, "Dad, Look. Look."

Squire stood at the trimming table, idly sorting through bunches of cut daffodils. He looked up expectantly. "Hey, buddy." And he held his hand up, palm forward, which was how Jackie knew to cross the room and slap him five.

And then, more triumphantly still, Jackie said, "Look!" The boy held up a small gewgaw, a molded but unglazed piece of plaster of Paris, a tiny vase shaped like a Jack-and-Jill watering can.

"Hey, Jake, that's fine." Squire took it with a show of admiration. "God, Jake, it's great, it's really great."

"You like it?"

"Sure I like it. I *love* it." He turned to the corner behind the table. "Look at this." He held up a galvanized steel watering can. "Just like mine."

The thrill could be seen breaking across the kid's round, fat face, a wave that picked him up and carried him into his father's arms, paradise.

Squire could never embrace this son — his pasty, boneless flesh, his swollen belly, the clinging smell of Listerine — without a stifled, guilt-inducing shudder of repugnance. The unwilled physical reaction had nothing to do with his fierce love for the boy. In a bizarre way Squire adored him, and drew a surprising consolation from knowing that Jackie, unlike all his other children, would be entirely his forever. He patted him, saying softly, as his own grandfather always had, "Cushlamochree, buddy. You're the pulse of my heart."

The boy pulled back, as he always did at that, and tapped his father's chest. "In there?"

"Yes. That's where I carry you. You're the greatest kid a dad could want."

Jackie looked into his father's eyes with acute fervor, always searching for some sign that he did not mean what he said, never finding it.

Squire heard someone at the door. He looked up and saw his son's namesake standing sheepishly in the threshold with a battered, swollen face. Jackie Mullen wore a fresh shirt and pullover, and his hair was slicked back, a sign that he'd just come from the shower. Squire took his son's elbow, turning him. "Look who's here, Jake."

As his godfather and uncle, Mullen was, with the nuns of St. Mary's and his teachers in Quincy, one of the few adults whom Jackie knew, but now the meanness in that face startled him. The boy drew back. His eyes darted queerly. Mullen did nothing to soften the impression he was making.

Squire said, "Say hello to your uncle, Jake."

But the boy only stared at the bruised face with his mouth open, his flycatcher. Squire reached into the nearby refrigerator and took out a fresh shamrock boutonniere. He pinned it on his son's shirt like a medal. "Why don't you go show Mommy what you made. Want to?"

Jackie nodded and pulled away. Squire said after him, "Tell Mommy it's a present you made for her, okay?"

The boy stopped and faced his father in a sudden fury. "It's for *you*, goddamnit!" He waved one hand, clutching the vase in the other. As he stumbled toward the door, Mullen cleared the way. "Are you crazy?" the boy howled. "I said it was for you!" And then he went through the door, bewildered and inconsolable, pounding up the sidewalk, away from the flower shop.

Doyle and Mullen stared at each other blankly. Squire never let anyone, certainly not Didi's brother, see how sad his son made him feel.

Ordinarily, Mullen would have apologized, but he just stood there, his bruises on display.

"You just back from the dead or what?"

Jackie shook his head. "You're not going to believe this."

Squire raised a finger, crooked it, then moved past Mullen, through the door, onto the street. He crossed to the small park, the Charlestown Common that anchored that part of the slope. When Mullen joined him, Doyle's manner was frigid, which made his eyes seem darker, which emphasized the natural ruddiness of his face.

"What happened?"

Mullen looked gravely across at the store. "You remember when Tucci's punks came in there, years ago. The one kid with acne, the other kid in the argyle sweater."

"Yeah, Jackie. I remember."

"You had a knife you didn't use. I never forgot that. They cold-cocked me, but you gave them the money."

"They gave it back."

"You made them think old Tucci was protecting us."

"What happened to you?"

"Tucci's punks, Squire. It felt like the same fucking guys. They know. They know what you're doing."

Squire stared at his old friend in silence for a long time. "What am I doing?"

"You're turning the tables finally."

"And they came to you?"

"I was checking the surveillance team in the North End. More or less routine, I thought. Collins and Pierce on Hanover Street, the Commonwealth branch that we have staked out. I was driving by when my fucking doors get yanked open, front seat and back both. Two wops, one with a gun. They make me drive down to Atlantic Avenue, into the lot at Bay State Lobster, which wasn't open yet. The lot was empty. They offered me money to tell them what you were doing. One asked if you was body-miked, Squire. That's the word he used, 'body-miked.' I didn't say anything. They kicked the shit out of me. Obviously."

"And then?"

"Before they left, they said if I told you, they'd make it look like I was the one that ratted."

"How would they do that, Jackie?"

"I don't know. Set me up somehow, I guess. I didn't say anything, but I knew they couldn't."

"Couldn't what?"

"You're making me nervous, Squire. Why are you fucking looking at me like that?"

"Couldn't what?"

"Make you suspect me."

"Suspect you of telling Tucci and Amory that I'm coming to the meeting tomorrow wearing a wire?"

"Right."

"I don't get it, Jackie. If they already know that, why did they jump you? Explain that to me again."

"I don't know. I guess it doesn't make any sense. Unless they just weren't sure."

"If they weren't sure, they could just strip me when I showed."

"You wouldn't put up with that, which they know. That's the point. After all these years, they know you." Mullen changed the level of his voice, lowering it to indicate a shift in the gravity of what he was saying. "This one fucker tells me something really strange, Squire."

"What?"

"That they can use your brother against me."

"Terry?"

"I guess so. 'Doyle's brother' is what they said. He's working for them. I guess McKay must of —"

"What is this shit, Jackie?" Squire slammed Mullen's shoulder, jolting him.

"I don't know. Honest to God, I don't know."

Doyle hit him again, driving him back off the curb into the street.

"Come on, Squire. Give me a break."

"I'll give you a break, you fuck! What does Terry have to do with Tucci? You telling me Terry is in with Tucci?"

Doyle seemed crazy suddenly, like his son — goddamnit! goddamnit! — or like his brother had acted behind Fenway. "Back off, Squire," Mullen said, but with no strength. "I come here to warn you, that's all, to save your ass. Isn't that the bottom line? You're just going to have to decide if you believe me, that's all there is to it." Mullen turned and started to walk away, knowing already what a mistake this was, the impossibility of fooling this bastard. Now he'd have to run. Brazil, for Christ's sake. Bangla-fucking-desh.

"Wait a minute, Jackie. Wait a minute." Doyle's voice was completely free of rage. He was shaking his head, his hands open. "I lost it because of Terry, the idea of Terry —"

Mullen turned back. "You did that, Squire, nobody else. You put Terry on the edge of this thing when you brought in the nigger banker."

"Doesn't matter. Come on." Squire threw an arm over Mullen's shoulder. "Come with me." Squire led the way across the street to his car.

Before getting in, Mullen said, "I shouldn't be seen with you."

"You're my brother-in-law. Come on, buddy, I just want to ride down to Old Ironsides, get some air." Mullen got in.

Doyle drove around the Common to Adams Street, then down to City Square. He waved at corner boys and honked at the parish priest. He was a guy without a care in the world. At the tourist end of the navy yard, afternoon strollers had begun their turn around the waterfront. The antique frigate sat at its pier like a Gothic cathedral, and the thin line of visitors gave off a pilgrim air as they approached the gangplank. But Squire pulled up shy of the official parking lot, at the pair of hooded pay phones on the sidewalk. Shore-leave sailors used those phones to call their girlfriends; Doyle thought of the phones as his. Ignoring Mullen now, he got out, picked one up, and dialed three numbers. Information. For the Ritz. A minute later he knew that Victor Amory had checked out. He dialed another number, which rang once and was answered without so much as hello. Squire said, "Just calling to confirm your upcoming cordwood delivery. When do you need it, and where?"

Still, for a long moment, no one spoke on the other end. Then a voice answered, "Ten days. At number seven."

"You got it," Squire said, and hung up. He checked his watch. Ten minutes, at the pay phone on the far side of the Mystic Bridge, in Chelsea. Squire returned to the car, drove back into City Square, and got on the ramp that led up to the bridge. "Let's get an ice cream, what do you say?"

Mullen could not break out of his moroseness. He had no idea, really, what to hope for, except perhaps an extension of the numb void that had replaced his feelings of fear and regret. He watched as the spine of the city's buildings fell behind them. Afternoon traffic was slow, and they had to pay the toll. But then, quickly, they hit the Chelsea ramp, and they pulled into a drive-in snack bar in the shadow of the bridge. Mullen stayed in the car.

With an ice cream cone, Squire walked to a weathered picnic table on the edge of the dusty lot, near another pay phone. He checked his watch, waited a moment, checked it again, and then the phone rang. He picked it up before the second ring. Tucci would be calling from the pay phone behind the gray-shingled store down the road from the entrance to his Weston estate.

"What," the voice said gruffly. Frank.

"Amory's gone."

"I know."

"You told him to go?"

Silence. Tucci had no fear of this phone being bugged, but he was cagey nonetheless.

"What's happening, Frank?"

"You tell me."

"I think our friends in the Bureau are trying to mind-fuck us, Frank. Don't fall for it."

"What are you telling me, Doyle?"

"Steady as she goes, that's what."

"Fuck you, Doyle."

Doyle felt sick, the sharp nausea of his knowledge that Tucci was off the hook, scooting away even now. "Whatever they told you, don't believe it. Believe *me*, Frank. After all these years. Believe me."

"What about this, Doyle? Listen to this." There was silence, then the click of a machine, then the whirring, hollow sounds of an underwater voice. "*. . . then we're doing seventeen, eighteen cartons a day . . .*"

"Cartons" was a word they used in referring to thousands of dollars. The voice was Amory's. Doyle listened, stunned. Then he felt, instead of nausea, a stab of pain in his chest, near his heart, when he heard his own voice saying fervently, "*At least that, Victor. And eventually we'll move fifty, sixty.*"

The voice snapped off. Then it was Tucci again. "I'm told you have seven more of those."

Eight reels of tape Squire had made during his meetings with Amory.

"And what are you telling me, Frank?"

"You want *me* on tape, Doyle, reciting the ABCs for the grand jury? What kind of stupid fuck do you think I am? You think I'm Kermit the Frog? You think I'm Irish?"

"You've got a tape, Frank. Doesn't mean it's me. The feds could have —"

"Amory said that was at the Top of the Hub. They got the Skywalk bugged, Doyle? That what you want me to believe? The fucking Skywalk? You want to know what I'm telling you? I'll tell you what I'm telling you. Watch your car, you got it? Watch your boat, make sure it's not leaking. Watch your fucking bicycle, Doyle! Watch your fucking skateboard! You get it?"

Was the wop threatening his kids? No. No. They didn't do that. They wouldn't. "Frank, don't fall for this. They've suckered you. Who'd you get this shit from? Mullen? Mullen is working for the feds now, straight arrow."

"Mullen is mine, Squire." Tucci could not resist. It was infinitely unnecessary to flaunt this, a cheap thrill his father would never have indulged, especially on a line with a prick he couldn't trust. But all at once, for the first time in years, Tucci didn't care. "Your chum has been mine for a long time. I had you covered. That's why I could go with you, asshole. But I always knew a day would come when I couldn't." The wavy lilt of triumph in Tucci's voice seemed impossible to fake, like the minute patterns on paper money.

Squire saw how he'd miscalculated, trusting too much — not Jackie, but his own shrewdness, and his certainty that Guido Tucci's son was a fool. Doyle held the phone at his mouth, mute, knowing nothing he said now would threaten Frank or dilute his sense of a long-sought and final supremacy. But *omertà:* Doyle fell back on silence, imposing the discipline of numbers on himself. At the count of thirty, he hung up.

In the car, at the wheel again, he said, "No problem, Jackie. We're just going to let things simmer for a while. Tucci's spooked, God knows by what. You're right about tomorrow. So we'll cool it." He pulled away from the snack bar, circled under the bridge, then back up onto it, going south.

"So then, I call Joyce and Farrell . . ."

"Yeah. Make them think *their* people telegraphed. Give them some shit about it. Be in charge. We got to keep them needing you."

"Okay. Yeah. Good."

Both men fell silent, each watching the back side of Charlestown come into view. Jackie found the air inside the car stale, and he cranked his window and opened his mouth for air.

"Want to come in and see Didi, have a brew?"

"No. No thanks. I'll just head downtown."

"You'll have to get a story up to explain your face. You don't want Joyce starting to think Tucci has a special interest in you."

"Good point, that's true."

"You'll think of something."

"Yeah."

"You always do."

Mullen looked sharply over.

Doyle was keen on his easy driving, an elbow out the window, a pair of fingers on the wheel. "Where'd you park?"

"Across from the Bouquet."

Instead of driving directly there, Doyle went to the top of Bunker Hill, to Monument Square, and pulled over across from his house, as if he hadn't heard Mullen's refusal. In the park to their right, half a dozen kids were cavorting on the sloping grass, a game of King of the

Hill. Doyle pointed. "There's Mark, there's Paddy." Two of his sons. "What is it, Jackie, the click in the brain at some point, when we stop enjoying wrestling?"

"I really can't come in. I should check in at the job."

"I'm going to drive you down to your car. Just wait here a minute. I got to get something." Doyle left the car and, after waving to his sons, dashed across the street, a loping stride. He took the stairs in a burst of hops and disappeared through the door of the stately house.

When he came out again, he was carrying a bulking green garbage bag.

"What's that?" Mullen asked, seeing threats everywhere.

Doyle opened the bag enough to reveal a pair of deep purple, velour-covered cushions, an Irish housewife's dream accessory. "I told Didi I'd pick these up," Squire said, as if that explained anything. He drove around the corner and down the hill to the store. When he'd shut the car off, he faced Mullen. "Come in with me. I want to show you something." He stared at Mullen so coldly now that Mullen dared not resist.

They walked to the store side by side, Squire clutching the garbage bag.

Mullen said clumsily, "What's up, Squire? Jeez, you're making me nervous. I feel like I'm up to my neck in wet shit, like the micks in that joke about hell, waiting for the Protestants to come by in their motorboat."

Squire ignored him. Inside the store, he led the way across the old uneven floor into the cluttered back room. "Come here, Jackie."

Even when he'd thought for a moment that he'd finessed Squire, the foreboding he'd felt since his fate revealed itself in the shadow of Fenway Park had not lifted. Now it positively choked him.

The back room. As boys, they'd cut flower stems on the worktable that still ran the length of one side wall. The back wall was the walnut and chrome door of the walk-in refrigerator, into and out of which they'd hauled bundles of daffodils and birds of paradise and cottage roses and palm branches, carnations and mums. For an instant, memory played its trick on Mullen's sense of smell: the sweet aromas and cool air had always made the walk-in seem enchanted, especially in summer. It had been years since the refrigerator had been used, except as storage, and it would be musty now.

Squire was on his knees at the third wall, beside the cluttered roll-top desk that both still thought of as old Ned's. It took a moment for Mullen to realize he was at the safe, opening it. The safe had two inner compartments. One was locked and required a key. The other was an open shelf on which banded bills and rolls of coins were stacked. Squire reached in for a single roll of quarters and put it on top of the safe. Then he straightened and leaned across to the desk. His eyes briefly met Mullen's, and he said, "Relax, Jackie. I want to show you something." He opened one of the several small desk drawers and withdrew a key. He bent to the safe once more and opened the second compartment. It held a cigar box, several glassine bags of white powder, a folded pair of rubber surgeon's gloves, and a Ziploc bag containing a black, oily-looking pistol.

Squire withdrew the cigar box. He opened it and, facing Mullen, fingered through a collection of small tape cassettes until he found a particular one. It was labeled *Amory-2*. He held it up to the light. "What do you know, Jackie?" he said. "The thickness of the tape on the take-up end of the little reel here is half what it's supposed to be. What do you make of that?"

Mullen could only stare at the cassette.

Doyle said, "You know what that missing stretch of tape is, pal? It's an exact measure of my stupidity — not for trusting you, because it isn't trust between a toilet bowl and the lever you flush it with; it's mechanics. No, my stupidity was in trusting myself. I guess I thought I really owned you, Jackie, like I own the shit that comes out of my asshole." Squire laughed, then replaced the tape in the cigar box, and the cigar box in the safe. He picked up the roll of quarters and faced Mullen again.

"Jackie, do you remember when my grandfather knighted me?"

"What?"

"When old Ned made me his squire. Do you remember that?"

"Yes."

"I'm going to do that to you now, pal. I'm going to make you a squire too."

Mullen took half a step back, shaking his head. "Your brother's the one who fucked us up here. Terry is who you got to watch for, not me. You know that. Terry's always been the one."

"I don't want to hear about Terry. I want you over there." Squire pointed to the refrigerator. "Move!"

"What, in there?" Mullen backed toward the door, but he was shaking his head. "I'll suffocate."

"No you won't. It's not airtight anymore, Jackie. No more than you are. It's quiet, and you can wait in there while I decide what to do with you."

"Come on, Squire," Mullen whined, but he did as he was told. Squire could kill him now, he knew. The fact that he apparently wasn't going to gave Mullen hope. He opened the door and backed in.

The space held old cartons and boxes, seedling cases and clay pots, the wire skeletons of wreaths and ribbons saying Mother and *Beloved Son*. The light bulb was long dead. Mullen had to push boxes aside to get in.

Squire took up a position in the threshold. "Now kneel," he said.

"What?"

"Kneel down here in front of me. I'm going to knight you, like I said." Doyle unzipped his fly and pulled his penis out. "Here's my sword."

"Oh, come on, Squire. Jesus."

"Do it, Jackie. Now."

"Blow you? Jesus, Squire! Blow you?"

Squire laughed wickedly, and Mullen thought, if I do this, maybe he won't need to kill me. Mullen knelt and opened his mouth wide.

At the last minute, Squire turned aside, adjusting himself, then back. From in close, he began to urinate on Jackie, who knew better than to pull away.

"Oh, shit, Squire," he said. The piss mingled with Mullen's tears. He slowly bowed his head to his lord of lords.

Doyle had his eyes closed as he continued hosing down his oldest friend. He went into a kind of urination ecstasy, and once, unconsciously, he spoke a word aloud: "Charlie."

Jackie, kneeling there, soaked, found himself wishing that he'd had to take the bastard's prick in his mouth after all, because this was worse.

When he'd finished, Squire said quietly, "Jackie?"

Mullen looked up at him, his red eyes burning.

Squire had clamped his fist around the roll of quarters and now brought it down on Mullen's face, hitting him once — he fell against Squire's legs; twice — Squire felt the bone in Mullen's skull crack; three times before Mullen collapsed. Squire snapped the roll of quarters in two and sprinkled the coins on the slumped, unconscious figure. "I dub thee Squire," he said.

He returned to the safe, removed the pistol in its Ziploc bag and the rubber gloves. He closed the compartment, locked it with the key, and put the key back in the desk. He closed the safe and spun the dial. He put the pistol and the gloves into the garbage bag with the cushions and knotted it. He took a roll of heavy plastic tape from the worktable, went back into the dead refrigerator, placed the garbage bag beside Mullen, then used the tape to bind his mouth, legs, and arms, in case the piece of shit regained consciousness, which he probably wouldn't.

✧

The offices of Bailey, Barnes & Coe occupied four floors of the Commonwealth Bank Building, which was always convenient, since the bank was the law firm's largest client. Unlike Bright McKay's city-facing office a dozen floors above, this conference room looked out on the harbor. Of the five blue-suited men and two tailored women at the broad mahogany table, only Terry Doyle was unaccustomed to this particular view, the islands moored like green vessels in the sharp blue water between the arching pincers of Hull on the south and Nahant on the north. The sea rose to the murky edge of the eastern horizon where the water met the sky in the blurring late light of the day. Doyle's focus kept shifting from the broad vista to tiny gleaming objects moving across his field of vision like motes. They were jets going in and out of the airport, which made Terry think of his son.

The conference room door opened. A receptionist leaned in. "Mr. Joyce is here."

"That makes all of them, then?"

"Yes, sir. Mr. Joyce of the U.S. Attorney's Office, Mr. Farrell of the FBI, and Mr. Patten of the IRS."

"Okay. Just one more moment."

The receptionist disappeared, closing the door without a sound.

The men at the table occupied themselves variously, adjusting a cuff, twisting the barrel of a Cross pen, centering a Rolex watch on a wrist bone. One of the women sat immobile, and the other held her pencil at the ready above a steno pad. The man at the head of the table looked at each of them. He was Brooks Otis, the chairman and CEO of the bank. To one side were Harold Van Buren, the bank's senior vice president, and John Logan, the Bailey, Barnes partner in charge of the bank's file. Next to Logan was a young attorney, the immobile woman. Her name was Roseanne Day. She was black, which had stopped Otis cold when he saw her in the corridor.

"Who's this?" he'd said *sotto voce*, pulling Logan back as she'd gone ahead into the conference room.

"She's a recently hired associate who —"

"Jesus Christ, Logan. Didn't you get the drift of what we're dealing with here? This is too fucking serious to be used as training for your goddamned —"

Logan had raised a hand in front of his own face with such an air of command that the chairman stopped. Logan had said, "After Harvard, and before joining us, she served as an assistant to the chief of the Narcotics and Dangerous Drugs section of the Criminal Division at Justice. She was the principal author of the department's official guide to the Bank Secrecy Act. I'm a real estate lawyer, Brooks, which until recently was all Commonwealth Bank really needed. This woman knows more about the law on money laundering than anyone outside of Washington — and that's what you need now." Logan had moved closer to his client and lowered his voice to add, "We hired her because we saw something like this coming."

By the time they'd entered the conference room, Attorney Day had taken a chair on the far side of the table, her back to the view, next to the stenographer, who'd shown no sign of noticing that anyone had joined her. Now, across the table, facing the women, were McKay and Doyle.

Otis said, "John, before we ask our visitors to join us, do you have anything to add?"

"No." Logan glanced at the woman beside him. "Do you?"

Day leaned forward. She wore a demure gray suit, and her hair was pulled back tightly in a small bun. A bright red scarf at her throat was one hint of flamboyance. Except for the other, an oversize, white-lacquered wristwatch that contrasted with her skin, she wore no jewelry. Her eyes went right to Bright McKay's.

"The bank's position is strong," she began. Her hand moved toward the middle of the table, toward McKay, a flaunting, it almost seemed, of the blackness of her fingers. "That is the point to have in mind." She glanced at Van Buren and Otis, but her gaze returned to McKay. "In sum, the reporting requirements of the relevant statutes are explicit. There is no question of a violation there. The act does not contain a separate administrative summons or subpoena authority. The provisions of the Financial Privacy Act take precedence over the Bank Secrecy Act. In relation to Mr. Amory, you have been bound by law to protect the privacy of the bank's customers, even from the government."

McKay nodded. "Until now, when we have reason to suspect deception."

"Correct. Currency law imposes its burdens on transaction originators, which in this case is the Sullivan Square Savings Bank. As second party, Commonwealth Bank is under no obligation even to report suspicion."

"Except as good citizens." McKay smiled broadly.

Day ignored him to make her further point. "There is no question of violation, no matter what the benefit to the Commonwealth Bank."

"Benefit!" Van Buren slapped the folders in front of him. "This was public service! We handled Amory's accounts, but he immediately collatoralized them, involving us in a massive loan commitment. Financing Ruggles Center involved no benefit, and we should lead with that fact." Van Buren realized that Otis was glaring at him, and so his adamancy fell away as he concluded, "Benefit to Roxbury, maybe, but not to us."

But Logan said, "Fees meet the definition of benefit, Harold. Your fees have been considerable."

Day repeated the phrase with special emphasis: "No matter what the benefit to Commonwealth Bank, there is no question of violation in the absence of evidence establishing *intention* to participate in illegal use of monetary instruments."

"And there is no such evidence," McKay said calmly, "because there was no such intention."

Day nodded. "Which this meeting supports, Mr. McKay. Your uncoerced and prompt notification both of bank authorities and federal authorities demonstrates the opposite of said intention." She sat back.

Otis waited until Roseanne Day, like the others, looked at him. "Well put," he said. He looked at his watch. "Comment?"

No one spoke.

"All right, Neville," Otis said, "it's your serve."

"Just call me Ace," McKay cracked.

Unknown to the others, Otis moved his foot to the buzzer buried in the rug. A moment later the door opened. Everyone stood. The receptionist appeared, showing in the three officials who, after handshakes all around, took seats on the visitors' side of the table, facing the view, beside Terry Doyle and Bright McKay.

Doyle listened as John Logan opened, emphasizing the bank's grave concern about irregularities only now apparent. Otis added a solemn word of his own before handing off to McKay.

McKay, carrying himself like a maitre d', passed over copies of the printouts that the others already had: the record of transactions on the Amory accounts in the months since they'd been opened. "Mr. Amory represented himself as a real estate developer from Florida. You'll note the steady inflow of sizable monies, which was generated, as we were given to believe, by the holdings of his several companies." McKay had fallen back on the stilted manners of the West Indies, and he spoke with more than a hint of *Masterpiece Theatre* in his voice. "But then I noticed over a period of time that, unlike patterns of income tied to real estate that I'm aware of, there was no monthly cycle here. Huge amounts of money arriving in Amory's accounts at random intervals, and that was what set me to wondering." McKay paused as the three feds flipped through the pages of the transaction record.

Colin Joyce, the assistant U.S. attorney, removed his eyeglasses to dramatize it when he looked up at McKay. "Set you to wondering about drug money?"

McKay shrugged. "It's the eighties, isn't it?"

"What'd you do with your suspicions at that point?"

"That's what we have you here to talk about. I made a request of the originating bank to provide us copies of the Amory account CTRs, and —"

"They refused?"

"Not quite. They said CTRs weren't relevant because all of Amory's money came in deposit sums under ten thousand dollars. Which, of course, given the amounts involved, is ridiculous."

"When did you make this request?"

"Today. And we immediately called you."

Bright looked briefly at Terry, who nodded curtly.

✧

Despite all their years, they had not understood what it meant that they were friends until earlier that afternoon.

Bright, in his office, had a headache that was squeezing his eyes together, and when his secretary had buzzed him that Terry was there, he told her to say he was in a meeting.

But the son of a bitch had walked right into his office and said, "Come on, I'm taking you to lunch."

"I don't eat lunch."

"You do today. Let's go."

They walked through the canyons of downtown to Quincy Market, hardly speaking. At a food stand, they bought lobster rolls and Cokes, and left the crowded corridor for a corner of the grand rotunda. They sat on stools, off by themselves. Above them, on the wall of acid-washed brick hung an antique sign, SANDERS PROVISIONS.

Doyle took a last swallow of Coke and wiped his lips with his napkin. He said, "Bright, I told you I didn't like our new partner."

"And I told you I didn't want to discuss it."

"I followed him from the Ritz this morning. He gave a suitcase full of cash to Jackie Mullen in exchange for information that Squire is working for the feds. Squire has set up Amory as a way to get at Tucci, and I have a sick feeling he's got you in the middle."

McKay looked up at the old sign. "God, they did a great job with this place, didn't they?"

"You've bought into a money-laundering scheme, and the FBI is going to blow it open. You have to talk to me about it."

McKay's expression was very hard. "You? Talk to you? Mr. Disapproval?"

"What the hell does that mean?"

"You know what it means."

"Bright, my attitudes are irrelevant. Maybe you want to make the case for putting drug money to constructive uses in the inner city, since the drugs that generate it are destroying its children. Robin Hood in the age of angel dust? There's a rationale, right? But do you know what? None of that matters, not now, my friend. The FBI is about to blow Tucci out of the water, and you with him."

"Well." Bright's voice was dead.

"You've met with Squire?"

"Yes."

"He's the puppeteer behind Amory. He brings in the money, what you've used to get the loans."

"Yes. Good old Squire."

"Shit!" Doyle looked sharply away.

"That's what has you so pissed, that Squire — ?"

"That Squire has you on tape, Bright. Mullen told me that Squire has worn a wire to every meeting he's had with you and Amory, and was planning to wear it to a meeting with Tucci tomorrow. An FBI wire, Bright. Now do you get it? You've been stupid."

"Wired? He was wired?"

"Yes. He knew how much you wanted the Ruggles deal, all that blue smoke you puffed into the newspapers. You were an easy mark for him. He got you, Bright."

McKay leaned back on his stool, his head against the brick wall. "Oh my God."

Doyle realized that guitar music had been playing, drifting out from speakers high up on the wall. He said, "Jackie told me Squire controls the tapes. The government may not have you yet."

"Why?"

"Probably because it keeps Squire in charge. Also, maybe it lets him limit his own exposure. Apparently he's been holding out until they nail Tucci, which now that Amory knows, won't happen."

"You've put this all together?"

"I should have been a prosecutor. Or a defense attorney. I want to be yours, Bright."

McKay stared at him in silence for a time before saying, "Your brother touched something in me that you've always hated."

Doyle nodded. "Your impatience. Your contempt for process. To get what you want, you'll do anything. But you're no John DeLorean. What you want isn't a fucking sports car. It's a new start for the neighborhood you were a priest's kid in. St. Cyp's. I know what that is to you. Squire could get to you because you want so desperately to give the Southwest Corridor back to the people it was stolen from, and that takes money."

"Which Amory gave us."

"Yes."

"Which you hated."

"Yes."

"This ain't Robin Hood," Bright said. "And it ain't the New Frontier either. It's been Boston's version of the Irish Sweepstakes. I bought a ticket. I took a chance. And I can see it coming already, how fucking sorry I'm going to be that I ever got in bed with your brother. But only because I'm caught. Do you understand that? If the deal could work —"

"You'd do it again."

"Which is why you hate me."

"Bright, you're not even in the ballpark. I don't hate you. You're my best friend. I love you." They were loaded words, he'd never said them to a man before, and it made no difference, really, that Doyle had succeeded in spinning the words out as if he and McKay were athletes or cops: Love ya, baby.

McKay looked away, his expression hard as ever. Still with his head against the wall, he flipped his eye patch up to his forehead, like half a pair of sunglasses, to rub his aching face. He said coldly, through his hands, "What you don't know about love would fill a five-inch floppy disk."

"That's true."

The guitar music, a chipper flamenco piece, cut through the steady rumble of the vast room's echoing conversations. Doyle said, "You think of me as your own personal puritan. You're like Joan in the way I burden you. I know that, okay? But, like I said, none of that shit is relevant now. I only have one thing on my mind at this point. Who moves in for the kill first? The FBI? Frank Tucci? Squire? Or you?"

"Me?"

"To protect yourself, Bright. To save your black ass."

"How can I?" When he looked at Doyle now, it was with an air of absolute vulnerability.

Doyle felt as if he were seeing him naked. "By listening to me."

✧

Patten, of the IRS Criminal Investigation Division, looked up from his notepad. "Mr. McKay, had you done business with the, ah" — he checked the reference — "Sullivan Square Savings Bank before?"

"No, sir. Not me personally. Although, before the Schrafft's plant closed, Commonwealth Bank had dealings with it, as you might expect."

"And had you done business with this Mr. Amory before?"

"No, sir."

"But you entered into transactions involving, ultimately, millions of dollars, and you recommended a loan arrangement."

Patten was overweight and perspiring, despite the air conditioning. McKay feigned the superior air that well-paid lawyers and bankers adopt with IRS functionaries. A British banker at that. "Mr. Patten, you know that banking, despite all regulation and government oversight, is a unique industry which, at the end of the day, is based on trust — the depositor's trust in his institution, of course, but also, every properly certified institution's trust in every other, in the banking network itself. Banks sometimes call themselves trusts, and with good reason. That's what's been abused here."

"But when you're dealing with these kinds of cash deposits" — again Patten checked his notes — "in the hundreds of thousands of dollars, it took you a period of many weeks to develop a suspicion."

Roseanne Day raised her pencil toward the IRS man, bringing the room's focus to her narrow black face, her lips the color of clay, her fine brown eyes, their steadiness fixed like glass. Her voice was irreducible: "Not 'deposits,' Mr. Patten. 'Transfers.' Accounts held by Commonwealth Bank received those monies by electronic transfer."

"But you knew from the start they were cash deposits at Sullivan Square."

"Yes," Van Buren said. "And we assumed Sullivan Square was in compliance with reporting provisions." Van Buren craned toward McKay. "You had reasons for assuming that. You knew people there. You told me —"

Terry sensed Van Buren's readiness to cut Bright loose, a move in that direction, and he jumped in. "That's why I'm here, gentlemen. I'm not only the principal developer in the Ruggles Center project that drew Mr. Amory's interest, but I am also the person who vouched for the Sullivan Square Savings Bank in the first place."

"You had done business with them?"

"No." Terry stopped, uncertainty clouding his face.

At that moment McKay concluded that Doyle could not do it, and to his own surprise, he did not blame him.

But Terry drew on reserves McKay did not know he had. He said, "My brother has an interest in it."

Patten flipped through a folder while Joyce and Farrell kept their eyes lowered. Patten withdrew a single page, a grainy photocopy of a charter document. "Your brother is — ?"

"Nicholas Doyle."

"There is no Nicholas Doyle listed here."

Sensing that the IRS man was not playing on the same field with the other two, Terry shifted toward Farrell. "My brother is a flower importer and wholesaler with wide-ranging business interests. He may have reasons I don't know of for staying behind the scenes, but he represented himself to me as an owner of Sullivan Square. He knew I was looking for major investment in Ruggles Center, and he introduced me to Mr. Amory. All of this has happened so fast — the suspicions surfacing only today — that I haven't had a chance to talk to him, but perhaps he can shed some light on all this."

Farrell looked across at Patten. "We'll follow that up," he said quietly, firmly, but to himself he said, Shit. Squire Doyle's name was on the docket now, and Patten's presence meant it had to be dealt with.

Farrell glanced at Terry: What the shit, Mac? Your own brother?

"So we had reasonable grounds . . ." Otis opened his hands, a show of helpless innocence.

"And Amory," Van Buren put in, looking across at Farrell. "Have you questioned him?'

"Mr. Amory seems to have left Boston," Colin Joyce said coldly, nailing Van Buren. "After closing his accounts with this bank late this morning. You, Mr. Van Buren, authorized a final wire transfer to the Kurfürst Royale in Basel in the amount of one million, two hundred and seven thousand, four hundred twelve dollars."

Van Buren glanced sheepishly at Otis, but it was McKay who responded. "If Mr. Van Buren had failed to do so, Mr. Joyce, he'd have been guilty of an outrageous and illegal malfeasance, as you know."

Terry Doyle, having sown his brother's name in the fertile soil of all that suspicion, let his gaze go to the view again. Through the black steel frame of the window, incoming airplanes lined up at intervals, as if to harvest the sun's late rays. Each fuselage glinted spectacularly in turn. Under the indolent sky, departing planes made their escape, leaping off the earth.

"How does it work, Dad?" Max had asked him not long before, having realized that flying was something to be afraid of.

"Just because we can't see the air," Terry had found himself answering, "doesn't mean it isn't solid. The airplane is supported by the mass of the air. All it has to do is keep going."

He thought of that answer now, how it applied to him. Just keep going or you fall.

Max. The boy knew nothing of the loneliness Doyle associated with his own childhood, and from which, in truth, he'd never shaken free. His own absent father. The current of his grandfather's affection flowing always over Nick. Sleeping in that room with his brother, listening to him breathe, wondering how, with someone so important so near, he could feel so alone. He'd never shaken free, yet what was this with Bright, even now, if not the bringing to some fruition of their kinship? Doyle often thought of that September morning two and a half decades before, when the figure of that tall, black BC kid by the Kennedy banner had made him feel he'd come home. Bright, who had served his aces after all.

Patten and Joyce capped their pens while Farrell spread his business cards around the table, in case anyone should have questions or further information. The FBI was coordinating the investigation, not the IRS.

"One more thing, Mr. Farrell, if you'll permit me." Brooks Otis leaned forward over his clasped hands, his gold cuff links showing. "This needn't be public, I assume."

"If it comes to indictments, Mr. Otis, of course it's public." The FBI man let his disdain show in the downward curve of his mouth. Farrell knew very well the game Otis was playing, and he was tired of it.

Doyle knew it too, but he recognized that the agent's attitude was toothless compared to that of Otis, who had no need to manifest his contempt. Otis was as superbly bred and educated as he was tailored, and men like him had learned above all to veil the certain knowledge of their superiority.

"But there is no question of Commonwealth Bank —"

"There is a question of everything at this point, I'd say, Mr. Otis." Farrell allowed what he'd been trained to keep buried to surface for a moment, and he frankly savored the bank chairman's washed-out, frightened expression before adding, "Of course, for the present, publicity serves no one's purposes."

Colin Joyce said, "And it's up to the U.S. attorney to determine what is presented to the grand jury."

"Grand jury!" Otis blurted. "You can't take this —"

Farrell stood, cutting the discussion off.

No one approached Otis as papers were gathered and chairs replaced. Farrell, in shaking Logan's hand, said, "You're fielding calls on this?"

Logan glanced at Otis, who nodded curtly toward Roseanne Day. "With her."

When Terry shook Farrell's hand, he sensed that beneath his cocky manner, Farrell had as much to keep covered, at least, as the bank did. Terry held Farrell's hand and his eye, giving him a chance to mention Squire. And he didn't.

After the group dispersed, Terry took an elevator down to the two-story-high lobby, which was furnished with oriental rugs and groupings of imitation antique furniture in which no one was ever expected to sit. He crossed into the branch office of the bank, withdrew fifty dollars from the ATM, then went to the opposite end of the lobby where the downtown branch of the Harvard Coop was located. He bought two cassette tapes, *John Williams Plays Bach and Scarlatti*, for Joan, and Michael Jackson's *Thriller* for Max. Then he returned to the lobby, boarded an elevator, and pressed thirty.

In Bright's office, once they had the door closed, the two men clasped each other by the arms, like a halfback and his blocker in the end zone. Bright had taken his coat off, and his shirt was stained with perspiration.

"Jesus Christ, Bright, you did it! I think you pulled it off!"

But Bright moved away, looking chastened. "Not everything. Van Buren just told me, with Otis at his elbow, to forget Ruggles Center. No loans from Commonwealth. They're cutting us off."

"Shit."

"I saw it coming."

"Screw them, Bright. We'll get it somewhere else. With Ted Kennedy on board —"

But McKay cut him off. "Same old fucking story. Back to zero for the wasteland around St. Cyp's. I hate that bastard Van Buren. He knew what we were doing as well as I did. Could you believe what he tried to pull on me?"

"Every man for himself, especially micks and coons. Boston is still Boston."

"You're Boston. You saved my ass."

"Not just me. How about Billie Holiday, your Lady Day lawyer. Where'd she come from?"

"A *new* Boston, Terry. See, it's true. But I got to tell you, when Logan first walked in with her, and it became clear that she was the quarterback, even I said to myself, Whoa! Where's Perry Mason? Get me James St. Clair." Bright laughed. "Serves me right for backing Shirley Chisholm." He moved to his desk. He took two cigarettes from a pack, Vantage now, not Gauloises. They lit up. Bright leaned on the edge of his desk. "The irony is, every point of law she made backed up what Squire had told me."

Terry looked up, then made a sudden, frantic motion with his hand, sweeping the air, mouthing the word "Bug!"

"Oh, bullshit, don't get paranoid on me."

Terry turned away. The weight of his intuition, now that he'd admitted it, only grew heavier, but he said easily, "Talk about paranoid." He looked out the window. "I was waiting for one of the airplanes coming in and out of Logan to crash. Those airplanes, man, hanging in nothing, defying the laws of gravity."

"Which is what you just did."

"When I —"

"In relation to —" Now Bright too looked at the ceiling, and he was only half joking when he then mouthed the word "Squire."

"I know," Terry said.

"A long time coming. You put his name on a list he has apparently succeeded in staying off."

"But you noticed how the FBI guy led away from it. Nobody followed up, they asked me nothing, not his address, not the name of his business, nothing."

"So maybe they know."

"It means what Jackie said was true. He's working for them somehow, or they think he is."

"I think they're confused, Terry. They don't expect shit like this at Commonwealth Bank, for one thing."

"Notwithstanding all its Latin-American branches?" Terry ticked his fingers. "Commonwealth Bogotá, Commonwealth Caracas. Panama City. What they don't expect Commonwealth Bank–Boston to do is report itself."

"Well, what you just did," McKay said, the nonchalant tone gone now, "whatever it meant to them, it means a lot to me."

The two men looked at each other for an ungainly moment. This time there was no question of a direct statement, however.

"But we're not finished," Terry said finally. "Or have you forgotten?" He joined Bright at his desk, picked up a pencil, and scrawled on a yellow pad the words "No violation in absence of evidence establishing intention!" And then he drew a circle around the word "evidence."

"I know," Bright said quietly, then whispered, "I think I said some things I wouldn't want on tape. Not now."

"He still has it, if we can believe Jackie. And I think we have to. So I'm going home to get it."

"You still call that home?"

"Did I?"

"Just now."

"Christ."

"I'm going with you."

Terry shook his head. "It's still no man's land over there for you. Why don't you buy a drink for Billie Holiday?"

"Shit, you know how women like that intimidate me. Are you still trying to get me married?"

"First, I got to keep you out of . . ." The last word he said inaudibly: "Jail."

McKay picked up the silence, and now when he spoke, it was in an even fainter whisper. "I'm going with you."

"Okay." Doyle put his mouth by McKay's ear, as if this would be the gravest secret of all. "We can't go into Charlestown until after dark anyway, when they can't see you."

19

THE WEEKLY HOLY HOUR at St. Mary's, with the rosary, the novena, and the exposition of the Blessed Sacrament, was one of the few things Didi Doyle did only for herself. She loved the church at night, the way the stained-glass window beside her pew was opaque because of the darkness outside, the blue candles flickering at the feet of Mary on one side of the sanctuary, and the tray of red ones on the other, at Joseph's sandaled feet. She continued kneeling while others around her left the church, banging the door in the back. She felt the blast of the damp wind intruding from the rainy April night, and a familiar shudder curled through her, regret that the service was over.

She buried her face in her hands, absorbed in the old habit of preparing to go home again by hurling herself against the rock of her disappointment, which knew of her existence no more than her rapacious children did, or her stone-hearted husband. "Jesus, Mary, and Joseph," she said. She still stamped their initials on every page of the prayers she uttered. She looked up and saw the monsignor, unvested now, removing the sacred vessels from the altar. And she realized it was time to go.

At home, the phone rang even before she'd removed her plastic rain hat or checked on the kids. Given that timing, she shouldn't have been surprised at whose voice she heard.

"Is that you, Deirdre?"

"Hello, Ma."

"But is it you?"

"Of course it's me."

"I called before, and where were you?"

"Molly is eighteen years old, Ma. Old enough to babysit while I go to novena."

"Is Jackie there? I'm calling for Jackie."

"He's not here. Why would he be here?"

"He gives me my medicine. I can't go to bed without my medicine. You know that."

"Did you call the Harp?"

"He said he was going to the flower store when he left here, to see Nick."

"When was that?"

"Before dinner. He never came home for dinner. I made meat loaf."

"Ma, it's nearly ten o'clock at night. The store's been closed for hours."

"But that's where he said he'd be."

"So call there."

"Nick doesn't like it if —"

"Nick doesn't care," Didi said, so wearily.

"Is Nick there? Is Nick home?"

"No, he isn't here, Ma." Didi thought of the placard *Thy Will Be Done.* Had that been her mistake, praying such a thing? Asking for it? Let this perfect emptiness swallow me?

"So would you check?"

"What, Ma? The store? Check the store for Jackie?"

"Tell him to come home. I need him."

Oh, brother. The poor dope, living with her still. Didi was in danger suddenly of feeling blessed.

✧

Terry and Bright parked the car on Main Street, near the church, two blocks away. They walked quickly in the light rain to the Common and cut into it. All the way across the deserted patch of grass, benches, and trees, they watched the building on the far corner. It was dark, rising in the mist, in Terry's mind, like the bow of the Spanish galleon it had been to him. Terry knew that the upper floors of the bowfront triple-decker were unoccupied, and that because of the staid character of the surrounding streets, especially on a night like this, there was no particular boldness in their coming before midnight. On the contrary, the neighborhood, with its light-sleeping elders and relentless busybodies, would be less suspicious of dark figures now than later.

Both wore windbreakers, baseball hats, and tennis shoes. They moved across the footpath soundlessly, and except for a rare tire-hissing speedster on Winthrop Street, no one else was out. Bright carried his hands in his pockets, as if to show as little as possible of his black skin. He was feeling like an interloper as they approached the flower store, not first because this was the Town, but because it was Terry's. In more than twenty years of feeling closer to him than to anyone, he had never been here, and the outrage of that was ambushing him — the violation of any real meaning their friendship had had. But then, of course, he quickly saw, as he often had before, that it was on his account, more than anything, that Terry had cut himself off from this root — or, rather, cut through this root inside himself.

At the door of the shop, as if it only then hit Bright what they were doing, he took Terry's sleeve. "Jesus, how do we get in?"

And Terry held up a single key in the glow of his broad grin. "You'll never guess where I got this."

"Where?"

"My grandfather himself. As I entered the seminary, presumably never to come home again, he slipped this into my hand and he said, 'Charlie, this is yours. Never hesitate to come home.' But do you know what the kicker was?"

Bright waited.

"His calling me 'Charlie' meant, really, he could only see me as his chaplain."

"Jeez, Terry, you always took that name so personally. It was just —"

"What finished me with Gramps was Cushing. When Cushing died that next year after I walked off the altar, Gramps said I killed him. I gave him his heart attack."

"But he didn't take the key back?"

"Shit, he'd forgotten."

"And you held on to it, I notice. Was that nostalgia, or hope?"

Terry shook off the question and put the key in the slot.

Bright said, "Here's hoping it still fits."

"This is the Town. You don't change locks in the Town."

"No alarm? You white folks are trusting motherfuckers."

"Aren't we, though?"

Inside the store, with the door closed, Terry took out the small Swiss Army flashlight he'd borrowed from Max, but he didn't turn it on yet. The plate-glass windows admitted ample light, and they stood there taking in the shapes of the room.

"Flowers," Bright whispered. "Smells nice."

"This is nothing compared to what it was. Gramps had flowers and potted plants all over the floor, with just an aisle." Terry made out the form of the old captain's chair in the corner, next to the brass cash register. He could feel the warmth of the old man's affection. "When he smiled on you, it was like being smiled on by the ancient king of Ireland, or by God himself. I wanted his approval more than anything."

"But not enough to kneel to Cushing."

"I was an arrogant fool," Doyle said calmly, as if to the vacant chair.

"Not to me, you weren't. It matters, what you —"

"What matters is finding the tapes Squire made of you, and getting our butts out of here."

"Lead, kindly Light."

"Squire has offices upstairs now, where we used to live, but my hunch . . ." Doyle crossed the room. The muslin curtain that had hung in the doorway, blocking customers from seeing into the cluttered back, was gone now. The doorway was simply open, but the darkness from the rear room seemed wall enough. Going through, Terry tripped on the threshold, stopped, and moved the loose board back in place. Then he snapped on the narrow beam of his son's flashlight.

The old roll-top desk, the massive worktable, the elaborately paneled walnut door of the walk-in cooler; as the cone of light swept the room, Terry half expected to see, lounging in those corners among flowerpots and flats, his grandfather, his brother, his brother's friend. He made another sweep of the room.

"There it is," he said, aiming at the floor safe next to the desk. Terry moved past some cartons to get to it. "My grandfather bought this thing from a salesman he felt sorry for. He was afraid he'd die and no one would know the combination. He made us both memorize it, and he used to make us open it, to be sure we could." Doyle laughed. "But whenever he got up to a hundred bucks, he put it in the bank."

"Smart man."

"But it became part of the routine anyway, part of what made the place his, like the brass cash register. I knew Squire would keep it, and I bet he uses it for more than a hundred. Here." Terry handed the flashlight over. Bright aimed the beam at the safe's handle. Terry knelt and began to finger the dial, but he'd blocked the light and had to wait while McKay adjusted.

"Shit," he said a moment later, when his jerk on the handle budged nothing. He bent and tried again. This time, when it worked and the massive door swung smoothly open, he bowed, as for applause.

Terry took the flashlight back. The safe's open shelves held bundles of bills and rolled coins and several packs of envelopes banded together, no tapes. "This door," he said, fingering the small inner compartment, its keyhole, "was never locked. I didn't know it *could* lock. Shit." He stood, reining an impulse to kick the thing. He felt, oddly, that Squire had locked the inner door expressly against him. He was turning toward Bright when the lights went on in the main part of the store behind them. After the stutter of the ceiling tubes, the garish illumination flooded in on them.

There was no time to think of hiding.

"What the hell are you doing?"

In the threshold stood a large woman in a raincoat and a plastic rain hat that shielded her face.

Terry snapped the flashlight off and guiltily slipped it into his jacket pocket, unconsciously protecting Max.

When the woman raised her arms to remove her head covering, Terry supplied the snarling face of a busing protester. He was caught in Charlestown with a black man.

"Didi!" he said when he recognized her. He took his Red Sox hat off. "It's me, Terry."

"Jesus, Mary, and Joseph. Terry, what are you doing here, besides giving me a heart attack?"

"You didn't seem that intimidated, Didi. Look who else is here."

"Hey, Didi," Bright said. "Long time."

"Bright?"

He held his hands out.

To everyone's surprise, surely including her own, Didi threw herself on McKay, embracing him. "I've thought of you a million times," she said.

"I've thought of you too, Didi." Bright kissed her forehead, and, shy suddenly, she pulled away from him. She looked at Terry and only shook her head. "And you, my old sweet T. You son of a bitch, you were going to come and visit. Your wife and I were going to become friends."

Terry said nothing.

"So what the hell are you doing here?"

Terry pointed to the safe. "Squire has something that belongs to us. I was trying to open this last door."

"What? What does he have?"

McKay said, "Tapes, Didi. Tapes he made of meetings with me."

"Wait. That's something I don't want to know about."

"It's important."

"And you can't find them?"

"This inside door is locked. I don't have a key."

She looked at Bright. "These tapes . . . ?"

"Will put me in jail."

She stared at him, then looked at Terry mournfully before crossing to the roll-top desk. She flicked open one of the small drawers, took the key out, and held it up. "This?"

Terry took it and knelt at the safe. Now the door opened. He saw the cigar box and took it out. He opened it. There they were, ten small cassette tapes — no, eleven. He looked up at McKay. "How many?"

"We met three times."

Each cassette was labeled, numbers and names. Flipping through them, Doyle read, "Farrell-Joyce, Farrell-Joyce, Amory, Farrell-Joyce, Amory, Amory, Amory." Then, in succession, he read, "McKay, McKay, McKay," and finally "Mullen."

He took Bright's three out, closed the cigar box, and slipped it under his arm. He held one of the cassettes up for Didi. "See?"

"Show *me*, Charlie," a voice said from well inside the other room.

Didi's eyes locked on Terry's, and he saw, like a bolt in the dark, her absolute fear. It was Nick. Terry put the three cassettes in his jacket pocket.

Even before Squire appeared in the doorway, the stench of alcohol wafted into the room. Yet when he stepped into view, he appeared as self-contained and erect as ever, dressed as always in neat, dark clothes. He said, "Am I invited?"

He made a show of taking in the sight of the open safe, of the cigar box under Terry's arm.

Terry said, "You have Bright on tape. The meetings you had about Amory. That's what we came for."

Squire looked at Bright. "So you told him." He paused for a sly wink. "Did you tell him everything?"

"In point of fact, Nick, your brother is the one who told me."

"That so?" Squire entered, pointedly ignoring his wife. He was not quite as steady on his feet as it first appeared. He made his way to the safe, closed the heavy door, spun the dial, then settled his haunch on the bulking steel cube, so that his face was at the level of his brother's chest. He smiled up at him. "So you remembered the combo."

"I guess so."

"I didn't think you were one for remembering, Terry."

"Some things."

"Ma called," Didi said. "Jackie never came home. Was he with you?"

Squire slowly faced her. She was standing a few feet in front of the walk-in. She looked frumpy and disheveled in her raincoat and canvas shoes. "Meeting Terry," he said, "I'd have expected you to do something with your hair."

"I wasn't meeting Terry. I was looking for Jackie. Where is he? Do you know?"

"No."

Bright said, "We should go."

Squire ignored him, still eyeing Didi. "But you showed him the key."

"Nick," Terry began.

But Squire held up his hand. "Didn't you?"

"Yes."

"How did you know where I kept the key?"

Didi shrugged wearily. "I have no idea how I knew that."

"You just knew."

"I guess."

"She walked in on us," Terry said. "She didn't know we were here. I made her show us the key."

"Made her? You *made her?* How did you do that, Charlie?"

"He didn't make me. I was glad to show him. Whatever it is you're doing, I'm on their side."

Squire took her statement in, his face a chillingly impassive mask.

"Let's go, Terry," Bright said.

Squire stretched his hand toward his brother without looking at him. "Give me my box."

Until that moment, it had not occurred to Terry to keep the cigar box — the other tapes, Amory's as well as Joyce's and Farrell's. But this defiance, so long in coming, had to be total. "I'm holding on to your whole collection," he said calmly. "It all implicates us."

"This doesn't involve you."

"When you involved McKay, you involved me," Terry said. "Once he's out, I'm out. That's why we're here. To shut down your sting. Isn't that what your handlers call it? Sting?"

"I should think you'd be proud of me, Charlie. After all these years. My doing what's right."

"What? A gangster's two-bit gofer finally sells out his *patrono?*"

"Jackie sold *me* out, get it?" Squire's knuckles were white with the downward pressure he was exerting on the safe. "Sold me out!"

Didi stepped between them. "Where is he?"

"Get home," Squire said sharply. He came to his feet and grabbed her arm. "Get home, you bitch."

Terry took his brother's arm just as fiercely. "Let go of her."

"Jesus Christ," he said coolly. "Look at this, will you? I mean, will you fucking look at this, or what? Aren't you a little late, asshole?"

"Let go of her, Nick."

Squire did, but shoved her roughly. "Get home."

Didi caught herself at the doorjamb. She looked back at Terry, and with a sudden plaintiveness asked, "Do you have a favorite song?"

Terry released Squire. "What?"

"A song. A favorite song."

Bright and Squire looked at Terry, as if only his answer could make sense of her question.

Terry knew at once what she wanted to hear. Without understanding how it could be a weapon, he knew it was, and so he gave it to her. "The Everly Brothers, 'Dream, dream, dream.'"

Didi looked triumphantly at her husband; it was the song she still drove him crazy with. How many times had he come in on her listening to it, singing it even? "When I want you . . ." In the old days she would dance around the bedroom, a hand on her hip, flaunting her nakedness while Squire watched, as if the song had reference to him. Before they'd stopped having sex, she had even hummed it sometimes in the drifting moments after orgasm.

She started to leave, but Squire said, "Wait." He hooked his fingers, stretched them palm side out. He tried for a cocky nonchalance but fell short, his voice quavering somewhat when he said, "So it's to be Trivial Pursuit, is that the game? Twenty Questions? Truth or Consequences? Will the real asshole please stand up?" He faced Bright, his eyes hooded, head nodding like a car toy. "Do you have a favorite night spot, Nightspot?" His eyes bulged open, a stagy imitation of William F. Buckley. "The wet spot on your sheets, perhaps? Sheets — there's a good idea!"

Bright touched Terry. "I really think we should leave."

But Squire reached out and grabbed his brother's coat. "And you, Charlie, now that we know your favorite song, perhaps you'll tell us who your favorite basketball player is."

"You're drunk, Nick."

"No, really. Was it Bean Nicolson?"

"What about Bean?"

"That coon embarrassed the hell out of BC, remember? When their all-time high scorer went to the slammer?"

Terry took a fistful of his brother's sweater. They each held the other now. "Was that you? You bastard!"

"My trained animal. Two years. We made a fortune off that baboon."

"You fuck. You ruined him! That was you?"

"You betcha."

"It crossed my mind, Nick. When the scandal broke. But you know what? I dismissed the thought because I was sure you wouldn't do that *to me*. What an asshole I am, huh?"

"You think *that* makes you an asshole, Charlie? Bean Nicolson, that's nothing. That's just fucking basketball. That's sports." He let his eyes go wide again and tried to do that Buckley thing with his tongue. "Let's move on to the world of fine art. Perhaps you'll tell us your favorite statue. Something by Michelangelo, perhaps?"

Terry took a step toward the door. But Squire, jerking forward, grabbed him again. "Or ask Joan."

"What?"

"Ask Joan what her favorite statue is. She'd say *Mick*-elangelo, of course, as if the wop was Irish. Why do they do that? Why do they say *Mick* instead of *Mike?* Ask her for me, will you?"

"No." Terry answered coldly. But he remembered Mullen sprawled on the street behind Fenway, desperately calling, "Ask Joan!"

"Ask her for me, okay?"

"There's nothing I need to ask Joan, Nick. Nothing." Terry did not move out of his brother's grasp.

Didi said, "You're a bastard, Nick."

Squire smiled to have scored on her. He dropped Terry's arm, as if finished. "Two can play your game, babe." But then Squire swung back to his brother. "Well, if you won't ask Joan, ask Max. The clue is Michelangelo. See if maybe Max has some unconscious feeling for —"

"Jesus," Didi said in disgust, and she started to leave.

"Didi!"

She stopped and faced Squire again.

He said, "If Jackie still isn't home, tell your mother she should call in. She should report him missing. Tell her to call Captain Lundgren and report Jackie missing."

"I saw him this morning, Didi," Terry said. "He wasn't in great shape."

Didi looked from one to the other. "What are you telling me?"

Squire smiled weirdly. "Truth or Consequences, babe. Trivial Pursuit."

They could all see a shudder move up her back and curl her shoulders. She went through the door, across the storefront, and out into the rain, slamming the door. The noise sank slowly below the surface of an oceanic silence.

This, Terry thought while staring into his smug brother's face, is where I am supposed to fall apart. He knew that he had spent his entire life avoiding this confrontation because of an inborn assumption that he would not survive it. And he knew that that assumption had been far from groundless. Apparently calm, in fact he was completely cut off from his own inner reaction to the things Squire had said. Max? What *about* Max?

Finally Terry looked over at Bright. "Okay, let's go." They began to move.

"About my box."

Terry faced Squire from the threshold. "If you want this box, you'll have to kill me for it."

Squire shrugged elaborately, but he could not hide his confusion. Had he just lost after all? But hadn't he played his ace? His Max? He hesitated before saying glumly, "I'm no killer. Don't you know that about me?"

"Nick, I know nothing about you."

"That's not true, Charlie. Just look at yourself. We're not so different. Whether you'll ever admit it again or not, we're brothers, you and me. Always will be."

Terry just shook his head. He'd come here to protect Bright, but now he saw how he had to protect himself — from the truth of what Nick was saying.

"Right?" Squire came unsteadily toward him. "Aren't we brothers?"

Terry backed away, clutching the cigar box in a way that drew Squire's attention.

Squire threw his hand toward it. "Hell, I don't need that shit anymore anyway. Take the tapes. I don't care."

Terry left, but not before having seen the meaning of all those years of kicking away the clutching hands that had sought to draw him back. Now he saw whose hands they'd always been.

✧

Squire did not move for a long time. The pops, he decided, he should never have had those pops. He'd felt so blue before, which was why, after wandering aimlessly around the Town for an hour, he'd found himself outside the Harp, saying, What the fuck. At the bar, he'd hoisted his beers like the other guys, and had done his best to join the annual April grousing about fat-assed Don Zimmer and that finger-fucker Haywood Sullivan. "I'll tell you the trouble with the Sox," he'd heard himself pronouncing at one point, as if he gave a shit. "Twenty-seven players, twenty-seven cabs!"

"What?" Slats Moore had asked, leaning in on him with rotten teeth.

"After games, they always leave Fenway separately," Squire explained. He'd read this in the *Globe*. "The whole fucking team, twenty-seven players, twenty-seven cabs. None of those guys are friends, and none of them loves the game. They just do it for the money. Fucking Red Sox."

"I'd do it for the fucking money."

"You would, you shitbag."

Brushed back by Squire Doyle, Slats had shut up and moved down the bar. "What's he doing in here anyway?" he'd muttered when the bartender set him up again.

Squire knew why he was so slow to move off the safe. It was not because of his wife or his brother, or because of Tucci either. After all these years, he was ready for Tucci, high fucking noon, scarface, the man who shot Liberty Valence. It was because of Jackie.

Two players, two cabs.

He'd never, in all the ways he'd pictured the last inning of this game, pictured it with Jackie blocking the plate. Right in front of the goddamned plate, in a Yankee uniform. Squire still couldn't believe it.

As if to prove to himself he'd been dreaming — dream, dream, dream — he pushed up from the safe at last and went over to the walk-in. The chrome handle, as always, was wonderfully cool in his hand when he jerked it down.

And there, when he pulled the door open, was Mullen, still curled on the floor like a giant shrimp, with coins scattered around him. He stank of piss. On his head was a stain of blood, which, in that shadow, seemed black. His mouth was still taped.

"Jackie?"

To Squire's surprise and relief, the figure stirred.

Squire stooped. "It's me, pal." He brought his face down as close as he could. Jackie opened his eyes, but they were so swollen. "You look like a fucking Chinaman," Squire said. He took his handkerchief out and began to dab at the gash on Mullen's forehead. "It's stopped bleeding. You're okay. Right?"

Mullen managed to nod.

"Atta boy, Jackie. Because you got to help me. Tonight's the night, pal. Will you help me?"

Again Mullen nodded, his eyes blazing, even through their half-shut puffiness, afire with pleading.

"Good, Jackie." Squire reached into Mullen's pocket and withdrew his creds folder, which held his ID and badge. He put it in his own pocket, then stroked his friend's head, his matted hair. He felt the old affection come streaming out of him, into his hand, his fingers, which moved tenderly at the edges of the wound. "You were there when all this shit started. You should be there when it's finished."

Squire felt sober now, himself again. The sight of poor Jackie had done that for him, because it was time. He felt moisture on his fingertips. Not Jackie's blood, which was all dried now, but Jackie's tears. "Oh, buddy," Squire said sadly, but he was farther from tears himself than he'd ever been.

✧

Squire had been to Tucci's place in Weston only three times in all these years, but he knew exactly where it was. He could have driven straight there if he hadn't wanted to kill time. He went to Memorial Drive, past Harvard, out to Lexington and Concord on Route 2. He drove carefully. It wouldn't do to be stopped in an unmarked State Police vehicle, wearing surgical gloves, with a State Police lieutenant bound and gagged on the floor of the back seat. In Concord, he drove past the famous bridge and along the Battle Road, which in the darkness seemed as rough and narrow as it must have to the Redcoats who'd retreated along it all those years ago.

Squire Doyle had a Charlestown Irishman's hatred of the British, and on the rare occasions when he thought about it, the Adamses and the Otises and the Hancocks and the Concord Minutemen, and the boys of his own Bunker Hill for that matter, were all versions of the great English-haters Padraic Pearse and Michael Collins — never mind that *their* revolution was more than a century later. And never mind that Boston's Irish hated the English today by hating the people who'd descended from the Minutemen, and who lived in the fancy houses, lit up like whiskey ads, that Squire was passing now. Those houses were set well back from the rustic but tidy roads, and Squire was quite aware that they would have no idea of his passing in the night. No idea of his existence.

What had Terry called him? A gangster's two-bit gofer? Following the curve of the road behind the splash of his own headlights, his mind on cruise, his heart empty, he knew it was true. He'd never pictured Jackie blocking the plate, and he'd never imagined he could come to this climax with such a void of feeling. He was acting out his oldest plan, more or less automatically, half wondering why he had long felt so passionately that it must come to this.

At midnight he drove past the gate of Tucci's estate. A pair of low, unostentatious brick pillars marked the driveway, which wound back into the dark of the moonless wet night. The house was not visible from the road. Nor were any watchers.

Down the road, an open field gave way to a mature grove of cultivated spruce trees. The branches of the trees had spread together, making a towering canopy, but the trunks of the trees were widely separated, and Doyle was able to pull the car into them. He shut the ignition off, listened for a moment, then leaned back. "Jackie?"

Mullen grunted.

"Good fellow. Not much longer now."

Beside him on the front seat were the two velour pillows he'd taken from his own sofa and a man's handbag made of smooth Italian leather, Tucci's own. He took one of the pillows, slipped out of the car, and set off through the woods.

Several minutes later he was on his stomach, crawling commando style across the sloping lawn behind the brick house and the garage building beside it.

Tucci lived like a fucking viscount.

The house was brightly illuminated by spotlights, which ironically were Squire's friends at this hour because the windows were all blanked with shades against the glare. Twice he froze in position, looking for guards. He was counting on their being posted in front, and he never saw them. He kept crawling.

The grass was wet, and soon so was he. He moved quickly, keeping the pillow as dry as he could. He reached the lip of the lawn, the circle of brightness, and the edge of a broad flagstone terrace on which summer furniture had already been arranged. He came to his feet and, crouching, ran along the shadowy edge of the light, angling toward the garage. There was no question of risking the house. One of the cars would have to do.

The garage had spaces for three automobiles, but Doyle knew those were for Tucci's Ferrari, Corvette, and Porsche. The garage would be alarmed too. He saw another three cars, sedans, parked on the washed-gravel apron in front of the garage. He crept to the gravel's edge. From there, Doyle could see out along the driveway winding away from the front of the house. And sure enough, a hundred yards out sat the dark mound of the guards' car. A Buick or an Olds. He saw the bright cinder of one of their cigarettes.

On the apron a dozen yards away, he noticed the black Chrysler that Tucci used. Hating the light, he crossed to it flatfooted, to keep from stirring the gravel. From inside his sweater he took out his wire-and-hook, prepared to slip it inside the window crack, manipulate it with his gloved hands. But then he saw the lock button, tall, erect. Unlocked. Jesus.

He looked around again. No one.

He opened the rear door and threw the pillow onto the shelf behind the back seat, beside the gooseneck reading lamp. He left and clicked the door shut without a sound.

Minutes later he was back at Mullen's car in the pine grove. He hauled Jackie up from the floor and out of the car, propping him against the rear fender. He ripped the tape off Jackie's mouth, taking skin from his lips, but the poor bastard was beyond a pain like that.

"Jackie, it's me. Can you see it's me? Squire?"

Mullen nodded. His face looked as if he'd been hit by a truck, but his eyes, what showed of them, achieved some focus. He mumbled something, a guttural noise.

"What?"

Mullen tried to press his lips together, but they refused to close. "Lees," he said.

"What do you mean, Lees?"

"Please."

"Hey, Jackie, you don't have to worry. It's me."

"You."

"Yeah, me. Now listen. We got to get some help out here, right? Right? Can you handle the radio? Can you talk?"

Mullen ran his cracked tongue over his lips, which fresh blood was moistening. He nodded.

"Can you say, 'Get me Captain Lundgren. This is Mullen. They got me at Tucci's in Weston. Help. Help.' Can you say that?"

Mullen stared at him.

Squire repeated: "'Get Lundgren. This is Mullen. They got me at Tucci's in Weston. Help. Help.'"

Mullen nodded.

"Say it, Jackie. I want to hear you say it."

"Please, Squire."

But Squire slapped him brutally on his head, opening the wound. "Say it. 'Get Lundgren! This is Mullen!' Say it."

"Get Lundgren. This is Mullen."

"'John Mullen.'"

"John Mullen."

"'Tucci has me.'"

"Tucci has me."

"'In Weston.'"

"In Weston."

"Good, Jackie. That's good. Now say 'Help.'"

"Please, Squire."

Squire hit him again.

Mullen fell against the car, sobbing.

"That's good, Jackie. Crying is good. Now say 'Help.'"

"Help! Help!" Suddenly, finding a voice neither knew he had, Mullen began to scream, "Help! Help!"

Squire clapped his hand over Mullen's mouth, silencing him. "Not into the fucking air, pal. Nobody can hear you that way. Into the fucking radio, okay? Do it like that into the radio."

Mullen's eyes were wide open now. His terror had pushed all the swelling back on itself. Doyle shoved him forward along the car, then reached in for the handset. He flicked the switch, then pressed it on and off repeatedly, an alarm signal. The speaker on the dashboard crackled alive, and a voice said, "Read you. Incoming, read you. Go ahead, incoming. Go ahead."

Squire pushed the handset to Mullen's mouth.

"This is Mullen," Jackie said. "Get Lundgren. Say Mullen, John Mullen."

Squire had his mouth in Mullen's face, and he formed the word "Tucci."

"Tucci has me! Help! Help!"

"Where are you, Mullen?"

"Tucci. Weston. Help! Help!" Jackie began to scream again, indifferent to the voice of the radio speaker.

But Squire heard the dispatcher repeat the words: "Tucci? Weston?"

"Help! Help! Please!"

Squire let him say it once more — "Please!" — before snapping the switch off.

"Good boy, Jackie. Good boy." Doyle dropped the hand mike. Now sobbing again, Mullen fell on him like a baby.

"I got you, pal. I got you. It's okay."

Squire eased Jackie back toward the rear of the car. "I got you." And indeed, carrying half of Mullen's weight, he did. Supporting Mullen in that way made retrieving the keys and opening the trunk awkward, but he managed it. "Right here, Jackie. Here you go."

Mullen had given up, and seemed not even to be aware of what Doyle was doing when he loaded him over the edge of the trunk and in. "You curl up in here, Jackie." And Mullen did, in a fetal position, with his back to Doyle. Perfect. Doyle fetched the second pillow and the leather handbag. Back at the trunk, leaning over Mullen, he unzipped the bag and took out Frank's gun. The gun Frank had given him years before. "I loaded it myself," Frank had said, the fool. Squire's bare fingers had never touched it.

He put the pillow against the back of Mullen's head, bunched in half. He pressed the gun nozzle into it. "You made a big mistake, Jackie," he said mournfully, "when you fucked with me." And he fired two shots in quick succession.

He dropped both the pillow and the gun on Mullen's body, amazed, now that he'd actually killed someone, to still feel nothing. He closed the trunk after saying, "Rest in peace, pal."

At the wheel again, he drove fast, an exact quarter mile down the road to the small, quainted-up country store, gray-shingled, tin-roofed, trimmed in Nantucket blue. A single gas pump, super unleaded, stood like a sentry, but Doyle knew that the place had closed hours before. Now it was isolated and dark. He got out and went to the rust-splotched pay phone on the side of the building, and he dialed the number that always gave him Tucci.

"Yeah?"

Even that brusque word was enough to know whose voice it was, and enough, Squire knew, to bring the listening FBI agent out of his midnight stupor. Because this line was tapped, they used it only to set up other lines. But not tonight.

"This is Frank. This is Tucci. I need you up here, quick!" Doyle was speaking as if he were the wop. He pushed all the reined panic he should himself have felt into a long-practiced impersonation. "I want that turd out of here. He's done. I did him. Get up here *now!*"

As Doyle expected, Tucci said nothing. It did not matter. It wouldn't be clear who was speaking from which end of the line if the Bureau chose not to raise the question.

"He's dead and I want him out of here now!"

Doyle heard the click, Tucci hanging up.

Doyle had an impulse to say, "There you go, boys. Wrap it in ribbons for Farrell." But he didn't. No indulgences tonight. No mistakes.

Back in the car, he felt under the dash for the detachable blue light, pulled its wires free, reached out the window, and slapped it onto the roof. He drove as fast as he dared back toward Tucci's, the light flashing. He did not hit the siren.

Not until he took the turn at the two pillars in Tucci's driveway. Then he gunned it, all light and noise, heading right for the car on the rise in which Tucci's two guards sat. He sensed their hesitation. Then, as he drew closer, their car began to move — backwards.

A lone police car screaming up Tucci's long, elegant driveway, Tucci's men fleeing in reverse, back to the phony Cabot-Lodge house — Squire began to laugh. He'd intended to flash Jackie's badge at them if they'd tried to stop him, but he wouldn't need it now.

At the gravel apron in front of the garage, the guards' car stopped. They got out and, after staring dumbly for a moment, fled to the house. When Squire reached the head of the driveway, he threw the wheel around, sending the car into a careening turn, cleanly reversing direction and stopping. Now the car was headed out.

He shut the siren off and pulled the blue hat in. Then he waited.

Nothing happened.

Moments passed. This was the hardest thing of all. He could just have called it good enough, but the risk was worth being that much surer.

A door opened in the house behind him. He sensed figures approaching, but he didn't look. Had he made a mistake?

But then he heard it, the sound of another siren in the distance, first from one direction, then another. Two sirens, three, four.

The figures behind him froze, then began moving back to the house.

Flashing lights appeared through the trees as the cars wound along Weston's roads toward the twin-pillared entrance.

"Right," he said aloud.

He got out of the car, taking the keys. He circled back to the trunk and put the key in the lock. "Right," he said again.

Then he turned and ran into the darkness, across the grass, toward the woods. He slapped his pocket for the bulk of Jackie's creds folder. I still have the badge, he thought. The feeling was, I'm not finished. The feeling was, I can do anything.

20

UPON LEAVING CHARLESTOWN, Bright said cryptically, "After all this, it's time for me to show you something."

"What?"

"How to take the feather out of your brother's tickler."

"I don't follow."

Bright did not explain. Instead, he took him to Buddies, the unmarked bar on Huntington Avenue across from Copley Place. Throwing the door open, he said, "Ta-dah!"

Terry at once recognized the crowd of men as gays. The revelation caused no emotional explosion in him, which meant he must, at some level, have known. He looked at Bright and said, "They'll have Glenfiddich here."

Bright led the way in, to a far room, a table apart. They ordered drinks. Terry placed the cigar box on the table between them. He was aware of one man's sly overture toward Bright, and of the easy greetings others offered. But if he felt surprised, it was mostly at himself. Charlestown had felt far more alien and threatening than this place.

Bright said, "I guess I'm at bat, huh?"

"Does that make me the pitcher?"

"I wish I'd talked to you about it before." Bright opened the cigar box and took out one of the tapes with his name on it. "If I've felt ashamed of anything, it's that Squire thought he had something on me. In relation to you, I mean. Your brother is a genius at making people feel dirty."

Bright's statement jolted Terry, the exact truth of it, in his own life.

"I wanted to explain."

"You don't have to explain anything to me, Bright."

"Lucy," he said, breaking into an impersonation of Desi Arnaz, "you got some 'splaining to do."

"No, you don't."

"All very modern, aren't we?"

"Do you *want* me to be shocked? Mr. Disapproval, you called me today. Is that what you want from me?" Suddenly Doyle did feel the push of his emotions. "Is that why, instead of just talking to me, you bring me into a gay bar? To rub my nose in it?"

"You see, you *do* have a reaction."

"Of course I have a reaction. The same way I have a reaction to your throwing in with my shit of a brother without talking to me. Why in God's name haven't you been talking to me? About Amory, about this."

"Because I've been embarrassed, Terry. That's why."

"Embarrassed? Jesus Christ, what kind of bluenose puritan asshole do you take me for?"

"That isn't it. You *are* a bluenose puritan asshole, but that isn't it." Bright was silent for a moment, then added, "I was afraid if I was up front with you, you'd cut me out."

"Bright, come on. I —"

"No. Let me say this, goddamnit! You asked me why I wouldn't talk to you. Well, let me talk."

"I'm sorry."

"I'm *not* talking about homophobia, okay? You don't see me as a nigger, I don't expect you'll see me as a queer. Okay? That's *not* what I'm talking about. Okay?"

"Okay."

"I was afraid, I mean, worried . . . Shit!" He took a swallow of his drink to control himself. "Afraid you'd stop allowing yourself to feel . . . for me . . . that you'd never acknowledge again, what you said today."

"That I love you."

"Yes." McKay's hands, framing the cassette now, were the focal point of all his concentration.

Terry reached across the table, touching him. "You mean, the problem is, if I'm straight, I can't love you?"

McKay looked up. His eye was crystalline, clear as a mountain pool. "But you are straight."

"That's right."

"And straight men are afraid."

"Of course we're afraid. The point is, so what?"

"I'm afraid of you."

"Of me?"

"Of my feelings for you. It's how I've felt about you for years. *You* are how I figured out that I'm gay. Which is why I could never say it to you, ever."

"Say that you're gay?"

"Not exactly."

"That you love me?"

"Right."

"Because you do?"

Bright nodded, and he pulled his hand away from Doyle's. He dropped the cassette back into the cigar box, closed it, and placed his hand on it as if it were the Bible.

Terry sipped his drink, then held the glass up. Bright clinked it with his, and that was that.

Later, they walked in silence along the Charles River. At one point, Terry nodded toward the shimmering water, golden reflections beneath the streetlamps of Memorial Drive. He said, "See that money in the river? The coins?"

Bright laughed, and said yes.

"That's what my grandfather always called those reflections, King Neptune's stacks of gold." Terry paused, then said, "I took a suitcase full of bills away from Jackie Mullen today. Christ, was it only this morning? I didn't tell you that part. Jackie had been bribed to blow the whistle on Squire, that he was working for the feds. Amory gave Jackie a hundred thousand dollars." Terry pointed ahead, to the Harvard Bridge. "I took it out there and threw it over."

"You what?"

"I threw it in the river."

Bright slapped Doyle's shoulder. "You're shitting me." At first he seemed angry. But then, in a lifetime's habit, he shook his head, simultaneously appalled and amazed at Doyle, what a numbskull. "Oh, Terry, you are some piece of work." But McKay recognized himself as the stupid one, for being surprised. "Some fucking piece of work."

"We're different, Bright."

"Are we ever. A hundred thousand dollars? Unattached? Are we fucking ever! And I'll tell you something else. One bum eye, race, and sexual preference are not what make us different."

"I know." Terry thought of the old joke, Caroline Kennedy and Martin Luther King's son. "What makes us different is, you're Protestant and I'm Catholic."

McKay responded with abrupt solemnity, "That's true. I believe in a God of love. You believe in a God of forgiveness. You *need* to see yourself as a sinner, the good things in life as temptations. Your idea of worship is the Sacrament of Penance. Mine is Holy Communion."

"Who are you kidding? You don't go to Communion."

"That's a detail," Bright said. "My point holds. It doesn't matter either that you never go to confession anymore."

"Except to you."

"Which is only fair, since this is my Communion." Eat your body, Bright thought, drink your blood.

It had started to rain. When they reached the bridge, they bid each other good night with a firm, somewhat formal handshake and a quick neck-pressing hug. Bright's cologne stirred Doyle's memory: the thrill of walking into Georgetown watering holes with him, how no one's girl was safe.

"What was that line from Blake you used to cite, picking up girls? 'We are put on earth . . . to bear the beams of love'?"

"I don't say that anymore. The beams of love are not a burden."

Their laughter now was full of affection one for the other, all they'd shared; but also, at last, it was bemused affection of each one for himself. What a pair they were.

Terry turned toward Cambridge, and Bright toward the South End. His apartment was on St. Botolph Street, half a mile up Mass. Ave. But Bright jolted to a stop. "Terry!" he yelled. When Doyle turned back, McKay called, "You're going to take care of those tapes, right?"

Terry held up the cigar box. "Shall I just toss it in the river?"

"I'd feel better if you burned them, the ones with my name anyway. Whose side is King Neptune on?"

"You want to do it yourself? Would you feel better?"

"No, no. I'd rather you."

"I'll take care of it," Terry said.

✧

The light in their bedroom was still on when Terry came home. Before going up, he took off his wet coat. He poured two Scotches. The drinks in his hands would tell her they had to talk. Explaining the day to Joan was his only chance of comprehending it. Still carrying Squire's cigar box under his arm, he went up the stairs, paused at Max's room. The boy's sleep was always bliss. Because of the drinks, he did not stoop to kiss him.

Their bedroom door was ajar. He pushed it open with his foot and entered quietly. Her light was still on, and the novel she'd been reading was a tent on the sheet beside her. The comforter was folded back. She'd fallen asleep with an arm flung across his side of the bed, but it was no invitation to wake her, and ordinarily he'd not have considered it. The edge of the circle of light from her reading lamp fell across her nightgown at her breasts. Her mouth was open slightly, her hair hiding one eye. The faint swelling and sinking of her body stirred him, and he was taken aback by the poignancy of the relief he felt just to be seeing her. His wife. His son. The feeling was, he could breathe again.

Because the room sucked in the dampness on a night like that, she'd had a fire in the fireplace, and now it was nearly out. He looked at his watch, surprised to find that it was nearly two o'clock.

Having put the two Scotches on the white table, in the white bedroom, Doyle turned his back on his sleeping wife and bent to the fire. He added kindling and a log, then watched it flare. He opened the cigar box and took out the three cassettes marked *McKay*. With the tip of his pen he coaxed the brown ribbon of the first tape out of its track, unspooling it. He balled the tape, yanked the last end free of the case, and dropped it onto the flame, which licked up at his hand like a famished animal. *Whoosh!* The tape writhed, curled, melted, and was gone.

He was working on the second cassette when Joan's voice floated across the room on a draft of warm air, a sensation he took in as much with the skin on the back of his neck as with his ears.

"What are you doing?"

He turned to look at her. She was up on one elbow, the sheet back entirely now, exposing her white nightgown, the languor of her body. A strap had fallen from her shoulder. The shining cloth, directly in the light, clung to the hot face of her breasts.

"I'll tell you in a sec." He continued to unravel the brown ribbon, bunched it, and dropped it on the flame. Then he burned the third tape in the same way.

He brought the drinks to the bed, swirling Joan's as he handed it to her. She was sitting up now, leaning back against the bedboard. Her novel was at her midriff, a shield.

He raised his glass in a toast.

The strap of her nightgown was back in place. The sheet was demurely at her knees. She had pushed the cone of the reading lamp away. The lamp, the fire, and the spotlight on the oil portrait were the room's only sources of illumination, yet the double of each one glowed in the reflection of the black wall of windows. The panes were streaked with rain, coming down hard now. The wind moved the branches of the great oak, but the bedroom was quiet.

Terry sat beside his wife. "You won't believe me," he said. "Nothing I tell you will seem real. I don't believe it myself."

"What?"

"Nick, Jackie, Bright — the end of a story that started a long time ago. Nick finally goes after his old enemy, the Italian gangster he's been fronting for. With Jackie, he sets a trap for him. But his bait is Bright, because of the bank. Bright gets drawn in by the man I told you about yesterday, Amory. I followed him this morning, and it all came unraveled right in front of me. All of it." Terry dropped his eyes. "You told me to leave it alone." He stopped, giving her a chance to speak. She said nothing. He added, "If I had, Bright would have been ruined."

Joan let her gaze drift, with his, to the fireplace. "Those tapes you just burned . . ."

"Implicated Bright. A money-laundering operation, including a loan-back scheme from Commonwealth Bank. Bright was using drug money to rebuild Roxbury." Terry shrugged. "Social justice, but still a major crime. The tapes were Nick's, made for the FBI, a contact set up, probably, through Jackie Mullen — all to bring down Tucci. But guess what? Before the tapes get delivered, Jackie betrays Nick. He warns Tucci. Their story is still being played out, I don't know how. But as of a minute ago" — he gestured toward the fire with his glass, then took a drink — "Bright isn't part of it anymore. He's all I care about."

"Your brother . . ."

"My brother has to play the hand he's dealt himself." He looked over at her, but her eyes remained fixed on the fire. "The point is, Joan, I'm out. Nick and I finished with each other finally. Nothing he does, or has ever done, involves me anymore. Do you understand that?"

She nodded, hugging the novel as if it were a child, but she said, "You just told me I wouldn't believe you."

"That I'm finished with him?"

She shrugged. When he looked, with her, toward the fire again, his gaze went instead to the painting on the wall above it. His beautiful wife, their son, the dream of love that had always seemed more the artist's or her father's than his. So enchanted. A line from Dostoyevsky popped into his mind, a poster quote from his seminary days, and he said it without meaning to: "Real love, compared to fantasy, is a harsh and dreadful thing."

He stopped, drank, started again. "As I walked home, I rehearsed, half out loud, what I would say to you. It seemed important that I should put into words what had become so clear to me." It seemed he was addressing himself to the woman in the portrait, and also to the child.

"I am your husband, Joan." This was what he'd said aloud to the Cambridge night, and he said it again. "There is no music in such a statement, but it's the second most basic thing about me. I am your husband. You are the only one who can change that, and maybe now you will, because it is that kind of moment. You may stop being my wife if you choose to, but me, I will never stop being your husband. That is the first thing I have to say."

He paused, not looking at her. His eyes went to the black mirror of the wall of windows. The trees were swirling in the weather. He spoke as to the images in the glass, going on record.

"The second is this: I am Max's father. That is the rock, Joan, of *my* life, *the* basic truth. And nothing can change that ever. Nothing past and nothing future. Not Nick. Not science. Not God. Not even you. I am Max's father, period. I am not asking you, I am telling you. Do you understand?"

He looked at her finally.

Tears were streaming freely from her eyes. He put his finger at her chin, turning her face to him. He said, "I know everything."

"Everything," she said flatly.

He took the book out of her arms and laid it aside. "And I don't ever want to talk about this ever again. Do you understand?"

Without warning she fell against him. He held her while she wept. He said, "I love you."

Then, later, after undressing, he moved the straps of her nightgown off her shoulders. She let the silk fall from her breasts, and she cupped his head as he lowered his face to kiss her nipples. His breath and tongue were cool on her body, and she realized with what sad heat she had been punishing herself all this time.

"I love you," she said.

He heard the familiar inflection — that *you*! — but for once he chose not to take it as a hint of there being someone else.

The complacency of their naked, spent embrace, not so long afterward that the fire had gone completely out, was interrupted by the shocking, shrill sound of the telephone. Joan could not imagine answering it, but Terry knew that the night of trouble was not over yet. He leaned to the table for the phone, while Joan pulled the sheet up and watched the rain streaking a pane of glass in the middle set of

French doors. The spring bough of the oak brushed the glass, a measure of the storm's energy.

She was aware of Terry's clipped responses on the phone, the wonder in his voice, the alarm. But such was her state by then, in the elation of pure aftermath, that she assumed somehow he would turn to her with something good.

She didn't imagine he would turn to her with, "Joan, there's been a robbery." He was cupping the phone, holding it away from her. He was as naked as she was, which made the words even more absurd, impossible. "A robbery at the Fogg. They ransacked your office. They took a print. A Michelangelo."

⟡

In the pitch dark, on foot, Squire easily slipped away from Tucci's estate. Without streetlights, the road along which he found himself running was like an endless black tunnel. He was aware of passing other driveways, but they would lead to houses whose garages had alarms and where dogs slept lightly. He felt the threat of rain in the air, which increased his sense of urgency, and it was only by a calculated act of will that he was able to pace himself. He trusted that what he needed, he would find.

A car.

He heard the noise of a car approaching from behind, and he plunged into the bushes just before the headlights came rushing around a curve. He crouched and watched it pass, then went onto the road again, feeling no calmer. He lit a cigarette, took a few quick drags, then tossed it into a small puddle. He forced himself to walk instead of running. He pictured the coming rain as an ocean liner, its huge bow steaming toward him without knowing he was there, a sole survivor in the night sea. He did not know why the weather should be such a threat.

It seemed a long time, but it was only ten or fifteen minutes before the road wound down into a valley across which a developer had spread a quilt of lots and houses, modest and tidy, with lights left on over front doors and in hallways to discourage burglars. These households would have dogs too, but Squire also knew that, along the road soon, he would find businesses that served the people who lived in the tract houses.

He felt lucky that it wasn't raining yet.

Around another curve he came to a Getty station, closed up for the night. The whiff of gasoline was strong. The car he needed, a dark, late-model sedan, like a cop car, was parked between the station office and a Dumpster. Before using his wire-and-hook, he froze one last time, to listen. The first crickets of spring, a stream running in the nearby woods, but otherwise not a sound. He had forgotten that he was wearing rubber gloves, and realized it now with satisfaction. Fucking A. He was infallible.

In quick order, he had the door unlocked, the ignition wires out from their casing beneath the dash, the wires hot together, and the motor running. He put the car in gear and took off. The headlights he did not snap on until he was half a mile down the road, approaching, miraculously, the ramp for Route 128, which would take him quickly to the brightly lit Mass. Pike. With the sky open and illuminated by the roadway lights and the lights of many buildings, even at that hour, he saw that the weather front was not an approaching ocean liner but a city, and he said its name aloud, as if reading stenciled letters on a prow. "Cambridge," he said, "to the rescue." When it started raining then, he began singing "American Pie," drumming the steering wheel.

Within a few minutes, his manic mood had evaporated. He was pulling slowly through the college streets toward Harvard Square. "And the three men I admired most . . ." By now he was reciting the lyric, quietly, without inflection, unaware that he was doing so. "They took the last train for the coast . . ." His eyes clicked from car to car, from building to building, as he drove, looking for signs of anything that could stop him.

At Mt. Auburn Street he saw the Florentine tower of the Catholic church, and on instinct he pulled into its parking lot. He got out of the car and, hunched against the rain, jogged across the lot to the rectory, as if he'd planned to do so all along. He peeled off the surgeon's gloves, pocketed them, and rang the rectory doorbell once. A few minutes passed, and he rang it once more.

The door opened. A stout, bald man in a bathrobe showed himself.

"Father?"

"Yes?"

Doyle held up Jackie's badge. "I'm Detective Mullen. May I come in?"

The priest looked wary, but he stepped aside.

"I apologize for the hour," Doyle said, entering, "but it's an emergency. I need you."

"But what — ?"

"A suicide. A would-be suicide. I got him to agree to talk to a priest."

"A suicide!" The priest shrank back. "You should call the counseling center, the health service."

"Father, the kid is a Catholic. We don't have time. Would you get dressed, please? In your clericals. It's important you wear your collar."

The priest stared at Doyle for a moment, as if he were trying to wake up. But then all his years of conditioning worked their trick, and he nodded. "I'll be right back."

"Do you have a phone I can use?"

The priest opened an adjacent door and turned on a light, an office. Then he rushed back into the dark, tamed reaches of the residence, up a set of unseen stairs.

In the office, beyond a Xerox machine, Squire opened the one door, a closet. Reams of paper were stacked to one side. A set of shelves held office supplies, including, he saw, heavy twine and plastic packing tape. He closed the door, noting that an old-fashioned rod key protruded from the keyhole. He turned it, click, and the bolt slid out of the door's edge like a tongue. He turned it back.

A phone sat on the desk. Three steps took him to it. A card attached to the phone listed numbers, and when he saw one labeled *Harvard Security*, he did a little dance step; it's a gift to be simple. He dialed the number. He pictured the pimply faced night-shifter, a graduate student, awkward in the blue monkey suit, the kid who said, "Security."

"This is Father Collins at St. Paul's," Squire said quickly. "I don't have time to say more than, I need a car here. I need you now. I have a student on the other line who's threatening to kill himself. He won't say which dorm he's in, but he's Harvard."

"Father, we —"

"He *may* deal with you. He most certainly *won't* deal with Cambridge Police."

"But we —"

"Who is this?"

"Private Simpson."

"Are you in charge?"

"I'm the night dispatcher."

"Well, get a car over here now, to St. Paul's rectory, Mt. Auburn."

"All right, Father."

"Don't call Cambridge. No siren. No lights. Do you hear me?"

"Yes, Father."

"I hope he'll tell me where he is, then your people will take me to him. Tell your people that."

"Yes, Father. Right away."

Squire hung up. He heard the priest clumping hurriedly down the stairs. Squire picked up a mammoth black volume the size of a telephone book, but bound in stiff boards. He went behind the door. The priest rushed into the room.

"All set," he began, and never saw it, or felt it for that matter, when Squire brought the book smashing down on his head. He collapsed unconscious.

Squire looked at the book. "Missal," he read. And he said, "You bet."

By the time the Harvard police car pulled up in front of the rectory, Squire had stripped the unconscious priest, bound him, taped his mouth shut, and locked him in the supply closet. He was just closing the collar on the black clerical shirt. The suit coat would be too short, but it didn't matter. He put on the priest's baggy raincoat as he hurried out into the teeming night.

"I have it," he said to the Harvard cop who'd just gotten out of the car. "Let's go."

Only one cop. Beautiful. No stripes on his shoulder, and no gun at his belt, a kid. Good old fucking Harvard liberals.

The young policeman's agitation was apparent when the engine died on him. He croaked, "Christ, I'm sorry, Father. Oh, Christ." But then he got the car going and dropped the lever into Drive. "Where is he?"

"At the Fogg," Squire said. "Don't ask me more. He's the night security man, and he says he's going to shoot himself."

"The Fogg!"

"Are they yours? The security people at the Fogg? Are they Harvard Police?"

"No, they're separate."

"Are they armed?"

The cop was driving fast now, heading up Arrow Street. The museum was only two blocks away. "I don't think so. I mean, if they don't let us carry guns . . ." The kid's voice shook, and his hands trembled on the wheel.

He reached to the radio handset on the dash and was drawing it toward his mouth when Squire roughly grabbed it away.

"Didn't they tell you? It's just *me*. Your job is to get *me* there, no one else. Otherwise, he's dead."

The cop cringed at the rebuke, but didn't resist. The car bounced through a pothole on Mass. Ave. and cut into Quincy Street, passing the staid colonial buildings that formed one wall of Harvard Yard.

Doyle thought of her, coming out of the pristine church, her bright green dress and the straw hat she carried, her loose blond hair, the movement of her thighs under the flowing fabric of her dress. That memory had shaped his fantasy more even than the image of her under him, those clothes wrecked, when, after all, she'd been like the others.

The car stopped. "You come with me," Squire ordered. "The other museum guards don't know what's going on. You have to tell them." Doyle's authority was absolute. He got out of the car knowing the young cop would follow, and of course, grabbing his nightstick from its clip on the door, he did. The doctrine of infallibility. Otherwise, the cop might have wondered how this priest knew to go down the side of the building instead of to the front.

Doyle had cased the Fogg, dreaming of this, years before. A way to get her; a way to get him. On the side was the unornamented staff door with the only buzzer. Doyle pressed it three times, urgently, then stood back. He swept his hand in front, so that the Harvard cop took his place exactly where Doyle wanted him. In the light, Doyle saw how drained of color the kid's face was. The rain, dropping from the beak of his hat, made it seem that he was crying. Jesus.

The door opened, but only a crack, the width of a security bolt. "What," a voice said gruffly.

The young cop put his stick in the opening. "Let us in," he said. "Hurry."

"You can't."

"It's an emergency. You've got a suicide in there. Somebody's trying to kill himself."

"There's nobody in here."

"I've got a priest here. Somebody in there called the priest."

Squire came forward. "How many are you?"

"What?"

"Night watchmen, security. How many?"

"Two."

"When did you last see the other one?"

"Half an hour ago. He's in the other wing."

"I've been talking to him on the phone. He's —"

The door opened suddenly, all the way. The guard was black, and hatless. On the shoulder of his uniform, a patch said WACKENHUT. A pistol rode on his hip. Doyle pointed at it and turned on the Harvard cop. "You said they weren't armed." He spoke as if this proved the suicide threat was real.

The Harvard cop, with abrupt authority, said, "Take us to him."

The guard hesitated, but one more careful look at the priest convinced him, and he turned to lead the way. Doyle followed immediately behind. The moment that the Harvard cop drew the outside door closed, Doyle smoothly reached to the guard's holster, unsnapped it, and yanked the pistol out. "That's it," Squire said.

"Oh shit." The guard fell against a radiator. He understood at once, and was now raising his hands.

But the young cop stood with his back to the door, aiming the nightstick as if it were the gun he had obviously been wishing for, and he kept repeating, "What? What?"

Squire aimed at his face. "Drop the stick." The kid did so, its clatter echoing in the closed corridor. "Over here, with him."

As the policeman passed in front of him, Squire grabbed his handcuffs from his belt and threw them at him. "Put one on," he said.

The kid had trouble opening and shutting the cuff on his wrist, but he managed it. Squire ordered him to push the other half through the protruding radiator pipe and to cuff the Wackenhut guard. They cooperated nicely.

"I won't be long, gentlemen. If you cry out, I'll hear. And then, when I come back, I'll kill you. Okay?"

The guard refused to look at him, but the Harvard cop nodded.

Doyle knew from a dozen visits, when he'd played museum-goer and she'd never seen him, where Joan's office was. He went there now, through dimly lit stairways and halls, to the second floor, off the atrium, without a thought for the other guard, the pretend suicide. Things were going too well to run into him — that was Doyle's conviction, and it seemed right.

The door to her office was locked. Shit. How could it be locked? He stood back, raised his foot, and punched it firmly against the door. But the door did not budge.

Easy does it. One day at a fucking time. Let's do this.

Squire knelt and studied the lock, picturing its notched traps and cylinder bars snapping into alignment. An old lock, a simple one. If he could just . . .

He straightened up and went down the corridor to the small table at the top of the stairs. It held tidy stacks of floor plans and exhibit brochures. There was a small drawer, which he opened. And there they were, fucking A. The dish of rubber bands and paper clips. He took a paper clip and returned to Joan's door, and only moments later he had picked the lock. He went inside.

As quietly as he could, he proceeded to empty the contents of drawers and files onto the rough-edge tile floor. He upended chairs and removed prints and paintings from the walls. He found an ink bottle and splashed its contents everywhere. And that was all. He left her ruined office as silently as he'd come. Message number one.

In the corridor again, he stood against the wall, not moving, listening for the guard. Nothing.

He went down to the first floor, took two quick lefts and a right, and, that simply, found himself in a room which, even in the darkness, seemed more charged than the others. *Terribilità,* she'd called it.

He waited for his eyes to adjust. Like the bow of that ocean liner appearing out of the mist, the huge statue gradually took form in front of him and above him. *The Dying Slave.*

"Don't touch," he remembered her telling him. The genitals came into focus at the level of his eyes. "Don't touch." But that had been the other statue down the hall, the naked woman. He *had* touched. The bronze lady had touched him. His bronze medal. His all-time hit.

Now let Terry say he had no need to know. Now let her pretend it had never happened. "I'm of the parochial school," he'd said, and he still remembered it as one of his better lines. What acid the memory of that Sunday afternoon must have been to her all this time. How she'd lowered herself. And then — her voice, "Oh, oh, oh!" — how he had.

Squire went to the long glass cabinet lining one wall of the room. He saw the drawings, but in the dark he couldn't see which was which. He fumbled for his matches, found them, struck one, and held it close to the glass.

The pope's tomb. They had drawings for the pope's tomb at fucking Harvard. He moved the match along. Three drawings, four, and then he saw them, drawings of the slaves, the two slaves. It wasn't *The Dying Slave* he wanted, but the other one, *The Rebellious Slave.* He saw it, the fist clenched, the face uplifted in defiance.

The match burned his finger, and went out.

He took the guard's pistol out of his coat and raised the butt of it to bring it down on the glass, smashing it. Buzzers and sirens began to blare at once, but he didn't care. He reached into the cabinet for the print, but its frame was bolted to the base. He smashed its glass and, pushing the shards aside, cut himself. He didn't care.

"The wonder," she'd said, "is that it doesn't speak."

But it did, to him. *I resist,* it said.

He had the paper free, bleeding on it. He rolled it as carefully as he could. Message number two.

He carried the print in the hand that wasn't cut and began to run. The noise of the alarms was like needles in his eardrums now, slave torture. In the corridor leading to the side door, the two men were still handcuffed to the radiator.

"Resist!" he yelled as he stormed down on them. "Resist!"

The Wackenhut guard cowered at the sight of the crazyman, charging the door like Geronimo, like fucking Spartacus, but dressed like a priest. To Doyle's amazement the Harvard kid, the terrified, pimply graduate student, if that's what he was, rose from his end of the radiator as Doyle approached, and he pointed his hand at him as if recognizing a ghost. Only too late did Squire realize that in his hand was a small gun, an unauthorized weapon the chickenshit had hidden on himself somewhere.

He heard a loud crack. For an instant the sounds of the alarms took second place to the gunshot. And in the same instant, an explosion went off in Doyle's chest.

Another crack.

He had his own pistol up, and he could have fired. But he didn't. Goddamnit, he didn't. A fucking Harvard kid. Instead, he thought of Jackie, as he'd looked years before, in his first blue uniform — that scared, but not that fucking dangerous. Like a third bullet in his chest, Squire felt a blow of remorse. Jackie!

He staggered past the cop, bounced off a wall, knew he was hit bad. He crashed through the door, out into the rain, clutching his gun and Michelangelo, blood pumping through the stolen clerical shirt, a dying slave after all.

✧

Terry hung up the telephone. He felt a twisting of his bowels, as if his brother had plunged a hand into his body and was choking him from the entrails up.

Joan had leapt out of bed, intending to dress and rush to the Fogg. She was still in the bathroom. Terry waited for the toilet to flush; when it did, he went in. She was standing before the mirror, more naked, if anything, than ever. He stood behind her. Their eyes met in the glass. "It's your brother," she said.

"I know."

"I took him there once. The Michelangelos seemed —"

"Joan." Terry took her by the shoulders. "I already told you. I know."

"Did he tell you?"

"Not exactly. He tried to use it as a weapon against me."

"It *is* a weapon. I use it against myself."

"Not anymore."

She leaned back against him, fitting her body into the soft curve of his. She had never felt such strength from him before, had never allowed herself to feel so needy of it.

He had his eyes closed, his face next to hers, an expression of inconsolable sadness. "I have to get over there," she said.

"I'm going with you."

Joan left him in the bathroom.

She was at her drawer, having pulled on underpants, and was now fastening her bra, her back to the wall of windows, when it happened — the explosion.

The center pair of French doors, against which the weather had been pushing the branches of the oak, blew in, shattering into a thousand pieces of glass and splintered frames. The black form of a man came crashing through, launched from the tree outside, and landing in a flayed heap on the white carpet.

The wind and rain whipped into the room. Joan heard her own scream as a noise from outside herself. She watched, horrified, first as a stain of blood spread out on the carpet, and then as the hulk began to rouse itself and come at her. A monster of blood, matted hair, and filth.

"The slave," he said, offering the crumpled print, as if in homage. But in his other hand was the gun, and he was raising that toward her too.

"Nick!"

Squire turned slowly and saw his brother at the threshold of the bathroom, beyond the bed. Perhaps it was Terry's nakedness, or simply the resolution in him; perhaps it was that Nick was too far gone already, but he seemed not to recognize him.

"Nick!" Terry said again, moving now, closing the distance, watching the gun as it came up. Once, Terry would have experienced the prospect of death at his brother's hands fatalistically, the inevitable end of their perverse story. But not now. And not ever again. He walked directly to his brother, preempting him. Before Squire could react, Terry had the gun firmly in hand.

Squire collapsed against him; his weight took Terry down. But Terry controlled their fall. He took Nick across his lap on the floor. Squire gave him the print. "Michelangelo," he said.

"You're in bad shape, Nick."

"Be my priest, Charlie."

"I can't do that."

"I killed Jackie. I committed adultery."

"I'm no priest, Nick. You're the one in a collar."

Squire laughed. "And you're the one with no clothes on. We switched places, Charlie." And then he looked up at Joan. "You did it to me, didn't you? You're really something."

Joan was too horrified to speak.

"You *did* kill me, like you said."

And then Squire slumped. The breath left him.

Terry looked up. Joan, clutching her unsnapped bra, her arms across her breasts, had not moved.

And to *his* paralyzing horror then, Terry saw the door open slowly, and there was Max in his hot-air-balloon pajamas. "Joan," Terry said, "go to Max."

Joan did, covering herself. As she took the boy, leading him back through the door, Max continued staring at his father, at his two fathers. Terry thought, And all we'd ever wanted was one.

The door closed. And Terry was alone with his brother, to whom he leaned then. He kissed his forehead. Already it was cold. "Oh, Nick," he said.

The ruined print lay on the floor beside Terry. Moments passed before he realized what a disaster, in addition to everything else, this would be for Joan. And, of course, wasn't that Nick's point in singling out her office? He lay his brother aside, picked up the print, and tried to flatten it. Torn and blood-stained, the drawing of a naked, bound, defiant man meant nothing to Terry.

He went back to the bathroom for his robe. He crossed to the table, thinking at first only to call the police. But then he saw the cigar box. And he realized at once the power it gave him: Joyce on tape, Farrell on tape, dealing with Nick Doyle, this murderer, this thief.

Farrell could cover this. Terry looked at the print again. Farrell could cover Joan. He opened the cigar box, fingered the tapes, a last gift, despite himself, from Squire. Terry picked up the phone and asked the operator for the FBI.

✧

Funerals. The Irish believe, if not in death, in funerals; and a good thing it was that week, when there were not two, but three.

First, a full-dress inspector's funeral for a policeman slain in the line of duty. The newspapers had been full of the story of Lieutenant John

Mullen's brutal execution. Frank Tucci, the mob overlord whom Mullen was investigating, had been charged with the murder and was being held without bail. The public was outraged, and the Middlesex County D.A. had called for a restoration of the death penalty in Massachusetts.

On a glorious, crisp April morning, seven hundred and fifty policemen, some from as far away as New Jersey and New York, all wearing white gloves and black armbands on the various shades of blue, filed into Holy Cross Cathedral near the elevated tracks of the Orange Line. The policemen joined a grief-stricken throng of Townies, including a special contingent of Mrs. Mullen's sodality ladies from St. Mary's. Mayor Flynn and Governor Dukakis were there, and the Requiem was celebrated by the new archbishop, Bernard Law, whose many distinctions included his having gone to Harvard College.

Joan Littel did not attend that funeral. To be with Didi, Terry went, but he moved through the motions of the Mass, the kneeling and standing, the blessing himself and the going to Communion, the dropping of dirt on the casket at the cemetery, feeling nothing.

Squire's funeral was at St. Mary's, in the Town. But this one was impressive too, attended by the men from the Flower Exchange, the K of C, truckers, dock workers, corner boys, merchants, union men, and liquor dealers — many of whom were also wiseguys, hustlers, straws, shills, and fronts. Every Irish neighborhood in greater Boston was represented. Who of those mourners had not been stunned, some even to disbelief, at the news of his sudden heart attack? And who had not seen it as a grief reaction to the death of his old friend and brother-in-law?

That was how Didi chose to speak of it. She moved through the rituals of both funerals with great dignity, thinking more than once of Mrs. Kennedy — not Jackie but Ethel, who could understand what it was to lose a beloved brother and a husband too. Like Ethel, Didi had her brood of children to worry over now, but also, like Ethel, she had her faith. And she had her late husband's brother. Terry held her arm at St. Mary's too.

And once more, he felt nothing.

Ethel Kennedy was on everyone's mind that week, because two days after the deaths of Jackie Mullen and Nick Doyle, her son David died of an overdose of drugs in a motel near the family's villa in Palm Beach. The clan's Easter reunion, to which Ted had invited Doyle and McKay, had become another communal act of mythic grief. On Friday, April

27, the family gathered for *its* Requiem at the Catholic church in McLean, Virginia. For the interment, they flew to Boston.

The newspaper that reported on David Kennedy's funeral also reported, in another story, that the ever-diligent FBI had recovered, in a Dumpster not far from the Fogg Museum, the priceless Michelangelo print, damaged but intact. The Bureau had no leads as to the identity of the thief.

And the newspaper noted, in a discreet item on the back page, that when the Kennedys arrived in Boston, they were joined by a number of family friends and political figures, and also former Kennedy staffers Neville McKay and Terence Doyle, and Doyle's wife, Joan. The unannounced service took place at two o'clock at Holyhood Cemetery in Brookline. Lasting less than twenty minutes, it was no one's idea of an Irish funeral.

The family plot dominated a rise known as Cushing Knoll, at the end of a tidy asphalt lane. Forsythia and mountain laurel were in bloom. Daffodils, late crocuses, and early tiger lilies had sprouted in bunches, dotting the rolling green terrain like Easter eggs. The scent of honeysuckle was in the air. A stand of arborvitae formed the backdrop of a large, upright granite block on which etched letters spelled KENNEDY. David's casket was centered before the stone, the family huddled on one side — the sisters, Bobby's other kids, John and Caroline with their mother, the new young in-laws, seeming lost — all in sunglasses. Looking at Jackie Onassis, Terry heard the gruff longshoreman's voice of Cushing: Leave the poor woman alone.

On the other side of the casket, mourners were more loosely clustered. Terry, Joan, and Bright stood close beside the coffin, near a pair of small tablets flush with the clipped lawn. The stones read, JOSEPH P. KENNEDY SR., 1969 and BABY GIRL, 1962. Terry had forgotten that Ted and his Joan had lost a child, but it was the thought of the old man that struck him most.

He nudged McKay. "Himself," Terry said. And he thought even the old crustacean would see the connection of then to now. The mob, rumrunning, and big Irish money were still the holy trinity, only cocaine and heroin had replaced bootleg whiskey. If Joe were alive, he'd have made the deal with Amory work, but through *his* bank instead of Squire's. And if so, he'd have had the pleasure now of seeing the capsule of his own space shot return to Earth in the fatal speedballing of his grandson.

For a shocking instant, as if inside Bright's head, Terry heard Bobby's voice asking, "with Aeschylus," as he always said, "Who is the victim? Who the slayer? Speak!"

Joan took Terry's arm firmly in her hand.

The archbishop, sprinkling water on the mahogany casket, said, "May the angels rush to greet you in paradise . . ."

And though the prayer went on, Terry said amen to that piece of it, thinking of the eager Harvard kid David had been, rushing to greet life. Then he thought of the twelve-year-old alone in the L.A. hotel room, watching his father's murder on TV. "Is everybody all right?" dying Bobby had asked. David wasn't all right, but no one knew it then.

And what of his own Max, after what *he'd* seen? Max was what had changed him, finally, for in Terry a son's ache had become a father's.

Terry glanced across at Ted, bent, old looking, too heavy. Yet strength was flowing out of him, into Ethel. From old habit, she clung to him. He was the father now.

An emotion hit Terry at last, what he'd felt none of at Jackie Mullen's funeral, or at Nick's. A wall fell on him, not glass but stone, *that* stone: KENNEDY. He tasted a bitter draft of this one family's longing. Here was what they'd become in the end, to him and to the nation, the very opposite of what the dead brothers had sworn they were: a forever fading symbol of what we see, want, strive for — and will never be. And he knew from the weight of his pity that he was not one of them.

Terry looked at Joan. He covered her hand with his own, aware for the first time that, in relation to her, unlike all these others, it had not occurred to him to wonder, Am I alone?